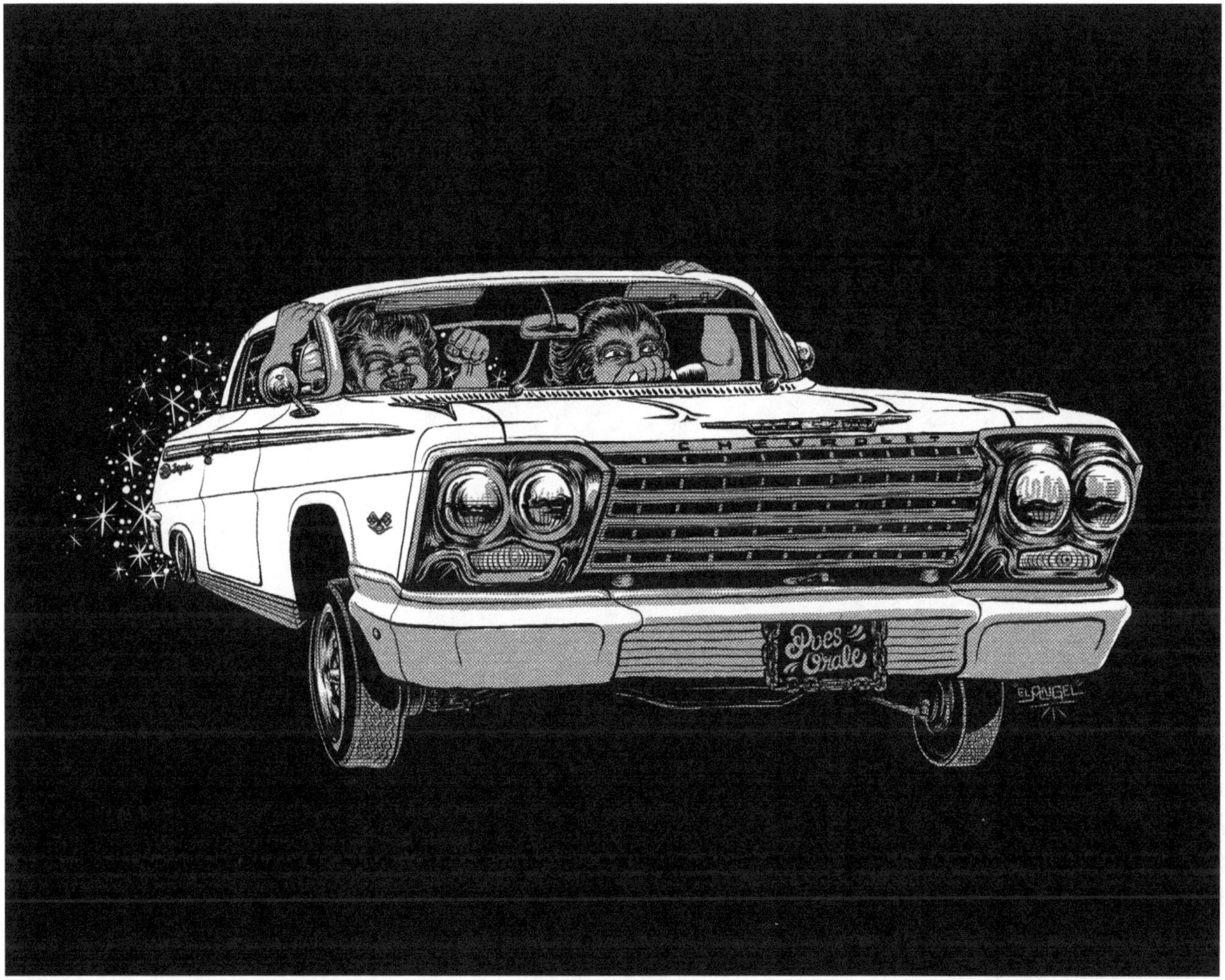

62 by Angel Diaz

Other Books Available from Broken Sword Publications

Alcohol Soaked & Nicotine Stained

Demon in the Mirror

AmeriKKKan Stories

¡Ban This! The BSP Anthology of Chicano Literature

Josh Divine's Ducktown

Lowriting

Shots, Rides & Stories from the Chicano Soul

Photographs By Art Meza

Edited by Santino J. Rivera

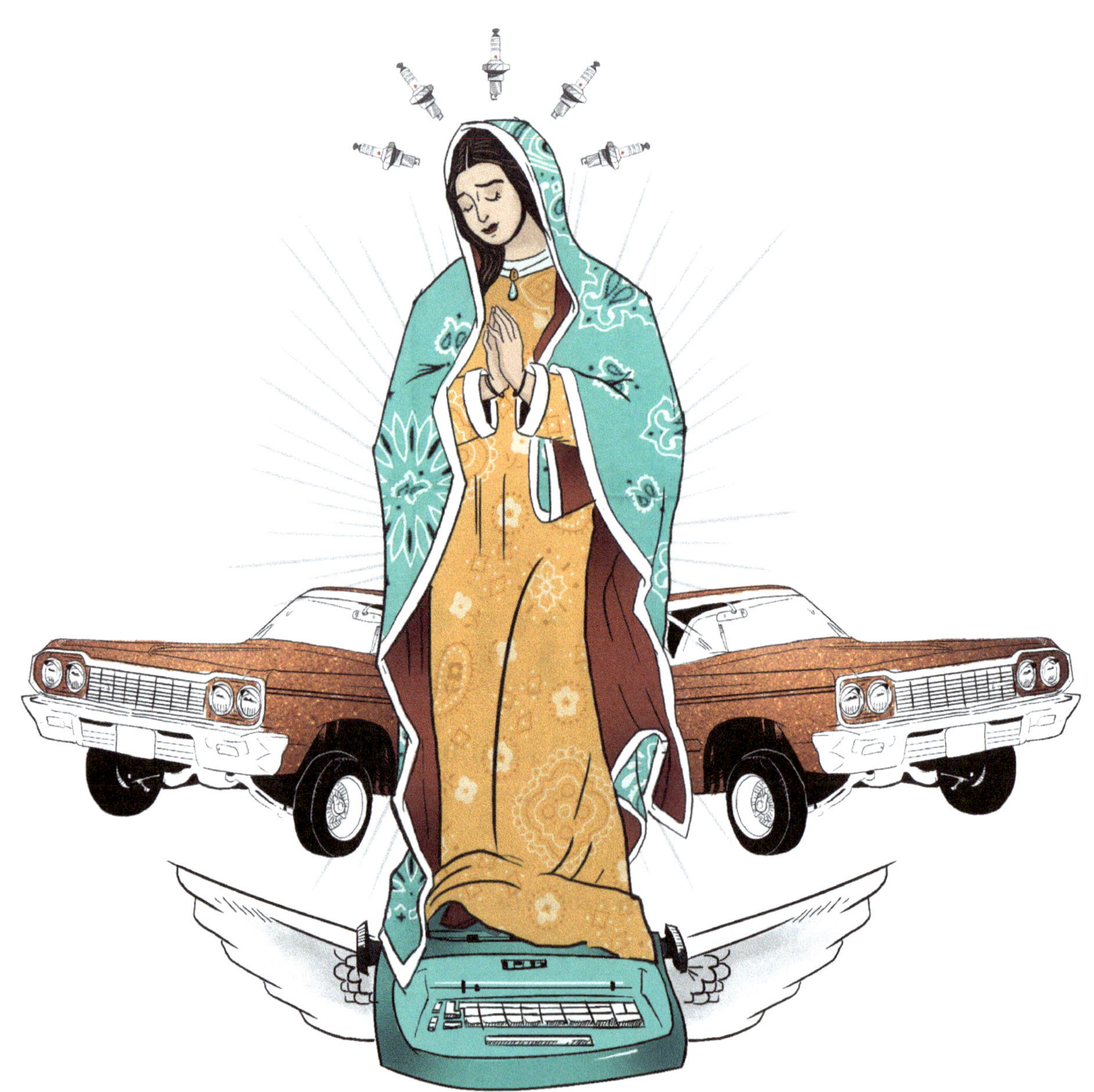

Lowriting

Shots, Rides & Stories from the

Chicano Soul

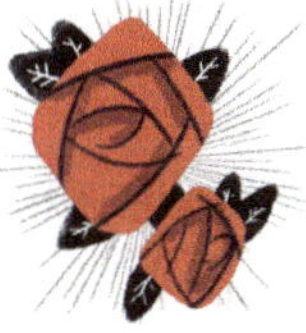

First Printing

ISBN 978-0-9896313-1-0

Published in the United States of America by **Broken Sword Publications, LLC**

Saint Augustine, Florida.

This book is a work of fiction. The names, characters, cholos, cholas, businesses, organizations, places, events and incidents etc. described therein are the product of the author's imagination. Any resemblance to actual persons or pachucos, living or dead, places in time and space and or 'things' in general are entirely coincidental and should be considered as such.

BSP, LLC assumes no liability should you get your feelings hurt.

Book cover design by Emilio Medina of **Muy Creative**. www.muycreative.com

On the back cover: Model Mayra Ramirez, photo by Art Meza.

Book layout by Josh Divine. www.joshdivine.com

Proofreading provided by David Diego Rodriguez aka Dr. D and Sam Lopez aka @texascubbie.

Broken Sword Publications, LLC

Saint Augustine Florida, USA

Web: www.brokenswordpublications.com

E-Mail: mail@brokenswordpublications.com

Twitter: @sjrivera @brokenswordpub

Acknowledgments

Livin La Vida Lowrider by Luis J. Rodriguez - Parts of this piece originally appeared in *Bello* magazine in September 2007 and Luis' blog at www.luisjrodriguez.com

Lowrider Oldies: The Unofficial Soundtrack to the Chicano Experience
by Allen Thayer – This piece originally appeared in *Wax Poetics* November 15, 2011.

A Father's Gift By Richard Vargas This piece originally appeared in *Kweli Journal* in December 2011

First and foremost I would like to thank Santino J. Rivera and **Broken Sword Publications**. This book wouldn't be possible without your support and belief in me and my work. I'll always appreciate it. *Somos Pocos.* I've dragged my family to many car shows gathering these shots. I'd like to thank them for their patience and their undying support. I love you. A big "thank you" goes out to the lowriding community for welcoming me and allowing me and my camera to be a part of and share the culture. Thank you to my tocayo, Art "Tudy" Beltran Sr., I'm glad we met, brother; your friendship is greatly appreciated. And thank you to other lowrider lovers/ photographers I've met along the way whom have been supportive and encouraged me to keep challenging myself and my skills. See you at the next show. I'd also like to thank every contributor for believing in this project and agreeing to take this ride.

- Art Meza

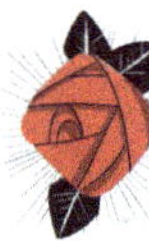

Dedicated to my family for strengthening me, Lowriters for doing the same for the word and our culture and the lowriding community for displaying their pride for all of us to see, Low & Slow.

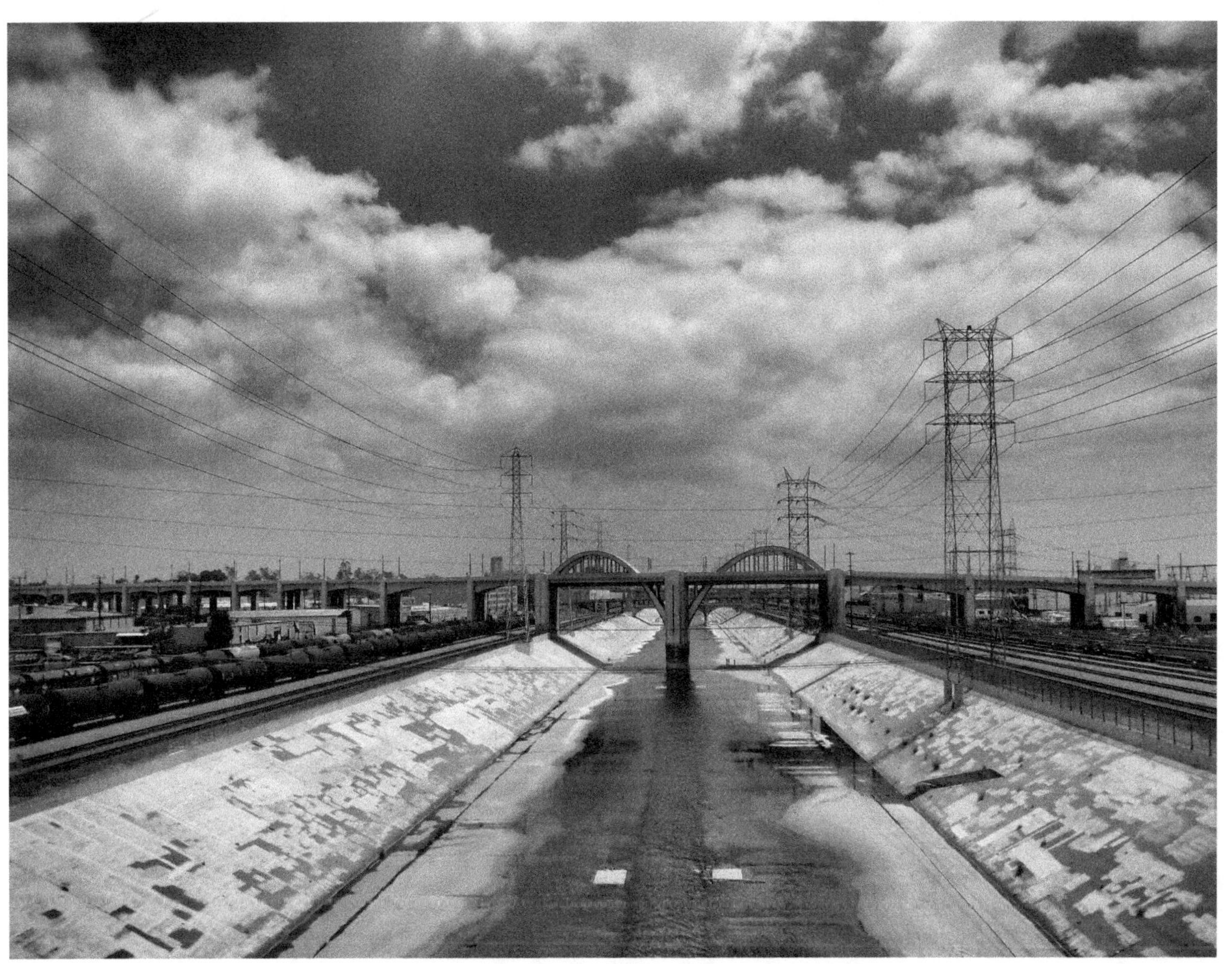

6th St. Bridge - L.A. River

Contents

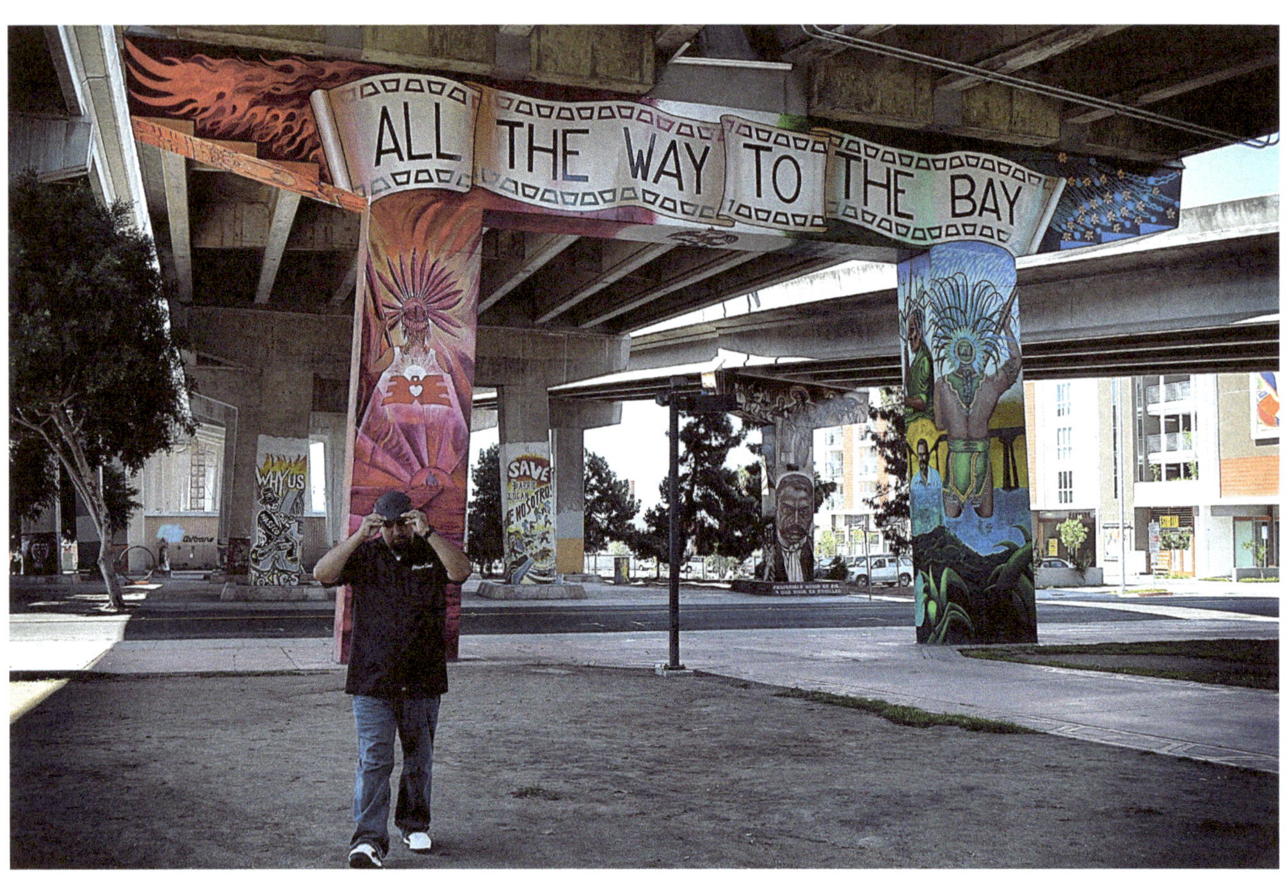

Chicano Soul – All the Way to the Bay, S.D.

Preface:

Low and Slow: Keeping the Tradition Alive

D***id you find your passion or did your passion find you?*** That's what Angel asked me as we stood on opposite sides of the circulation desk where I work. Angel stops in at the library every few days and we chat about different things going on. On that day I told him about my first Artwalk exhibit and handed him a flyer.

He was impressed.

But Angel doesn't know that I don't consider myself a photographer. In fact, I shudder a little every time I hear that word and my name in the same sentence. Let me explain…

I get a lot of '*I didn't know you were a photographer*' comments. I mean, I do take photographs but I don't know all the technical terms like "aperture" or the differences between the many lenses I see online or in ads. I just know they're expensive.

I like to edit the pictures I take and for me, that's where most of the fun is. I get to push pixels around and mold the image into what I want just like a potter does with clay.

So did I find my passion or did my passion find me? I don't know. At this point I wouldn't call it a passion but it is a lot fun.

I appreciate the compliments I get, especially from those I consider great photographers, but I'm just a guy who has always enjoyed classic cars – lowriders to be exact. I appreciate the hard work and sacrifice that goes into building them. I don't personally own one…yet. But in the mean time I feel that I'm doing what I can to keep lowrider tradition alive.

Lowriding is worldwide now but it began with Chicanos. Whether we're talking about zoot suits, Chicano Park in San Diego, or lowriders cruising somewhere, Chicanos have always taken pride in what is ours.

I first experienced lowriders as a kid watching the movie *Born in East L.A.* Watching a car bounce up and down the way it did was unbelievable to me. I mean, cars aren't supposed to do that. I grew up in the Boyle Heights section of Los Angeles where lowrider sightings were common. You'd see them cruising around school every day as the 3 o'clock bell rang.

Now that I'm an adult, I go out and look for lowriders. Though I don't own a lowrider of my own, I hit every car show I can. I appreciate their beauty, their owner's creativity, and the overall need to be original or have something all their own.

About a year and a half ago, I began snapping pictures of lowriders with my phone, editing them, and sharing them with friends and family online. It was simple and most importantly, fun. With the constant support and encouragement from friends and family I began to take pride in every image I shared.

My wife and kids gave me a digital camera for Christmas and by the following Father's Day I moved up to a DSLR.

During my learning process I was approached with the idea of featuring my photography in a book – this book – which is more than just an automobile-centered picture book. *Lowriting* is a collection stories, poetry, memories and fantasies about lowriding culture straight from the soul – the Chicano soul. And it just so happens that my photos get to accompany those stories. For that, I am honored.

I've have not yet taken any formal photography classes so I still have a lot to learn but this book is proof that I am headed in the right direction.

'Built Not Bought' is a popular saying among custom car builders and one that is spoken with a great amount of pride. We all know anyone can buy a lowrider but pride is something you trade your blood, sweat and tears for. I hope what I have done with my camera here conveys that same pride.

I would like to thank you for picking up this book – I think you are going to enjoy it.

Art Meza, Photographer

October 20, 2013, Los Angeles, Califas

c/s

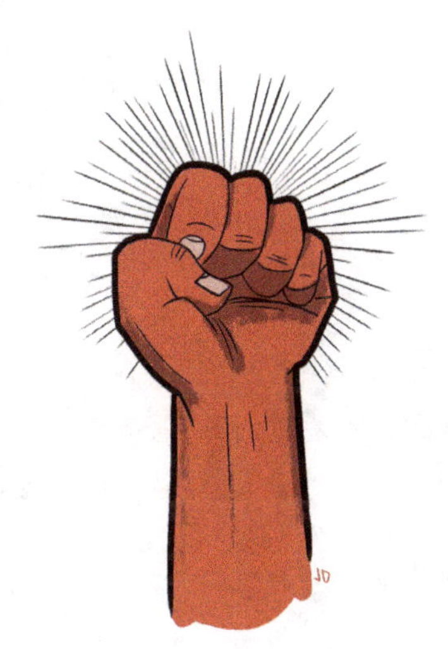

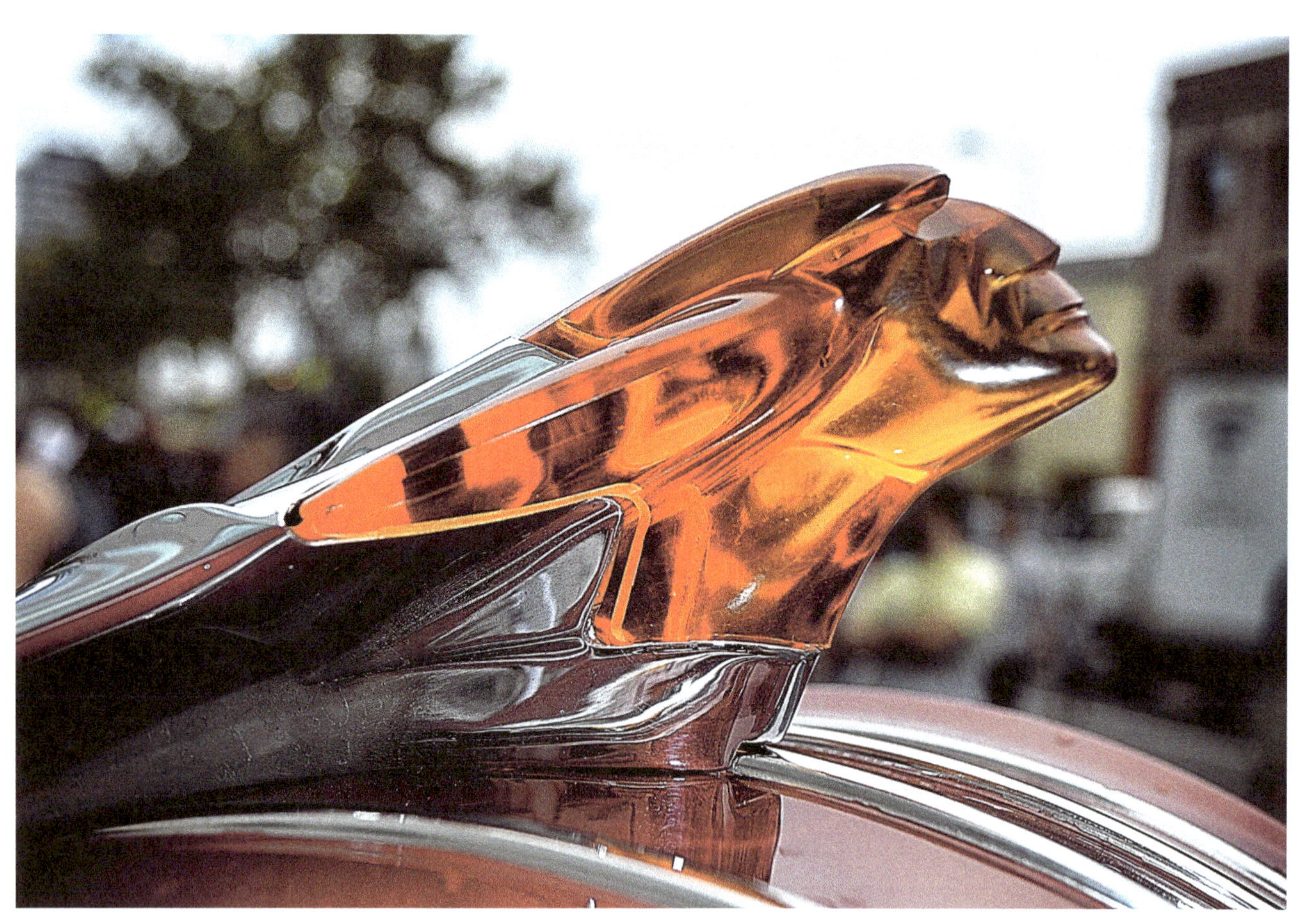

The Chief – 1954 Pontiac Star Chief

Editor's Note:
This is Lowriting

Once upon a time, in a land far, far away I owned a 1973 Chevy Impala lowrider. It was a two-door with a 400 cu. in. engine that sounded like God clearing his throat every time I punched the gas. That car made me feel alive and no other vehicle has made feel the same way since.

My ride was a deep shade of burgundy with black interior and it sat on Crager Starwire rims in the summer and moon hubcaps in the winter. I loved that machine. I bought it from my uncle and after I did, life would never be the same.

For one thing, I developed the magical power of automatically attracting the police anywhere I went. Without fail, I only needed to get behind the wheel to ensure that the chota would appear in my rearview mirror like an apparition from Hell.

I have never in my life been fucked with by the cops more than when I was driving that car.

This was during the 90's in Denver, Colorado and cruising was popular. We would cruise Federal Boulevard and 38th St. for hours in search of the next party and a young lady's phone number. You would see cars tricked out all night long and parking lots became the spots to see and be seen.

Denver was much different back then. There was little to no gentrification and there were a ton of car clubs and lowrider shows came to town all the time. This was the era of La Raza with *Kid Frost* showing us what the homies in Cali were up to via cable TV. I along with many others from my generation, wanted to belong.

Truth be told, I was much more into the ladies than I was the cars but getting behind the wheel of that Impala garnered respect and envy everywhere I went. It gave me a chip on my shoulder that I miss. Back in those days, the Mexicanos drove these really loud trucks with ridiculous decorations and blared loud ranchera music in traffic. *Bomp-bomp-bom-bomp!* In sharp contrast to this, I drove a wicked lowrider and played loud rap music while leaving burnt rubber on the asphalt. They idolized Chente. I idolized Che. The White boys were clueless to both worlds and the cops preyed on all of us.

We were in our own little universe and we clashed all the time…but man, was it ever fun.

That car brought me many moments of pride and more than a few tense situations with the cops, the ladies and other homeboys cruising the boulevard. Though that car did not have a happy ending, I look back on those days fondly and reminisce about the bad old days, especially now that I find myself in a stock family mobile, deep in the trenches of a suburban wasteland.

Such is life.

The thing is – these kinds of cars really are *special.* And I would argue that they are more so than muscle or sports cars. I'm sure anyone that has a love affair with a vehicle says the same thing, but lowriders have a certain magic about them. Just ask anyone who has ever owned one and you will be privy to a secret world of sparks on asphalt, red and blue light shows and more than few tales of love, lust and the law.

Lowriders are not something you read about in literature. You might see the cars in popular culture and definitely in magazines but rarely do you hear the stories behind the cars or the people that drive them or even admire them. These kinds of stories are usually passed down from one generation to the next.

Until now.

I have said many times in public and in print that I enjoy publishing books that I would like to read. And so here we are. Now, I cannot definitively say that there is not another book like *Lowriting* out there somewhere, but if there is, I've never heard of it.

The question is, *Why?* As Luis J. Rodriguez points out in his essay, lowriding is worldwide. It now spans the globe and permeates just about every aspect of pop culture that exists. You see it in films and on TV, so why is there no literature dedicated to the subject? With the amount of history behind these cars and their culture, you could get a PhD in lowriding…if such a thing existed.

Certainly there have been photo books about the cars themselves – I have seen them myself. There are also pseudo-history books detailing the evolution of the lowrider movement but there are no books that tell the stories that go along with these cars. Why?

This baffles me until I walk into any major bookstore and find the "Hispanic" section, which usually consists of the same seven or eight books. You would figure, with the population numbers that Chicanas/os have now, there would be more books, certainly some telling the tales of the low and slow tradition. Alas, no. We are still segregated on the bookshelf, relegated to our own "specialized" and tiny section. This must stop. I have set out to try and help change that monotony and censorship with the books that I publish and *Lowriting* continues that tradition.

The images in this book arouse a desire to want to know more about the cars and the people behind them. I mean, just look at them! Beautiful! I tried my best to pair these iconic photos with stories and artwork that would evoke the same emotions you once got from being behind the wheel of vehicles just like these. Or maybe it stirs memories of a family member or friend…or a rival! Trucha!

Photographer Art Meza has captured some of that lowrider magic with his lens and though he's humble about it, I think you will agree that there's definitely some enchantment going on here.

One of the things that I like most about Meza's work is that it's not garish. Having grown up on *Lowrider Magazine*, and all of its incarnations, I grew familiar with the stylized photos of "exploded" and posed lowriders; doors open, hood and trunk open and half-naked women on display.

Not to say that those photos are not great but they are what's expected – the lowrider norm if you will. Meza's work speaks to another era, one which gets glossed over by popular culture. Lowriders and lowrider culture mean different things to different people but the media and entertainment industry often miss the class, the stylization and the pride that goes with these rides.

I would like to think that Art and myself captured some of that here in this book.

You will find amazing stories and images in this book. Each of them is crafted with the same pride that any lowrider masterpiece encompasses. These are the stories from the people who have built these cars, driven them, grown up with them, loved them and lost them. There is some heavyweight talent in here and for that I am both honored and grateful to each person that has lent their voice.

These are the shots, rides and stories from the Chicano soul. This is Lowriting.

Santino J. Rivera, Editor/Publisher

November 2, 2013, Saint Augustine, Florida

"Our pachuco realities will only make sense if you grasp their stylization."

- El Pachuco, Zoot Suit

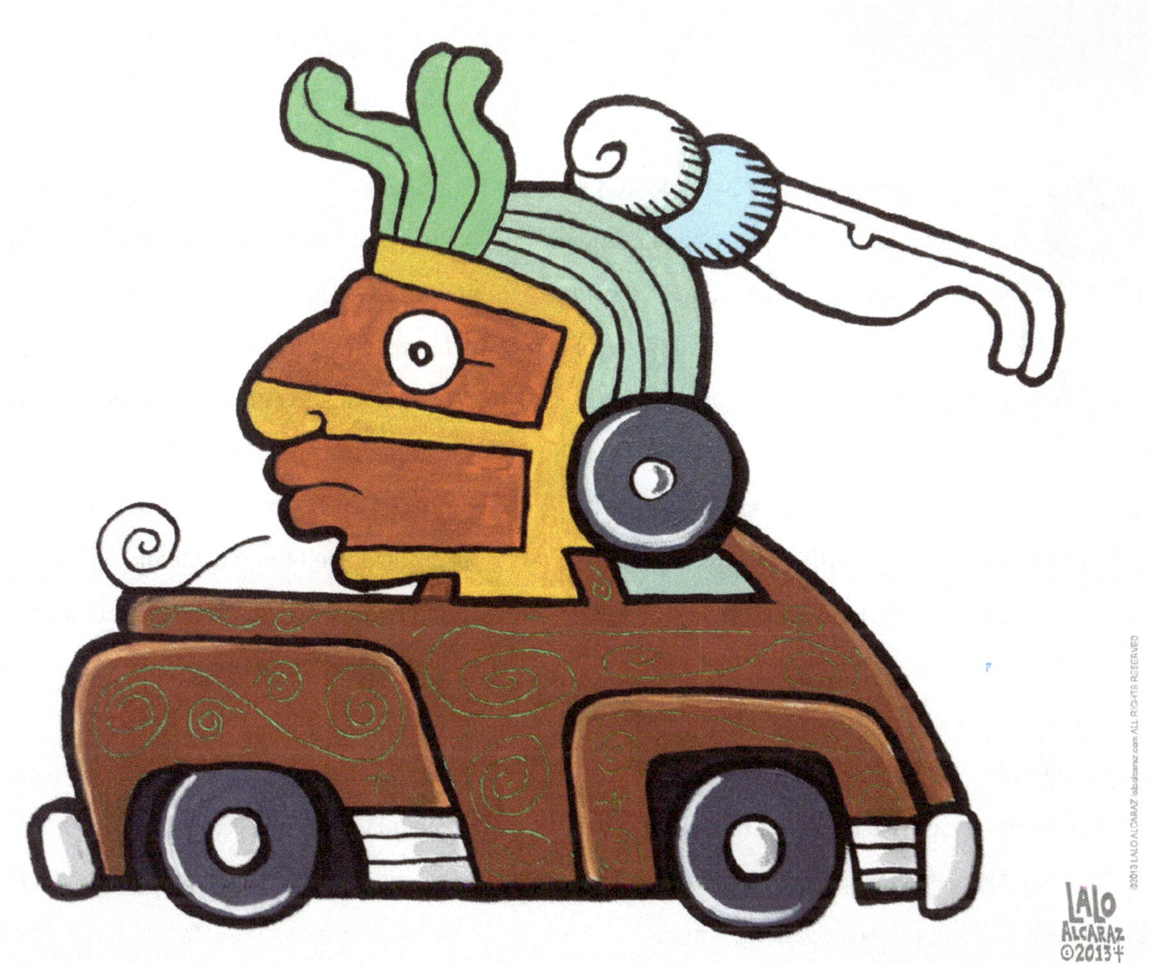

Low God by Lalo Alcaraz

Tokyo: Living La Vida Lowrider

By Luis J. Rodriguez

A row of bald-headed, broad-shouldered young men stand together in the middle of a small smoky dance club called "Sound Base." They wear well pressed Dickies pants, "locs" (wrap-around shades), extra-long flannel shirts or long cotton athletic shirts in black and gray. A few had T-shirts with images of lowrider cars as well as "cholas" and "cholos." In the club's parking lot, adjacent to a lumberyard, several lowered 1950s and 1960s Detroit-built cars display airbrushed murals and shiny chrome, the one exception being a caramel brown 1941 Chevy truck.

On the stage are two members of Quetzal, one of East Los Angeles' most popular bands: Quetzal Flores and his long-time companion, Martha Gonzalez. Flores strums a *jarana*, a traditional stringed instrument from the Mexican Gulf port state of Veracruz. Gonzalez is seated astride a *cajon*, also used extensively in the *Son Jarocho* tradition of that state, and thumps with her hands and fingers a driving cadenced beat as she sings in Spanish and English, words heavily tinged with Mexican/Xicano cultural and political significance.

DJ dGomez (David Gomez) of Monte Carlo '76, another East L.A. musical group, stands over the turntables. Well-known Xicano street favorites – from the 1960s to the present – emanate from the speakers, including El Chicano's "Viva Tirado," the Village Callers' "Hector," Slowrider's "Sandoval y Teixeira," and War's "Cisco Kid." Later that evening, English-language poetry laced with *calo*, the street slang of L.A.'s Mexican streets, and Spanish echoes across the densely filled hall. Even famed harmonica player Tex Nakamura, formerly of the L.A.-based band War, guest plays another *jarana* during Quetzal and Martha's set.

This could have been Boyle Heights, Highland Park, or Montebello. It could have been any place in Los Angeles or California for that matter. This music, this style, this way of life is mostly California-based and bred. It's called Xicano – a clearly defined musical, cultural, and social stance that is also unabashedly anti-racist, anti-exploitation, anti-oppression while indigenous-rooted, intellectually grounded, and linked to the social movements that arose out of the Mexican barrios, migrant camps, and factories in the United States during the last century, particularly at the height of the Civil Rights struggle.

However, this concert and reading didn't happen in East Los Angeles or East San Jose—it took place in an industrial, mostly isolated, section of Chiba, about two hours' drive outside of Tokyo.

In Japan.

Tokyo is exactly how I imagined it: lights, sounds, shops, orderly, clean. It is massive, daunting, the largest metropolitan area in the world. A hard city to enter, to understand. To embrace. And despite a large number of tourists it's extremely culturally cohesive. Not like New York City or Los Angeles with their renowned variety of voices, faces, and colors. Yet in sections, the city can be absorbed, appreciated. Re-imagined.

Tokyo is also a world-class city, incorporating various social expressions and phenomena while also innovating them. In Tokyo you feel the ancient and the modern.

Mind you, I've been to many cities and countries over the past 30 years as a lecturer, journalist and poet. Places all over the United States as well as in Europe, Canada, Mexico, Central America, Puerto Rico, and South America. While many of these cities are picturesque and vibrant, I've also visited soot-covered, trash-strewn locations with gaping poverty (starting with those in the United States). Some of these were tragic (New Orleans after Hurricane Katrina or San Salvador after the Civil War); others had intense character and energy (like San Francisco or Mexico City).

In Tokyo so much comes at you at once, including tons of advertisements. So many products to sell. This city is the epitome of modern technological commercialization. Most people I saw on the street were in business suits. Yet

Tokyo is also a city of books, of poets, of artists, of restaurants. The landscape of glass and steel seems void of actual nature, yet I found truly serene and well-manicured green spaces. In the streets and clubs there are songs, dance, theater, and a sea of languages. I danced one night at a salsa club in Roppongi, mingling with Peruvians, Brazilians, and many Japanese.

I came to Tokyo in November of 2006 to interview and follow Shin Miyata, then 44, an independent record producer who has brought East L.A. and other Xicano music to Japan through Barrio Gold Records/Music Camp, Inc. I also arrived during Miyata's promotional tour for Quetzal and Martha, accompanied by Gomez. Besides "Sound Base" in Chiba, we ended at the Tower Records/ Shibuya and the Bird Cafe in Shimokitazawa, Setagaya-ku where the house rocked with *Son Jarocho*, political songs and Xicano oldies. I was honored to read my poetry accompanied by *jaranas* and even Tex's harmonica.

I was surprised at the crowds that came to listen to us—including my poems. They genuinely appreciated our presence. In fact, it felt cool to be Xicano, Mexika/Azteca, to be from the urban barrios of Los Angeles.

In Japan, I met with lowrider car aficionados, *cholo*-attired radio Djs, and young Hip Hop/Xicano clothing store owners. Xicano culture has a foothold here, not large, but significant. *Lowrider Japan* Magazine at the time had around 70,000 readers.

The Xicano culture is rooted in the Mexican people—those who lived in the U.S. Southwest before the United States took more than half of Mexico's territory after the U.S. invasion of Mexico in 1846 to 1848. The many Mexican migrants who came in subsequent waves from Mexico across more than 150 years after that also shaped this culture. The first big wave was during the 1910 Mexican Revolution in which a million refugees created the first barrios of L.A. and other Southwestern and Midwestern cities. Some of their children became Pachucos, the so-called "zootsuit gangsters" that eventually evolved into the *cholos*, emulated by poor African Americans, Whites, Cambodians, Salvadorans, Armenians, and others who've landed in L.A. in search of a better life.

Much of our struggle as Xicanos is to be seen for

what we are—indigenous, not Mexican or American, yet willing to defend both when needed. Xicanos have been in all major U.S. wars, including winning more congressional medals of valor than any other ethnic group during World War II. But most of our fighting here has been against racism, against bad schools, against the lack of decent jobs, and against terrible housing.

Today the United States has an estimated 30 million Xicanos and others of Mexican descent. Of the 12 million undocumented immigrants here, more than 60 percent are from Mexico.

As a Xicano, I understand the Japanese need to find its own creative center, its own cultural and economic pulse, away from the influence of U.S. capitalist power and finance. To choose its own past and destiny. Choice is important for Xicanos as well. We are trying to achieve the same, even after several generations of being inside the belly of the United States as estranged and often second-class citizens. We reclaim our heritage beyond the Spanish conquest (where others "Latinos" tend to start) all the way to the Native peoples of the Americas—their teachings, rituals and history—to claim the whole continent. We draw from a time when there were no borders and therefore no demarcation of who belongs here and who doesn't. We have a fatherland and a motherland.

In time, many Xicanos created their own way of talking, dressing, acting. While much of this is in the barrio-based street gang culture, most of it is not. In Japan, I met people who seemed to appreciate this expression. To honor it. To make it theirs. The lowrider cars I saw came directly from the streets of Los Angeles—they had to be real, from the source-land of Lowrider Nation. Xicanos chose not to totally assimilate the often hollow and bland "American" culture, while at the same time enriching it with our art, speech, clothing, and style.

As a Xicano I found a connection, an affection – a sense that Xicanos are important in Japan. The Japanese know the power of their choices. But they also seem to gather in the world, not as an isolated and patronizing people, but truly enraptured with unique and wholly alive cultures such as Xicano.

They understand that being Xicano is both a necessity and a choice.

In the United States where I was born and will

remain until I die, I fight for a better land, country, culture, and economy. I fight for Xicanos to be recognized and respected, but also for anyone else to have the same—as far as I'm concerned, we all belong here, even when some of us (like African Americans) were brought as slaves and others (like the Spanish or English) came as conquerors. But something has to change—so that we are equal, fully entitled to the rights of any human being, and properly treated under the law and in the hearts of the people.

My experience in Japan is that, at least at the level of culture, Xicanos can find home even in such a faraway land. This should be a right for everyone, especially in a world where being uprooted and homeless seems to be the poignant feature of our time.

If I can stand next to a lowered 1940s Ford truck with magnesium rims in Tokyo, something I could have done in East L.A., and still feel the same sensation of joy that such a car can bring in both countries, then I know—It's time for borders to come down.

Of course, this is a controversial subject. There are concerns about trade and home markets and so-called terrorism scaring most developed countries to close in on themselves. But we have seen how our divisions by race, by nation, by religion, and even by gangs have lead mostly to fear and violence. I imagine a world with no borders, but also where people can be their own special kind of human expressions, not homogenized, but truly unique and driven by their own innate purposes and dreams.

Ari gato Japan. Thanks. Or as we say in Nahuatl "tlazhokamati" – or in Spanish "gracias." Thanks for being open to me as a Xicano and poet. And for letting me know and savor your own magnificent culture and heritage. "Tokyo *Rifa*" as we say in the barrios of East Los, meaning this place lives, demands respect, cannot be erased.

Con Safos

††

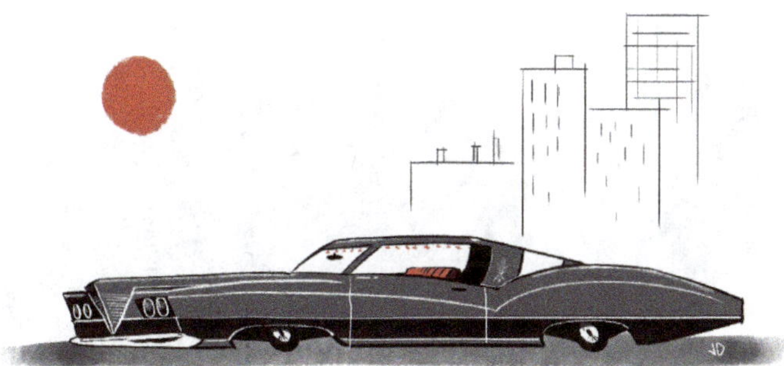

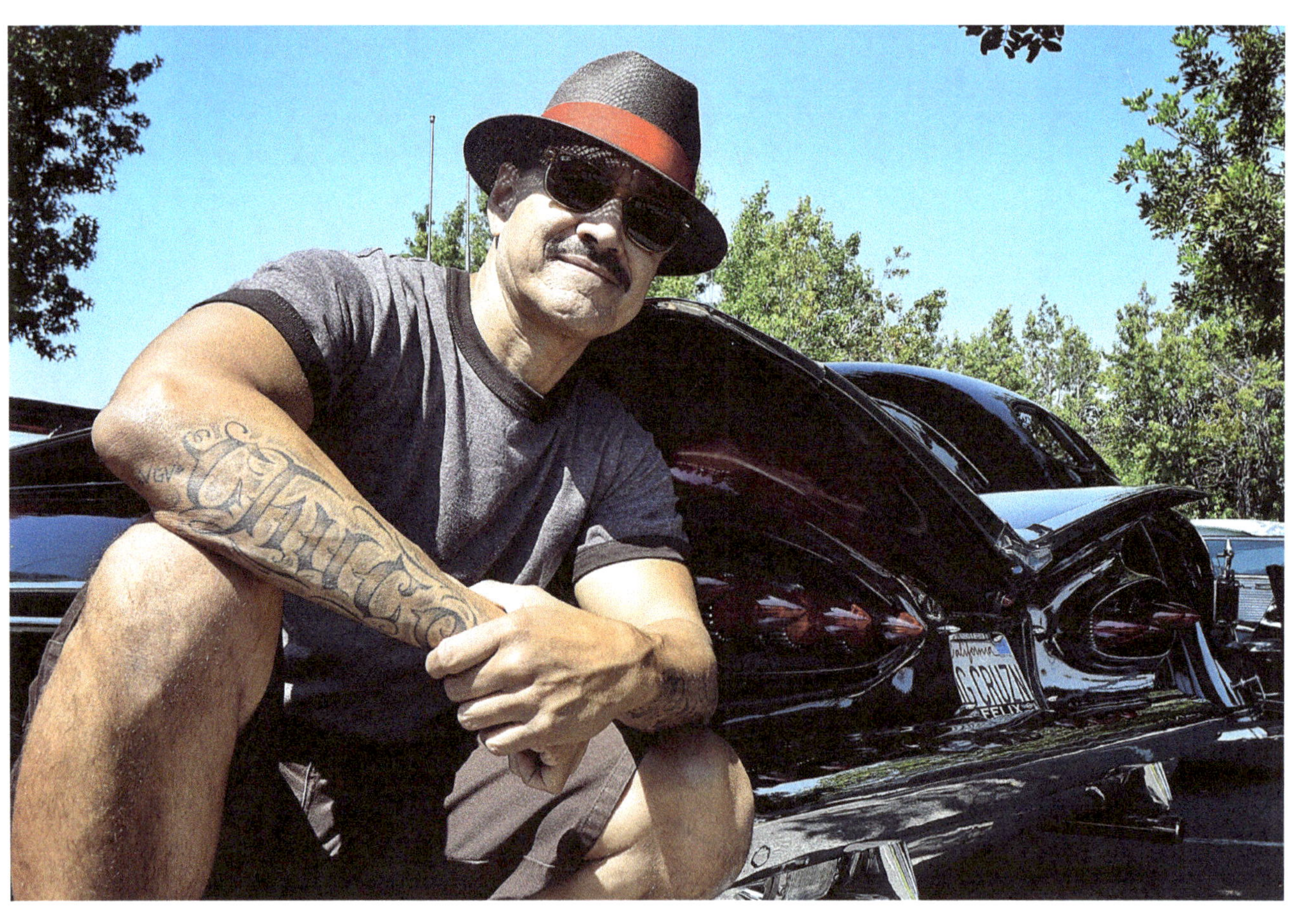

Danny De La Paz – '59 Chevy Impala

An Interview with Danny De La Paz

Boulevard Nights & Lowrider Dreams

By Santino J. Rivera

I was first introduced to actor Danny De La Paz not in person but on the big screen when I saw the film *American Me*. The character that he played in that film, Puppet, made a strong impression on me back in the day and I will never forget how shocked I felt by his transformation on screen from loving older brother to a stone killer. What I didn't realize at the time was the amount of skill De La Paz brings to his characters.

An accomplished actor of both stage and screen, De La Paz brings raw emotion to his characters and an edge of realism that gets left out of most gang and prison films. It's hard to explain it unless you genuinely feel it – and in *American Me*, when he strangles his little brother, played by Daniel Villarreal (Little Puppet), I felt genuinely sick to my stomach. I also felt betrayed. Why? Because De La Paz is a highly skilled actor who plays the role so well that you believe he and Villarreal really are hermanos – at least I did.

When he looks to the sky and says, "Goddamn me…" it is a powerful moment and arguably, one of the most powerful twists in the film.

As luck would have it, both Puppet and Little Puppet are in *Lowriting* but this time under different circumstances.

It wouldn't be until years later that I would be introduced to De La Paz as Chuco in the now iconic film *Boulevard Nights*. Of course, I'd heard about the film through older family members over the years who would revel in its unique and gritty story but I did not personally catch on until years *after* I owned (and lost) a lowrider of my own.

As Chuco, a young De La Paz brings to life a Chicano character in turmoil. Chuco has influenced and touched generations of people and continues to do so through the rebirth of classic films being shared on the internet. You'll find images of Chuco all over social media. Thanks to everything old being new again, the film continues to fascinate and provide a snapshot of what lowriding was – and what barrio life was like – before the gang violence and drugs of the 80s, as well as Hollywood, changed everything.

Again, De La Paz lends his talents to a character that is brimming with both emotion and chaos. You can feel Chuco's frustration and identify with his sense of wanting to belong to something. De La Paz had a special insight into this character and was able to relate to him better than most actors would be capable of. He has a way of enriching the characters he plays with a sense of realness and it shows on screen.

The film, just like lowriding culture in general, was no stranger to controversy. Late film critic Roger Ebert wrote that he was met with leaflet-carrying protestors frothing at the mouth about fascism when he went to the theater to screen *Boulevard Nights* for a review. According to Ebert, the protestors had linked the film as part of a plot by the "fascist ruling class" to "poison the minds of thousands."

1979 was popular year for so-called gang cinema with *Walk Proud*, *The Warriors* and *The Wanderers* all released that year, but it was *Boulevard Nights* that spoke to the Chicana/o community and to the culture of lowriding.

To say that De La Paz has become a Chicano icon in the lowrider community and to Chicana/o cult film fans is an understatement; in his own words he considers himself an ambassador of the Chicano culture.

Boulevard Nights, now regarded as a cult classic and legitimized by both cable TV as well as retail and bootleg sales, went from being chastised as a negative and stereotypical gang flick to one that is not only treasured for its authenticity but hailed as a moment in time for the lowrider movement. It's shown regularly on Turner Classic Movies, has been written about in several books and even taught from in some Chicano Studies curriculums.

If you check out reviews for the film online, you will find that people regard De La Paz's *Chuco* character as the real deal. This kind of validation means the world to the actor and he spends a great deal of his time interacting with fans at lowrider shows around the country and even the world.

It was an honor to interview Danny De La Paz for *Lowriting* and get his insights on lowriding culture, Chicanismo and the culture of Hollywood where Chicanos are concerned. Without further ado, here is my interview with Danny De La Paz.

SJR: I watched an interview with you online where you talked about your experience growing up in middle class Whittier as being kind of like the TV show *The Wonder Years*. Were you exposed at all to lowriders or lowrider culture as a kid in Whittier? Or did that exposure come later when you got into acting?

DDLP: As a youngster I was not exposed to lowriding or lowrider culture. I grew up in a middle class neighborhood in the city of Whittier, a suburb of Los Angeles. Many people who are not familiar with Whittier think immediately of Whittier Boulevard which runs through many cities, including Whittier itself, until it ends in Downtown LA. They get confused thinking Whittier must somehow be just like East L.A., where cruising the boulevard had at one time reached iconic status. My childhood in Whittier in the sixties was more akin to that of Kevin, the boy in the television series *The Wonder Years*. On the weekends my parents, my sister, and I would often visit my aunt who lived on Record Street in East L.A. just off the boulevard, a mere ten miles or so from our home in Whittier. The journey west down the boulevard was always an eye opener for me as we drove through Whittier then Pico Rivera, Montebello and finally into East L.A. There was quite a contrast between the two cities. I would later retrace this exact route on my way to work each morning while shooting *Boulevard Nights* in the summer of 1978. It was during this period that I was immersed into lowriding culture as well as other aspects of the Chicano experience of which I was not familiar. The character of Chuco Avila was 16, though I was actually 21 during the making of the film.

SJR: How did you get the part of Chuco?

DDLP: I was working at a lumber yard in the Spring of '78. I was also represented by an agent at a good agency in Hollywood at the time. One day my agent called at my work to tell me about an audition for a new film which at that time was called *King Cobra*. I went to meet the casting director and that's what got the ball rolling regarding my being considered for that role. That was in April, let's say, and I was called back numerous times over the next two and a half months before the decision was finally made to go with me. I was a theatre-trained young actor with only two small television credits under my belt. They took the time to make damn sure I was the one...so many actors were clamoring for that role. It was one of the juiciest parts of that year! I had a strong sense that this was my breakout opportunity. I was a huge James Dean fan, still am, and this was *my* James Dean role in my *Rebel Without a Cause*...and for the same studio, Warner Bros! My blood, sweat and tears are in every frame of that film which eventually came to be retitled *Boulevard Nights*.

SJR: What did your family think of Chuco and of *Boulevard Nights* back then? And now?

DDLP: Alfredo and Margaret De La Paz were my parents. I recall them being as supportive as they could, during this very important transitional period of their youngest son's life. They were both extras in the film during the wedding and reception sequences. In fact, they both did some extra work on *Walk Proud*, another gang related feature shot just prior to *Boulevard Nights*. When the film was finally finished and ready to be screened, many of my family members attended private, invite-only screenings at Warner Bros. Studios, who were set to release it nationwide in a couple of weeks. After seeing it I think we all were a little in shock but impressed at the same time. My parents very much liked my performance and I feel they were very proud of me. The film opened in theatres all across the country on March 23, 1979. I could definitely feel this was a life changing experience and somehow I knew things would never be the same from that day forward. Boy...was I ever right about that! My parents have both crossed over and I thank them from the depth of my heart for all that they gave me. LOVE U, MOM AND POP!!!

SJR: You've said that in other interviews that you identified with Chuco very strongly – can you talk a little bit about that? Does that speak more to Chuco's desire to be accepted by the culture or your own?

DDLP: When I say I identified with the character of Chuco I mean insofar as the inner life of the character, his feeling isolated and alone even within his familia. It's important to take into consideration the fact that I was hiding my sexuality from everyone at that time; having to hide something as significant as that causes one to be affected in such a negative way, the impact of which bleeds into every aspect of your life. I felt isolated and had no one to turn to for advice or guidance. Chuco was a youngster on the verge of manhood. There was no father present in the household and his absence is never dealt with in the film. Chuco is very close to his older brother Raymond, but his carnal is deep into a relationship with a woman whom he plans to marry. Between his job and his relationship with her, Raymond has little time to spend with his younger brother. There are things that a young man does not feel comfortable talking to his mother about. So ultimately he turns to his homeboys for the validation he so desperately desires. In a way, perhaps my acting career was my form of validation. It offered an identity…I was that kid…"the good actor." I don't know – it's all very complex. I don't remember having a need to be validated by my culture…but I related to Chuco's inner conflict. There but for the grace of God…

SJR: Tell me about the role lowriders play in *Boulevard Nights.*

DDLP: Lowriding is as much a part of *Boulevard Nights* as any of its central characters. At that time, in the late seventies, many people not familiar with lowriding associated the whole scene with gangsters and gangsterism. If you were a lowrider you were considered a "gangster with a car." *Boulevard Nights* helped dispel this erroneous myth by showing that lowriding and gangsterism was in most cases mutually-exclusive. The car and the effort put into its presentation represented a transformation for Raymond in terms of the way he saw himself, past and future. It takes a great deal of effort, time, care and finances to create a rolling work of art and all that effort would be seriously threatened by anyone involved in the gang life. Their car would become a target. The character of Raymond had been a gangster in his past, but put all that behind him to seek a different life for himself which included a job at a car shop and his pride and joy: a 1972 tricked out (for the time) Monte Carlo with a beautiful paint job and tight tuck and roll upholstery. His brother Chuco also has a car, but it is not fixed up. There is no sense of pride associated with Chuco's car, mirroring a lack of pride in himself as a person, his self-esteem, and the value he places on life. Lowriding, and Raymond's involvement in it, represent much more than just a pastime or a hobby; it symbolized change. Raymond went from a kid perhaps angry at the unfair absence of his father, to a youngster seeking validation from his gang, to a man with something to build and care for and oversee. The car is a representation of its owner and in Raymond's case, it was a stylish and clean machine. *Boulevard Nights* was the first major studio release (Warner Bros.) that dealt honestly and effectively with the subject of Lowriding. Cruising is an anthropological phenomenon with roots in the mating rituals of Mexico and elsewhere, where the young gather, usually on Sundays, and walk in circular fashion around the plaza seeking to connect with each other and enjoy the fruits of their youth. Cruising just took it from the feet to the foot pedal. If you removed the element of lowriding from *Boulevard Nights* you would have a totally different film, so large a role did it play. Instead of being out in the street wreaking havoc, Raymond could now be found with a respectable job at a car shop using a different kind of gun, loaded not with bullets, but with staples.

SJR: How do you view *Boulevard Nights* all these years later?

DDLP Let me put this whole thing in perspective. It's been over three decades since *Boulevard Nights* was released theatrically nationwide. Video was then in its infancy and there was no Blockbuster or other rental outlets. Cable TV was also in its early period with stations like Select TV, ON TV, The Z Channel, HBO and others just coming on the scene. After its initial run in theatres *Boulevard Nights* was released to these cable outlets where it found a new life. Soon VCRs and video tapes were de rigueur and people began making tapes of their favorite films. *Boulevard Nights* was not officially released to VHS tape until the summer of 1988, ten years after its production and nine years after its premier. VHS tapes back then were very pricey. I believe the retail price for *Boulevard Nights* was somewhere around $80. But there were all those recorded-from-cable tapes floating around…and so begins the journey of the little film that could. A journey that began with placard-carrying Chicano protesters marching in a circle in front of theatres where the film was playing, who, though not having seen the film, but felt compelled to decry its "destructive and negative stereotypical portrayal" of a culture that was sick and tired of being misrepresented by the media. Many of these protestors later became educators who would show *Boulevard Nights* in their classrooms as part of their Chicano Studies courses. How ironic then that this little film should itself be misrepresented by the very same people, the *Raza* themselves. The colonized were mimicking the behavior of their colonizers, and so the cycle was complete. But *Boulevard Nights* was not affected by any of this for one reason and one reason only…THE RAZA LOVED IT. Chicanos identified with the struggle of a Chicano family like the Avilas and the challenges faced living in an environment like that of East LA. The Raza embraced it and it became a part of the Chicanada, passed from generation to generation. It is even more beloved today when so many feel nostalgic and reminisce about a time when things were perhaps not as dark and complex as they have become for the modern Chicana/o. I am constantly amazed and deeply moved by the strong feeling of love that so many Chicano people feel for me because of my work in film. To them, I am their cultural ambassador, a role which I take very seriously; when I meet these beautiful gente their eyes light up like a Christmas tree and I sense a genuine excitement and enthusiasm emanating from them towards me. I have been invited to weddings and quinceañeras and baptisms and pachangas of every type. Though I know none of these people personally and would otherwise be considered a total stranger, I am nonetheless treated as though I were a member of their family. I cannot help but be blown away by this and also very, very grateful to have been a part of something this impactful. To receive an Oscar for their work is what many actors strive for in their career, the ultimate validation of their work by their peers. What I have achieved is something even more fulfilling and much larger in scope: the love and acceptance and *validation* of my Raza, my culture, the people who understand what it feels like to be Chicano, and the pride and gratitude for all that that represents in this life. *Boulevard Nights* gave all that to me and I will forever be grateful for the honor of being given such a blessed opportunity. To be a part of a movie now considered a Chicano Classic.

SJR: What was the impact of *Boulevard Nights* on mainstream America at the time and now?

DDLP: Though the film has been shown on TCM Turner Classic Movies as part of a Latino Film Festival, and also as a videotape, it was consistently a bestseller for both Blockbuster Video and Tower Records/Video, and despite the fact that the Los Angeles Time's highly revered critic Charles Champlin gave it a favorable review at the time, BN is still so far under the mainstream media radar that it barely registers.

In 2009 Warner Bros. finally released an official "DVD" of the film 30 years after its release. After all that time what the unsuspecting public finally got was a video transfer to disc as opposed to an actual transfer of film digitized and made into a DVD. It's not even presented in widescreen so the viewer is subjected to the very tacky pan and scan scam. Warner went and released all their older "vintage" titles this way. What a shame.

BN was gorgeously photographed by John

Bailey, a highly regarded cinematographer for whom BN was his first film as the main man, THE cinematographer, and not the first assistant as he had been up to that point. The look of the 35mm film is crisp and clean with beautifully composed shots and masterly lighting. Today I don't believe anyone who works at Warner Bros. has ever even heard of the movie. Perhaps when I pass they will give it a brief mention. Probably NOT! [laughs]

SJR: Any great behind the scenes stories from the set of *Boulevard Nights*?

DDLP: As far as great behind the scenes stories go... when we began principal photography in July of '78, the film had just changed titles from *King Cobra* to *Boulevard Nights*. At first, the role of Chuco was seen as a supporting role in service of the role of the elder brother Raymond played by Richard Yñiguez. Yñiguez was the closest to a Chicano movie star as we had at that time, having starred in two projects that drew large television audiences, *TheDeadly Tower* and *River of Promises*. Both of these projects featured Richard in full leading man status as police detectives, very respectable roles for a young, very easy on the eyes Chicano who Richard very much was in those days. As filming progressed and the producers began to view the dailies (the scenes that had been shot the previous day) they began to see my performance and realized very quickly that they had quicksilver on their hands. Soon after that, new pages of script began to arrive on the set that featured more and more of my character. I went from a supporting role to the central dramatic focus of the film. Richard could see this happening and once commented to me how he thought it was the best thing for the film. His character was still in front, if not center, of the story, but my character Chuco was the driving force behind the story. I will always remember Richard as a kind and generous person who grew to love and respect me and who shared with me some of the wisdom he had gained up to that point in his career. We got along famously and the whole shoot was a very enjoyable experience! I also remember being very insecure about playing a Chicano gangster because of the specificity of behavior involved in taking on a role like that. It was akin to doing

Shakespeare for me, like visiting another planet and trying to be accepted as one of them. I was always seeing the real cholos watching us film or hanging out in the area and praying that they, of all people, would believe me to be authentic and real. One day we were all just hanging around waiting for the crew to light the set and I overheard some real homeboys saying "who is that homeboy?" referring to me..."I've seen that vato before, aye." It was at this juncture that I realized they believed that I was a real homeboy and had no clue that I was, in actuality, about as real as Pee Wee Herman! Wow... was I ever relieved. Standing there in my baggy Dickies and my Pendleton with those B52 collars, I knew I had succeeded at least on some level. That moment was a milestone for me, so much so that I have always remembered it.

SJR: Do you or have you ever owned a lowrider?
DDLP: I do not now nor have I ever owned a lowrider.

SJR: Has lowriding changed since those days?

DDLP: Not only has lowriding changed but we have changed as a people, Chicanos have changed. We've come full circle from a point where we lost touch with our cultura as we travelled down the yellow brick road of assimilation, to the point now where our Chicano youth have *embraced* their Chicanismo and redefined it, in a sense going back to the egg and drawing from within themselves a new fervor and pride for being Chicano. I am so happy to have lived long enough to see this. Yes...lowriding has also changed. It's become much more respectable with fathers and sons bonding over the restoration of first a bicycle, then a car when the boy has reached a certain age. Car shows are beautifully produced up and down the state of Califas as well as all over the country and the world for that matter. An exhibition of lowriding at the Peterson Museum in Los Angeles made history and really showed how far lowriding has come. But *Boulevard Nights* put lowriding on the map. George Lucas, the esteemed filmmaker of Star Wars fame, was himself a lowrider cruising the streets of Modesto Califas as a teenager. That's how he came to make *American Graffiti*. People in Japan were fascinated with Lucas' film as well as the Cheech and Chong films but *Boulevard Nights* placed lowriding in its proper context; for lowriding is very much a creation spun from Chicano culture and is inextricably connected to the Chicano experience. The Japanese are as enthusiastic about lowriding as any Chicano I have ever encountered. My Japanese homeboys are my carnales, Chicanos in their heart. It's a beautiful thing to see them in their full Chicano regalia with their magnificent lowriders. When *Boulevard Nights* opened in 1980 in Japan it started a movement. I have visited this wonderful country many times and have some amazing stories to share…maybe in my memoirs! [laughs] So yes, I believe lowriding is more sophisticated today than it was back in the day because technology has introduced new techniques and possibilities taking restoration and artistic expression to a whole new level. But the spirit of lowriding has not changed. It is still an expression of a singular pride, a connection to *cultura* that will never die as long as there are Chicano hearts beating somewhere on the planet.

SJR: In your opinion, was *Boulevard Nights* an authentic portrayal of lowrider culture of the time?

DDLP: YES. I believe it was. I suppose you could look upon the movie as a photographic record of the lowriding scene at that time in the late seventies. There was, of course, much more to lowriding than can be seen in *Boulevard Nights*, but as far as the accuracy of pinpointing where lowriding was in regards to its evolution, I think the film is quite accurate.

SJR: Tell me about your experience as a Chicano actor in Hollywood.

DDLP: Having come from a small-ish town some thirty or so minutes from Hollywood, I was quite familiar with the famous dream factory that lay essentially in my backyard. As a child of ten and eleven I actually had an agent and was submitted for movie and television projects. This would be in '66 - '68 or thereabouts. I was way too shy and intimidated by the whole thing at the time so I let it go. I remember once auditioning for the young boy in *Elvis Goes to Acapulco* or whatever that

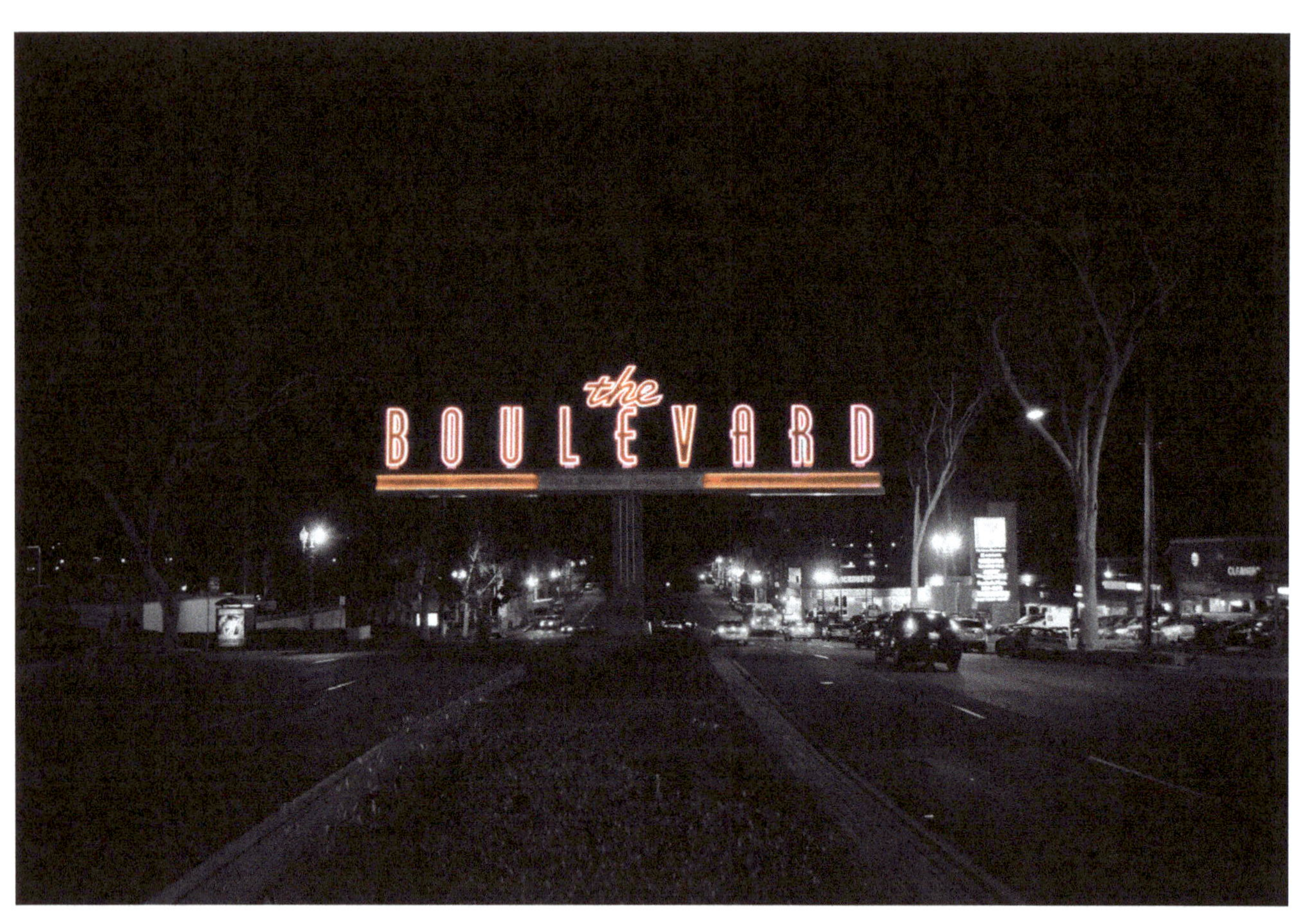

On the Boulevard, San Diego

movie was called but it really wasn't until I got to high school, my freshman year, that I joined the drama department, and things began to gel for me. We had a teacher, she was young and attractive and very enthusiastic about theatre and the arts in general. It became apparent to me from day one when I first set foot on the stage, that I was right at home in that dark sacred place known as *The Theatre*. I flourished in the numerous plays we did over my four years in high school and started to gain both experience and confidence. I very much belonged there. By the time my senior year rolled around I found myself with my first professional job which began in the spring and therefore required me to miss school so as to meet my newfound professional obligations. I took night school and graduated along with my class. I was on my way. Three years after my high school graduation I landed that coveted role in *Boulevard Nights* and so began a journey that I am still on to this very day. When I got involved with the Hollywood system I gained a perspective of what it's like from the inside. I observed how dishonest the writing was when it came to Chicano or Mexican people. I was always asked to modify my performance so as to fit into a predetermined set of stereotypic parameters. Television was the worst offender, but films came in a close second. Because my last name was De La Paz, it was accepted as a foregone conclusion that I would be a drug dealer or a gangster or some sort of victim desperately in need of my superior Anglo's good graces. It was comical in a way because I am a very intelligent and articulate person who was classically trained as an actor and knew my craft as well as anybody my age. I wanted better written roles but found that my choosiness led to my taking roles that though eventually offered, I really wouldn't have done if there were no money involved. In short I felt unfulfilled. I did get the opportunity to be in some wonderful films that I am very proud of. Many of my fans are only now beginning to discover these films and are impressed to see the variety of characterizations I was able to assay. Westerns, political thrillers, even comedies, I have done them all. Overall, I found working in the industry to be untenable for me as my mental health was a bit questionable to begin with; adding Hollywood into the mix only exacerbated my mental and emotional anguish. Today after many years of reflection and personal growth, I have decided to return to the scene of the crime so to speak; to get back up on that horse and ride, hopefully into the sunset of my so-called golden years. Perhaps the best is yet to come.

SJR: After a lifetime of experience and recognition, do you identify more with Chuco from *Boulevard Nights* or with Big Puppet from *American Me.* Or neither? I ask because you must still feel a strong connection to both characters if your tattoos are anything to go on.

DDLP: Let me begin by saying that I love both those characters, Chuco Avila and Puppet, with all my heart. I tried to imbue each with heart and soul – my blood, sweat, and tears are all over that screen. I identified with Chuco's sense of isolation; even his homegirls could not penetrate that solitary place. And Puppet…I really believed he loved his brother deeply, that he did what he did to save his family from the nightmare he had created, an act the shame of which caused him to utter those now iconic words repeated back to me so many times over the twenty one years since the film's release. I am so glad that my Raza did not hate me for what I had done. It was, in fact, a metaphor. Puppet and his younger carnal stood for every young Chicano who out of sheer ignorance and mental conditioning kill their own Chicano "brothers" each and every day on the streets of barrios across this nation. Some people got it, some people did not. I have to identify with my characters or I cannot bring to them the understanding and empathy necessary to create truthfully from the heart. I have their names tattooed on my forearms to honor two very significant experiences in my career as an actor and in my life as a proud Chicano.

SJR: What do you see for the future of lowriding?

DDLP: I really see lowriding going deeper into connecting with Chicanos in a very practical way. Lowrider car clubs can give back to their communities and reach out to the youth, offering an alternative to the gang lifestyle. I see lowriding becoming more proactive and focusing more on helping others. I have already seen this happening today. I hope it continues to evolve in the most positive way for Chicanos and humanity alike.

SJR: Could you ever see *Boulevard Nights* being re-made?

DDLP: Not so much remade as REIMAGINED. I have the seeds for a wonderful sequel of sorts that more echoes the original than copies it. I hope to get to that project in the foreseeable future. What trips me out is the fact that after 34 years, this movie, so identified with the lowrider movement, has never inspired one single lowrider to do a mural tribute to the film. I have seen *The Sopranos*, *The Godfather*, *Scarface* etc. but never *Boulevard Nights.* I find that quite remarkable. Scarface etc. but never *Boulevard Nights.* I find that quite remarkable.

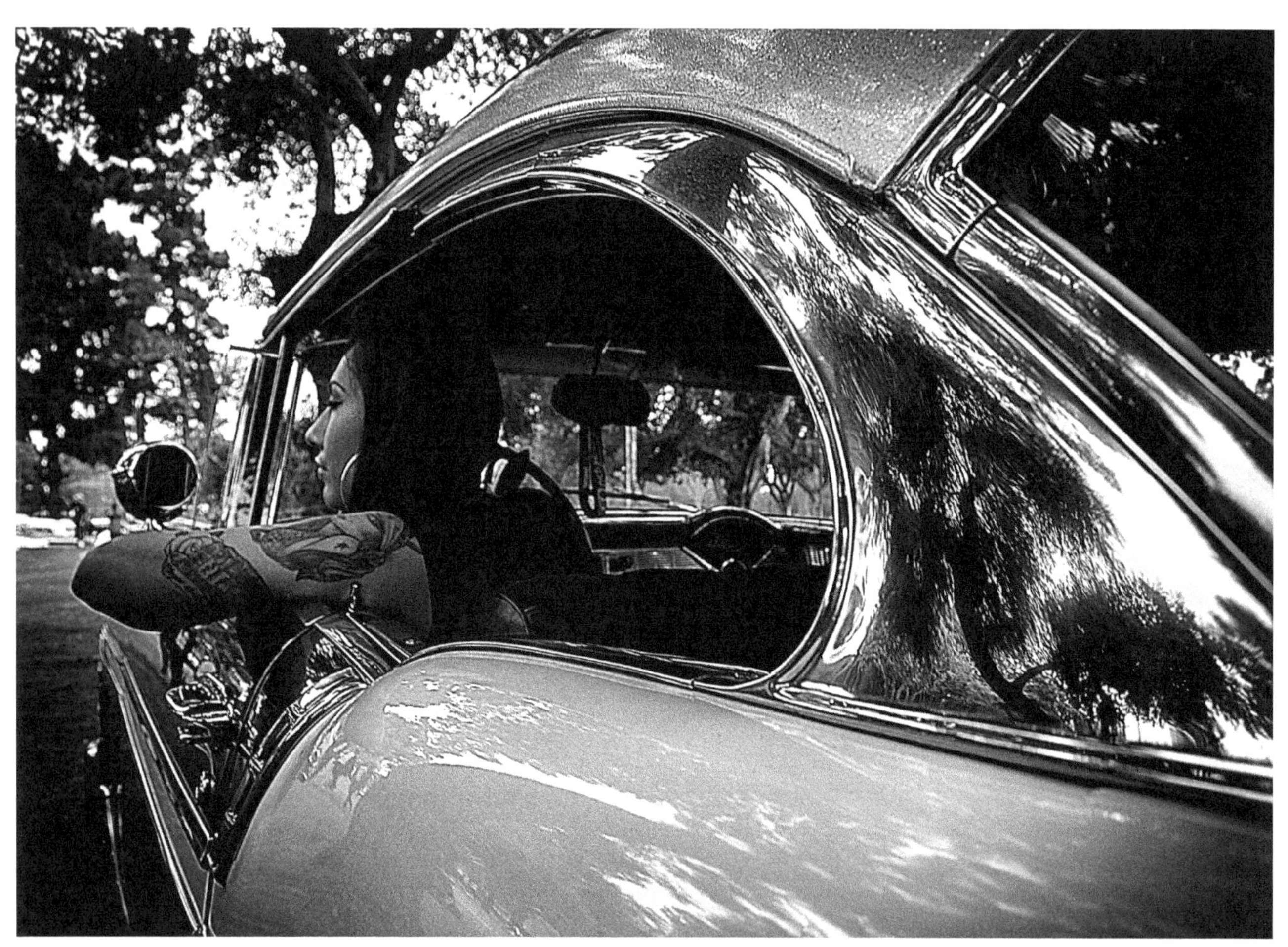

Dreaming Casually, Mayra Ramirez - '56 Chevy Bel Air

To All The Cholos I Ever Loved Before

By Andrea J. Serrano

I can't help but want you
you break into me like poison
sweet absinthe that takes me back
to days gone by and
guys like you
whispering "mi'ja" softly in my ear
just before nuzzling my neck
a barrio king
and me
hoping to be queen

The memory of your kiss
keeps me warm the way your Pendleton used to

The smell of yesca mixed with Tres Flores still makes me hunger for you

Remembering our bodies smashed together
with the urgency of young love
steaming up the windows in the backseat
of your homeboy's '85 Regal

still makes me tingle

I can't help but turn my head twice
when I see a full bigote and goatee
I watch you walk down the street
white t-shirt slung over your left shoulder
tattoos blazing against your brown skin
and I imagine you
humming Brenton Wood songs in my ear
dark brown hands running over my body
under my shirt
into my flesh
making every part of my body scream out your name
in innocent delight

I wish life hadn't changed

I wish we hadn't changed

Shit gets heavy and we had to choose
and I sometimes regret
that I didn't choose you
Maybe growing up
broke us

and leaving you behind
was a natural part of life
but it hurts to wonder
what happened to you?

what happened to me?

I want to remember
your smile
your skin
your voice

I want to remember a simpler time
when being your lady
was all that mattered to me

When it's cold outside
and I'm alone
I wrap myself in Pendleton memories of you
do me a favor
whisper "mi'ja" in my ear
for old time's sake
let me be your barrio queen
just one last time

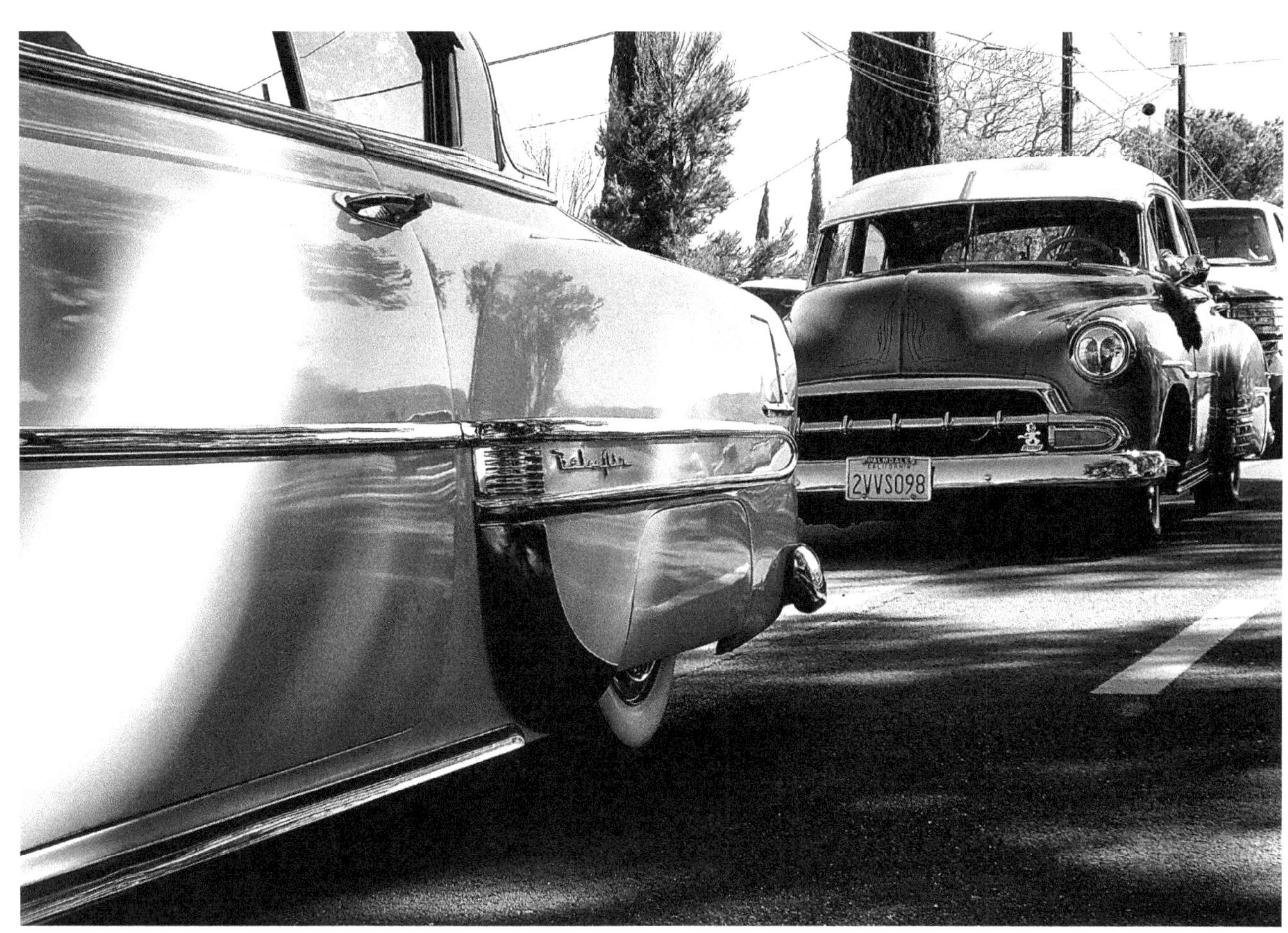

Pachucos Cruisin – 1954 Chevrolet Bel Air

A Prayer for Nuestra Señora la Reina de la calle Central

A Litany (with a nod to Juan Felipe Herrera)

By Andrea J. Serrano

I cruised the hell out of West Central Avenue
aka Route 66 that sliced through Albuquerque aka Burque
I cruised because it's what young Brown kids did on Saturday nights
because I had to lie to my mom to get out of the house
because I was looking for the love of my life
and I found him over and over and over again
because Sonic Drive-In banned cruisers from their parking lot
because low and slow was the best life advice I had ever received

I cruised because good Catholic girls weren't supposed to
because I was too young for downtown bars
and too Brown for the "nice" part of town
because the finest guys in Burque shined up their ranflas at
Crystal Clear Car Wash before hitting the Ave.
because my older sisters cruised San Gabriel Park and Tingley Beach
and never took me along for the ride
because those same places were outlawed by the time it was my turn

Central was my rite of passage
and in a world where nothing is sacred anymore
the cruise was as sacred
as the moon that hung like a communion host
on the tongue of the night sky
watching over me
worrying about me
the way my mom did

I cruised because there was a Lowrider exhibit in the Smithsonian
because Española, NM
is the Lowrider Capitol of the World
but West Central was the cruising capitol
of my world
my heart

I cruised because Breton Wood sang Oogum Boogum
and Dr. Dre rapped Nuthin' But A G Thang
because the mayor said I couldn't
because Albuquerque Police Department said I couldn't
because my parents said I couldn't
because someday I was going to grow up
because Central between Atrisco Street to Coors Boulevard
was my entire world

because I didn't have my own ride
but I dreamed of a firme '78 Monte Carlo
black cherry with pink diamond tuck interior
because I still dream of that ride

I cruised because I could

Sometimes, on Saturday nights
West Central calls me
says she still waits for me
sometimes I answer and hit the Ave.
because I haven't forgotten

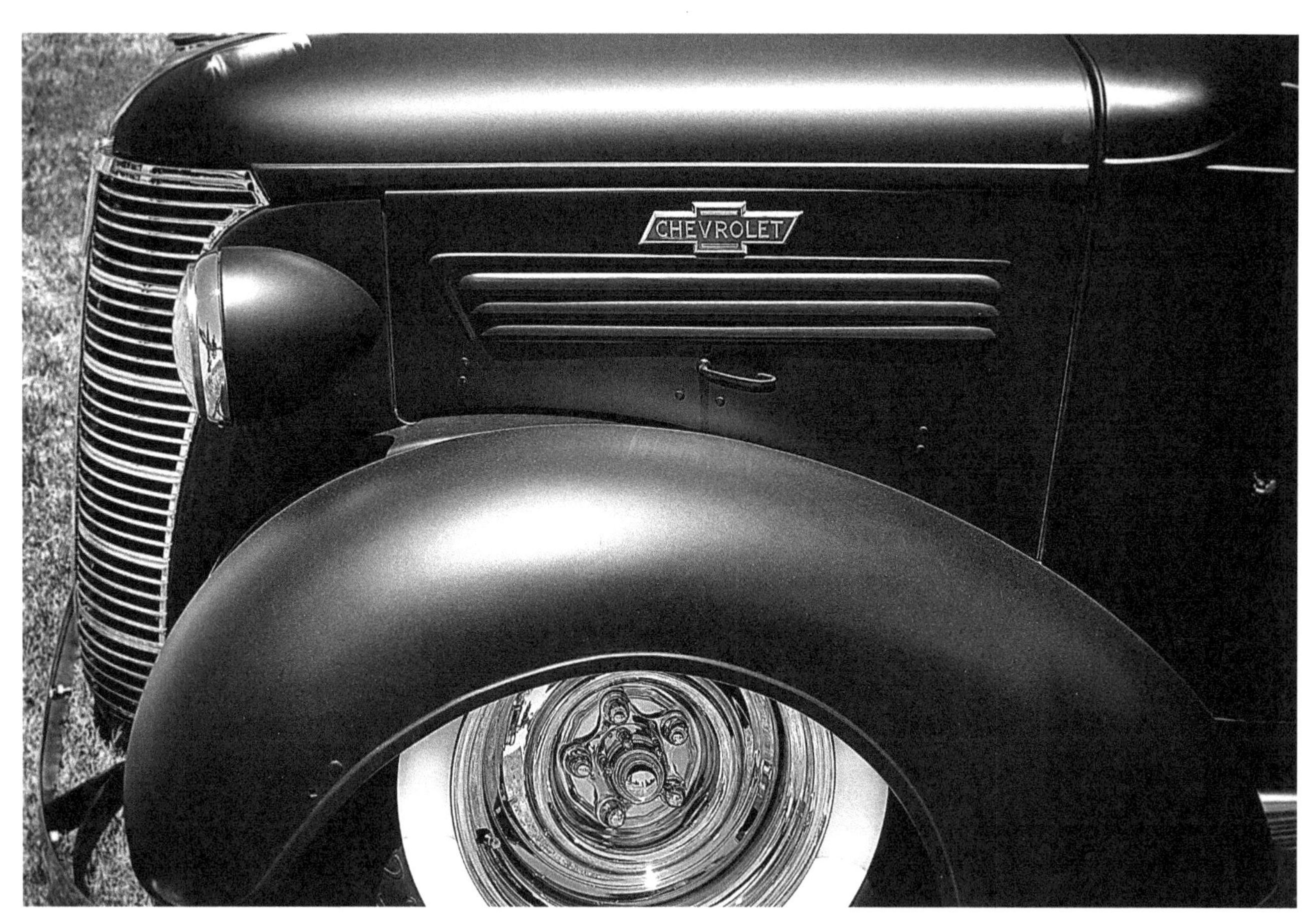

38 Special – '38 Chevy Pickup

Chimayó Chevy Pickup, Step Side '69

By Anna C. Martinez

she chuckled at his question by numbers as
she remembered them by
car/make/model
American mostly Chevy
diamond tucked leather pleated overheated
heaved
over the front bucket seat into the back
on her back
windshield beaded of breath excreted

root beer Bel Aire revving high
racing stripe black and white
Malibu tight checkerboard leather
she wonders whether this one will be back

step side, '69
blue Chevy pickup rumbling fingers fumbling
steering column stick shift encumbering
static on the a.m. and aqua net 'do
hips bumping

the knob rolling back from Wolfman Jack to KRLA
sixteen candles
a thousand miles away
she begs him
stay
begs

low cigarette pack low Impala
candy apple
diamond tucked
both ignore the glamour shot
tucked in his driver side visor
lo mucho que te quiero, que te adoro
eyes her over
flick of the finger
switch sends it hopping
she locking fingers around his neck
white leather to squeal the spread of her legs

blue Chevy pickup rumbling
fingers hovering over the phone
running through smoke swirling
from red tip of borrowed cigarette dangling off her lip
lifts the shade just in time to see

Chevy pulls away
watches feet chasing down racing down
naked down the street wrapped in a bed sheet chasing down tail lights hoping for red
so much unsaid it's speak now or

Malibu
now driving blue silver plush interior wire spoke wheels dropped to the floor T-Bird
who loops around the old Sonic and
had said it once but his whispers touched just too much
but two years gone by she didn't think twice to hop in his ride
cruised her through town showing her around
to his friends and their
dart away eyes and
she runs fingers through his hair
touching him there
just to hear it said
under breath

coldassmetalshellwhiteSuburban
doublebarrelshotgunrack
hollowedoutnoseatintheback
woolenhorseblanketthrownover
jaggedfloorboardcancerspots and
splinteredbitsofalfalfaandhay and

hick don't even try to say it

not colder though than black '72 Camaro
down by the river to smoke a toke
he keeps pouring her Crown
she can't wait to pee
squats down behind the monkey peanut tree near the edge
where he shoves her in
head over panties
water washes over
WHATTHEFUCK
struggles up for air
through wet web of hair
mid November
stabbing icicle air
pulling up levis
stumbling to shore
teeth rattling
screaming battling
fucking dripping
red river
on black leather
wondering whether she
will come back

combats all
but the blood red
shackle of hickeys choking her throat and
purple and blue
five-finger prints between her thighs
but she survives

funny
as she just hopped in that ride down Riverside Drive
so that he could see her drive away
as he sat parked and watching in that pínche blue pickup Chevrolet

she chuckles again remembering them
even the most recent
Hyundai gray
didn't make the cut
so
what a reminisce from red tip
of freshly licked and rolled smoke
billowing from her sun faded wine and silver

Chevy van
where she vows that she still can
though young face fades away and

strong legs less tanned and brown
better keep your eyes on the road son
better slow this vehicle down
wine plush recline captain's chairs
rear end continental spare
8 cylinder
8 track
Player
fingers through her gray
jet black back in the day
and that's alright with her.

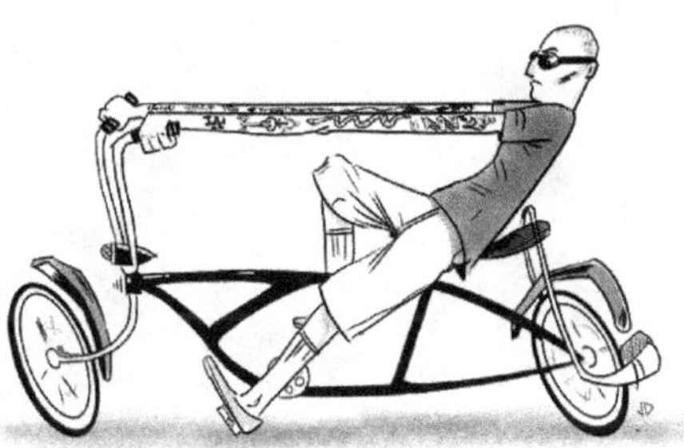

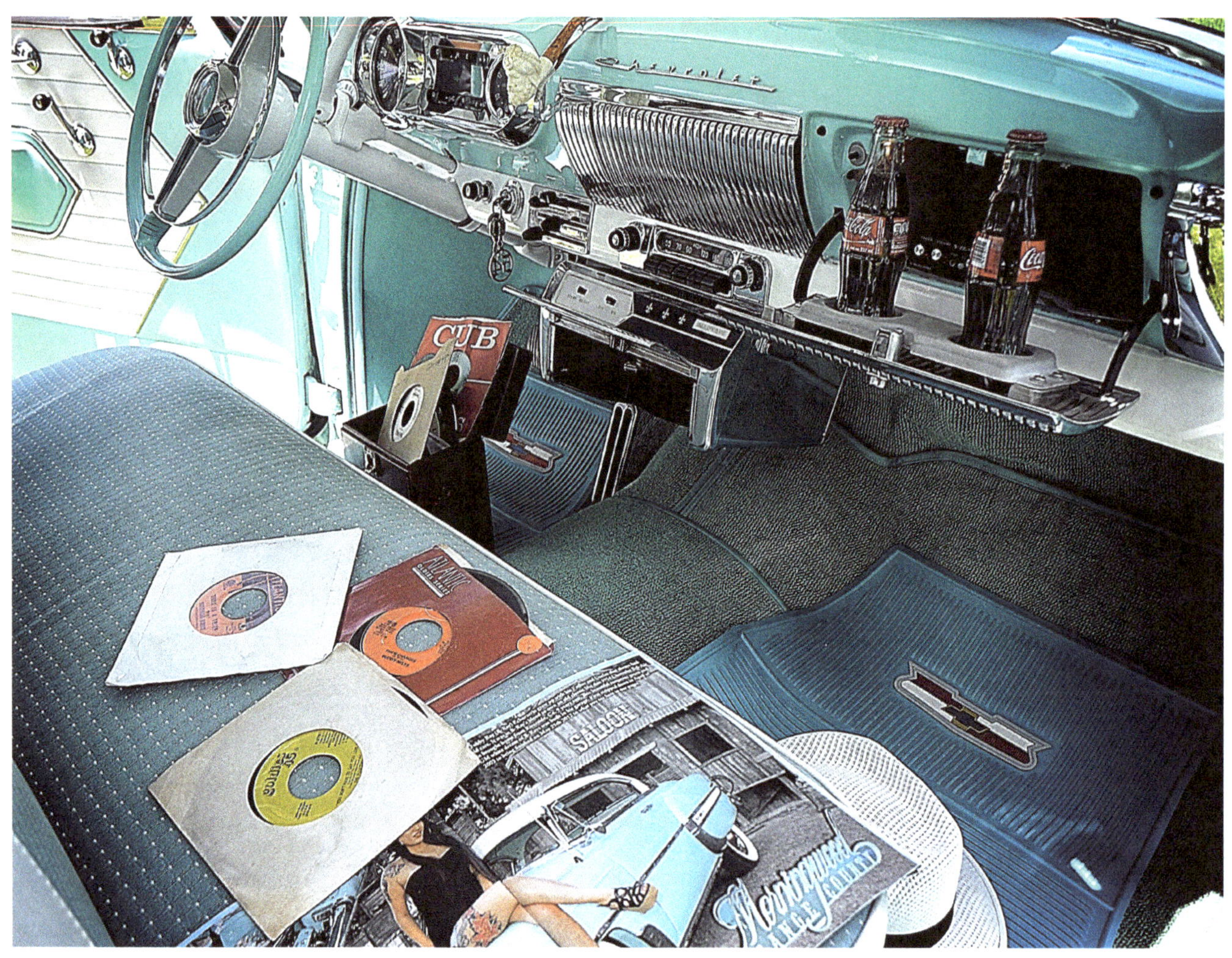

For the Record - 1954 Chevy Bel-Air

Lowrider Oldies:
The Unofficial Soundtrack to the Chicano Experience
by Allen Thayer

"I love the rare soul music of individuals that never got their voices heard and never got radio play. Their music, their records only stayed within their region. And that's kinda like us; our voices aren't really heard outside our region and our neighborhood."

–The Homeboy Mad, Souleros Ball founder, Chicano activist, and Streetlow Magazine editor

Chicano lowriders in search of the perfect musical mood to enhance their slow procession look to the past and present for a certain sound and feel: desperate and delicate harmonies proclaiming love, hate, or reconciliation set to dramatic arrangements and a tough R&B rhythm track. For more than fifty years, lowriders, neighborhood record collectors, and local DJs have collectively cataloged an unfathomably deep canon of R&B, doo-wop, and harmony soul, collectively known as oldies.

"The car attracted the girls and the music got them in the mood," writes Ruben Molina in *The Old Barrio Guide to Lowrider Music*, "so the neighborhood record collector was just as important as the neighborhood grease monkey."[1] But you don't have to have a lowrider to appreciate these songs. Swirling in and out of laughter and conversation at a family BBQ, lovingly dedicated by a wife over the radio for her incarcerated man, or drifting out of a slow-rolling, shimmering lowrider, oldies are the unofficial soundtrack to the Chicano experience.

"If you're a Chicano, you're supposed to listen to oldies, have a lowrider, just dress like I'm dressed right now with the Pendleton, your brim hat, your Winos with your *pantelon* all creased up." Soulero Sal is the youngest, at eighteen, of the informal

Northern California network of Chicano soul music collectors. He's still working on getting that lowrider, but he's got all the other bases covered. When we met in October of 2010, Sal proudly confirmed that his 45 collection was exactly forty-five records deep. He lives in the predominantly Hispanic agricultural community of Salinas, and since graduating from high school just months ago, he's been working at McDonald's to support his record habit.

Some of the most impressive soul music collections are in the hands of Chicanos. Of course, not every Chicano is an expert in rare soul music, but it's fair to say that the average Chicano from the barrios of Los Angeles, the Bay Area, or any number of smaller California and Southwest communities has a deeper knowledge of and greater appreciation for soul music than the average citizen, with or without papers. "When they ask for a song, they know what year it came out, who recorded it," says Johnny Morris, a Los Angeles DJ on KGFJ. Once, he says, a thirteen-year-old girl called in to request "Fork in the Road," the little-known B-side to the Miracles' hit "Tracks of My Tears."

"My parents used to always have parties at the house—I must've been, like, twelve years old, and a lot of the music they played was like Smokey Robinson and the Miracles," says Tommy Siqueiro, Soulero Sal's mentor and a San Jose local. "Ever since I heard that sound, I wanted to collect anything that had those *oohs* and *aahs* in it." He wasn't the only one. More than three hundred miles to the south, Ruben Molina had his oldies epiphany at about the same time:

> I remember being picked up from junior high school by a friend's uncle. He was a laid-back vato from East Side Clover who drove a 1954 Bel-Air dropped to the ground. He pulled up in front of the school, and as we piled in, the oldies streaming from his eight-track tape player filled my head. I don't remember what song was playing but I knew right there, that was the sound for me.

Today, both Tommy and Ruben are considered *veteranos* of the oldies scene, one in the North and the other in the South, and each playing a critical role in supporting and influencing the next generation of Chicano record collectors. The traditional tensions between the Northern (*Norteño*) and Southern (*Sureño*) Chicano communities in

California and the considerable distance between Southern California and the Bay Area means that the scenes stay separate despite their shared passion for the same music.

For generations, oldies remained a well-kept secret within the Chicano community, leaking across ethnic and cultural lines via local radio shows, the twelve volume *East Side Story* LP/CD series, and innumerable legit and less-than-legit bootleg CD compilations. Just in the past few years, this sweet-soul secret has leaked out to the broader community of music collectors, musicians, and the general public. As Chicano collectors have infiltrated eBay and established a beachhead on YouTube and Facebook with video clips of their rare soul records, they are expanding the canon of classic oldies while exposing collectors and general soul music fans to the delicate beauty of these slept-on B-sides.

A quick listen to records by Raphael Saadiq, Lee Fields, Sharon Jones and the Dap-Kings, Amy Winehouse, Kings Go Forth, Mayer Hawthorne, Cee Lo Green, or even R. Kelly reveals a growing trend, however marginal, in popular music that favors soulful sounds, innovative arrangements, and an emphasis on sentimental songwriting. Andy Noble, bandleader of the contemporary sweet-soul group Kings Go Forth and rare-vinyl dealer, appeals to the oldies infidels. "Whaddya fuckin' want?" he says. "Hip-hop-tempo bangin' drums with four dudes just killing sweet harmonies. I mean, c'mon, most people our age have not grown up with that music, have not heard of it, and they hear it and it fucks them up. It's so good!"

From Pachucos to Chicanos

There's nothing wrong with enjoying oldies over computer speakers, the hi-fi, or a crackly radio connection, but it goes without saying that oldies should ideally be experienced from the comfort of a classic lowrider with the windows down despite the fact that at a cruising speed of seven mph, there's not much of a breeze. Whether you call them "lowrider oldies," "Chicano oldies," or just plain "oldies," this musical tradition is inseparable from the Chicano culture and specifically its lowrider subculture. But before there were Chicanos riding around in lowriders to the sweet sound of oldies, zoot suit–wearing *Pachucos* cruised the streets in bombs—customized 1930s and '40s sedans—on their way to juke joints to swing dance to raw jump-blues.

It's convenient, but lazy, to imagine that the demographic mix in the Southwest U.S. has always been the same mix of Caucasian, Hispanic, Black, and Asian. But, as Ted West writes in *Car & Driver* magazine, "before the dust bowl and World War II brought hordes of new Anglos from the Midwest and South, Chicanos, like the Anglo pioneers, were simply 'Californians.' Until the 1930s, most Anglos spoke some Spanish as a matter of course. But in the wake of the Anglo migration, Chicanos suddenly became foreigners in their own land—strange, olive-skinned people 'so stupid they couldn't even speak English.'"[3] This mass domestic migration to California naturally put a strain on the minority Hispanic population, especially in the young and thriving city of Los Angeles.

The younger generation of Mexican-Americans borrowed and adapted styles from other recently migrated minority groups, like their appropriation of the zoot suit from the Black jazz scene. Their parents didn't much care for their extreme fashion statement, and the U.S. government went so far as banning the style. Because of the war raging in the Pacific, basic commodities were rationed, and wasteful use of most staples was outlawed. By their very design, zoot suits required an unusually large amount of fabric, which, in addition to their unconventional style, brought negative attention to the Mexican American youth who wore them. Long before organizing migrant farm workers, Cesar Chavez wore a zoot suit. In *Lowrider: History, Pride, Culture,* Paige R. Penland quotes Chavez: "The style hit California in 1937 or 1938. They looked kind of weird to everybody. From 1940 through 1944, people were wearing them a little more."[4] They called themselves Pachucos. With their flamboyant, arguably unpatriotic, costumes and their automotive counterpart—customized and lowered older-model family sedans—Pachucos were easy targets for the Anglo police force.

"That was the beginning of low and slow," said Victor Vega, an advertising agent for *Lowrider Magazine.* "Cruising in Mexico was done walking around the plaza, flirting with the girls. Here, we do it in our cars, on the boulevard, checking out the girls. In White culture they like their cars jacked up in the back and fast; we have to be different so we have them low. The U.S. is a car culture and whether you're White or Chicano your car is an expression of yourself."[6] The same was true for Cesar Chavez, who not only dressed the part, he fixed up a couple of bombs. Penland quotes Chavez: "The one we had for the longest time was a 1940 Chevy. In those days you went the opposite—we lowered the springs in the back. Fender skirts. Two tail pipes."[7] Pachucos transformed junked, hulking family sedans into slow-rolling sculptures of metal, paint, love, chrome, and grease.

Around the mid-'60s, when the civil rights movement crested, a new kind of Mexican American emerged. In contrast to Pachucos, who were marginalized, seen as hoodlums and rebels, Chicanos embraced their indigenous heritage while forging a new political and cultural identity. What was once a racial slur, the word Chicano became a badge of honor distinguishing modern, politically aware Mexican Americans from their disenfranchised parents. "A Chicano is a Mexican American with a non-Anglo image of himself," said Ruben Salazar, the Chicano activist and journalist killed by the L.A.P.D. while covering an anti-war protest in East L.A. in 1970.[8] Salazar pits Chicanos against mainstream society, basically saying that they are anything that mainstream Anglo (read: White) culture is not. Ted West echoes Salazar's sentiment, referring specifically to how lowriders embodied this new political ethos:

> As surely as long hair and dirty clothes in 1967 expressed young America's contempt for its government in war, 5.20" x 14" tires on tiny Cragars supporting a '64 Impala with no ground clearance express the refusal of young Chicano American to be Anglicized. There has never been a clearer case of the automobile being used as an ethnic statement. You can look at it from an automotive engineering standpoint and say it's an atrocity. But if you do, you haven't seen it. This isn't engineering, this is community consciousness.

Just as the automotive designs evolved dramatically from the 1940s to the 1950s, so did popular music. The stew of jazz, blues, and swing that thrived in L.A. during the '30s and '40s gave birth to thriving local rock and roll and R&B scenes, which were hardly distinguishable from each other in their early years. Young Mexican Americans were enthusiastic supporters, though rarely performers themselves, of these new sounds. Chicano music historian Ruben Molina writes, "This 'cool' sound was gathering a ground swell of support during the mid-forties among Chicano teens and musicians who did not feel the same appreciation for ranchero and mariachi music as their parents did."[1]

Due to the massive influx of workers from the Southern states and Texas in order to man the factories cranking out hardware for the war in the Pacific, Los Angeles' ethnic mix began skewing decidedly darker with Black, White, and Brown additions. Molina explains that alongside the Mexicans from Texas came "African Americans from the South and from Texas, so they kind of congregated at work, and the music kind of jumped over. Rhythm and blues slowly became part of Chicano culture."

Cesar Chavez's evolution from a frustrated and marginalized zoot suit–wearing, carrucha-driving Pachuco youth to a proud, lowrider-cruising Chicano activist represents the cultural and political shift within the Mexican American community during the middle of last century. The Homebody Mad, a Chicano activist and *Streetlow Magazine* editor, explains why for more than half a century Chicanos have celebrated the same musical aesthetic: "I think it was just the music of the time when we really found ourselves: the way we talk, the way we dress, you know, the cars that we drive, and the music we listen to."

"In the early days, they [the Chicano audience] liked exactly what the Black audiences liked," recalled legendary L.A. bandleader Johnny Otis.[11] Otis and his band used to play every Sunday at Angeles Hall in East Los Angeles. Chicanos were big supporters of the African American music scene in Los Angeles in general, but a handful of White Los Angeles radio disc jockeys would soon discover the Chicano listener had a special appreciation for R&B and soul ballads.

*

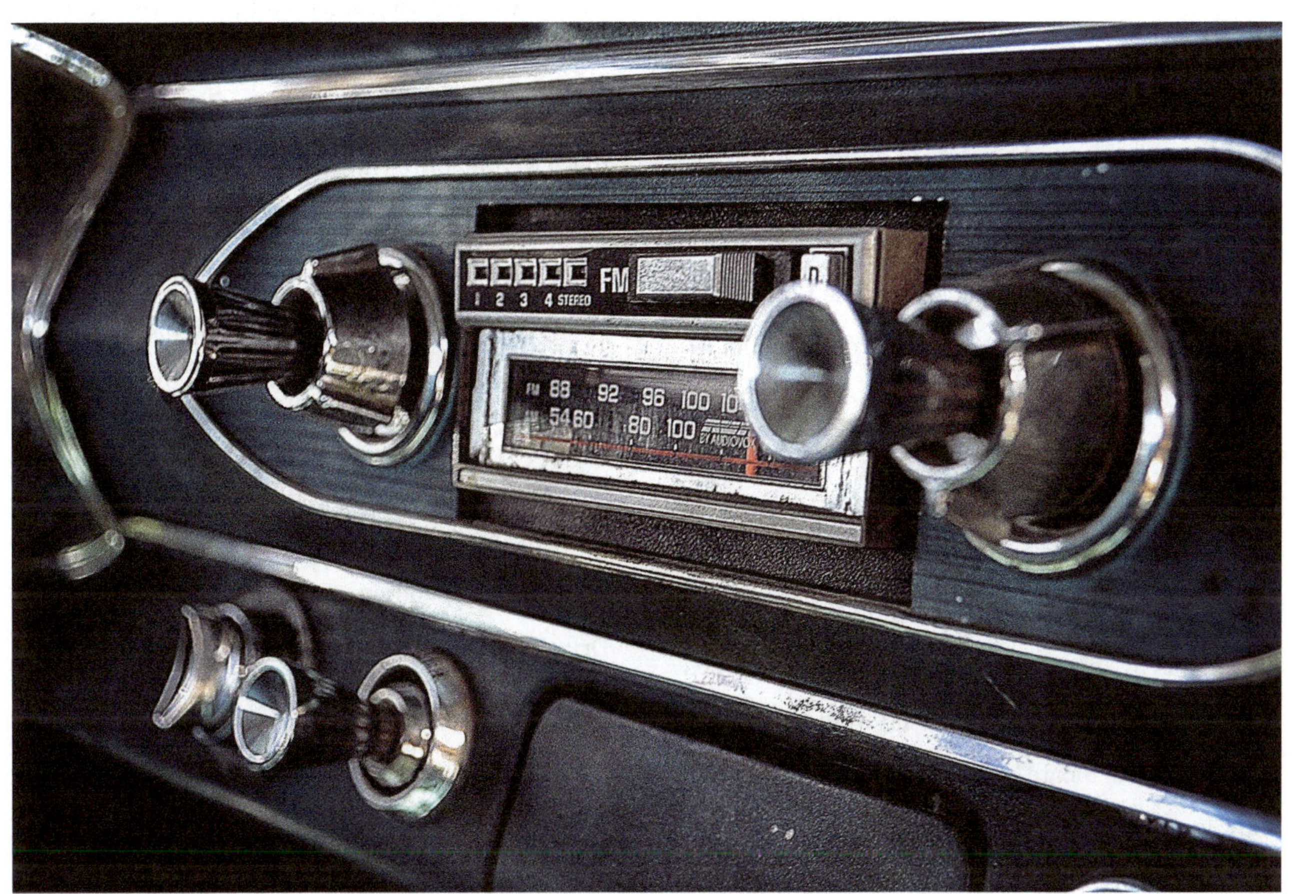

On the Radio – Chevy Nova

Oldies But Goodies

Thanks to the White baby-boomer nostalgia vehicles like *American Graffiti*, *The Big Chill*, and *Happy Days*, and the near-monopolization of radio by Clear Channel, for most of us, the word "oldies" suggests a stagnant pool of overplayed Motown hits and bubblegum pop. Not so if you grew up in Southern California listening to DJs like Hunter Hancock, Dick Hugg aka Huggy Boy, or the man who started it all, Art Laboe, who was the first DJ to revive yesterday's hits, in the process inventing the oldies format.

"I used to pass out a list of songs at this afternoon show of the Top 20," Laboe explains of his famous live show from Scrivner's Drive-In in Los Angeles that started in 1954. "And I would say, 'You pick 'em, you dedicate 'em, and you get 'em.'" Laboe's show appealed to young listeners over the airwaves, as well as droves of teens who packed into cars and cruised to the drive-in to make dedications in person. "So I was just playing whatever people would bring in, their own records sometimes, that kind of thing," Laboe remembers. "Around late '57, they were starting to ask me for older songs like the Penguins or Johnny Ace or the Dominoes, Little Walter, songs like that." In an era when popular culture was evolving at a breakneck pace, the idea that a radio disc jockey would play old songs was unheard of. He started reincorporating some of these past favorites into his list of available request songs, calling them "oldies but goodies."

Laboe's revolutionary new format of including contemporary selections mixed with the tried-and-true oldies proved to only strengthen his already impressive share of listeners, and it wasn't long before other DJs started biting his style. Laboe's drive-in shows attracted a diverse cross-section of L.A. youth, depending naturally on which Scrivner's Drive-In he was broadcasting from, but by the early '60s, Laboe made a connection. "You'd see a car go by with all metallic blue just shining, and on the side it would say 'Earth Angel' or 'In the Still of the Night' or one of those '50s song titles, mostly the ballads of the Black artists like the Flamingos and so on," Laboe explains. "The oldies became anthems for the lowriders. They came to the drive-in, a lot of them, because they live in their cars in Southern

California, especially Chicanos. And they started coming to my dances in El Monte."

"The good times continued after the dances were over," Molina writes about the impact of Laboe's weekend dances. "Car clubs would pack the streets around the dance halls showing off their cars and trying their luck with the girls, who came streaming out of the dance hall. Not only was El Monte Art Laboe's weekend headquarters, it also became a magnet for Black, White and Chicano youth and aspiring rock 'n roll stars."[12] Bands like Thee Midniters and Cannibal and the Headhunters drew their inspiration from the combination of sounds favored by local oldies DJs and the British Invasion. Thee Midniter's first and biggest hit, "Whittier Blvd," was a brassy and raucous cover of the Stones' "2120 South Michigan Ave." Molina, who grew up in East L.A., says the live music scene fed off the oldies radio format. "The bands that were forming to make up the 'East Side Sound,' they had to know these songs, because when the dance was ending and you wanted that last dance with a girl, you wanted one of these songs. So all the bands knew songs like 'Sad Girl' or 'The Town I Live In.'"

The arrival of the British Invasion simultaneously inspired young Chicanos to pick up guitars, and threatened the emerging radio genre that their community celebrated. "The music business is always a moving target, so it moved on," Laboe says, referring to commercial radio's capitulation to the aggressive come-ons of the British Invasion onslaught. "But the Chicanos embraced this doo-wop ballad type of music, sometimes called the 'East L.A. Sound,' and they still do." The fact that the then nascent oldies format survived had as much to do with its charismatic DJs as it was the loyal Chicano audience. "None of [the radio DJs] were Chicano, but they quickly learned that we were their audience," says Molina. "They learned how loyal the Chicano could be to something targeted at them."

Art Laboe might have invented the oldies request-show format, but Huggy Boy is the first name off most lips. The appeal of Huggy Boy was as much about the sentimental ballads he featured as it was about his off-the-cuff interactions with his audience. The popularity of the oldies request-show format, according to Ruben Molina, has something to do with the macho Chicano culture and not wanting to directly admit your mistakes. So, if your woman catches you with some other chick, "you go to Huggy Boy, and you make a dedication," he says. "And everybody's listening, so next thing you know—*bam*—you're back together with your girlfriend because she heard your dedication."

Oldies Para Siempre

It's understandable that the White teens would abandon R&B for the new rock sound, but what about the Blacks who up until that time were partying, cruising, and romancing to the same music as the Chicanos? The Homeboy Mad has a theory: "The only difference between Blacks and Chicanos—we definitely had a similar struggle, a similar history—but for whatever reason, Blacks are always redefining their culture every decade from rock and roll to doo-wop to soul to funk and so on. Chicanos are more about tradition, and we like holding on to our traditions. We don't really like change too much. We like who we are, and we're proud of who we are."

That's not to say that any Chicano worth his Winos only rolls to harmony soul recorded before 1969. What Chicanos refer to as oldies is a loose term that describes a certain sound and tempo characteristic of songs found across a half dozen decades and about as many genres, but most particularly doo-wop and harmony soul. And the songs are typically ballads with evocative lyrics that tell a story. "It's kind of like elevator music," Molina says, "something cool that you listen to [while cruising]. And then when you're alone, if the lyrics are really good, then it has a double meaning."

Most of the time, oldies serve as a mellow soundtrack to pass the time as Molina described, but these songs can have a much more profound meaning when requested over the radio as a dedication or when played at weddings, funerals, or other significant family gatherings. "Ballads became an integral part of the ritual of a community that stages huge elaborate weddings, throws engagement and coming-out parties, and as early as junior high school celebrates the pairing of one boy to one girl," write David Reyes and Tom Waldman in their book *Land of a Thousand Dances: Chicano Rock 'n' Roll from Southern California.*

"The Hispanic community typically uses oldies song titles to express what they feel towards their loved ones, whether it be love or hate or let's work it out. It could be any one of those three," says DJ Tony C., who a few years ago fulfilled a lifelong goal of becoming an oldies radio DJ in his hometown of Salinas. On the weekly Saturday night request show he cohosts, "the line is constantly off the hook, people calling for dedications and requests." Beyond the obvious role of providing a memorable soundtrack to any given Saturday night, his show serves as a lifeline to two isolated communities within reach of his radio signal. "A lot of the women who call in to my show have men who are incarcerated," Tony explains, "and this is one way of getting to them and saying, 'I love you, baby, and I'll stay by your side.'"

The U.K.-born R&B dance scene known as "northern soul" represents the A-side to oldies' B-side. Molina confirmed the analogy: "They're like our brothers, man. You know, it's just the working-class people, they get together on Fridays and play their records, but they like the A-side, the dance side." Both genres developed in local communities outside of the national spotlight, allowing them to more freely incorporate a wide spectrum of popular styles into their playlists so long as the songs had that certain sound: strident and upbeat for northern soul and mellow and sincere for oldies.

"You got the Louisiana swamp-pop mixed with the Chicago soul and the Philadelphia soul," Molina says. "Whatever was smooth and had this thing about it that was cool, that kind of became the lowrider sound." Northern soul, like oldies, has an accepted canon of classics, cataloged first on Laboe's *Oldies But Goodies* compilations and continued by Tony Boosalis's twelve-volume *East Side Story* series. Also like northern soul, oldies is a living genre with collectors and DJs continuously adding songs to the canon through official and unofficial CD compilations, radio shows and more recently with collectors showcasing their rare acquisitions online. "*East Side Story* [compilations] are basically just like common oldies to us. That's like puppy love to us," Soulero Sal says. "We're tired of hearing that, so we wanna hear other stuff, rare stuff that we never heard before."

Lowriding the Internet

"You should check it out and tell people to check it out: the whole culture of the Latino sweet-soul guys on YouTube," says Andy Noble excitedly. One of his band's early singles, "High On Your Love," is already considered a lowrider classic thanks to this community of Chicano soul music collectors online. "That culture is alive and well online."

For the first edition of his pioneering *The Old Barrio Guide to Lowrider Oldies*, Ruben Molina started by documenting his own impressive collection of doo-wop, harmony soul, and Chicano soul. Then he hit the car shows and record shows and met with other collectors to see what the gente were listening to in other barrios. Molina says the landscape has changed since the first edition primarily because of the Internet: Before [the Internet], there wasn't really any new stuff coming in," he says. "It was basically the same kind of oldies. But then the record collectors started to look deeper into the Chicago sound, the New Jersey and D.C. sounds, things that never popped up over here on the West Coast.

For collectors who started recently, the sounds they found on YouTube were revelatory. One such collector, known online as Soulera5150, has always been a oldies fanatic, but after exhausting the classic oldies found on L.A.'s K-EARTH 101 or bootleg CDs, she turned to the computer. "There's gotta be more out there," Soulera remembers saying to herself. "So I hooked myself up to YouTube, and I went in there and was like, 'What's this? I've never heard of the Flint Emeralds or the Fuller Brothers.' I never heard of all these groups, so I started getting into it more and more, and I says, 'I gotta have these records.'"

With every leap in technology, a new generation emerges to master it. A few Chicano record collectors from the Bay Area came together "to advance [their] collections and further one another's knowledge," and in the process, they injected some seriously rare and unheard soul into the vibrant online community of oldies lovers. They prefer to remain anonymous to avoid legal hassles around their influential compilations. The Homeboy Mad collaborated with these collectors for his Souleros Ball—a recurring event celebrating the musical side of the Chicano movement featuring the spinning of rare oldies—and says, "What they did is brought it to a whole new level as far as recording an actual sought-after 45 and putting it on YouTube to share the music with other people." One of these collectors added via email, "I find it fascinating to see a rare piece of history spinning right before my eyes, not to mention the awesome label designs and color variations. To me, that's what the YouTube soul scene is all about." These mysterious collectors also coined the term soulero, which is rapidly becoming the household term for Chicano/a oldies collector.

Souleros Unidos?

"For me, it's a badge of honor," says Moe—aka Moses and the Ten Commandments of Soul—about being a soulero. "I know I can walk up and down the street and somebody will say, 'Hey, you wanna hear something different? Ask Moe, he'll have it for you.'" In spite of his fair complexion, Moe comes from a Chicano family in San Jose. "I have five [half] brothers that are full-blood Mexican, and because my brothers were brown and I was light, I didn't always fit in," Moe says with his brimmed hat perched on top of his closely cropped dome and the ever-present box of 45s at his side. "But then one day, I started collecting these oldies, and it was a symbol of acceptance, because everybody started to see that I knew what this music was about."

Like Moe, Soulera's a recent convert to the black crack. "It's like a freakin' car payment or a house note," she says, referring to the price tag of a rare soul 45. But every time she hears another must-have tune online or at a homie's place, it's only a matter of time before she's compelled to scoop it up from a European dealer who certainly snagged it for the flipside. "That's how we do it, and we don't care. I could feed the whole family beans and rice for a week: 'Where's the meat, mom?' 'Can't afford meat; Mommy bought a record!'"

The increased access to rare soul records from countless previously inaccessible localities, combined with the simplicity of sharing these nuggets online, is creating a stage for souleros to show off, to compete, and to interact about their shared passion for oldies. While it's unlikely that a shared passion for oldies will erase generations of hostilities between North and South, a beef that

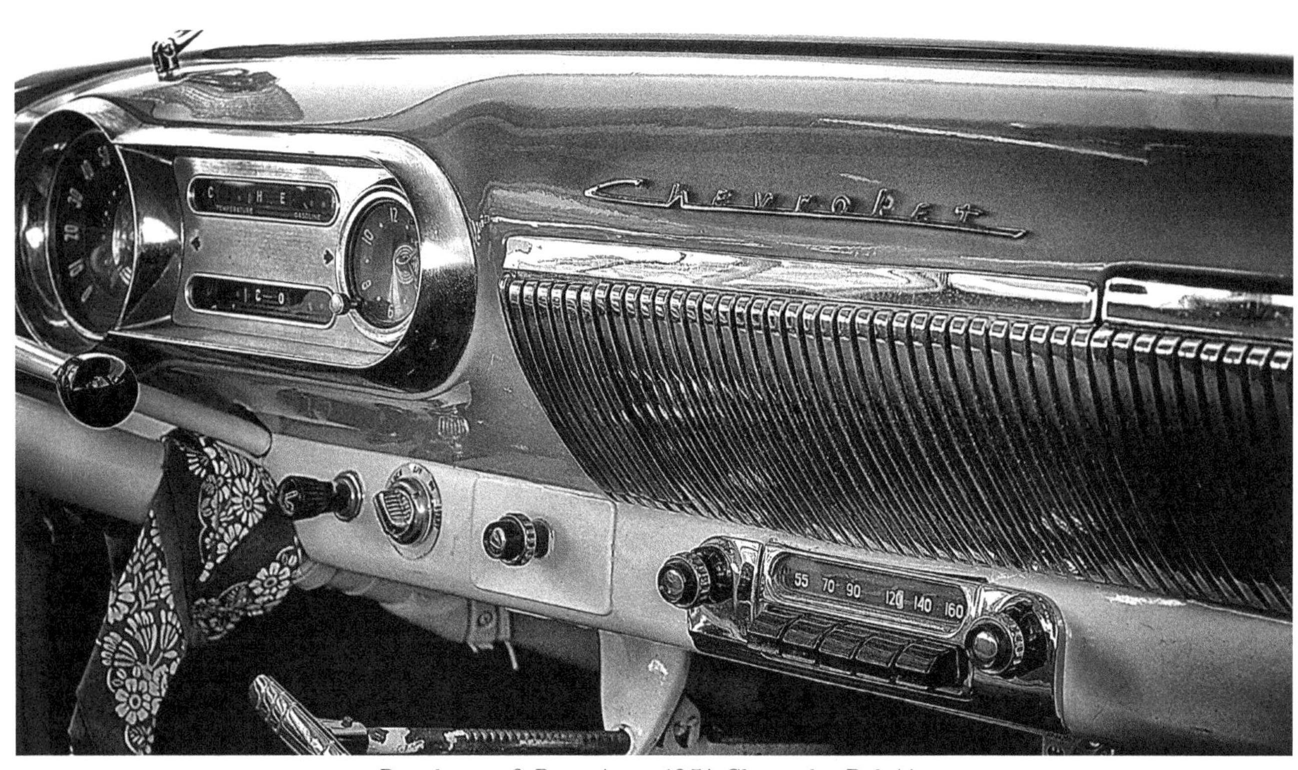

Bandanas & Bow ties – 1954 Chevrolet Bel Air

runs deep and has origins in the California prison system, the very fact that there's dialogue is progress. Tommy Siqueiro, one of the original collectors from Northern California, explains his personal philosophy towards this historical rivalry: "I try to promote unity between the collectors there and here. I think it's the love of music or it should be a West Coast soulero thing. We should all share the music, not hide it from each other, because it's all about love."

"Most of the lowriders that I hung out with weren't into fighting, they were into cruising around, getting high and picking up chicks," Cheech Marin of Cheech & Chong fame told Lowrider Magazine. "Which is right there for me."[14] Cheech's generalization holds for a majority of lowriders, but the reality is that Norteño and Sureño allegiances run deep. The family identity that's so much a part of Chicano culture can be a double-edged sword. It may bring people together, as seen with the loose network of Northern California Chicano record collectors or their counterpart in Southern California, but it can also fuel traditional rivalries. "With the Chicano," Ruben Molina says, "it's this never-ending loyalty, and I think that's why there's a lot of problems with gangs and stuff like that, because people are very loyal to something that they love, and they never get rid of it. It becomes a part of you, and it's handed down."

Souleros Ball Revue

Chicanos have single-handedly kept alive the careers of countless R&B and soul performers long after their fair-weather fans moved on to the next fad. Barbara Mason, Gene Chandler, and Brenton Wood all speak candidly about the support of their loyal Chicano fans. Legendary R&B bandleader Johnny Otis said, "I would have had less of a career if not for the Chicano audience. They were the most loyal and responsive, and they would show up everywhere we went."1

For Joe Bataan, an Afro-Filipino New Yorker without a drop of Latin blood, the enduring support from his Chicano fans is a pleasant surprise. Back in the early '90s, following a long spell away from touring, Joe Bataan returned to the West Coast to find that "kids were getting tattoos of my songs on their arms," he says. "They were telling me stories of how they grew up with my music. Then I started to realize, my popularity in Southern California hadn't diminished, but it had really grown." Both lesser-known and better-known artists, like the Young Hearts and the Moments, are still singing to enthusiastic audiences thanks to shows organized in part by Ruben Molina in the south and Tommy Siqueiro in the north.

While nostalgia and tradition are a major part of the oldies culture, eager ears are always looking for new artists with that old sound. Mayer Hawthorne, Kings Go Forth, Lee Fields, and even the Australian combo Cookin on 3 Burners are contemporary favorites, as are the headliners for the fifth Souleros Ball. Myron & E, whose Timmion Records B-side "I Can't Let You Get Away" is a lowrider favorite, headlined the July 2011 show.

The Homeboy Mad came up with the idea to organize the first Souleros Ball to showcase the musical side of Chicano culture. Each ball has been bigger than the previous one, drawing more DJs and collectors and lowrider car clubs to listen to rare soul 45s, dance, and have a good time. It was a first having a contemporary soul act playing an oldies event, but the real stars of the show were still the souleros and their impossibly rare records. "It's all about bringing us all together and keeping our culture alive, and the rare soul music plays a huge part in that," writes the same Bay Area soulero who prefers to remain anonymous, "and I don't think it will ever come to end."

Soulero Sal debuted behind the turntables at July's Souleros Ball. Tommy Siqueiro says of his protégé, "He's the next generation. I'm inspired by him, because he calls me viejo and looks to me as a father of music, and he wants to be like me. And if being like me means collecting records, being a good guy, and staying out of trouble, then more power to him." Tommy, who jokingly refers to himself as "a businessman by day and a cholo by night," says that collecting oldies has kept him out of gangs. "I've never hurt nobody," he says, "never been in prison, never been in jail. I just love music and love lowriders."

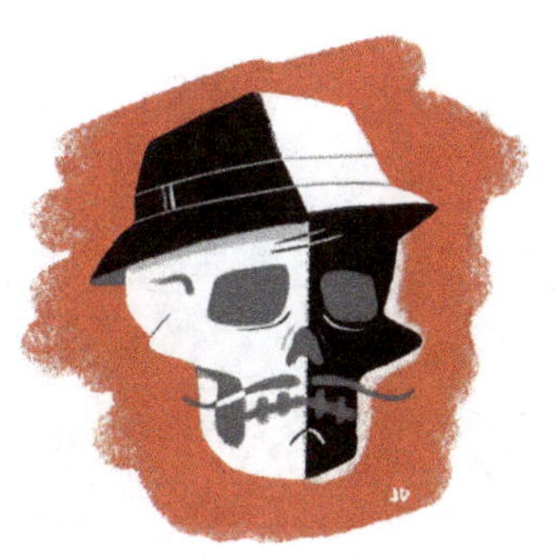

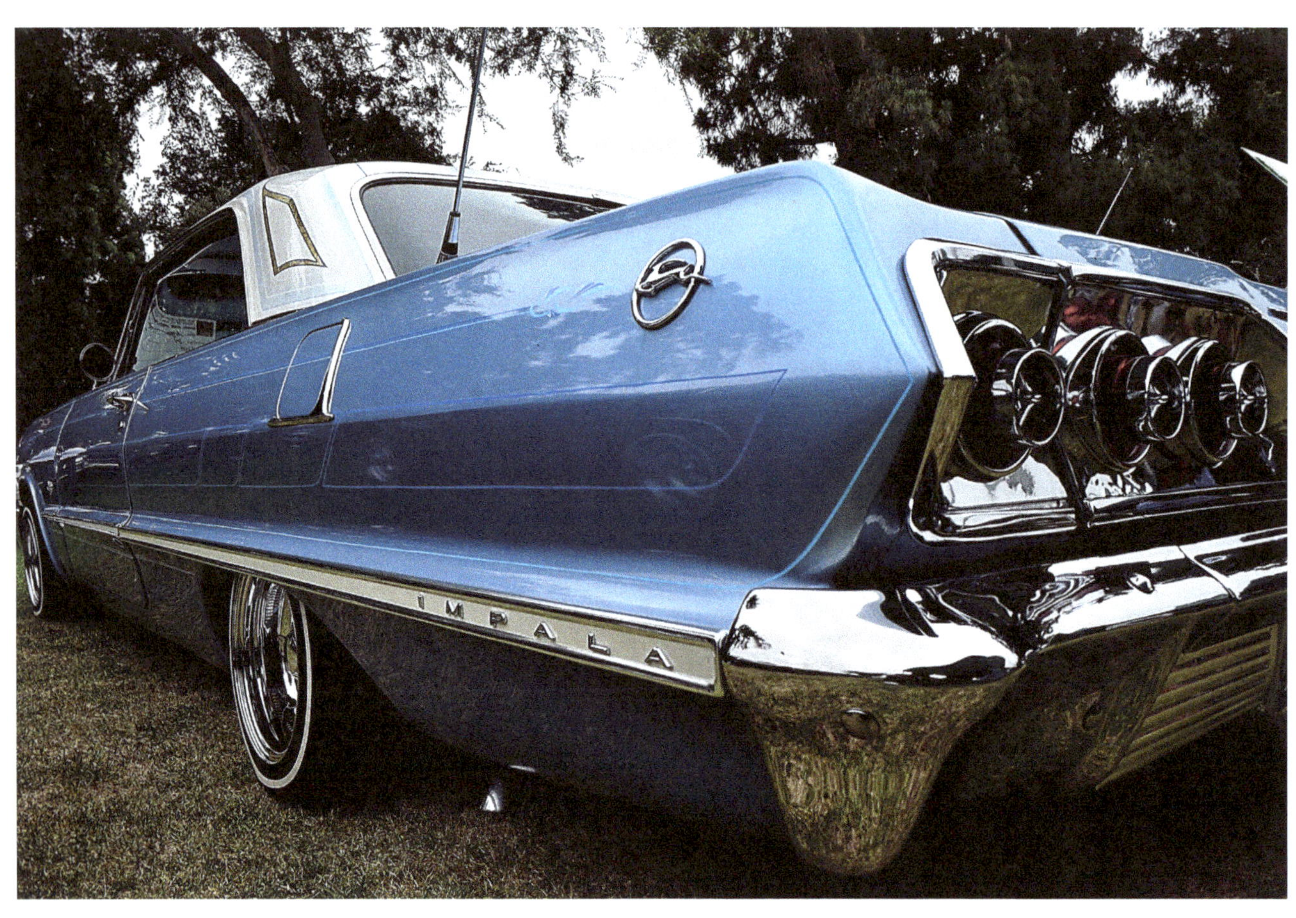

In the'63 – '63 Chevy Impala

In the Six Three

by Enrique Arroyo

Always washed it like it was mine
Inside and out
Earned me shotgun every time
Metallic light blue
Chrome accents and bumpers shine
Always had it ready to roll on time
The year, 1979.

Hopped on the 110 by Pico
Heading to the Eastside
Riding shotgun con El Mero Mero
GQ's "Disco Nights"
Earth, Wind & Fire's "September"
And KRLA on the radio
Getting us ready
For another adventure to remember.

Cruising The Boulevard
Every ride in best dress
Speed to a minimum
Getting closer looks
The 63 turning heads
The firme hynas, looking fine too
The looks we got were like a scorecard
Could've got a trophy every night.

Heading home
West on the 10
Wave-like pavement
Like the ocean swells
Smooth, long hops
Hood bouncing in slow rhythm
Elbow out the door
Cuz you know
It was good to be me
I was only 11
Already stylin
In the 63

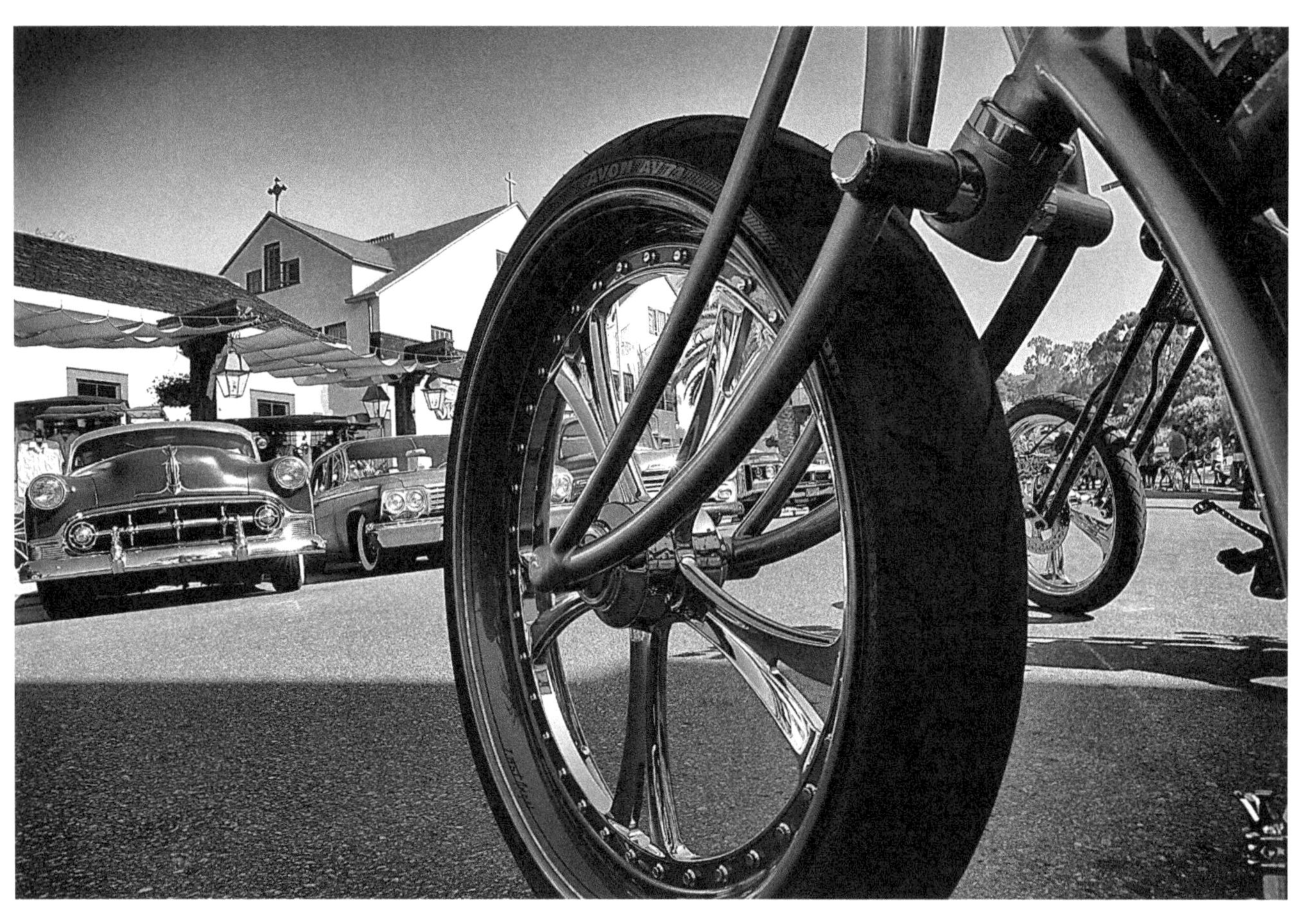

Us & Them - '53 Chevy Bel Air

Cruisin' Classics

By Jason Hoyt

There was nothing like the sweet and savory aroma of chorizo con huevo to help break up the lagañas in my eyes. Ah, Saturday mornings in the barrio. When I was a kid I loved getting up early to just spend time with my brother John who was better known as "J.D.". I always knew that Saturday was going to be an awesome day, because we spent every Saturday the day working on our classic Sting Ray Schwinn low rider bikes trying to see what more we could add to our never ending project to best the homies.

We would start by getting dressed putting on our

khaki Dickies, house shoes and a flannel button down shirt. We would eat an awesome Mexican breakfast then do the little chores around the house dad wanted done. We would eventually go outside to the side of the house where we had our little work area with some old beat up chairs and tables. We also had our old stereo the kind that kind of looked like a chest that was made of wood and sat on the floor. It had a door that opened on the top and stayed propped up to reveal a record player and an AM/FM tuner. We already had the station set on 980 AM with Dan The Man's Cruising Classics to keep us company. The oldies but goodies always help set the mood for the day.

My story might be like that of other little brothers, you see, my big brother, John, was my hero. I looked up to him. Everybody in the barrio knew J.D. Even the cops would drive up to me and say, "Hey where's J.D.?" I guess they had a hard time keeping up with him. He was either at the park shooting hoops or on that Sting Ray with the Apehanger handle bars, sissy bar, banana seat, white walls and little dice for the stem covers. We were just some poor kids from the barrio that took pride in our favorite pastime. Our dad worked really hard to support us. He was a single parent, my mother passed away when I was just 10 years old. So we took good care of the few belongings that we had. Whenever we wanted something to add to our bike sometimes we would have to pick up aluminum cans or go mow a lawn. We learned the value of a dollar early on in life. We would save up our pennies and look for that one piece that would make our bikes stand out above everyone else's. Once we had a little wad of cash saved up, Dad would take us to various stores that sold parts and accessories for bikes. Every time we would go in to one of these stores our eyes would light up upon seeing all the sparkling and shiny assortment of bells and whistles that were just waiting to be that one piece that was going to make our bikes the best low riders in the Sixth Ward.

Around lunch time, if we had any cash left over, we would get on our low rider and take a cruise to the neighborhood drugstore for a burger and a shake. This drugstore had the best burgers and shakes in town. It was a remnant of the mom and pop businesses left on Washington Avenue. This was no Walgreens, it was much better. It had a built-in diner counter with shiny bar stools to sit on and there were only about five aisles filled with the necessities: Aqua Velva, Aqua Net and other items that any resident in the barrio might need on a Saturday night. I remember that on Fridays Mrs. Gant, the owner, would give out free candy to all the elementary school kids who happened to pop in. She died some years back and shortly after the drugstore closed down. But while the burgers n shakes were still coming our Friday ritual of collecting our free candy never faltered. We would hang out read all the comic books and when my brother had an extra buck he'd get one for his collection. Then we'd jump on our low riders, pull our paños over our eyes until we were barely able to see and only button the top of the flannel so the shirt tails would flap in the wind. This was something only we low riders understood. We would ride to the park to hang out with the homies and compare bikes sometimes even trading parts.

I am sharing this little story to commemorate my hero, my big brother John, who lived and died on his bike. He was always on his bike even when everyone else outgrew theirs or stopped caring for riding anymore. As we grew older we went through just about everything that any Chicano kid goes through in any barrio. Some of our bikes were stolen. Some kids would rebuild and start over. Some of us moved on to different kinds of bikes and some were just too poor to rebound. But my brother always found a way to get another bike. You could bet your pay check that you could find J.D. on his bike. Sadly enough, he took his last ride in October of 2011. I was told that he fell off his bike and into the Buffalo Bayou. My brother couldn't swim. My only consolation is that John died in a place where he found solitude. He loved riding those trails that lined the bayou. He is dearly loved and will forever be missed. What I would give to have our old low riders back.

But anytime I want to relive those unforgettable memories all I have to do is close my eyes and listen for the laughter of my brother as we race each other through the streets of the barrio.

In loving memory of John G. Hoyt b. 03-02-1980 d. 10-20-2011.

††

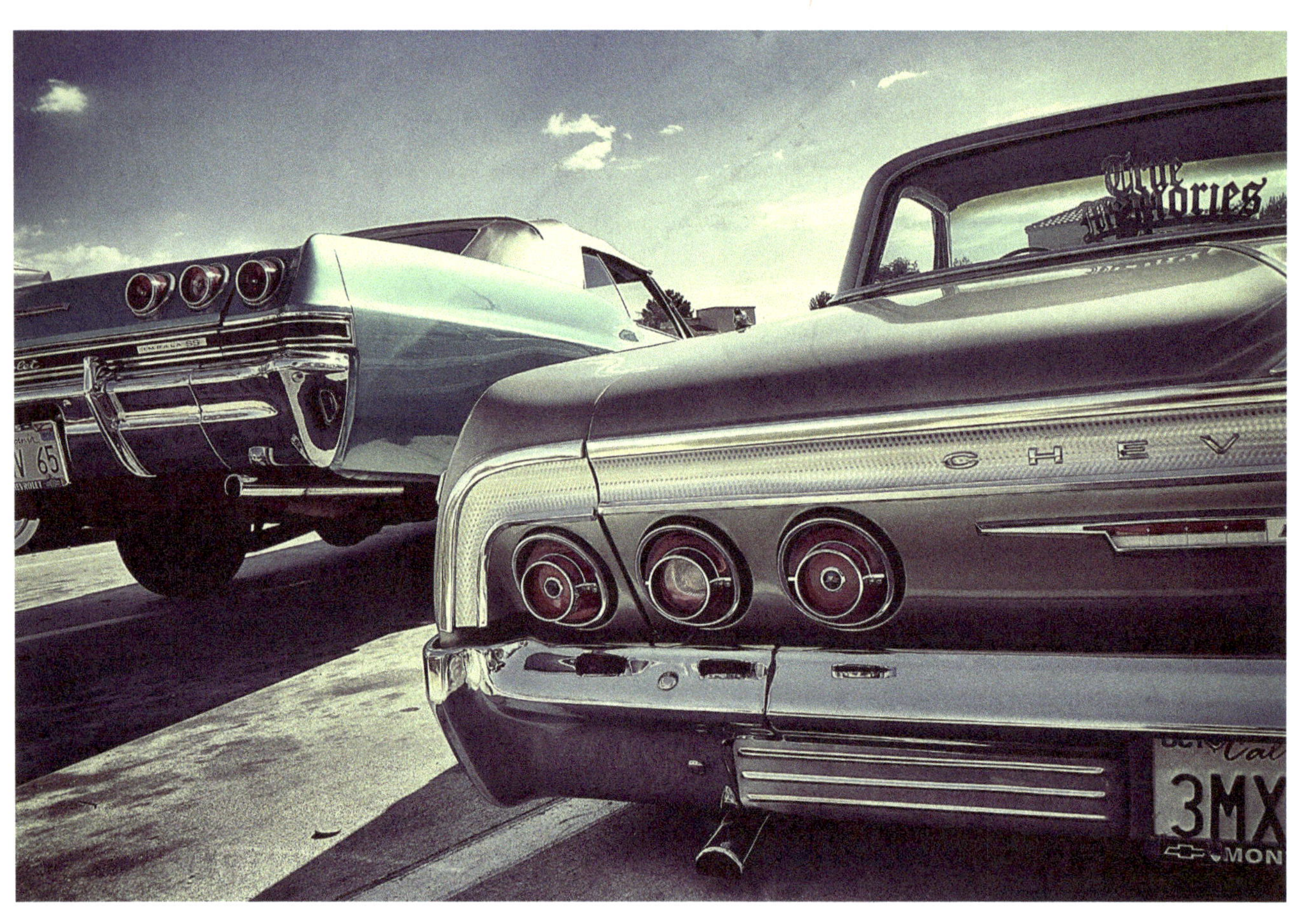

Highs & Lows – '65 & '64 Chevy Impala

Rose Ranfla

By Nancy Aidé González

Riding in the '63 Impala
cruis'n el corazon del barrio
passing by
carnalitos y carnalitas running through sprinklers
abuelas y abuelos on the porch talk'n about the old days
cholos playing handball at the high school
women in the beauty shop getting their hair did
rollin' past
taquerias panaderias heladerias

Bumping
I'm Your Puppet
La La Means I love You
Thin Line Between Love and Hate
Sabor A Mi
through the streets of Califaztlan

Chrome spoke wheels spin
low and slow
variations of pink paint layers glisten

hard top covered in a garden of hand painted gypsy roses

lean back upon velvet pink interior

flip the switch

hit the hydraulics

dip and raise

dip and raise

hop hop hop

off the ground in the intersection

the journey has just begun

let's chase the immensity

of the moment

in estilo.

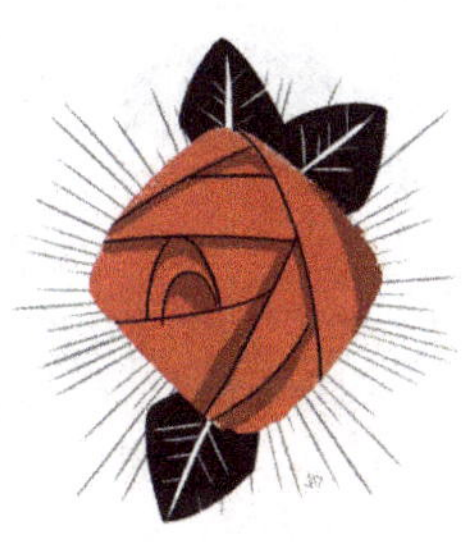

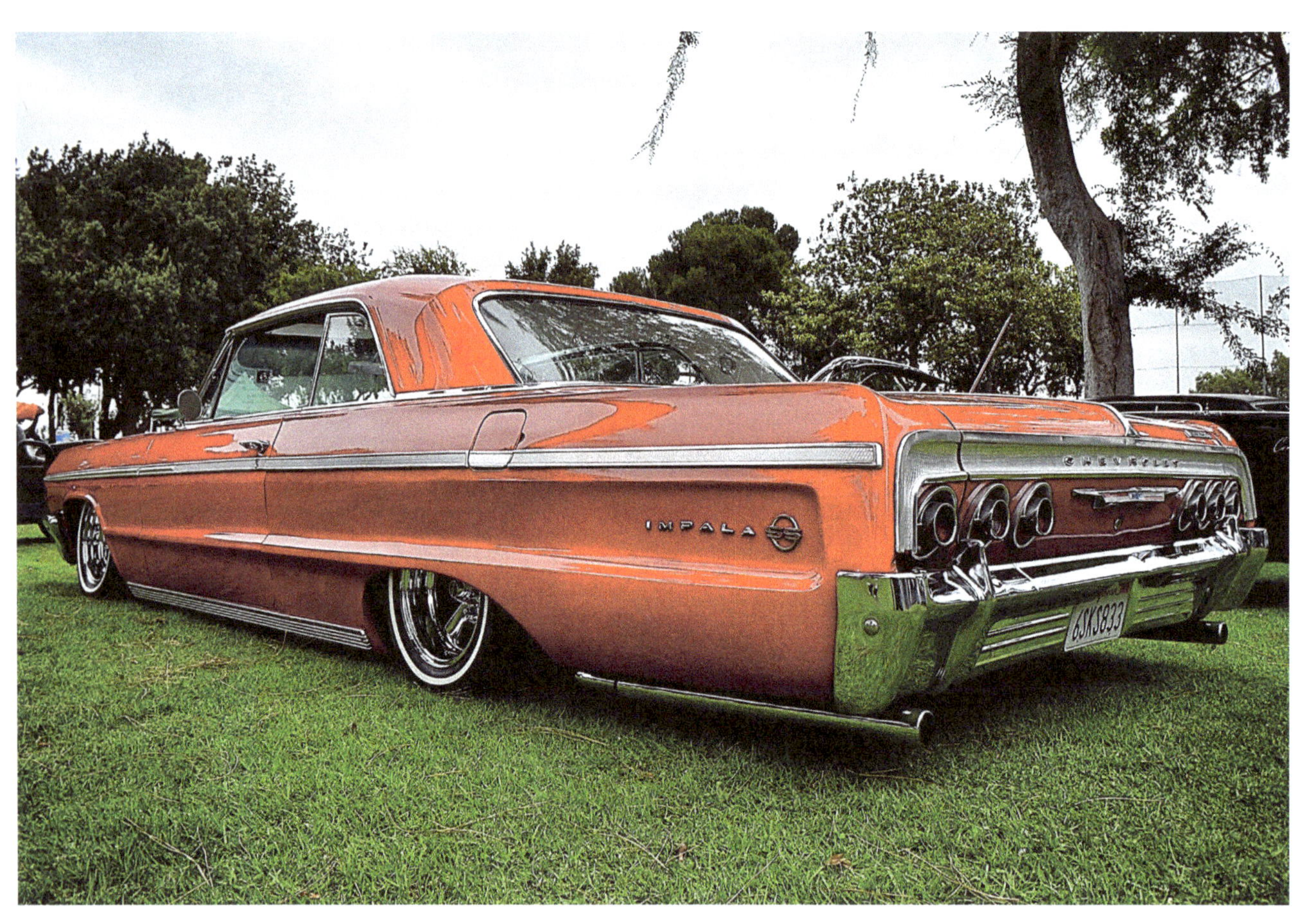

Redrum - '64 Chevy Impala

Paula

By Nikkeya West

1964 Impala

327 Engine.

Firme.

Smooth

The smell, the leather, it all soothes.

If I don't make it home tonight take care of Paula she's my life.

I run my hand down your life side,

I open the door,

I think upon all the memories you store,

My love,

My ride.

Mi razon,

Mi paz,

To them I'm just some heathen,

To Paula I'm the King.

Motivation.

Determination.

Rims as my ring.

Forever Paula,

You're my queen.

To you I'm not just some wetback on the Southside.
Not the fuck up or the "wrong guy"
I'm a man when I drive.
And Paula she's been good to me.
She rides so suave.
No hyna can compare,
When all the bullshit blows over,
She's all that I have there.
Every night's a risk,
A gangster I may be,
But all I got is Paula,
And Paula,
She gots me.

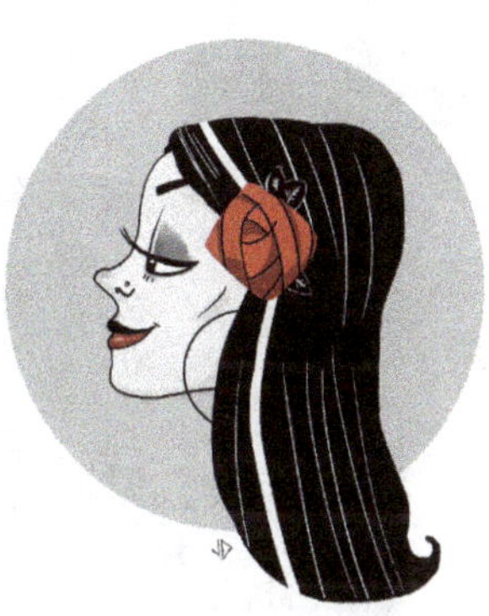

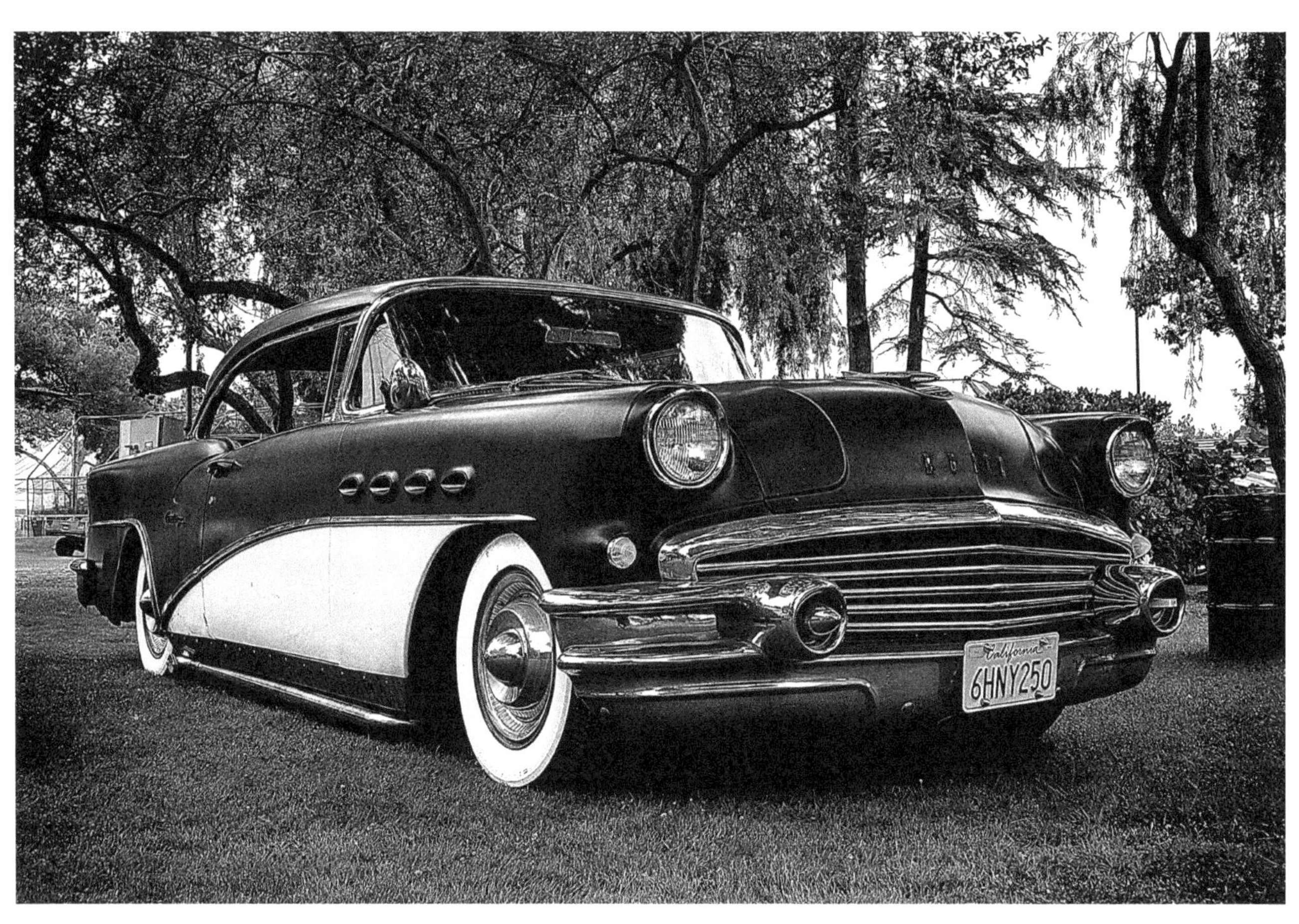

The Road Master – '56 Buick Roadmaster

Road Master '56

By Luis Alberto Urrea

Tio Chente rolled out
Low and slow
In Gabardine, fedora
High-belt trousers

And Calcos

The color of his face
Color of his fenders
And his doors, roof
Yellow as his eyes
No smiles
Ever, loco, smiles

Blew the Aztec vibe
V8 high priest
Never over 50
Pinches miles

An hour, Brodie
Knob on the wheel

See-thru orange
In case he needed to
Spin out the Buick

But Tio Chente never
Turned back once
Cruising from TJ
To Korea smoking
Domino unfiltered

Old vato only
Wanted to be buried
In his ranfla
His stone saying:
Roadmaster.

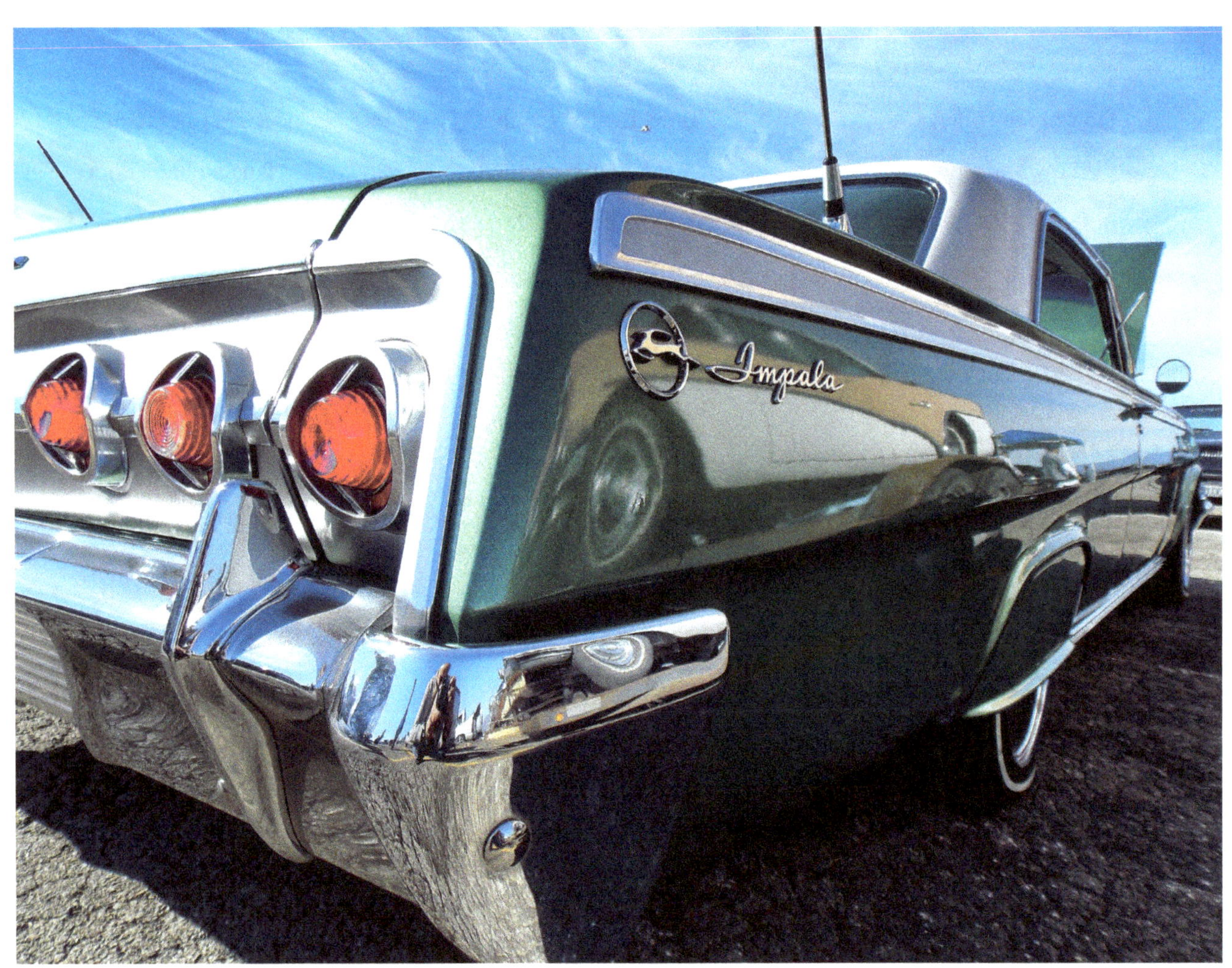

For the Good Times – '62 Chevy Impala

The Way I Feel

By Tara Evonne Trudell

the way I feel
shiny '67 Impala
chrome mirroring
my reflection
black velvet
welcoming
my intent
curves
of steel
invoking
sliding caress
I feel chakras
light up
dinging
pinball machine style
I stop my walk
to stare
and admire

my wide open smile
acknowledging
this work of art
puro Vato heart
reminding me
reminiscent cool rays
falling down
moon shine
inviting me
cruising a ride
black derby filled
embraces
on a dark starry night
can't help the way I feel
when I see
a shiny '67 Impala

c/s

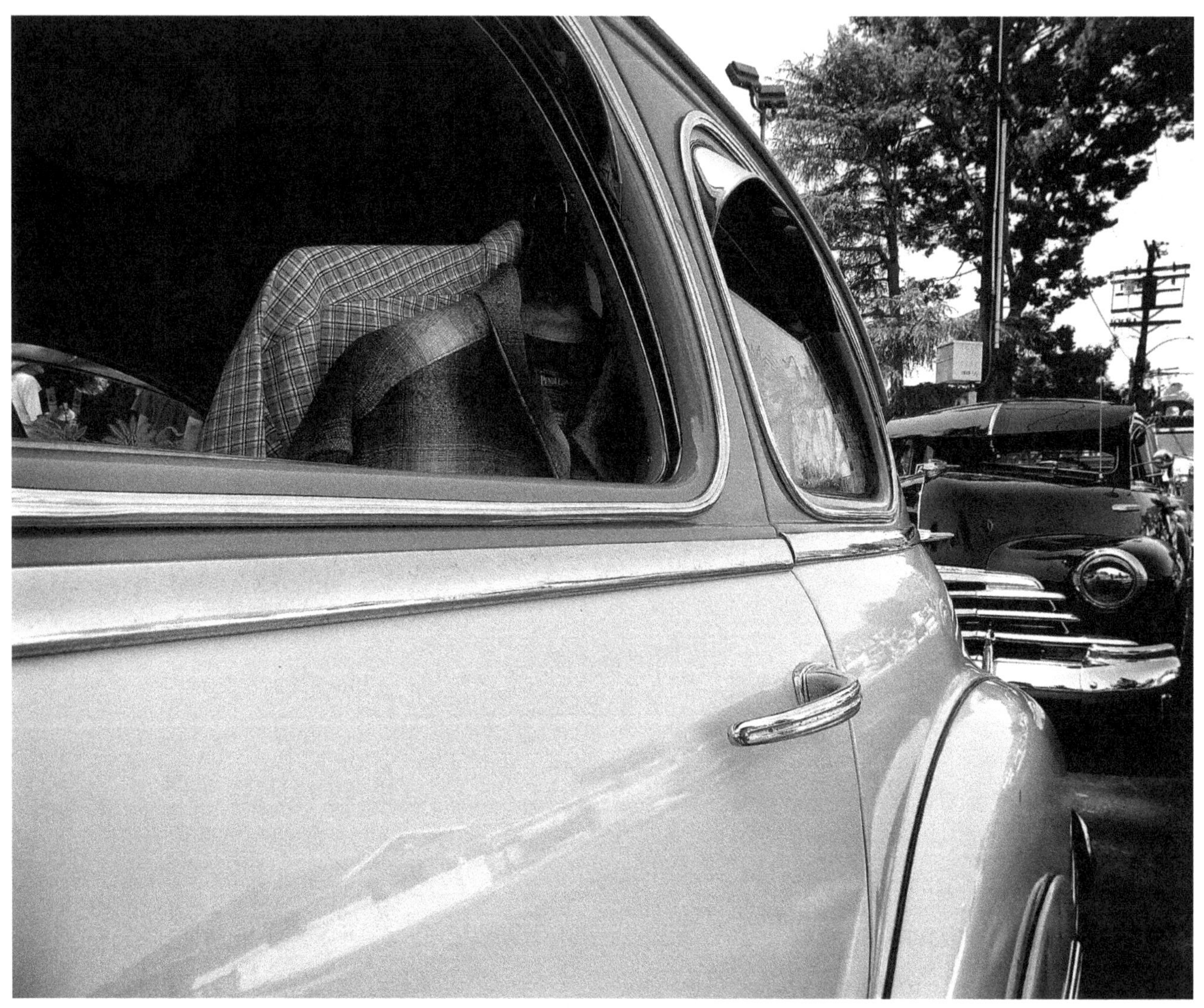

Veterans of Style – 1948 Chevrolet Stylemaster

Ode to a Cholo

By Tara Evonne Trudell

ode to a Cholo

on the birth

of the Sixth Sun

to the Vato

who brings

his brown

to the surface

of being Chicano

representing

Mexican first

never a question

of the great lie

the big divide

of hispanic

working hard

on trying

to brainwash

him in concrete

lifestyles

Fantasy Heritage

breeding
crazed minds
his resistance
alive
in canyons
of nopales
y ocotillo
ode to the Cholo
taking pulse
to pen
flowing words
for his people
standing on
street corners
handing out
strong words
on paper
the Vato
writes poetry
¿y qué?
ode to a Cholo
ironing board
steam pressing
Pendleton creases

calm and slow
the iron flows
steam rising
smell of tamales
cooking on stove
reliving his love
for his Abuelita
singing softly
Los Panchos
under warm
breath
ode to a Cholo
when the women
pull their purses
closer
passing him by
with worried glances
how bad ass
he is to smile
and nod
continuing
his stroll
never saying
a word

never looking

back

ode to a Cholo

walking his path

fighting revolutions

leaving hearts

shedding light

his polite way

keeping eyes

on his brown

people

never wavering

Zapata's vision

ode to a Cholo

con safos

siempre.

c/s

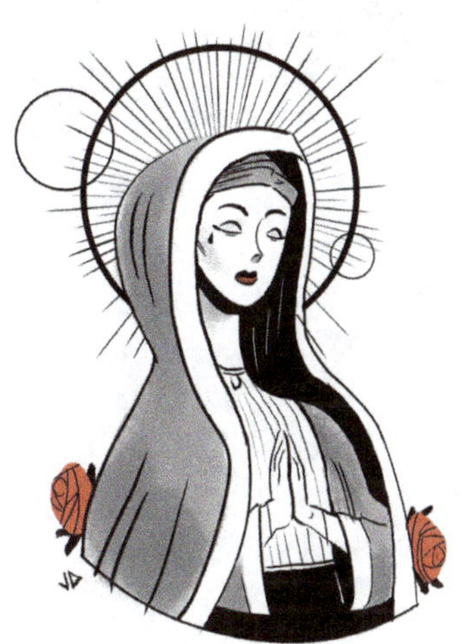

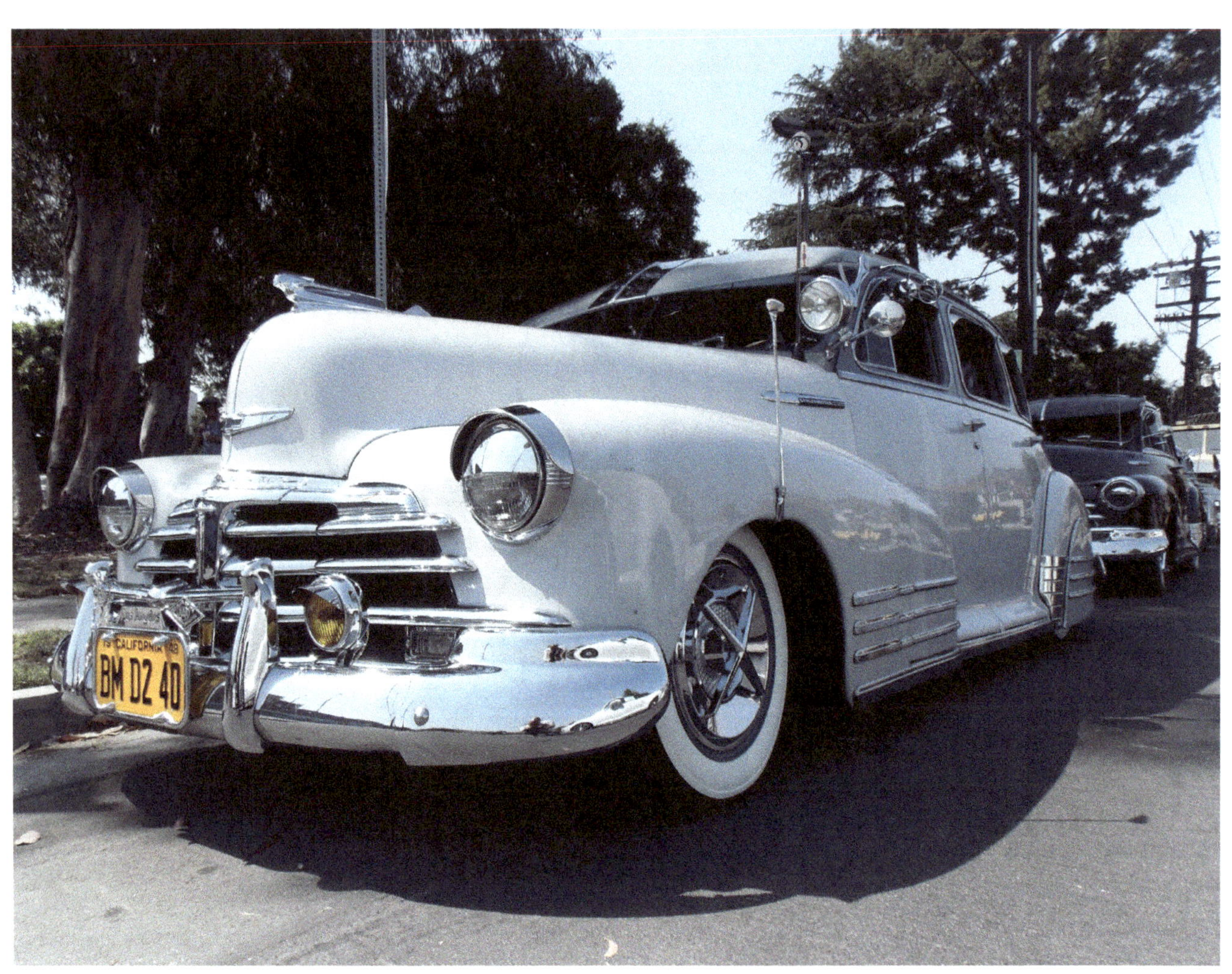

White Knight – 1948 Chevrolet Stylemaster

Chilidogs & Homeboys, To Go, Please...

by Jim Marquez

I was drunk one Saturday night. I needed some sloppy beef to sober up. With chili. What better place than Original Tommy's over on Beverly Blvd, off Rampart, just outside of Downtown Los Angeles?

But I should've known better. You just can't go there late on a weekend night without the bullshit starting because every degenerate waste-of-sperm wannabe 'gangsta' goes there after a drive-by or a sexual assault of some sort.

The only good thing that can be said about these assholes is that for some reason (I intend on asking God about this the minute I stumble into Heaven), they get to be with the hottest women on the planet. So, thankfully, the eye-candy is pretty good after a lonely booze. I am but a nerd and a drunkard and I am fuckin' jealous. Freely admitted...

That being said, there I be, slouched against my car, chowing down on my usual heart-bursting crap of a double chili-cheeseburger, chili-cheese fries, and a chili-cheese dog. Nasty shit, yup, yup, but it does the trick, soaks up the alcohol; allows you to get back behind the wheel and have an even chance of getting home without getting pulled over.

Slamming into a family of six on their way back

from an outing never crosses my mind. There are far worse things on the road to avoid other than me: Cops.

Between 12 midnight and 4 A.M. lie the true fear in this City of Angels and God help you if you're Brown or Black.

Now, parked next to me, to my right, in this lot, is a beat-to-all-hell, rusted out, puke-green Chevy Nova. 1986? 87? Hatchback. Christ, yeech! How the fucker is still running I have no clue, but it sits there, offending the casual passerby, or the horny drunk trying to sober up. At the wheel is a Latina, fairly hot, staring into her Smarty-Phone, fidgety, waiting for whoever the fuck is supposed to be bringing the food. Judging by the look in her red eyes it appears she's trying to will this person into being via the fading glow of the screen attached to her face.

On the other side of her is another car. Huge fucker. Talk about old-school L.A. gangster. Mickey Cohen style. Bulky. A steel behemoth. Whitewall tires the size of a bus. Rounded trunk, space for four bodies. A white steering wheel as big as an extra-large Little Caesar's. Gear shift on the column. An ancient bastard. Mid 1940s. Maybe Later. It had a black lacquered finish/sheen that it might as well have been melting glass you were staring into. A Plymouth.

When I was a kid my mother used to have one just like it. Though not cherried out like this one, fuck no; permanent dust clung to every surface of its stripped interior, for some reason mom never had a good enough answer for the two bullet holes that adorned the truck's lid, and the tranny begged for an early death every time mom shifted going uphill. It felt like the bottom carriage was going to drop out from underneath us and we'd have to climb those hills Fred Flintstone style. Scary shit.

Homeboys, cholos, mechanics, and varied interested parties offered mom tons of cash for that thing; wherever we'd go they stop and point and ask her what she wanted for it; like moths to the flame. She'd always decline though; she needed it to take me and my brother to the doctor, to school, shopping at Kmart and Sears, and to visit our nana in Boyle Heights on Esperanza across from the cemetery. But money became tight, and eventually she sold the car for $500. A thousand years ago that was an incredible amount of scratch, actually a lifestyle changer and she gratefully accepted. Years later she told me selling that Plymouth was one of the biggest mistakes in her life.

There's a man behind the wheel of this Plymouth now. Latino. Shaved head. 30-years-old? Next to him is not a drop dead gorgeous Latina baby momma, but possibly the baby herself. Jail bait.

That Fucker.

They sit and eat. The windows are tinted. Lowered. Halfway.

We're in the main parking lot. Across the street, separated by Rampart, is the smaller, secondary lot. There's an LAPD cruiser in the far corner shining a floodlight on a group of young men at their three cars parked next to each other. Latinos. They are gathering to talk before coming over this way to order up but their convivial banter, in Spanish, is interrupted by the prying pigs. The men wear short cropped hair, open shirts over wife-beaters, baggy jeans. Maybe ten guys. Late 20s. I try to ignore it.

My food, finally, is beginning to achieve its desired effect. And that's when I see the passenger approach the lone girl and the crap-Nova next to me.

He's a huge bastard. Shaved head, neck and chest buried in garish jewelry. He's sporting that constant, bitter, menacing, thousand-yard prison glare that these assholes seem to have in reserve whenever out in public, and he doesn't walk per se, but swaggers, or lopes, some kind of bad clown pantomime that's supposed to show he's a badass and that nobody better fuck with him but all it achieves from those of us who are educated and have seen far, far worse (a gaggle of skinhead Nazis {white laces on black boots} in an east Berlin bar once, watching me drink my shot and beer and considering cleansing me from the earth but as luck would have it a Turkish taxi driver happened by and saved my life just as the music cue to the chase scene began), he rates a yawn and a shake of my head as I turn away, careful though not to catch his eye.

He throws a bag of food into the Nova girl's lap – ah, what a gentleman, but hey, she puts up with it – and swings open his passenger door a little too wide and there!

I think I heard a slight thump as the door tapped the Plymouth next to him...Or it could have been a mouse farting, it was that indiscernible.

It took a full second before the driver of the Plymouth sais, as the giant was already halfway into his car, "Hey, homes, watch the ride-A."

The giant stepped back out of his car, leaned toward the driver and said, "What jusay motherfucker?"

"You heard me. Watch the ride-A. You hit my car, homes."

"What jusay motherfucker?"

The gorilla straightened up, cracked his neck; simply believed, as most socio/psychopaths often do, that he hasn't done anything remotely wrong. He whispered,

"You better watch your motherfuckin' mouth-A or I fuck you all up-A."

The driver smirked, shook his own head incredulously and said, "Alls I'm sayin', homes, is to watch my car-A"

"Don't ju homes me motherfucker! I'll fuck you all up-A! Your bitch too, right here in front of the fucking cops. I don't give a fuck!"

Veins pulsed at the side of his forehead. His nose flared, swayed left and right.

"Fuck-A, take it easy-A, why you gotta be all hard and shit? Talk that shit."

"Fuck you-A! I'm not the one with the problem!"

"Fuck you-A! I'll take you anytime bitch...just not right here."

"OH YEAH?!"

The gorilla's voice cracked and boomed, no longer human. He began hopping in place like he wanted to take a piss or he badly needed another bump of coke and he hollered,

"WELL COME ON THEN MOTHERFUCKER! I LIVE AROUND THE CORNER, DOG! SHOW ME YOU'RE A MAN! COME ON! PROVE IT! I'll ALWAYS BE BETTER THAN YOU! SHOW ME YOU'RE A MOTHERFUCKIN' MAN! I'll FUCKIN' FUCK YOU ALL UP MOTHERFUCKER!"

The dude's face blistering red, spit flying, eyes wild, head twitching, contorting, about to explode. (What, abandonment issues? Poppy cornholed him in the ass too many times? Mommy suck dick in front of him to pay the rent? Uncle Chewy jack him off too hard after the Dodger games? Fuck off. Get over it. You be a man motherfucker…of course I didn't say any of that.)

I look over at the oblivious pigs and the maniac

finished with,

"YOU FOLLOW ME HOME AND WE SETTLE THIS SHIT LIKE MEN-A! THEN AFTER I STILL FUCKIN' KILL YOU ALL! LET'S GO MOTHERFUCKER!"

"Naw, man, you see, you get all stupid and shit-A"

"That's on you bitch!"

And then the driver actually opens his car door, begins to step out.

"COME ON THEN, FUCKER! RIGHT NOW IF YOU'RE A MOTHERFUCKIN' MAN!"

The sexpot at the driver's side grabbed his arm and brayed, "Nooooo, youstuuuuuupid or what-A?! Come on, let's go home, pendejo!"

"I'M WAITING MOTHERFUCKER! UNLESS YOU LET YOUR BITCH DO ALL YOUR TALKING FOR YOU!"

Clearly the driver was at a disadvantage because of positioning. The ape was standing, and the driver, much smaller, would be coming out of a seated posture. The jackass, no doubt having never heard of the concept of 'honor', would've hit the driver before he was even out of the car.

"You know what-A?" the driver sighed, relented. "Fuck you, homes!" The driver sat back down and closed his door.

"Whatevers-A!" the mutt grunted and turned.

Both engines rumbled to life (well, the Nova coughed and spit, the Plymouth purred). But just as the animal stepped in his car he picked up an empty plastic bag and tossed it into the driver's lap.

"MOTHERFUCKER!"

The driver screamed and put the car in park and flung open his door just at the asshole jumped into his car, giggling like a school girl. The jailbait again screeched, "NOOOOOOO! COME ON STUPID!"

And the driver quickly conceded once more.

Now, while all this high urban drama is taking place cars are coming and going. It's always a tight squeeze in that crappy lot and tonight was no exception. Cars honked and headlights washed out the bloated and sweaty faces of those of us gathered at, on, or under their vehicles trying to sober it up.

The patrol car across the street pulled up to the Latino males in that second lot. The pigs approached the group, hands quickly unhooking their holsters, hands at the butts, gripping, withdrawing their weapons and before these two cars could leave they had to wait for an earth-killing SUV to clear the space as it too was attempting to back out.

Physics being what it is, the battling homeboys had to wait their turn while the SUV made its move and its obscenely large and blinding beams splashed over the Plymouth bringing to light all of its contents: the driver, the jailbait, and remember, all tinted windows only partly lowered, so only now did I get to see one more person rising and sitting up on backseat.

A young man. No. Check that. A boy.

Shaved head. 10-years-old. He was pointing a .44 Magnum at his side window, square in the spot where the gorilla had been standing. If the boy had chosen he could have taken the ape's head clean off with one shot.

As the SUV passed the boy slowly lowered the cannon. The other idiot had no idea what could have happened to him if he had indeed unleashed that first punch.

I could hardly believe it.

These dickwads were willing to shoot and spill blood and kill each other at a burger joint at 3A.M. while an LAPD cruiser sat 40-feet to my right over the barely audible tap of a car door brushing another while leaving no obvious markings.

As a child I used to see those commercials for TIME Life Books. 'The Old West' series. The announcer on TV would bark in a fake, twangy, Ritalin-induced stammer, "OLD BART WAS SO ORNERY HE ONCE SHOT A MAN JUST FOR SNORING!"

Christ, I'm not naive, I know people have died in this City of Angels for much less, but I was in the direct line of fire here.

Knowing the history of these fools it's doubtful that any of them take target practice at the local NRA-KLAN meeting up in the Glendora hills, aka Land of Fathers Who Molest Their Daughters.

The asshole and his woman tore out, raising dust and old chilidog wrappers.

The Plymouth and its mini-cannon cautiously pulled away, signaled left, then, exited the opposite side of the lot. Nice and quiet. I finished my food feeling very damn sober.

And the pigs. Man, the fucking pigs...

They continued to flash their lights at the young Mexicans, waving their guns, pointing, hollering, giving orders, making them empty their pockets on the ground. Cursing them. Scolding them. Saying shit like, "WHAT ARE YOU DOING HERE?! YOU DON'T FUCKIN' BELONG HERE! KEEP YOUR FUCKIN' HEADS DOWN! TALK FUCKIN' ENGLISH YOU FUCKIN' COCKSUCKERS! BUNCH OF FAGGOT WETBACKS! YEAH YOU MOTHERFUCKER! LOOK AT ME! YOU THERE! YOU WANNA SUCK MY NIGHTSTICK? WHO'S GONNA BE THE FIRST MOTHERFUCKER TO SUCK MY FUCKIN' NIGHTSTICK?! WHO'S IT GONNA BE TONIGHT, HUH? I'LL GIVE YOU A RUNNING START WHOEVER SUCKS MY STICK FIRST! YOU MOTHERFUCKERS YOU! YOU'RE USED TO RUNNING, RIGHT, PACO?! TALK FUCKING ENGLISH, PACO! TALK FUCKIN' ENGLISH! THIS-IS-FUCKING-AMERICA!"

And all the while more drunks and hopheads streamed in and out of the parking lot.

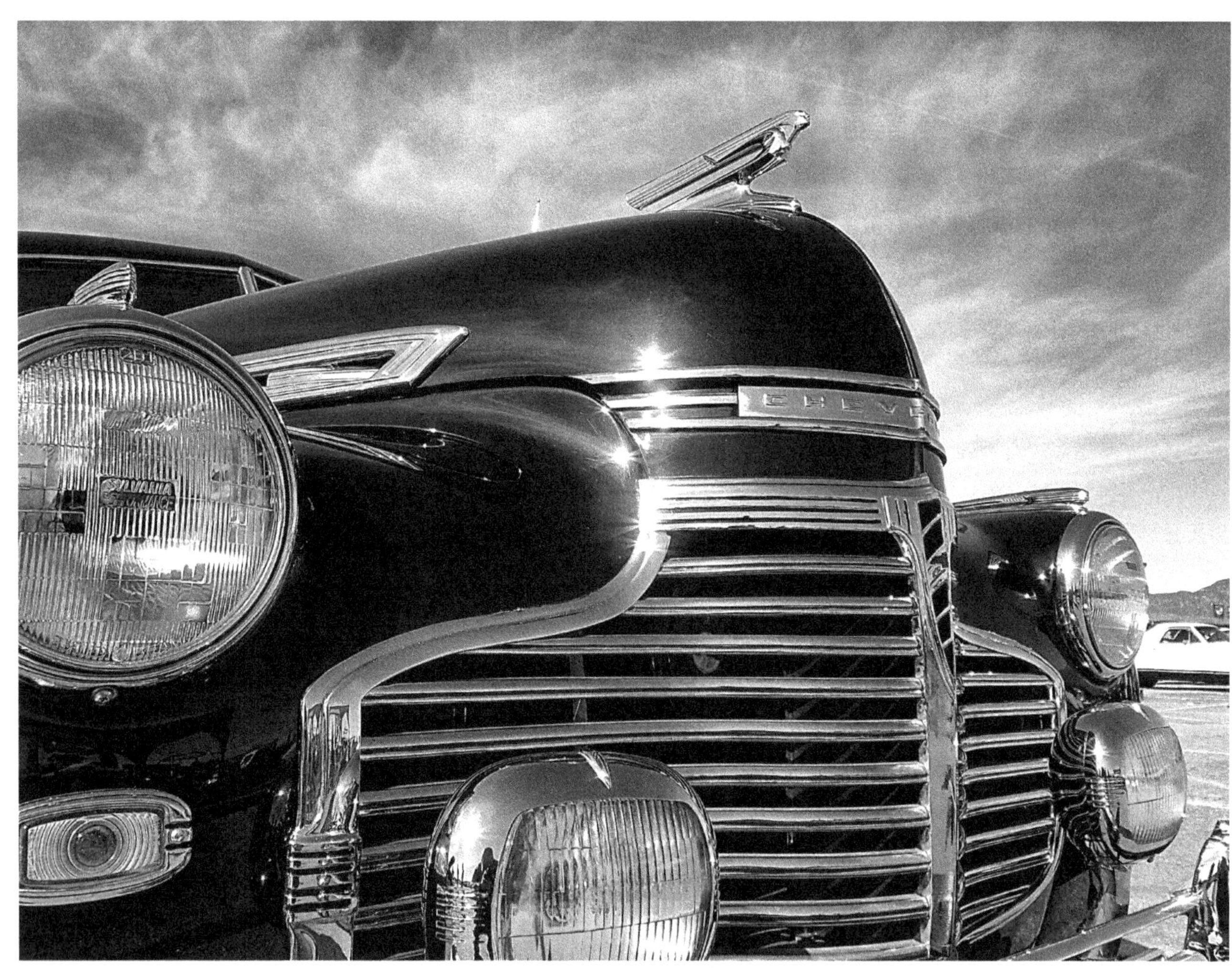

Taking Flight – 1941 Chevy Deluxe

Lorca Green

by Gina Ruiz

In the 1970's, we lived off of Florence in Southeastern Los Angeles, in a city called Cudahy that was so crappy we called it Crudahy. There was nothing good in that town. Nothing. It was economically depressed. There was nothing but roach-infested, cheap tract housing and even crappier apartments. There were a few "real" houses but they too, were nothing to write home about and just stood there as hold outs to a time before tract housing for steelworkers. That end of the L. A. River was nothing like the Los Feliz part of it that had delicately tiptoeing egrets, green rushes and the hills of Griffith Park surrounding it. No, this side of the river was all concrete, stink, florescent green algae and junk.

Our street was a dead-end. It wasn't a *gaba* neighborhood where such things are called cul-de-sac's in a tone that implies that somehow made it safe. No, to us it was just a dead-end street and had nothing to recommend it. Our street was so bad to the Bell Police Department (yes, that City of Bell) that they came four in a car, in full riot gear just to cruise. Cudahy didn't even merit its own police station.

The *vatos* on our street were bored, with not much to do. We'd sit out on summer nights, drinking cheap cola and watching them stand around, looking cool and bored. There were no parks, unless you went to the other end of it, and only the White folk went there. We just hung, sitting on curbs, being bored, eventually getting into trouble.

Those guys weren't scared of anything or anyone, well except for the moms and grandmas in the neighborhood. I'd seen more than one of them running as fast as he could to escape a *chancla*, or in my mother's case a broomstick. She'd run as fast as her short, fat legs could carry her too, shouting, "Stay away from *mis hijas, pinches cholos*." Those guys would haul butt and run, but they'd be laughing till tears ran down their faces as they ran from the abuse.

There was one escape and that was the river. We'd slip onto Florence (technically Bell) and scoot under the bridge. We'd run down the concrete river. We'd play ball, we'd find things, kick at old junk. Maybe the guys would spray paint their names and / or that of their girls or neighborhoods in Old English script:

El Ruben con La Smiley c/s

Little Payaso y La Giggles por vida

El Junior rifa!

Little Dopey *con safos*

I would go to the concrete river, ignore the green algae that seeped onto the cement around me, find a quiet spot under the bridge and read. There was always a book in my pocket.

One day, we found an old car, or parts of a car I should say. The rusted out, stripped frame of it sat in the shallow water, partially hidden by debris. Only the graceful hood remained, rising up out of that unnatural green water, an algae-encrusted rust beast that still believed it was the beauty of its youth.

I looked at it and it seemed to be saying, "Save me, I'm too beautiful to end like this."

Ruben and the other *vatos* from the street hauled it out of the water and dragged it into an old tunnel. The car became our *raison d'etre.* Piece by piece, in shop classes and in garages, each of us contributed something to the car. Maybe Junior happened upon some paint. Maybe Oso lifted some tools from the hardware store. Maybe, just maybe, I might have pilfered S.O.S. pads from under my Tia's sink that we used to buff away rust and grime. All summer long we found ways to patch it together, hidden in that storm drain we called a tunnel in the concrete river.

It didn't become real to us though; it never became more than bits and pieces of an old car, until the day Little Dopey got out of juvie. He'd been locked up for petty theft for six months and while in there, had been missed, especially by me.

Little Dopey was my particular friend though I never called him that. His real name was Carlos and it suited him far better than that ridiculous nickname. He looked scary, with tattoos on his face and covering his neck, but he always stopped by the 7-11 and brought me bags of candy when I was younger. I looked up to Carlos who always showed up with small presents that my mom would have smacked me for taking because they were most likely stolen. It didn't matter to me if they were – Carlos had no money but he had a big heart and to my romantic, book-reading mind, he was the Robin Hood of the barrio.

Carlos also knew cars like nobody's business. He was magic that way. The day he saw the old piece of junk we were working on, he lifted his inked chin, pointing at the car with it and said, "1941 Chevy Deluxe Coupe. Bomb" and immediately took off his immaculately pressed blue cotton shirt, folded it neatly and handed it to me.

"Don't wrinkle the shirt, mija," he said as he crouched down and disappeared under the car.

We waited nervously, almost breathlessly for his verdict. When he came up, he had a smile on his face. When Carlos smiled, it was like the whole world would just light up. His smile changed his face, which he always kept in a study of fierceness. He most-always looked pissed off and scary. When he smiled though, you could see the guy he really was inside. The kind guy that always brought candy or food to kids that didn't have any, the guy who stole in order to buy groceries for his old abuela who was barely existing on her small government check, the guy who would stop to help you, no matter what. All that showed in his smile and it was blindingly bright and warmed your soul up with its light.

Carlos stood, carefully dusted off his khakis and stepped around the car and opened its now rust-free hood. After a half hour or so of muttering to himself half in Calo, half in Spanglish, he closed the hood, flashed that lightening smile again, winked at me and said, “Firme. Needs a radiator, a few belts and some brakes but I can get this bomb up and running. We gotta move it from here though, the damp is killing it. Car’s have spirits you know and this one is saying it doesn’t like the agua, homies. It’s had enough.”

No one dared talk smack when Carlos got all mystical and shit. Nah, man, his abuela was a mean-assed curandera, so no one even blinked an eye when he talked about the car having a spirit. We did eye the car a little differently though.

That night, Carlos walked me home from the concrete river. It was one of those perfect pre-summer nights, where the air smelled like the jacarandas that shit their petals all over the sidewalk on Florence, leaving gross-looking smears of brown and purple mush, but a heavy, intoxicating scent. We talked about his time in juvie and he gave me shit about dressing like one of the cholas.

“Don’t get all chola’d out, *mija*,” he said. “Keep the makeup off and your nose in that book you always have. You should go to college esa. This vida loca ain’t for you.”

In turn, I told him about school, the books I was reading, talked to him about poetry and problems with my stepfather. Carlos was the always best listener and a really good friend. When we got to my driveway, he winked and hopped over the concrete block wall and I was left to make my way in and deal with the hell that was my home.

My home life wasn’t great. In fact, it was shittier than the neighborhood. My mother was an abusive drunk; my sisters were mean and my stepfather lecherous. I hated them all. It was no wonder I escaped into the worlds of my books and spent as much time as I could away at the concrete river. That night I stepped into the usual pile of dirty crap on the hard tile floor, opened the fridge and saw, the usual – a piece of moldy old cheese, some watery Kool-Aid with no sugar and a beer. I don’t know why I expected any better. Once again, my mother had sold her food stamps for booze and there wasn’t anything to eat.

Rummaging around the cupboards, I found fideo and started frying it for sopa de fideo. My sister Carlotta (Lottie) popped her head into the kitchen when she smelled food.

"Whatcha cooking?"

She sniffed appreciatively as she expertly braided her long thick hair. She had a startled look that came from her plucking her eyebrows all the time. I never said so but privately, I thought she looked like a bald, blue-blacked hair chicken.

"Fideo."

"There's nothing else?"

"Nope. The usual."

She whined, "I thought Mom got her food stamps today."

I rolled my eyes and poured water and a can of tomato sauce into the browned pasta.

"Get real."

"Fuck! She spent them already?"

"What do you think?"

"Fuck. I guess me and Tina are going to have to go steal some cartons of cigarettes and sell 'em to that crazy dude again."

She curled up her lip, Elvis-style and yelled for our other sister Tina.

"Teen! Yo, get your face outta the mirror and get in here!"

"What?" bitched Tina, clomping into the kitchen with her makeup half-done.

"Mom spent the stamps."

"Are you serious?"

"Yep."

"Crap. Whatcha making, Elena?"

The last sentence directed at me with not a little scorn. Tina didn't think much of me. My weirdness, always reading my books bothered her. Yet, God forbid either she or Lottie would cook. They did try and clean every so often though and they hustled to get us fed so they weren't all bad.

Tina too had dyed her hair that weird blue-black that she thought was so cool. Her already long lashes were caked with about a whole bottle of mascara and her eyes shadow was just about every color and all the way up to her drawn-on brows. She looked like a clown.

"I should think it's obvious. It's fucking fideo, the same as last night and the night before."

By then, I was beyond fed up and snappy with both of them.

"Oyela. Talking *que* fancy and shit."

This from Lottie, and a recurring theme too;

you'd think they'd come up with better ways to pick on me, but no, it was always about my vocabulary or my books.

"Well, fancy or not, it's fideo, either eat it or shut up."

"Fuck that" Lottie said. Tina and I are going out, we'll get food outside."

"Planning on bringing anything in?"

"I don't know Elena, are you going to do my history homework for it and Tina's too?"

"Guess so."

"Then we'll bring some carne asada or something and we'll get some cash."

I didn't even want to know what they were going to do for the cash. I tried not to think about my sisters that often. They took off and left me, as usual, with the task of handling their homework while they went out and flirted with the vatos.

I ate quickly. Where my mom and her current husband were, I didn't know, but I planned on being in bed before they got home. I sure didn't feel like dealing with drama and whatever fight was sure to ensue, nor was I looking forward to Andy's leer as he stared at my chest right in front of my mother. She was so oblivious.

I got lucky that night. My sister's homework was easy enough and I did it quickly, and then did mine as well. I washed up, left a plate for my mother and scooted into bed.

Around midnight, my sisters slipped in through our bedroom window giggling and whispering. Tina threw me a bag from Carl's Junior and I sat up to eat the still warm french fries and burger they had brought. In exchange, I whispered between bites that their homework was done and in their Pee-Chee folder's all ready for school tomorrow. We heard my mom and her husband stumble in, clearly drunk but they were too busy getting busy to bother us. I could almost feel Lottie's eye roll as they got loud and the bed started thumping against the wall. She grumbled and pretended to snore loudly.

"That's so nasty," whispered Tina.

"Yep."

"Night, Elena."

"Good night, Tina."

I pulled my pink sheet up over my head and smiled a little at the embroidered roses I could feel against my cheek. My grandmother had stitched them for me and it was one of my few nice things. Counting the days till it was summer and I could spend the three months with my grandparents, I fell asleep.

***

Summer arrived all too slowly, and then, like summers do, it was over all too fast. Autumn brought cooler days and still Carlos and the guys worked on the old Coupe, now in his grandmother's overgrown backyard. It was shaping up, becoming the beautiful and sleek lady that the hood had promised it would be. Carlos often said that the car and I were growing up together. All the way into winter, he worked on the car even when the other vatos had long become bored with the project and found other, less productive things to spend their time on. It had become important to him, a symbol - of what, I don't know…probably status and achievement.

Most days it was just Carlos and me and every night he'd walk me home, then jump that wall with his a smile and a wink.

Soon it was spring again and I turned fifteen. There would be no quince for me, though my mom enjoyed taunting me about it whenever my grandparents mentioned the idea. She could be shitty that way, but mostly she was bitter about her own life and her daughters but especially me. It gave her some feeling of power. I understood that on a basic level, but it still hurt.

That spring was a wet one and Carlos moved the car into his grandmother's garage. I often sat on a rickety old stool, absently handing him this tool or that and reading aloud. He loved hearing stories; non-fiction and history were cool too, but his all-time favorite was poetry.

At school each day, I'd spend my lunch hours in the library, poring over the poetry section to find something I thought he would like. The day I read to him Federico Garcia Lorca's *Romance Sonambulo*, he stopped all work on the car and just sat his haunches, transfixed, almost enraptured.

"Verde, te quiero verde," he said over and over after I was done reading.

"Read it again, *mija*."

And so I did, over and over in the days and weeks to come. I renewed it three times and finally, in an old second-hand bookstore, I found our own copy for twenty-fives cents and bought it with my change I had hoarded. He smiled his rare full-lipped smile when I brought the used copy and even rarer, he hugged me.

"That Lorca vato, he's cool eh."

"Yes."

"Bueno, you read him, I'll work, but first I got something to show you, mija," he said with a wink.

"Ooh! What?"

"Watcha"

He went over to a locked cabinet in the garage and pulled a rusty key out of his pocket. When he opened it, I saw paint, real car paint, not just some paint the vatos brought from the last house their dad painted. No, it was real car paint and it was the loveliest shade of silvery green. I looked at Carlos in wonder.

"It's beautiful. Where did you get it?" I asked and gazed down into the shimmery paint.

"Here and there, mija," he said and laughed. "Nah, my Uncle Javi has an auto body shop down in Lincoln Heights and I worked for him and took this as pay."

I smiled. I didn't like having to worry about Carlos going back to juvie.

"It's Lorca-green, mija. The carrucha's name is Lorca."

This he said with that dreamy look he often good when talking about spiritual, *c*urandera-type stuff. In another time, Carlos would have been a shaman, a seer, a wise man. In this time, he was just another vato, but somehow set apart a little from the rest.

I looked up at him smiling. I loved that he would call the car Lorca and paint it the green color of our poem though I didn't have the heart to tell him Lorca's last name was really Garcia. But the naming of the car and the poem connected us somehow in a very deep and soulful way. Carlos, I know thought of me as the little sister he never had, but I had one big-time crush on him and this was damned romantic.

Now my days were spent wearing a mask as Carlos carefully layered paint on Lorca. When the car was fully painted and dried from its last layer of paint, he took the airbrush and wrote on it: *Verde, te quiero verde.*

While I was at school, Carlos had haunted the junkyards coming back with old grills, chrome numbers, hood ornaments and other odds and ends that he piled in the back of the garage. Some had gone on the car, others stayed in his pile of parts. He'd talked another uncle, this one with an upholstery shop, into re-covering the seats in a buttery cream vinyl that almost looked like leather, or at least we thought it did. What did we know?

Not too long after he had painted the car, Carlos showed me his latest treasure: four white wall tires and some chrome rims that he had polished up to a high shine. He even had found a chrome visor for the windshield and carefully installed it.

"Wanna go for a ride in the carrucha, mija?" he asked, grinning that Dopey grin.

"Can we?" I was dying to.

"Pues, si. It's running, my tio hooked up the pink slip and a license plate for it, so we won't get stopped. I have my license. Not too far though, this ain't ready for the Boulevard yet."

He was speaking about Whittier Boulevard, the place where people drove up and down showing off their cars. Lorca, with its shimmering green paint job, sparkling chrome and sleek lines was bound to be a hit on the Boulevard.

I'm sure my eyes were shining. I clutched my book tightly and hopped onto the new smelling vinyl seats. I breathed in the good, clean smell of Carlos and the car and sighed happily. This was my perfect moment in the sun. The guy I loved, his beautiful car he had turned into a poem and me, reading him poetry (this time from Pablo Neruda) as we slowly cruised around his block. I remember he'd even got the old radio working and after I finished reading, he turned it on and the song that played as he took me for the last spin was *Tell It Like It Is* by Aaron Neville and Carlos sang along in a voice nearly as good as that of the singer.

That was my last good memory.

***

The next day, I woke up excited and happy. It was the last day of school and I'd be going to my grandparents over in Los Feliz for the summer and leaving Crudahy behind for three peaceful months. I was going to be getting out of school, and then catch a bus to my grandparents.

School let out early and I ran all the way home, eager to get going. No one was home when I got there, so I quickly packed and hopped into the shower. While changing in my bedroom, I thought I heard a noise and called out for Tina or Lottie.

Nothing. I called out for my mother dreading the confrontation but still there was nothing so I resumed combing out my hair and braiding the long, wet strands of it, still daydreaming of my perfect day with Carlos and Lorca the car.

I heard another noise and annoyed, I turned up the radio, thinking my sisters were trying to scare me.

I can hear the song now as I tell you my story. *Taste of Honey* was singing Boogie, Oogie, Oogie and I was dancing around the room as I packed up my few critical items – books that were making the trip to my grandparents with me. On my last disco spin, I whirled right into the body of my stepfather Andy who had snuck into the room. I yanked away hard, and screamed at him to get out of my room.

He was just too creepy.

In answer, he yanked me by the arm, almost pulling it out of the socket, till I was pressed up against his beer-smelling body. Ugh! I yanked away and he pulled me back. I was angry and scared, struggling and fighting as he held me tight against him. I managed to lift my knee the way Carlos had taught me and caught him a good one right in the nuts.

"You fucking bitch!" he yelled, his spit flying all over my chest as he stumbled down to his knees, reaching for his crotch.

I ran. I got out of my room and flew out of the house down the driveway, not even realizing my shirt was gaping open. I just ran. I ran till I got to Carlos' house but there was no one home. The garage was empty too and then I remembered; Carlos was working at his uncle's today, paying off in slave labor the cost of the green paint.

Frantic, I ran back out onto the sidewalk and the street was empty except for what appeared to be my stepfather's old Chevy, slowly turning the corner.

Fuck!

I had to get away, but where? The concrete river is all I could think of. I would get there, hole up in one of the tunnels and wait for Carlos, then sneak out and have him get me to my grandparents.

Bell cops sure weren't going to believe me. They treated us neighborhood kids like criminals whether we were or not. All we were to them was Mexican trash.

So I ran. I didn't stop, I didn't think, I just ran. My wet braids slapped against my back noisily as I ran. I made it over the bridge on Florence and down into the riverbed and climbed into one of the tunnels. There I sat gasping for air until my breathing calmed and I realized my shirt was half open. That's when I started to cry and tried to button it, fumbling because my hands were shaking. I gave up and cried for an hour. Then I got cold. It was cold and damp in the tunnel and it smelled like moldy water and urine.

I started to freak out, thinking about possible rats. Still, I stayed there, till it seemed like enough time had passed for Andy to stop looking for me and for it to be time for Carlos to be home.

Carefully, I crawled out of the tunnel, my cramped muscles screaming. I was hungry and cold and wanted the last dregs of sunlight to warm my skin. It was too dark in the tunnel to get a look at my arms, but they hurt, so I knew they were bruised from where he'd grabbed me.

I hiccupped and a shiver ran down my spine. I didn't know what to do and stood blinking in the light for a moment when I got out of the tunnel where Lorca had spent is first weeks with us.

I smelled him an instant before my hair was being pulled hard and I flailed and scratched but with nothing to grab onto as he dragged me caveman style back into the tunnel.

"Bitch! Thought you would get away? Thought this place was secret, huh? Fucking whore, I know you come down here with those cholos. Probably giving them all what you tease me with while I'm stuck fucking your fat mom. Bitch! Whore!"

He hit me again and again as I tried to get away, scooting on my back through the slimy water in the tunnel where he'd thrown me. With each blow, he'd call me whore. I screamed and fought, his face was dripping blood onto mine from the scratches I'd dealt him, but it was no use. He was biting me, the

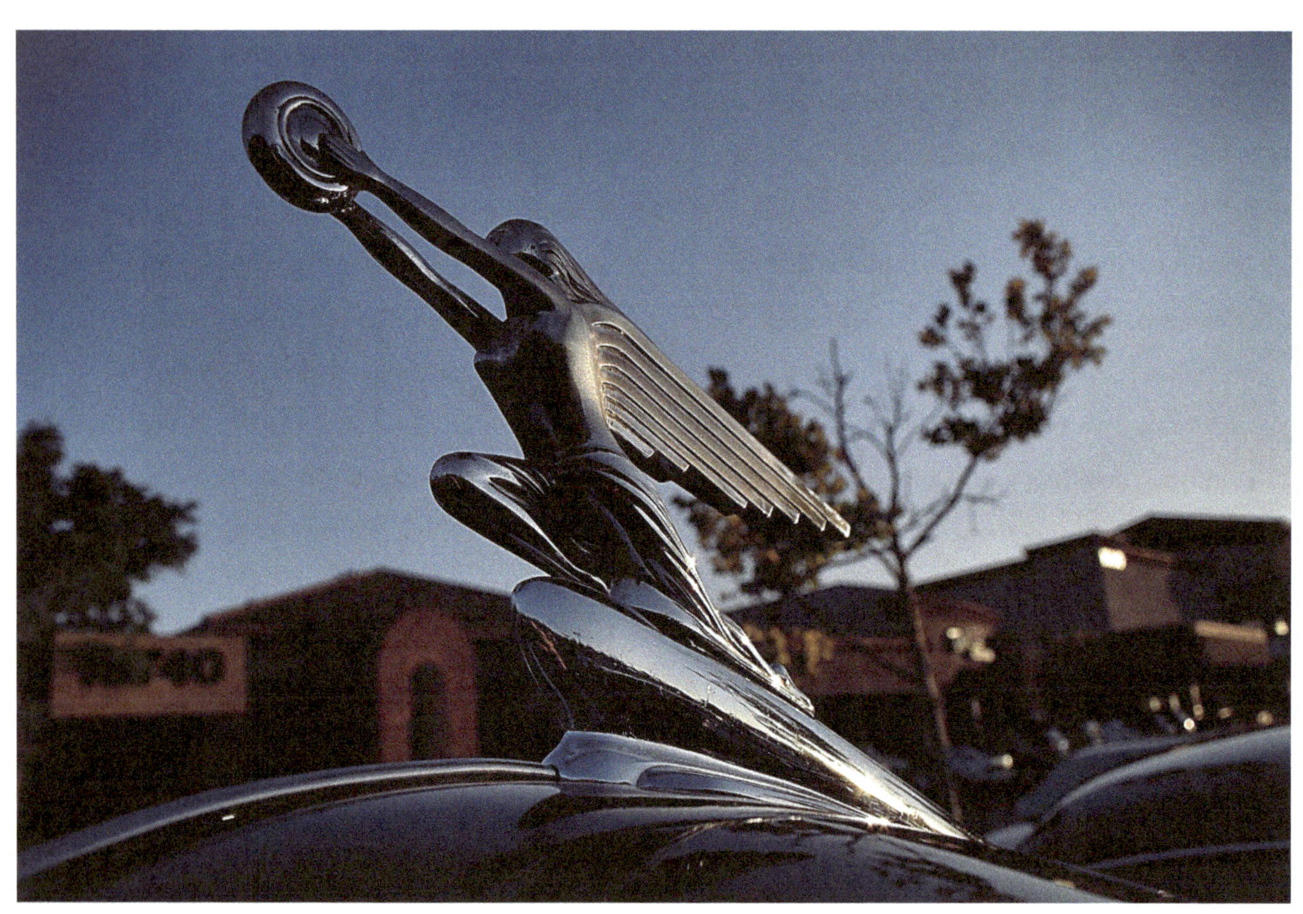

Goddess of Speed – '38 Packard

smell of beer was making me gag and then I felt his clammy hands on my breasts, as he shoved his knee in my crotch hard.

"Remember this bitch?" Knee me will you?"

He kneed me again and I howled from the impact. Then he was yanking my pants off and I screamed again as he tore into me right through my panties. I struggled even more but there was no stopping him. I bit him and he yanked me up by my bra strap and slammed my head down on the wet cement. Then he did it again.

Then I didn't feel anything.

I woke up in the passenger seat of Lorca. It took me a day or two to realize that I was dead. I just sat there crying softly, till the day Carlos got into the car, put his head down on the wheel and cried. Seeing him cry stopped me cold. I tried to reach out and comfort him, but my hands passed right through his body and that freaked me the hell out.

It took them two weeks to find my body. My mom didn't even look for me. She'd figured I ran away and good riddance. It was my grandparents and Carlos that looked. That is to say, my grandparents went to the police, dragging my mother along with them sullenly, while Carlos haunted every block, every hiding place he knew of and every library looking for me.

One day Carlos rounded up the guys and girls and everyone looked and up and down streets until Ruben and a couple of other guys from the hood decided to ask my stepfather about me. They knew something was shifty, so they beat him. They kicked the living shit out of him until he spilled where he'd left me, still calling me a whore. Carlos busted his jaw then.

The guys wanted to kill him, but Dopey shook his head.

"Nah man, let him die in prison," he said. "They'll make him someone's bitch in there."

He dragged Andy to the police station in his uncle's car with Ruben and the guys holding him down in the back. It was then the cops put that yellow tape around the concrete river and opened up the tunnel.

I don't know how I came to live in Lorca. Carlos knows I'm here though. He brings me books of poetry and places them like altar offerings in the passenger seat. It is he who now haunts libraries and old bookstores. He cruises up and down the Boulevard on Fridays and Saturdays, sometimes with the guys.

No one is allowed to sit shotgun, ever. If they ask, he simply says, “That seat’s Elena’s” and no one ever dares question him.

His grandma died a few weeks ago and he moved Lorca and I to Lincoln Heights. He turned to me just the other day, almost as if he could see me and said, “You know what, mija? We’re going to be happy here. Watcha.”

I just smiled at him, picked up my book and began to read to him from the new copy of Octavio Paz he’d put on the seat that morning.

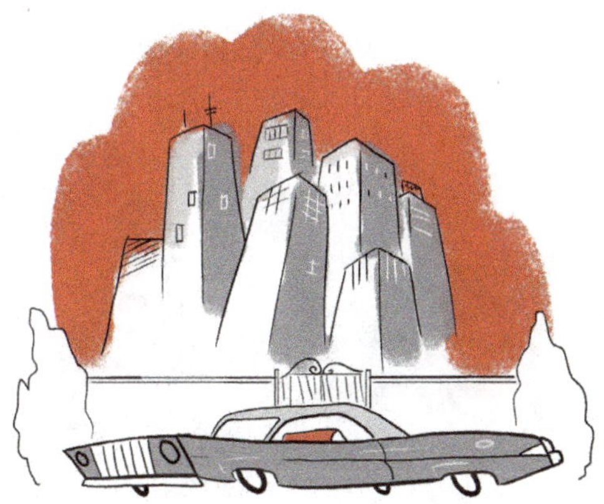

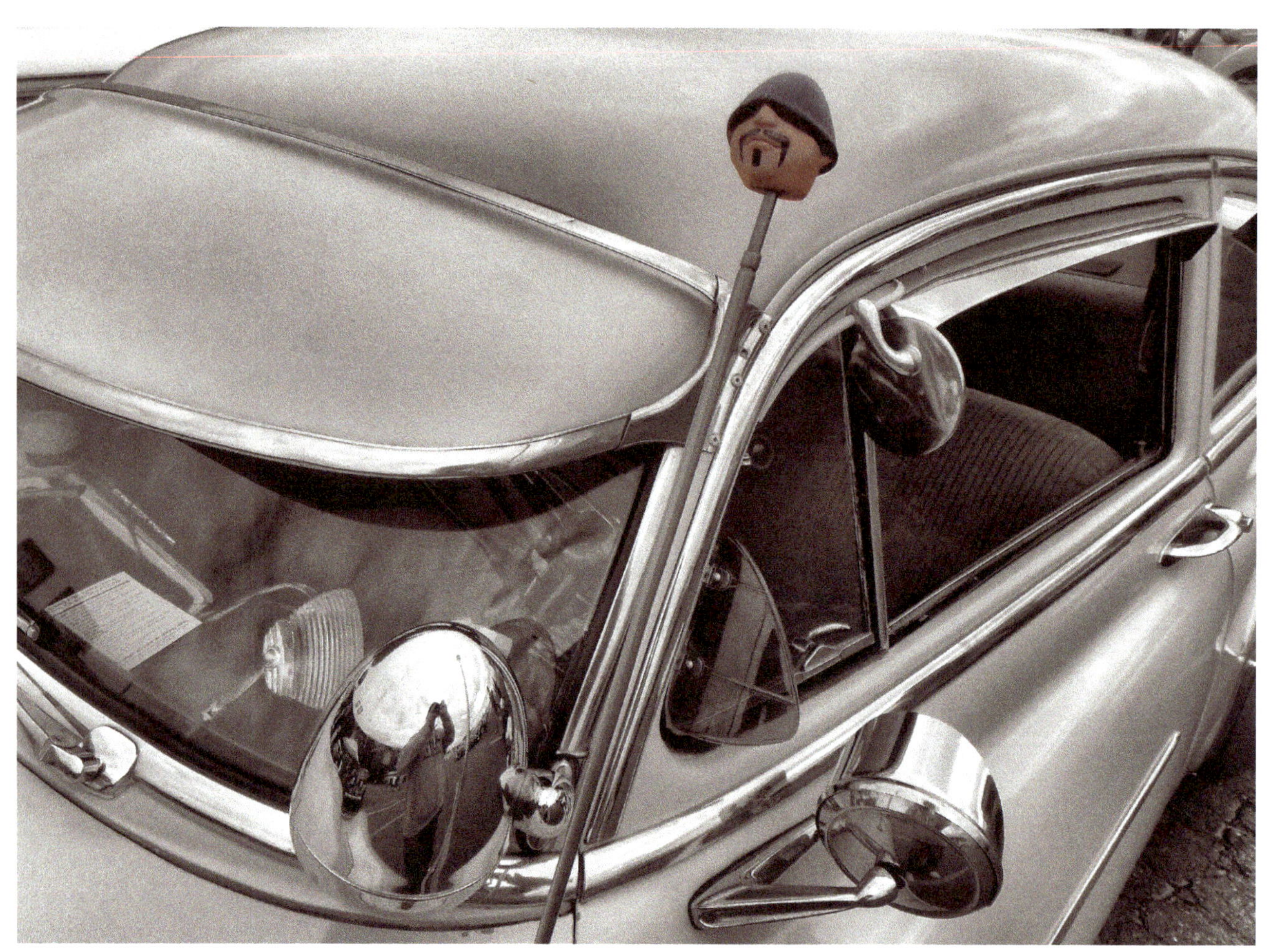

Lowriting — 1950 Chevy Deluxe

Sleepy

By Daniel Villarreal

FADE IN:

EXT. EAST LOS NEIGHBORHOOD - DAY

Heat waves blur the vista of telephone wires and aerials that spot the crowded rooftops.

EXT. DUKE'S HOUSE - DAY

A steel reinforced door opens, letting out loud music and BOBBY, a fine young vato. He's quick tempered and very sensitive. BOBBY exits the house looking pissed. He dispatches a cone shaped party hat from his cholo head.

Next out is DUKE. He's tall, thin and obviously the group's best dresser. He twirls a ring of keys while in mid conversation with JO JO, the leader of this clicka. Trailing them is SLEEPY. He is often either daydreaming or high or both. Sleepy's got his arm around his cousin CHINO, the youngest of this group of teenage Mexican-American gangsters.

SLEEPY

Chino. Fucking surprise party, alright!

(SLEEPY squeezes CHINO'S head with his hand. Chino gets all excited.)

CHINO

Watch this!

(CHINO does his best Harry Houdini and very theatrically, reveals a joint.)

CHINO (CONT'D)

Happy birthday, Sleepy!

SLEEPY

Shit. That's some good trick...You ready for the beach, homie?

(CHINO shrugs.)

SLEEPY (CONT'D)

Fuck, sure you are.

(The boys move along.)

SMASH CUT TO:

EXT. DUKE'S GARAGE - DAY

JO JO pulls up the garage door as an engine roars to life. DUKE backs out of the garage in his 1951 midnight blue Chevy Suburban.

EXT. DUKE'S DRIVEWAY - DAY

The Suburban comes to a stop and shuts down. DUKE calls out.

DUKE

Check it out, suckers! Old school style.

(DUKE pumps the music: 'It's Okay' by The Sunglows.)

EXT/INT. DUKE'S DRIVEWAY - DAY

The homeboys sing along to 'It's Okay' as they primp the Suburban.

Inside the wagon DUKE is up by the dashboard. He works on the leather, makes it shiny. SLEEPY does the same to the blue on white seats.

BOBBY sits in the back, sulking. He's not helping.

EXT. DUKE'S DRIVEWAY - CONTINUOUS

Outside the wagon CHINO belts out the song as he goes over the driver's side front tire. He works on the chrome rims and spokes.

Jo Jo goes around Chino humming the song and cleaning the windows. He ends up at the back of the Suburban looking in on disgruntled Bobby. Jo Jo mad dogs him.

JO JO

Lazy bitch.

(JO JO hits BOBBY in the face with a wet paper towel.)

EXT/INT. DUKE'S DRIVEWAY - DAY

The homies pile into the wagon as The Sunglows do their thing.

DUKE's the driver. JO JO rides shotgun. SLEEPY and CHINO occupy the middle seat since BOBBY's already taken the back seat, the big baby.

DUKE turns the wagon on, looks back and pulls out of the driveway.

EXT. DUKE'S STREET - DAY

The wagon swerves onto the street and they drive off.

EXT/INT. DUKE'S STREET - DAY

The Suburban cruises down the street. The song ends. A moment of silence, then...

SLEEPY

So, who invited Pebbles? She's such a whore.

(A few groans from the guys.)

CHINO

She scares me.

(The guys laugh.)

SLEEPY

Yeah, well, I don't like her.

(DUKE puts out his hands like 'What the fuck?')

EXT. DUKE'S STREET - CONTINUOUS

From outside the Suburban, there's some animated talk going on. As they turn the corner they pass a makeshift shrine with flowers and candles around a framed photo of some fallen homeboy.

EXT/INT. DUKE'S STREET - CONTINUOUS

(DUKE drives.)

DUKE

Sleepy, you know your party today?

(SLEEPY nods.)

DUKE (CONT'D)

That was Pebbles' idea. She came over real early and put up all the decorations.

(DUKE gestures like 'What have you got to say to that?')

SLEEPY

She did that?

(SLEEPY thinks about it. Shakes his head.)

SLEEPY (CONT'D)

I still wouldn't fuck her even if she was the last pinchi vieja left in the 'hood.

(Nobody argues this point.)

EXT/INT. DUKE'S STREET - DAY

CHINO looks out the window and says to no one in particular...

CHINO

Man, Pebbles trips me out big time.

(JO JO looks like 'enough already about this shit!')

JO JO

Why? Just 'cause she likes to fuck? Everybody fucks, homie. It ain't no big thing.

(JO JO turns to Chino.)

JO JO (CONT'D)

Your mommy fucked your daddy and here you are, fucker.

SLEEPY (to Jo Jo)

Wait a minute. Are you saying Chino's mom's a whore?

(SLEEPY leans forward towards the passenger seat.)

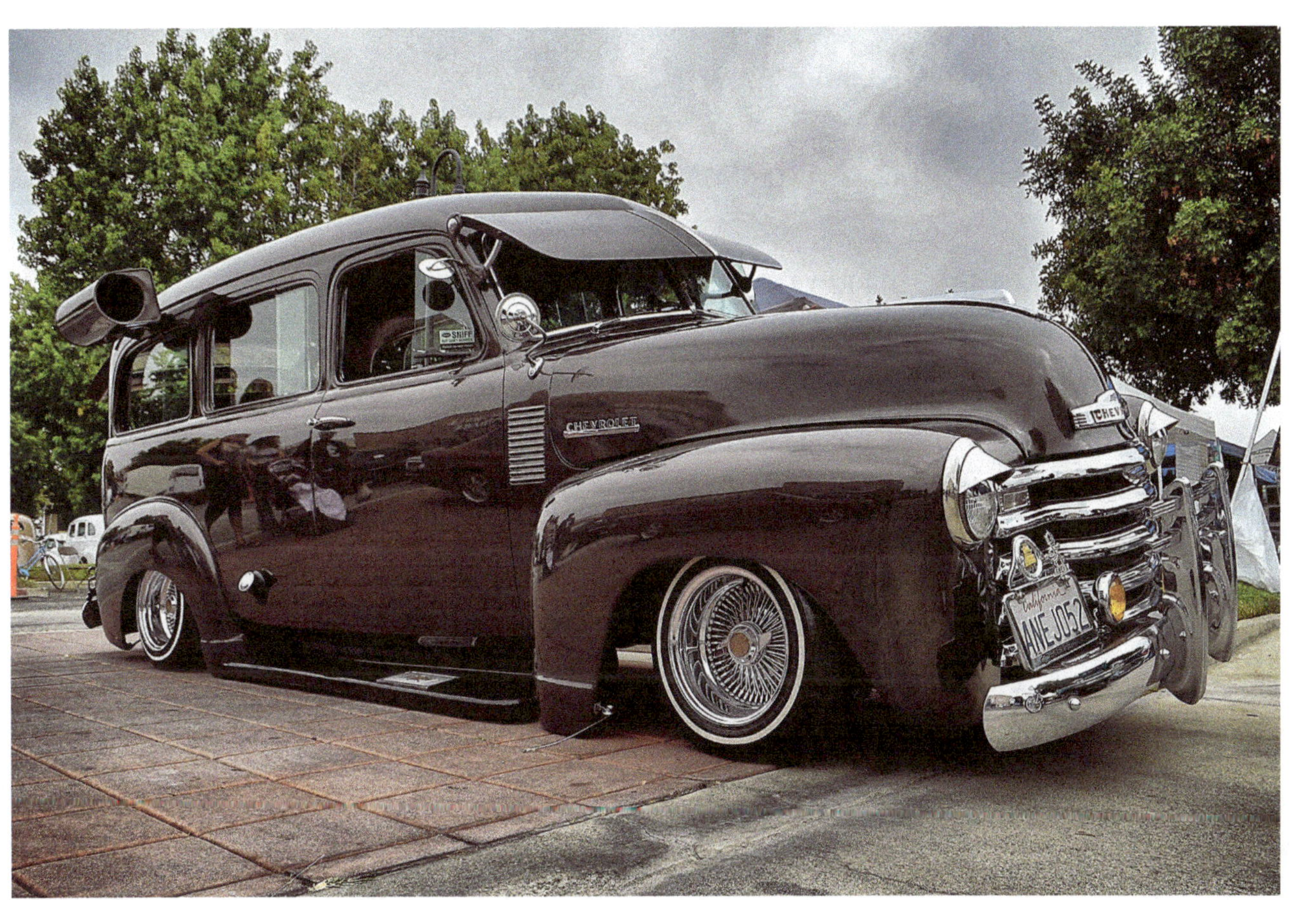

O.G. SUV – '52 Chevy Suburban

SLEEPY (CONT'D)

That's my aunt you're talking about now.

(JO JO defends himself.)

JO JO

Hey, I didn't mean it that way, alright?

(Slouching back into his seat SLEEPY directs himself to CHINO.)

SLEEPY (to Chino)

Homie, don't pay Jo Jo no mind.

(CHINO blows off SLEEPY as he tries to keep up with the 'whore' thing.)

CHINO

Fuck you, Jo Jo...

(BOBBY's been stewing in the back and almost shouts through SLEEPY up to the front seat.)

BOBBY

Fuck you, Jo Jo! Don't be calling Chino's mom a whore.

(JO JO is growing more and more irritated.)

JO JO

Hey, you know what? Fuck all of you. I'm just saying fucking's fucking.

(JO JO drives his point home.)

JO JO (CONT'D)

If that makes Pebbles a whore then my ma's a whore and so is yours.

(DUKE speaks out as if he's going to have the last word on the subject.)

DUKE

My mom ain't no whore but you wanna know something...

(DUKE pulls into a gas station.)

EXT/INT. GAS STATION - DAY

The Suburban pulls up to one of the pumps and DUKE throws it in park. He finishes his point.

DUKE

Pobre vato, Huerito... His mom's a whore, for reals... Sucks dick for a song.

(JO JO thinks DUKE's crossed the line.)

JO JO

Homes, you best not be saying that to Huerito's face.

(DUKE raises his hands as if to say 'I'm just making a point.' He gets out to pump gas. Sleepy follows.)

EXT. GAS STATION - DAY

(DUKE handles the pump as SLEEPY leans on the Suburban.)

SLEEPY

Duke, don't be talking that shit about Huerito's mom. She's got all them kids to feed and no man.

(DUKE pulls SLEEPY off the wagon.)

DUKE

Well, if you can see that then why can't you see that maybe Pebbles is a nice girl?

(DUKE triggers the pump and nothing happens. He points to the attendant in the window.)

JO JO (O.S.)

Sleepy, go put down for the gas.

(SLEEPY heads towards the cashier window as the discussion continues in the wagon.)

DUKE (O.S.)

(to someone in the wagon)

Pendejo, get your feet off my seats.

EXT. GAS STATION - DAY

(SLEEPY approaches the window and notices an OLD MAN sitting in a lawn chair. He holds rosaries and mumbles prayers to himself.)

SLEEPY (to attendant)

That pump over there.

(SLEEPY points in the direction of the wagon.)

EXT. GAS STATION - DAY

(SLEEPY walks back to the wagon. As he leans into the window his shirt raises just high enough to catch a glimpse of the PISTOL tucked into his waistband.)

SLEEPY (to CHINO**)**

Hey, trip out on this old viejo.

(CHINO and the guys are too caught up in their

discussion to respond.)

EXT. GAS STATION - CONTINUOUS

(TWO YOUNG BLONDE GRINGA BEACH BUNNIES arrive and sit on the steps of the gas station convenience store.)

SLEEPY (O.S.) (to himself)

Watcha...

EXT. GAS STATION - DAY

(SLEEPY squats down in front of the bunnies as they giggle and fidget with their skateboard.)

SLEEPY

Nah, really, I ain't lying. I've never been to the beach. First timer.

(The girls giggle and slurp their Slushies.)

BEACH BUNNY #1

Yeah, you don't look like you're going to the beach.

SLEEPY

C'mon. It's my birthday...I swear...

(SLEEPY places CHINO's gift joint on the

skateboard. BUNNY #2 picks it up with her foot and passes it to BUNNY #1 who is all smiles.)

EXT. GAS STATION - CONTINUOUS

(DUKE's Suburban's doors burst open. The homeboys spill out with fists swinging. BUNNY #1 peeks around SLEEPY to view the ensuing melee. SLEEPY does his best to keep the ball in play.)

SLEEPY

It's cool.

(BOBBY goes flying. DUKE is losing his breath laughing as he tries to get JO JO off CHINO.)

JO JO (to DUKE**)**

Look! CHINO'S the puto! He tried to grab my ass. Did you see that?

(BOBBY tears off DUKE's sneaker and tosses it into the wagon. He pig piles the lot of them.

SLEEPY sighs and slowly makes his way back towards the wagon.)

(DUKE frees himself, hops in the wagon, flips everyone the finger and takes off.)

EXT. GAS STATION - DAY

(CHINO and BOBBY have JO JO pinned down.

SLEEPY watches the Suburban drive off.)

SLEEPY (to himself)

Fuck...

(SLEEPY turns to the girls and finds them gone as well, halfway down the road already.

He frowns and looks back toward his homeboys.)

The beach is not happening today.

The dark blue ocean shimmers in the distance.

FADE TO BLACK

††

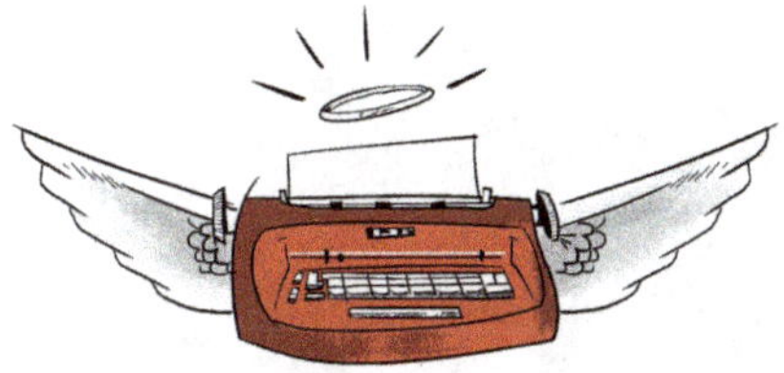

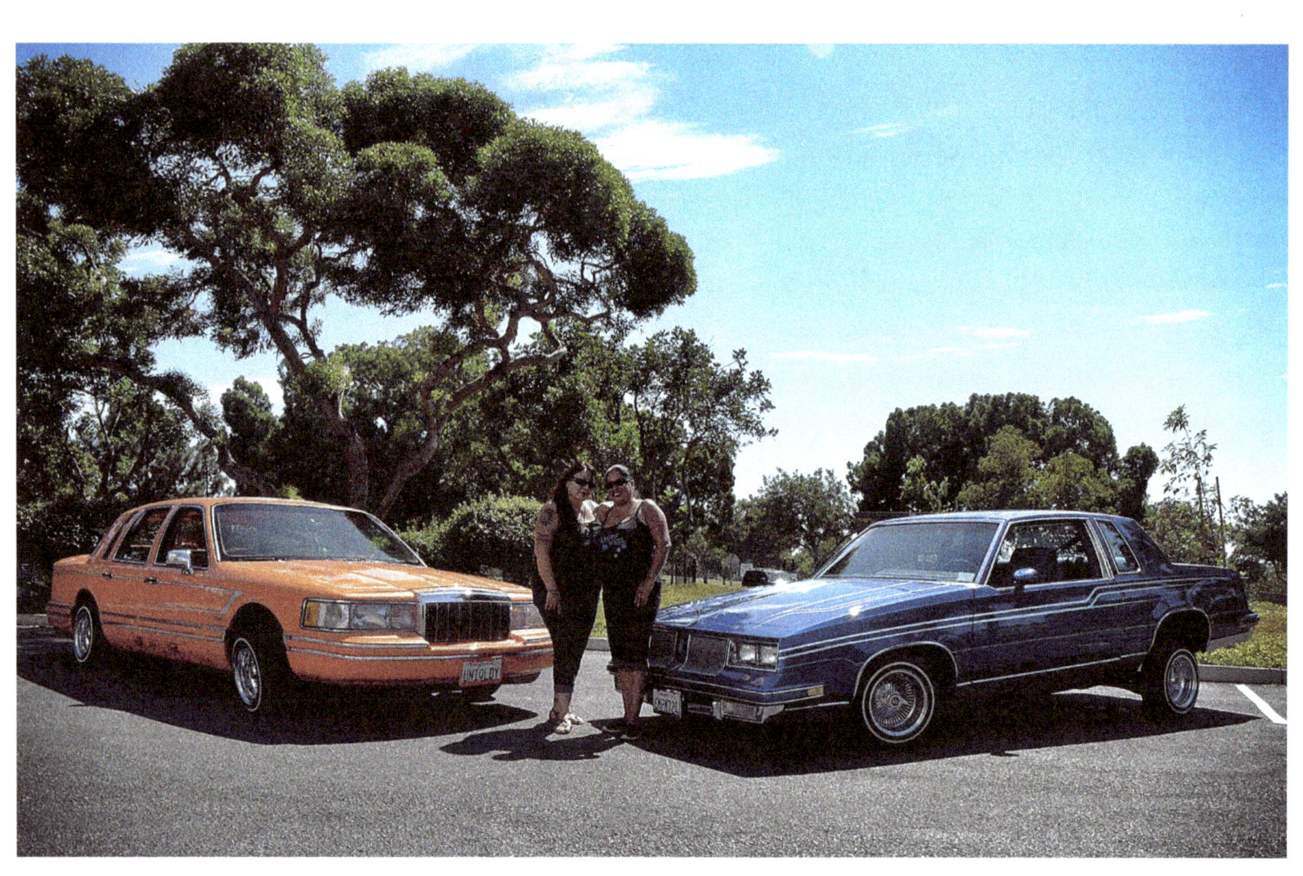

The Unique Ladies – 1990 Lincoln Towncar, 1980 Oldsmobile Cutlass Supreme

Cruising into the Future

By Gloria Morán

This year (2013) was the triumphant debut of my short documentary, *The Unique Ladies*, which follows an all-women lowrider car club in San Diego, California. Triumphant, because it took nearly seven years to complete, despite major health delays and financial woes. Being a light-skinned guera filming in a community of color, I'm often treated as an outsider; it takes some flexing of my hood knowledge to gain rapport and confidence, often involving me to reveal how I came to the idea of making a documentary about women lowriders. *And how did you get into lowrider culture?* I'm often asked by Chicana/o lowriders that I meet while filming. I'll offer a shorthand explanation; of growing up with a Chicano dad from East Side Stockton, California, where a Sunday afternoon of chillin' with the homies was quite common for us, and we frequented the impromptu cruise, local lowrider show and concert.

The palpable emotions of entering lowrider culture resurface when I explain my connection to the culture. Each time I tell my story, I can still go back to that hot Stockton afternoon at the fairgrounds, where a huge lowrider show was well underway, and I trailed my *papi* everywhere.

"I can't see, *Papi*, I can't see," I said tugging at my dad's pant leg.

A crowd was formed around something spectacular, and I was determined to see it. I was so close, but being only five years old, I was too short to see over the gathering of people, so I needed help from my *papi*. In one swoop he lifted me up to sit on his shoulders so I could get a glimpse of something truly magnificent; a tricked-out, fully customized, VW van lowrider. I squinted at the sun's reflection on the smooth shiny roof with chrome trimming. Lowered completely to the ground and sitting gently in the grass this car commanded one's attention. Balanced on his shoulders my *papi* made his way closer to the vehicle, up to the "do not cross" rope—also part of my fascination, instead of using velvet rope like most display barriers this car lover used hollow plastic tubing filled with a moving liquid that changed colors, alternating hot pink and green. The car itself was white with details of neon palm tree green and bright flamingo pink. The interior was a clean and creamy white, from a white shag rug to the white leather bench seats trimmed in the signature neon green and pink, there was just no stopping the beauty and detail of this vehicle. With its side panel door open, the pavement pounding bass was cranked up and next to it was the TV/VCR media area and mini-kitchenette.

Silently staring, I took it all in while my *papi* snapped photos. I wanted to stay for a while but we started moving on to the next car, I looked back, and watched the gap in the crowd my dad and I left fill with more onlookers. After that, I was hooked.

Sometimes I feel guilty about not falling in love with a "classic" lowrider--not a *candy* colored impala, a clean bomb, or a gleaming Caddy. The VW van signified a new aesthetic that was burgeoning in lowrider culture; a new generation of enthusiasts were participating in the culture, transforming it to their ideas and monetary capabilities. This was the late 80s and early 90s (think: hammer pants and gravity-defying aquaneted hair) when the demand for the "classic" lowriders was either driving their cost up considerably or drying up any availability. The alternative then became the use of non-U.S. cars that were fairly affordable, leaving the opportunity to invest significant income into their modification. Nissan mini-trucks lowered within a half-inch off the ground, speedy Honda civics with airbrushed murals on every panel, and of course the one of kind lowriders like my friend, the VW. Sometimes when I go to car shows now I long for those masterpieces of re-defiant ingenuity and over-exaggerated detailing. It seems the "new" affordable alternative to the "classics" are the luxury vehicles of the late 80s and 90s, Lincoln Towncars, big Buick Regals, and of course the staple favorite Cadillac. This is the lowrider scene I re-entered through my filming, but the vehicles and their owners still maintain every characteristic of rasquache sensibility where inventiveness, recycle and reuse are king.

When I first entered the lowrider scene, I was a young scrunchy-wearing, blond-haired *huerita* running around in leggings and t-shirts (one of my dad's designs with a Pachuco gangsta-leaning with a 40's Bomb in front of the El Castillo pyramid of Chichen Itza). While my *papi* never owned a lowrider he did cruise with his homies back in high school. His stack of *Lowrider* magazines reached almost to the ceiling, each month adding to the pile after he read the latest issues, which I then read, and placed on the top of the stack. Photoshop had just came out for at home use and my dad invested his money and bought a t-shirt business. He was determined to use Chicano imagery in different ways but still keep it part of the lowrider style. He played with the Chicano aesthetic by proudly celebrating the Pachuco image back-dropped with the green white and red of the Mexican flag, and old school English writing that read *Pachuco Nation*. My favorite shirt was of a blue 1940s Bomb orbiting the Earth with the top caption reading, "The Chicano Space Program," and completed at the bottom with, "Cruising into the Future." Lowriders have been at the forefront of merging history and technology, and I consider making *The Unique Ladies* part of that gamut, where digital technology allowed me to cruise into the future with cementing an untold history of women's work and participation in the lowrider space.

The Unique Ladies looks at lowrider culture through the eyes of women. The car club featured in the film is composed of two central members, Patricia (Pat) Gutierrez and Sherry Yafuso.

Lowriders in their youth, they shelved the practice for the demands of marriage and motherhood. Now with children who are grown and out of the house, they've delved back into the lowrider lifestyle they know and love. My initial undertaking of this project began in 2006 with my senior thesis as an undergraduate at UC Santa Cruz, comprised of mostly phone interviews with varying members of the lowrider world. I wanted to write and publish an alternative history of lowrider culture and explore the possibilities of the future of women's involvement in the lowrider scene. I first met Sherry and Pat via telephone – the first time I called Sherry she had to reschedule as her boyfriend just purchased a new lowrider and they were taking it for a spin. When I heard this, I knew she was the real deal. Pat and Sherry both exuded excitement and passion as they spoke about lowriding, growing up Mexican-American, and finally fulfilling their dreams of owning and customizing their own lowrider. The result became nearly five hours of audio interviews, documenting their life's paths and how each ended up became "firme hynas cruising the boulevards."

While my dad led my introduction into lowrider culture, I look back at certain incidents that now stand out, where my dad couldn't communicate verbally the problems with his young daughter imbibing lowrider culture. Mainly at issue, was the portrayal of women. Sitting atop my dad's shoulders during the concert portion of a lowrider show, I was introduced to some of the 90s classics: *Lighter Shade of Brown*, *Kid Frost*, and *Angelina*, just to name a few. Bouncing on top of my dad's shoulders I would get sucked into the show, but in a brief moment it would all be taken away and I would be dropped off his shoulders with my new view of only people's backs. I was removed so that I wouldn't witness the bikini and wet t-shirt contests that serve for entertainment between musical acts. My dad never explained to me why I was taken down, hence everyone's cheers confused me as it seemed I was missing out on something exciting. I later discovered what I was missing, ironically via reading my dad's *Lowrider* magazines.

Those *Lowrider* magazines – sometimes it was perfectly ok for me to look at them, but sometimes my dad would fervently tell me no. His indecisiveness was indicative that he couldn't or more likely didn't know how to communicate why women's bikini clad bodies graced themselves upon the glossy hoods of these vehicles I so admired. *Lowrider Magazine* would consistently feature a selection of photos from the bikini contests at their car shows. That imagery was very "effective" on my six-year-old psyche. I got into a lot of trouble once because I wanted to mimic the women in the those magazines. Dressed in a plain white Hanes t-shirt and a pair of black high heels my grandma had bought for me to use when I played dress-up, I made over-exaggerated poses each time making clicking sounds as if a photographer was really in front of me. My mom was on the phone when she walked past my room and witnessed my activities – she immediately hung up, and she told me to stop.

"Were you mimicking the women in your papi's magazines?" she asked me.

I nodded silently. That night we had a conversation about what I saw in the magazines and the meaning of the phrase "sex sells." I'm thankful for that talk; it opened me up to realizing that I could be a girl into lowriders, and that the only way I could participate didn't have to be as a scantily-clad model.

Utterly determined to turn my written thesis into a documentary, my mom made an investment in my filmmaking career and we split the cost of a prosumer camera. Informed about the Lowrider Indoor Super Show in San Diego in August of 2007, I coordinated with the ladies to film them prepare for the event, and participate in the show. The night before meeting the ladies, and shooting for the day, I called Sherry, whom I still had not met in person.

*

"We're all meeting at 6 am over at Peter Piper's in National City," she told me.

"Peter Piper's?" I asked, curious as to what type of establishment this was.

"Yea, ummm, you got Chuck E Cheese's where you live? It's like that, a place to take the kids," she replies.

I got up the next morning at 5, nervous, excited, all with a growling tummy. I drove down the 5 freeway, my driver's side mirror dangling by its wire in my borrowed silver dented Mazda—worried that I would be mocked for driving such an atrocity among such car aficionados.

Arriving at Peter Piper's I'm furrowing my eyebrows, squinting at the bright San Diego morning sun. Stepping out of my car I walk over to a blue Lincoln (I remembered Sherry's car from a photo she sent me) and finally meet Sherry face-to-face. She's very petite, her features are a lot softer than I had gathered – all the photos I had seen of her she was wearing thick black sunglasses and bright red lipstick. Her hair is pulled back in a Janet Jackson ponytail that spills out of the back of a baseball cap that reads *Unique Ladies* in blue cursive embroidery with her matching black tank reading the same. Before I reach out to shake her hand her arms are warmly outstretched and ready to embrace me. She treats me like she was my niña, like she had known me all my life. She takes me around the parking lot and introduces me to the other lowriders that are going to the show as well. Included, was Sherry's boyfriend Ronnie with his sick, tricked out yellow and brown El Camino. Mayra, mother to two *Unique Ladies Bike Club* members, and her root beer float colored Lincoln, in tow with her daughters' chrometastic lowrider bicycles flanked in purple and pink.

"We're still waiting for Pat," Sherry informs me, "She texted me a minute ago saying that she was on her way, and she doesn't live to far from her soooo…" right then Pat swoops into the parking lot blasting One Way's *Cutie Pie* in her cream and gold Lincoln Towncar.

"Hey gurl!" Pat calls out to Sherry. They give each other a big hug and take a step back to check out Pat's lowrider.

"It's looking good, really good," comments Sherry.

Sherry introduces me to Pat. I had only known her through her sweet voice and infectious laugh from our phone interviews. Whenever she spoke about her future plans for customizing her car I envisioned her as always speaking with a smile. And that is how Pat talked to me, warmly with a smile and sincerity.

"It's good to finally meet you gurl, I was wondering if you were still coming, you drove right?" she asks.

"Yuuuup, from San Francisco," I tell her.

"Daaaaaaaaang, and there aren't any women

lowriders up North?" she asks me pointing her gold and black detailed acrylic nail upward.

"None that I could find," I told her, "Besides, I really wanted to check out your rides."

"Well, we're gonna take off right now and meet up with some folks at Chicano Park. You ready to go? Got all your stuff? You can ride with me."

I began to tingle. Chicano Park. Chicano Park, I said quietly under my breath. I had heard about Chicano Park, its one of those must see/must visit/must have a spiritual moment places in Chicana/o Aztlan. I felt so unprepared, not just with filming, I felt unprepared to experience Chicano Park that I grew up hearing about from my dedicated Chicano Movement parents. But, there was nothing else to do but hop into Pat's Lincoln, strap the camera tightly onto my hand and go.

Pat hops onto the 5 Freeway heading North, driving about 40 miles an hour in the slow lane. We make our way to Chicano Park with six lowriders behind us. We pass by a lowrider with a flat tire, and two other lowriders parked in front and behind with their owners helping the one with a flat.

"That's what we do," Pat says pointing at the flat tire situation, "We're all family so we're down to help you out."

I nodded quietly, enamored by the kinship this community fostered.

I press record and cram myself against the passenger door, trying to keep steady as we roll and bounce into Chicano Park. We park and wait for more lowriders to join together to create a long caravan to the San Diego Convention Center where the indoor show was to be held. I was trying to cram a spiritual experience behind the camera lens. From what I saw, I was mesmerized. Long concrete columns of murals that chopped up a large green park. Some were fading, but their life was still in them. Faces of the icons- Pancho Villa, Adelita, Frida, and of course the La Virgen.

There was a moderate homeless population spread about in different corners of the park. A police car patrolled through the park, driving directly on the grass- driving slow and checking out both the homeless folks and the lowrider folks. *Disrespectful*, I thought. No one else batted an eye about it, so I pretended it didn't bother me. I simultaneously appreciated and gaffed at the fact that everyone at the park felt so comfortable in that space.

Although the sun is already out, Chicano Park remains cool due to the the tall concrete bridges blocking out the warmth. Pat gets out of the car and starts greeting other lowriders that are waiting for their club members to gather. Pat lights up a cigarette and quickly hides it behind her back when she sees that I am filming. All I could think about was how much I wanted a cigarette myself, barely 7 a.m. and I'm overwhelmed.

All of Pat's lowrider friends were standing away from me- creating a circle of avoidance- like I was the girl who farted. Maybe they could tell that I was uncomfortable, and that I didn't want to start filming them right away. So, I just started shooting b-roll--the murals, a car cruising by, details on some of the vehicles. Through my headphones I covertly hear conversations about how long of a wait there will be to get into the convention center. Today, the lowriders bring in their cars and set up so the next day is for them to enjoy. I have been told to expect a long day, we won't be done until 6 p.m.

We hop into the car and I try to mount the camera so that is sticking out of the window to get a moving shot. We pass by the lowrider council mural- a blue background with Impalas, bombs, and car club names scripted above. A little girl runs past the mural. I am quietly ecstatic. A golden shot.

As we move out from the park and begin the slow journey to the convention center I look behind me and through Pat's back window, seeing nothing but shiny cars behind me.

"Do you want to stand up through the sunroof and film the cars behind us?" Pat asks me.

The car is still moving pretty swiftly but I figure that since we're off the freeway I would be ok.

"Here, here, wait," Pat exclaims, "Can you stand up on this?" Pat spreads out a worn out towel rag, "It's not you, I just want to protect my upholstery."

Slowly making our way to the convention center, I ask Pat to tell me how she got started in lowriding. I am basically asking her questions I have asked her before, but this time, it's on film. She starts talking to me about growing up in Bakersfield, about her husband being a member in Groupe car club. But, I can't hear, Rick James "Superfreak" is too loud. I begin to ponder: how can I politely ask a lowrider to turn down the tunes that always keep them going? But I don't. I figure, that's a request for when she's known me a little longer.

Arriving in front of the convention center we pull up in line and Pat turns off her car. She turns to me and says, "We're gonna to be here a while…"

Barely 8 o'clock in the morning, and it's already 98 degrees, so instead of baking in the car, we step outside and Pat gives me an exterior tour of her ride. The blaring sun plasters my shadow on the golden pearl flake paint of the car.

By noontime the ladies and I are inside the venue. Then began the hours of tireless prep; polishing chrome, cleaning wheels, dusting, more polishing, display and decorations set-up, and did I mention the polishing? As the rest of the day unfolds, I gain their confidence and start to feel comfortable in what turned out to be my best day of shooting.

We end the long day with the best tacos of my life. After seven years of filming the ladies, albeit slightly repetitive, I still love reentering the lowrider scene. I can close my eyes and appreciate the freshness of that first time I forayed into the lowrider scene, perched atop my *papi's* shoulders.

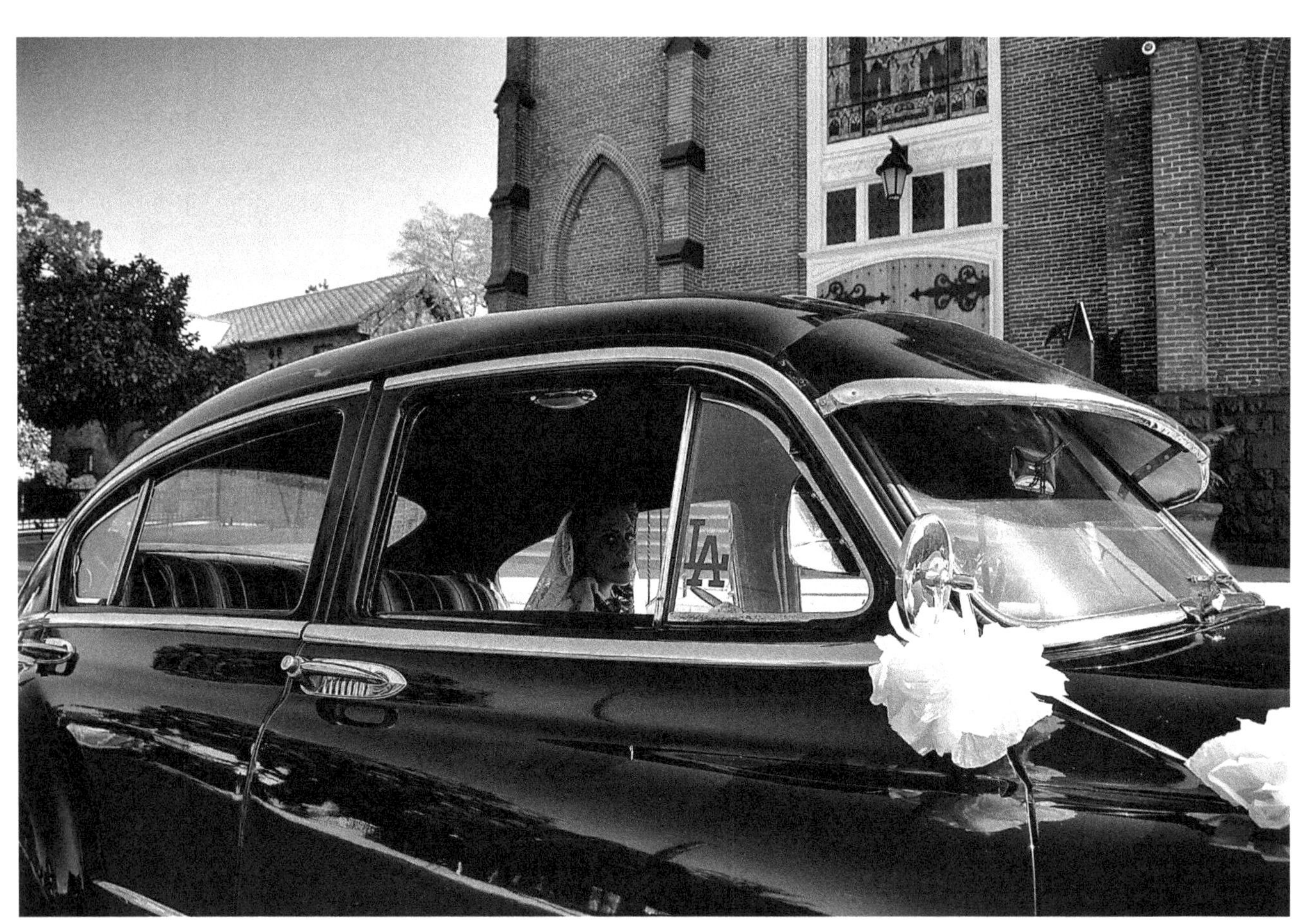

Pachuca Princess, Noelle Reyes – 1951 Chevy Fleetline

Princess Pachuca

by Noelle Reyes

Otra vez…..

Another boda!

With a family this large,

it seemed like there was one every other month.

Paper flower making time.

Handmade streamers

for the wedding lowrider parade of candy cars.

She loved helping her Ma and Tias.

To hear their comadre sessions was better than

anything on TV.

She loved creating.

It sent her into major day dreamer time.

Each fold her little fingers made to the tissue

paper was a wish.

Back and forth, over and over.

Little lady hands working hard to manifest her

dreams.

Prayers to keep her focus.

She didn't want to be married.

She didn't dream of a big poofy lace dress.

There was no need to be distracted by anyone's glitter flake.

No pinche prince was gonna come for her in a lowrider.

She wanted to create her own pinstripe paradise.

Creating luscious lace airbrush patterns and twirling around the city.

The queen of her own universe.

No Vatos Allowed!

And this was her prayer:

CON/SAFOS

with respect

guard this heart

branded corazon

message to all

insults will be spit back

sincere warning

powerful energy

bursting passion

all threats reversed

don't mess with this love

forbidden to touch

unless it's real

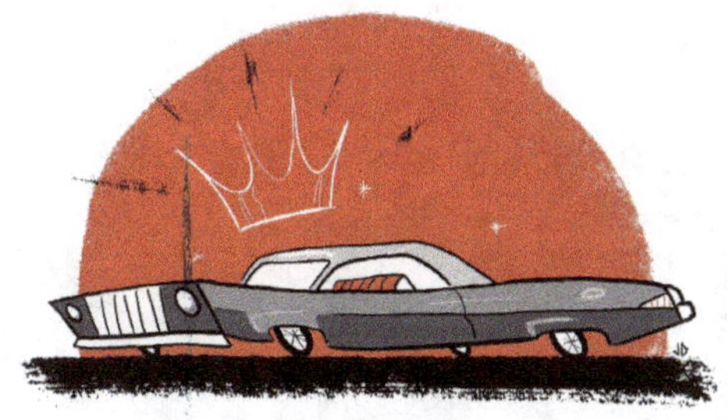

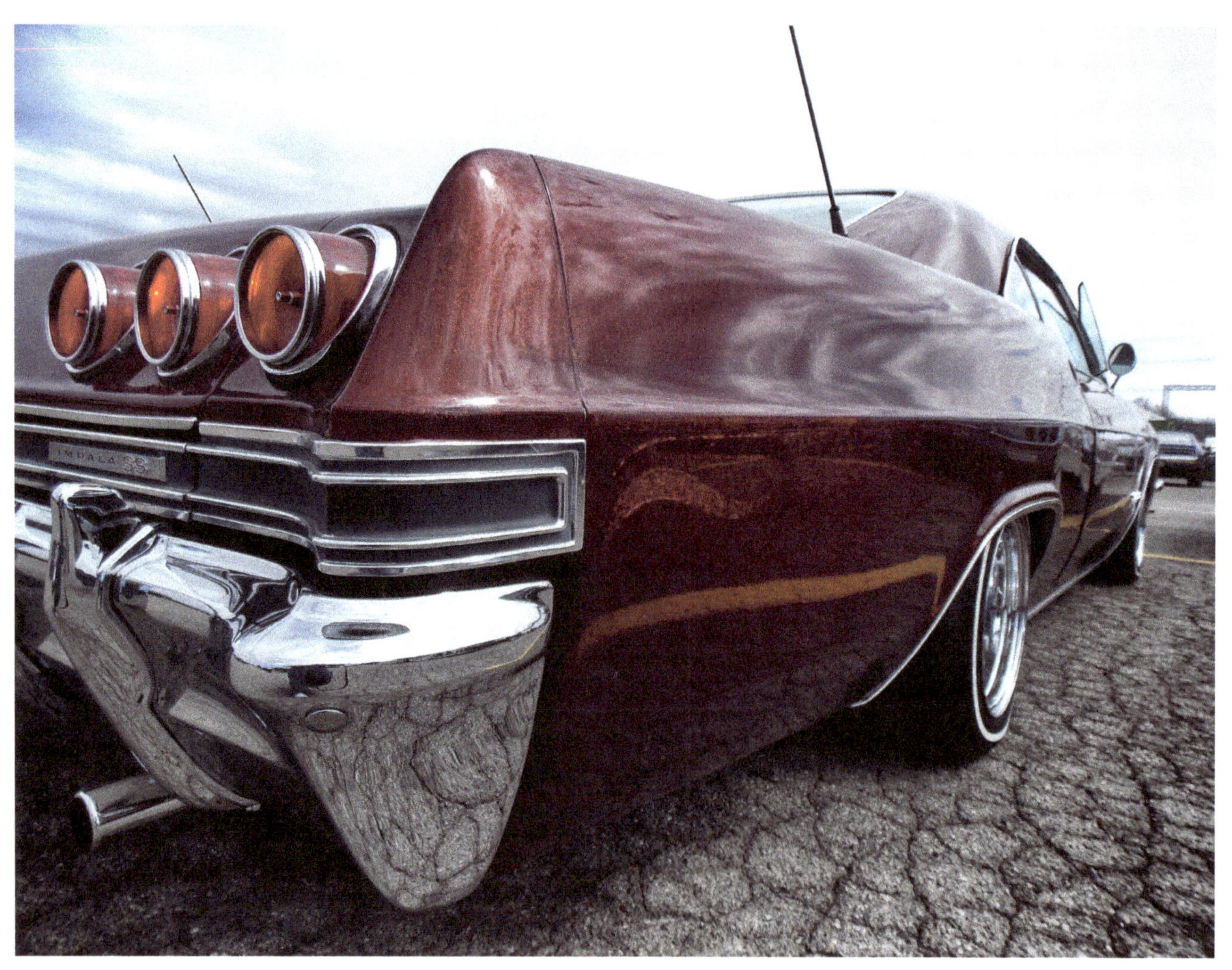

Candy & Concrete – 1965 Chevrolet Impala

Reminiscing

by Raúl Sánchez

Me and my Impala
cruising Hollywood,
tilting at Crenshaw
rear tail tilt at Western

left side up at Vine
past Cahuenga
all the way to Las Palmas
straight up at Highland

cops lurking for dragging
sparkling tail pipes
grinding,
bandanas hanging

Pendleton high button shirts
flowing.
José, Chuco, Rudy and me
riding 'ranflas'

on lower than low
Hollywood streets.
We cruise the night
riding high on purple 1965

Chevy Impala
custom paint
crushed velvet seats
smooth ride—

the pride of the hood.
Tierra, El Chicano,
Third World music blasting
speakers loud

we scratch our way back
to Atlantic Boulevard
East Los El Chante homes!
homies got to sleep too esé!

hang over morning deal
menudo, pozole, birongas.
Tonight we cruise downtown
Main and Broadway our way

across the river

Low riding, riding low

riding 'ranflas'

on lower than low American streets.

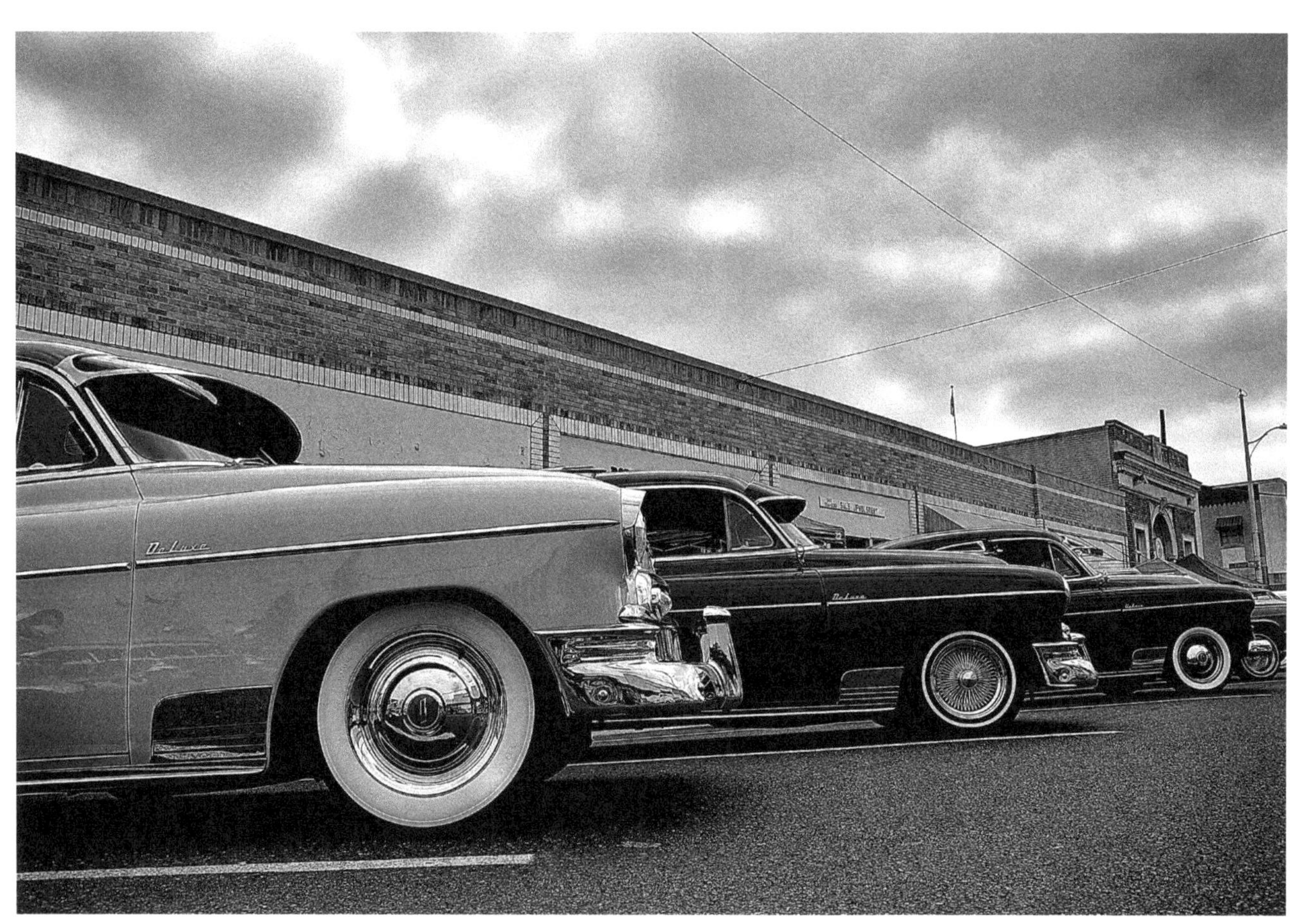

3 of a Kind – 1949 Chevy Deluxe

Quemando Llanta - (Burning Rubber)

by Raúl Sánchez

Órale vatos,

acá

on this side

of Aztlán

pónganse al alba

dejen de cabulear

Chido tacuche

buenos tubos en los calcos

agarren su jaina ya!

dejen de pestañear

pónganse chancla

el borlo va a empezar

rolas, birongas, refín

pisteando con Don Ramón

el ruco. La ranfla old Impala

quemando llanta

los locos tirando chancla

cumbia, simón, polkas de jalón.

Andrés pásame las tres,
quiero sentirme
aviadoooooor Ese
tomorrow al jále
los varos hay que ganar
sin feria no baila el mono

Dale gas Barrabas
échale vapor Nicanor
let's go cruise Whittier Boulevard
aguas con la chota
slow down man,
cool down in the hood

East Los best
with the boys makin' noise Ese!
Old school esteicis
buttoned up lisa
wango pants
next to the carruja
gold spoke wheels
whitewall tires
pearl flake

and clear coat

air brushed

Cuauhtémoc warrior

así mero man!

desde mi cantón

Tlaltécatl les da bandera

hay nos vidrios

carnales y carnalas

Wachenle!

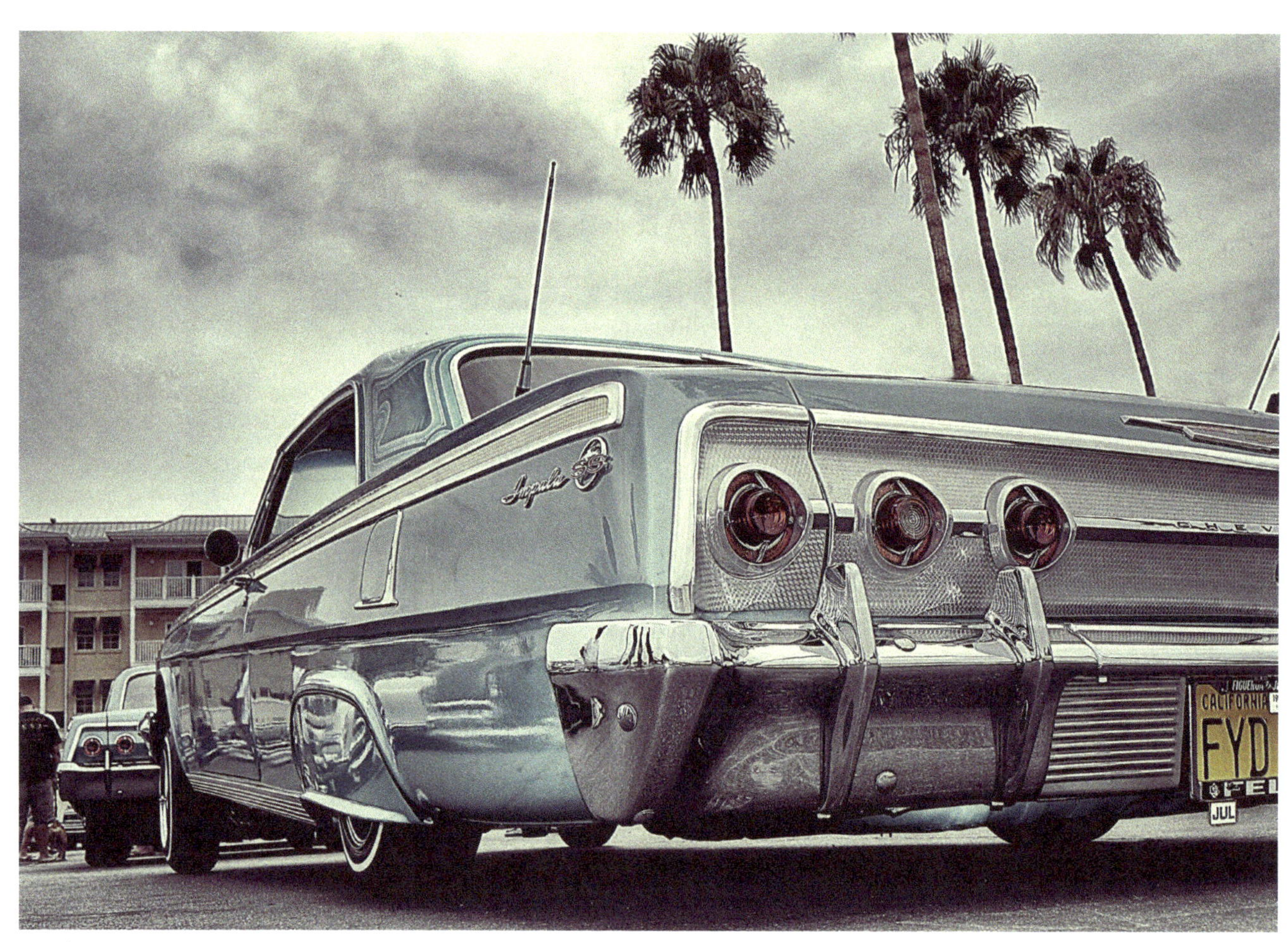

City Livin' – 1962 Chevy Impala

Chevy Impala

by Raúl Sánchez

Chicanos

Hitting the streets

Elevated shocks

Vintage cars

Yelling, órale vato!

Ideal custom cars

Mexican-Americans

Pump these up

Aztec motifs on the doors

Los Angeles, East Side

Aztlán!

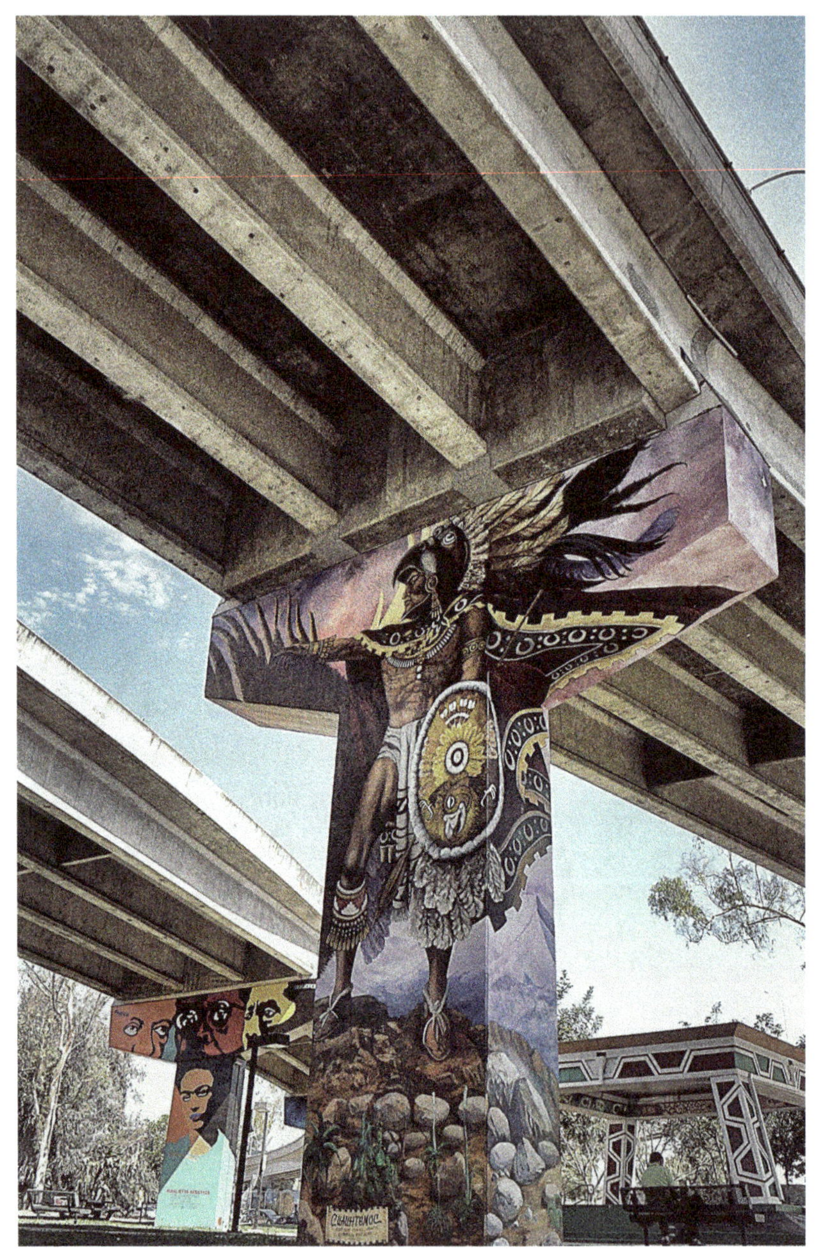

Cuauhtemoc, Chicano Park, S.D.

Chicanismo

by Manuel Gonzalez

I used to cruise a lowrider
A firme '63 Bel Air
Everything was original
Except the hydros
I even took the pilgrimage
To Espanola, New Mexico
The lowrider capital of the world
And I got respeto for my ranfla

I remember when I was a Cholo
With the creases in my kakis
Razor sharp
My Pendelton buttoned at the top
And those corduroy bedroom slippers
You remember those Chopos!
And that grease I put in my hair
Tres Flores
That shit kicked my hair back
Just right
Every night

And it never completely washes out
But that's not what being Chicano is all about

Then I learned my Chicano history
About
El Movimiento,
Caesar,
Che,
Tijerina,
Aztlán.
The walkouts
The boycotts
The riots
The resistance
And I was pissed that I wasn't taught all this in school!
But I still hadn't figured out
What being Chicano is all about

Then I became a militant Chicano
With my fist in the air
Trying to conquer the establishment
I started spelling the word "Xicano" with an "X"
Because that's the way the Mexica would have spelled it
I stood at the pinnacle of the pyramid of the sun

And I was ready to throw myself to the bottom
For any cause
But I still hadn't figured out what being Chicano is all about

Then I finally accepted my meztiaje
That means I have the blood of
Indigenous
And
Spanish
Flowing through my veins.
From the Conquistadors and the Moors
To the Azteca and the Tolteca
I could see the class and regalness of the Spaniard
Like the tragic beauty of the bullfight
And the precision and discipline of flamenco
But I also put my hand in the soil
And I felt mother earth
La tierra
I pray to the four directions
And I understand the harmonious balance
Of duality
But I still hadn't figured out what being Chicano is all about

I never got a tattoo teardrop

Or Mi Vida Loca tattooed
Between my thumb and finger
I never did a drive by or
Spray painted my placa on the wall
But that has nothing to do with what it means to be
Chicano

Chicano is the fire that feeds my soul
It's blood of my ancestors running through my veins
It's the passion in my heart
Chicano is the love for mi familia
Chicano is the love for mi cultura
Chicano is the love for mi Raza
It's about having respeto
Respect
It's about being humble
But knowing when to fight!
Chicano is the
Burning
That's inside me
That moves me
Motivates me
Makes me who I am

My name is

Manuel Gonzalez

And I am

Chicano

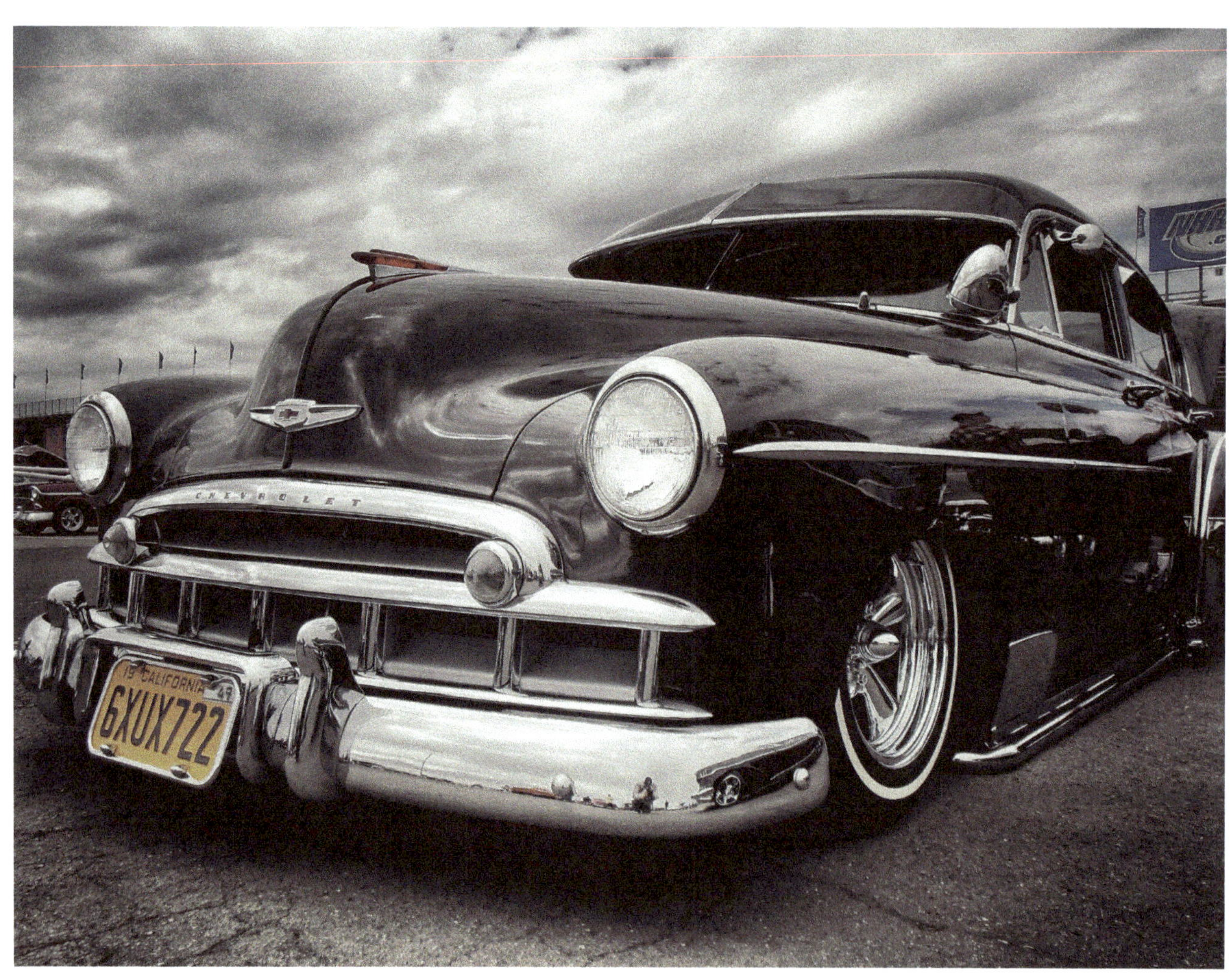

Before the Storm – '49 Fleetline

Guero's '49 Chevy black bomba and the Hand of God

by Benjamin Quiñones Reyes

Names have been changed to protect the innocent

"I*t's gonna take a miracle...Yes, it's gonna' take a miracle*," the sweet spiritual sounds of Deniece Williams bumped out from Guero's '49 Chevy black bomba. It was about love and liberation and you could feel it. When Guero cruised his black Chevy bomba was like an ice cream truck serenading the whole neighborhood with sweet harmony.

It felt like a flowing peace treaty in the East L.A. badlands, where gang-banging and drive-by's (bueno para nada), unworthiness, self-hate, heroin addiction and drug overdoses, reigned supreme. Darkness always seemed to be hovering in East L.A., like a vulture, always ready to swoop in and take life with it. It depleted our energy.

But Guero and his bomba gave us life. That firme ranfla was a spark and it was more than the wax he applied to it.

It was a spirit.

Everyone in the neighborhood seemed to know Guero, but no one could tell you his last name. Still, Guero was the neighborhood star. He could pop-a-wheelie on his Schwinn beach cruiser for blocks.

Guero was a sophisticated vato that always looked clean. He ironed his own khaki pants and plaid button-up Pendleton shirts. Guero shined and he always had the baddest hyna.

I remember he would give me cash for running to the liquor store and buying him those old school Listerine mouthwash glass bottles. Clean & fresh; that was Guero.

Guero was no longer gang-banging either; some said he was born-again, Victory Outreach or something, but he never preached. He just did it for

God. The vatos respected him. He was an upright dude, a loyal vato that still kicked it with the homeboys.

The barrio gang was deep, made up of mostly younger vatos in their 20s but there was a core of veteranos; dudes that handled it. They led up front.

It was by this time that the darkness had blown in crazy thick to the barrio; it crept in and you could feel it. Someone had started picking off the older vatos from the neighborhood one by one...

PA!

Flaco at the liquor store...

PA!

Listo in the alley...

With sniper precision... *PA!*

Boxer outside the party.

The deaths felt very coordinated, like the rivals were being exact about whom they were taking out - the veteranos.

Disruption ensued. Everyone in the neighborhood scattered. Darkness hovered, waiting.

Despite all of this, Guero still cruised in his '49 Chevy bomba.

"It's gonna take a miracle...Yes, It's gonna take a miracle," the sweet sounds harmonized the neighborhood until you couldn't hear it no more.

In every East L.A. neighborhood there was at least one crazy vato loco. Ours was my best friend and neighbor Danny Villa. Danny was a Mexican Merlin; he was an alchemist in the truest sense, trying to convert some man-made concoction into gold or liberation.

Danny smoked everything imaginable to man: PCP, Primos, P-Dogs, Double-dipped Coolies but mostly lots of yeska. He loved cannabis; he said it helped him with his imagination and thinking. Danny excelled in math; he took honors calculus in high school (when he actually went to class), most of the time though he ran numbers for some Mafiosos.

Danny was a savant, a real genius who smoked only because he was bored. Reality bored him. I remember he used to do these impressions from the film *Sid and Nancy.*

"Boring, Sidney, Boring!" he would say.

He was a character.

Danny and I used to hang out in front of his

porch - it was the spot. He would usually party with a bunch of the neighborhood homegirls. And this one night we were listening to Evelyn "Champagne" King and the feel good music of Shalamar.

There was a wall that lined along Danny's driveway and always seemed to be tagged by some vato or another. Part of Danny's driveway was always in the dark because the street light was shot out by the homies.

While we were partying and drinking Budweisers, I went to relieve myself on the side of Danny's house. I could sense something strong as I stood there and pissed; a hand miraculously came out of the shadows and began to spray paint on the wall. All I could make out was the hiss of the spray can and a hand magically moving. The writing was clean and assertive, no fear.

I focused like a hawk and could make out a large spider web tattoo on the hand. I tried calling Danny, who was occupied with one of the homegirls, turning up the volume on some "Forget Me Nots," by Patrice Rushen, but Poof! the shadow disappeared.

"Danny!" I called to him. "Danny, come here!"

I pointed at the wall.

He picked up his old 12-gauge Mossberg shotgun hidden behind an old sofa on the porch everyone kicked it on.

We both approached cautiously - out of the shadows and into the light.

On the wall it read:

Mene, Mene, Tekel, Parsin.

I didn't know what it meant. I couldn't even begin to pronounce it. I just thought it was another neighborhood placa - a new hieroglyphic way to write it out.

"Mene, Mene, Tekel, Parsin," Danny read it out loud.

He took a big hit of his yeska and began to break it down.

"It's biblical," he said, "It's written in the bible."

Danny's parents were both hard core Catolicos and his aunt and uncle were Jehovah's Witnesses. If anyone could decipher this shit, it would be Danny.

Danny took another big hit of his yeska; he held it in for a while...and then blew it out.

"It means: 'The writing is on the wall,' carnalito. Someone's time is up."

Danny's eyes got big. We both knew what that

meant.

For the next couple of weeks the neighborhood was quiet; most of the vatos were hiding out, afraid to be the next one picked off by rivals. The only daily constants were the Sheriff's staccato thump-thump-thump helicopter blades, the ambulance's hi-pitched sirens, the barking dogs and of course Guero cruising in his '49 Chevy black bomba bumping the sweet sounds of "*It's gonna take a miracle...Yes, it's gonna take a miracle.*"

It felt like when serial killer Richard Ramirez, aka the *Night Stalker*, was still on the loose terrorizing the barrio and you didn't know when or where he would strike next.

One night Danny and I were hanging out on his porch with a bunch of homegirls listening to Teena Marie's "Square Biz."

He pulled out a .25 Beretta handgun and showed it off to the hynas.

"The same one James Bond carried carnalito!" he said with a big grin.

He walked toward the old couch, pushed the homegirls off and pulled out a huge rifle.

"M14! My uncle who was in the Marines shot the Chinos in Vietnam with it! Orale!" he said with an even bigger grin.

I shook my head in absolute disbelief.

He quickly changed his tone and took a moment to think: as if the Mexican Merlin was pondering the unification of the general theory of relativity with electromagnetism.

He took a hit from the yeska and leaned forward, making sure no one else could hear him.

"You know what I heard, carnalito..?" Danny blew out some smoke and leaned in even closer, "My cousin told me they found two dead gabachos dressed up as cholos in a parked Regal."

I was silent.

"Word is those were the dudes blasting the neighborhood. They ain't no rivals. Chale! Those putos were chotas. They knew what they were doing, carnalito."

Danny's cousin was a Sheriff and at a recent backyard family gathering he made the mistake of blurting out some inside information while taking shots of Mezcal and singing, 'Para todo mal, mezcal y para todo bien tambien'."

Danny took another hit of the yeska.

"The Sheriff's won't confirm it, carnalito, but they said these dudes died of natural causes - no holes or slugs. No blunt trauma – nada. It was like someone just turned off their light switch," he said. "Fucking brilliant strategy, ese."

I stood there overwhelmed, trying to take it all in.

Danny blew out more smoke and almost whispered in my ear.

"And you know the crazy part about the whole thing, carnalito? My cousin said they found inscriptions on the gabachos that read: '*Mene, Mene, Tekel, Parsin*' just like we saw on my wall that night."

"Get the fuck out of here, loco!" I told him as I pushed him away.

But we both looked at each other in disbelief.

And sabes que? The shootings in the neighborhood stopped. The light shined again.

Later on, one sunny Sunday, Danny and I were kicking it on his porch barbecuing and talking shit when Guero cruised by in his '49 bomba.

I looked up and Guero leaned back holding the steering wheel with his left hand, and reached out the window with his right hand and waved.

There, out of the shadows and into the light, I saw the large spider web tattoo on his hand. It was the same hand that held the spray can that night.

It was the hand of God.

"*It's gonna take a miracle...Yes, It's gonna take a miracle*," blared out from the classic bomba.

It was a bombshell.

The sweet sounds had new meaning, a revelation. The message was:

I'm with you. I got your back. You can count on me.

I was humbled and smiled.

My faith had been strengthened by God, Guero and his '49 Chevy.

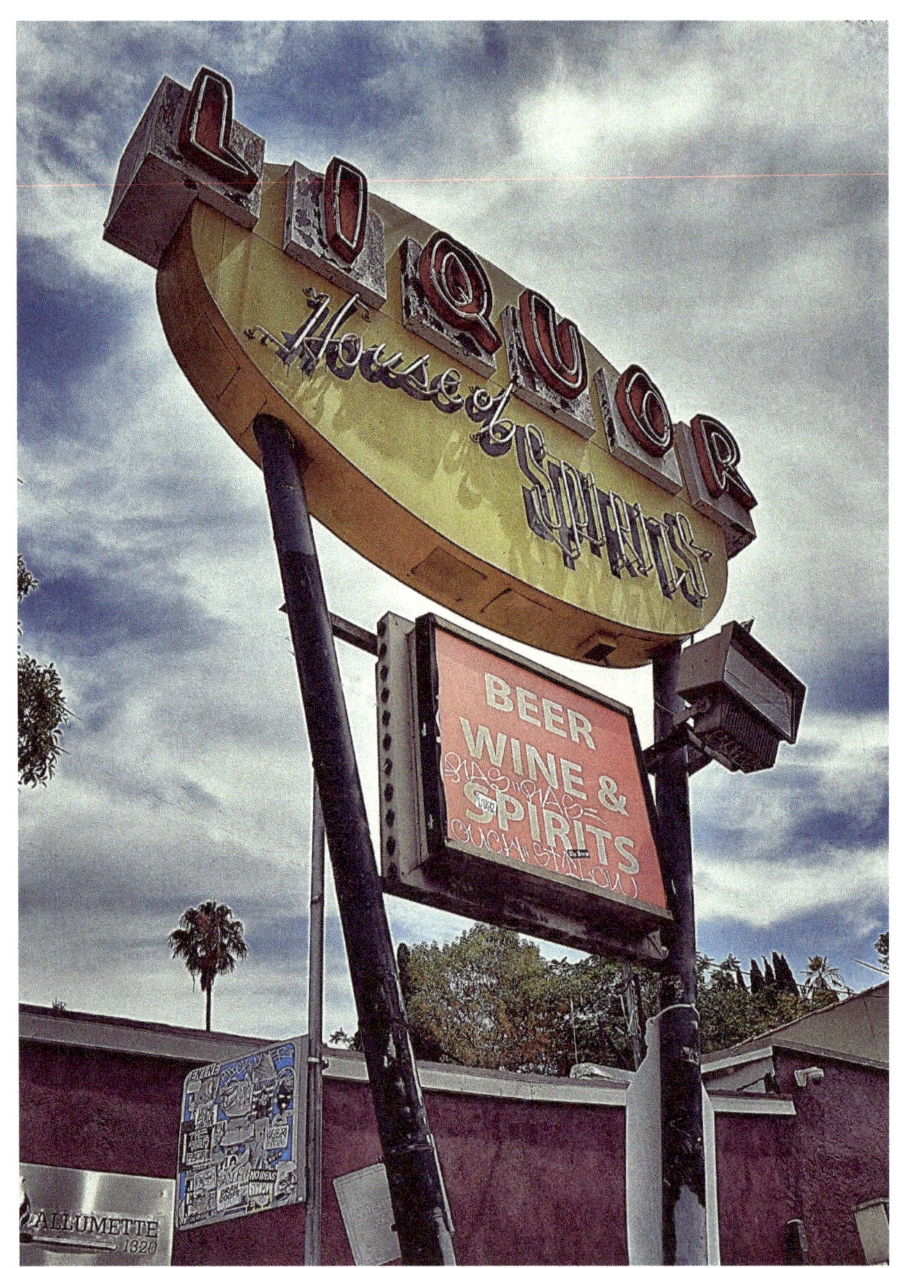

House of Spirits - Echo Park

Beer Run

by Viva Flores

Wrought iron swirls adorned the windows and there was a hastily built fence outside the small rectangular house where I grew up. Up until the time I was a teenager the whole yard had been completely covered in grass, until my older brothers all moved away and my dad decided he didn't want to upkeep the lawn anymore. I stayed the longest of us four, like I was supposed to, but was never expected to do any yard work. Soon after that a cement truck rolled up the driveway and pumped smooth grey sludge over it all, making the house look like it was surrounded by an empty parking lot. Years later, when it was sweltering hot, I especially liked sitting outside on the hood of my faded white Cutlass after my parents had gone to bed. I would silently roll a joint, smoking and watching all of the late night cars park at the convenience store across the street. I'd wonder who was inside, and where they were going.

When I was six I wrote a letter to McGruff the Crime Dog, a cartoon bloodhound I'd see on television that was first introduced in the eighties to combat societal drug use. Similar to Smokey the Bear, McGruff was staunchly against illegal activities and substances. In the handmade construction paper card I sent him I also made a solemn pledge to never do any drugs. Six weeks later I received a package in the mail filled to the brim with McGruff paraphernalia; stickers, masks, and even a small badge I wore proudly, vowing to keep the neighborhood safe.

I wondered what McGruff would think of me now.

"Sorry, fucker. I guess I disappointed you too," I said aloud as I pulled out a small sandwich bag filled with what my homie Redbeard had called "Lima-Limon."

I have always especially appreciated the moment when you're holding the marijuana bud suspended between your thumb and forefinger in joyful anticipation; then rubbing it until it dismantles into itself, unraveling into something pliant and gentle. I like to fold the rolling paper almost in half, and then make sure the crease is sharp, lick the edge of it slowly so I can tear a little piece off. I learned that from someone somewhere along the way, it's so you don't get as much paper in your smoke.

With the folded rolling paper sitting in my left hand, I'll reach over with my right and take a small pinch out of the little broken up pile and then line it smoothly along the crease, until I reach that perfect thickness. The tricky part is keeping it straight, holding the tiny paper on each side with both hands so it can be rolled. I'll start to smooth it with my fingers, pressing it closer and tighter together and then carefully twist each edge until the ends are perfectly shut. The really good rollers know how to make the side you light different than the edge you put between your lips. I'm not sure why I never picked up on that skill.

When we first started getting high I liked the papers that had cherries or peaches printed on them, but now I don't mind the little ones that come with packs of rolling tobacco. I like to roll them long, thin and tight, joint hanging out of my mouth and then light the fire.

A softly revving lowrider slowly pulled into my sight. It was a ruddy-hued or maybe tan Monte Carlo. I watched blankly as it parked across the street, tires lined up against the fading curb. It took me a moment to figure out what was going on and then I took a deep hit and held it, watching interestedly.

Beer run.

I've been witnessing beer runs since I was a little girl. As soon as my mother would see a car creeping up that curb with the lights off, she'd call me inside frantically and then quickly lock the door and have me run and turn off all of the lights in the house.

"Para que no nos vean", she'd say.

We'd sit cowering inside, huddled close together until we heard it; sometimes shouts or breaking glass and then always the sound of a car door smashing shut and then an engine booming and tires squealing away.

Once I remember hearing the sound of gunshots. I can still remember clearly the taste of a dry mouth hanging in fear. We were afraid, always afraid of the men who stole beer and held up stores with little black guns and folded bandanas covering their menacing faces.

Criminals. Criminales. Bestias. Beasts.

Redbeard broke it down once when we were blazing.

"Pussies," he declared. "Only chapetillos steal beer like that. Desperate high schoolers and shit. Ain't no real motherfuckin' criminal going to risk getting chased down by some dumbass good Samaritan, or the cops for something as stupid as a thirty pack. The real motherfuckers think before they act, I assure you," he declared diplomatically, and then taking a hit, breathed out, "The real motherfucking criminals buy their beer before midnight."

Post-beer run is another story. The cops have to show up and sometimes shut down the store depending on how severe the situation got.

This one was in progress.

I watched the Monte Carlo exhibit the telltale combo of running engine and lights off. Laughing a little I thought of Redbeard. Just by the looks of the car, I knew he was right. What kind of pendejos would try to pull off a beer run in such a noticeable car?

"Hijole", I whispered, taking a hit. "Either these fools want to get caught, or they just don't give a fuck."

It was a shame, really. How could a regal ride like that be used as an accessory to such a mediocre crime? Even from several feet away I could tell that whoever had put it together had shown a lot of care. That was somebody's baby.

The first thing I noticed was its color, which was a very clear and brilliantly glittered shade of pearl ivory. It wasn't too lifted, either. You see that mistake made a lot with these cars, some overzealous G overlifts the rear and then it looks like a fucking beetle with its ass in the air. The tires on the Monte had class; they were small yet thick and in the center showcased delicate gold plated rims. No visible hydraulics or decals on it either, no gaudy details or airbrushed tetas anywhere in sight.

Just my style.

It was the kind of car I'd always dreamed about cruising down a boulevard on a Friday night, filled with my laughing homegirls, red lips blazing. Why would anyone with love for their ride be so fucking reckless?

"Alright," I said out loud. "I'm fucking thirsty."

I slid off my hood and lightly dabbed some saliva on my forefinger to put out the joint, and then carefully placed it safely on one of the windshield wipers, and walked across the street toward the sitting car.

The driver's side window was open and without too much hesitation I stuck my head into the vehicle, peering inside. There were five little vatos, teenage boys, wearing expensive department store sweaters and scrawny-haired, speckled faces. They were maybe football players from the looks of their half-assed muscles - most likely Junior Varsity.

They all looked up at me and froze.

"You guys going to do a beer run?" I asked.

Not one of them responded. Instead they all began looking at each other confusedly, meeting each other's darting eyes. It was obvious to me not one of these fools owned the car. The driver looked was about seventeen and had probably borrowed it from his pops or big brother. Damn shame, if only they knew where their baby was.

"Look, I know you are, and frankly, I don't give a fuck what you guys do. I live in this hood though, and I was on my way to the Good Time for an orange coke. Can you wait until I do that? If you jack the beer they might shut down the store and call the cops, and I smell like herb, 'cause I've been blazing it."

Again, no one answered me, and instead they all

rested their gaze on the driver, who after a moment of hesitation met my eyes and responded with, "Okay, but don't fuck us over."

"Thank you," I said.

We had an agreement.

I backed away from the car and headed in the direction of the store. Once inside I went toward the back and grabbed my soda from the cooler, all the while sizing up the new evening clerk; a chubby brown-haired girl with large brown eyes framed with shaggy bangs. She had a very noticeable pair of pendulous breasts that seemed to shake nervously with every customer she rang up. A nametag spelling out "Anabel" hung silently off the store's mandatory orange smock. I wondered if this was her first beer run and how she'd react to it.

"You'll be alright, Anabel," I whispered to myself silently as I paid. "Those guys were pussies for sure."

I felt their relief when I walked out of the store and passed in front of their car silently with my soda and a last-minute decision Hershey Bar. It was dark but I could see that the guy sitting in the back right of the car walked out and slowly made a beeline towards the store.

I lit my joint back up and waited, puffing excitedly. A few minutes later there was a loud smash, and then I saw him running for the car, a thirty pack in each hand.

The Monte Carlo revved and then boomed with the door swinging open as he threw the beer and jumped in behind it. The car took off all bat out of hell and shit, as eager as they were.

I couldn't believe those pendejos actually waited for me to buy a soda.

"Dumbfucks," I laughed.

††

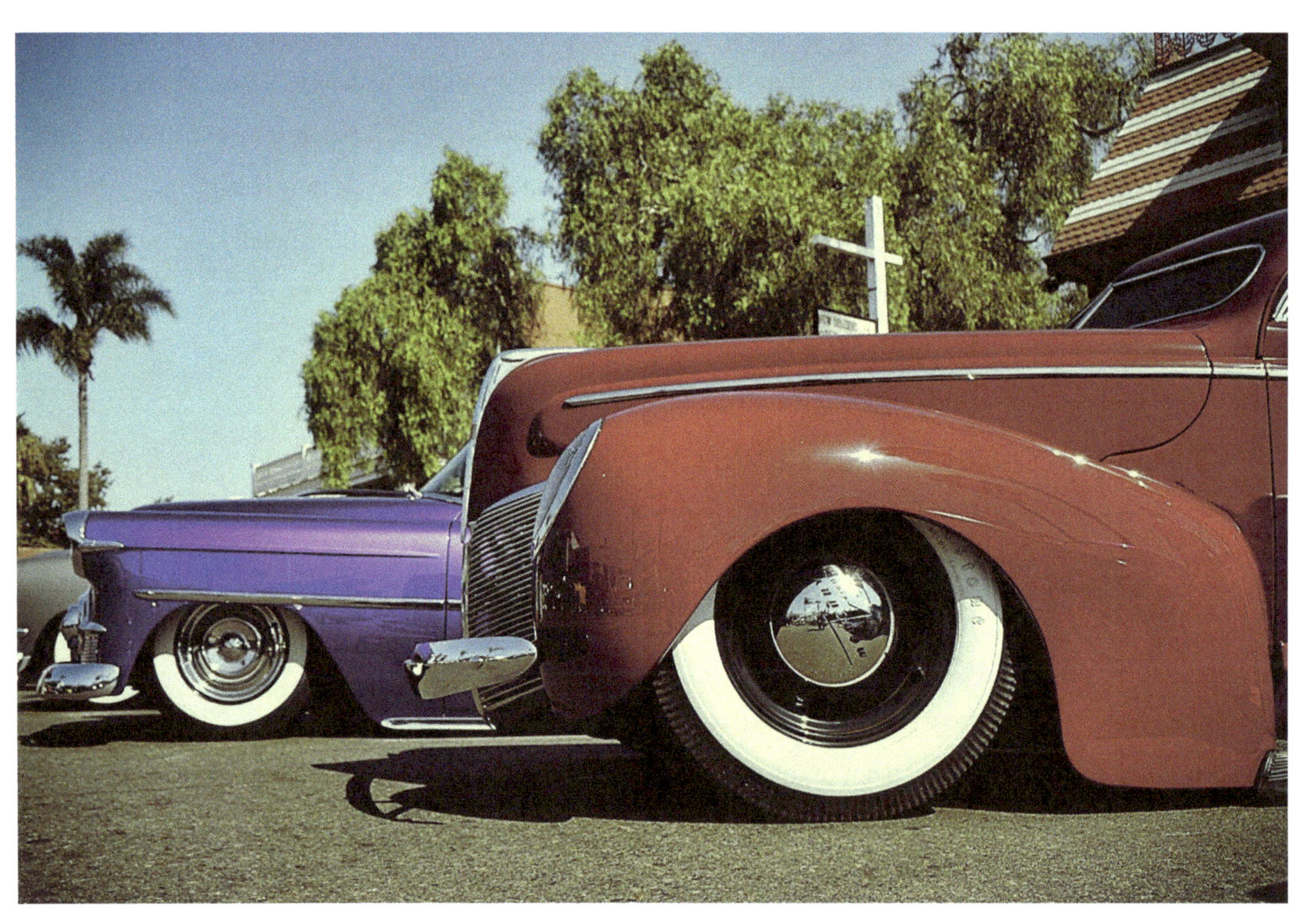

Kustom Made – '40 Mercury, '53 Chevrolet

Lowriders: Time and Money Well Spent

By Xicano X

Lowriders are nice, but too much money and time is wasted on them, when that money and time could be used for something else, related to Raza empowerment."

This was the comment a Chicana/o Studies professor made in reference to the money and time a person would invest in a lowrider. I'm sure this professor is not alone in this train of thought. Whether radicalized or not, I'm sure the above sentiment has been echoed throughout academia, and in communities by activists that feel there is too much else to do to waste so much money and time on a car that grabs the attention of the Chicana/o public; especially when there are so many other issues that *need* to grab the attention of the Chicana/o public.

When I first heard it coming from this radicalized Chicana/o Studies professor, I was in a bit of shock. I guess I tend to think that anything related to Chicana/o culture, becomes part of Chicanismo, which in turn becomes part of the toolkit, used to teach about Chicanas/os and our causes, and the existing diversity, in these here United States. I've always admired lowriders, and even that perspective from the professor hasn't really skewed my own outlook. I understand that perspective, but I don't agree with it. Mostly, I would find myself admiring the artwork displayed on them. Yes, the many different shiny parts on them would grab my attention as well, like a deer caught in headlights. But I would mostly enjoy looking at the artwork, ranging from the religious with the La Virgen De Guadalupe to the indigenous past with the Aztec men and women splayed throughout, the messages or names of vehicles displayed in a variety of fonts, but usually in an elegant cursive style.

As a matter of fact, the "American Dream" for me and my junior high friends wasn't about a lot of money or owning a home, it was about owning a '64 Impala that we could convert into a lowrider. That was the particular car we wanted to own, no idea why, other than it was a cool-looking car. Of course, none of my circle of friends ended up owning an Impala lowrider, nor any other type of lowrider for that matter. Unless you count one of my friends who had a Cutlass Supreme he had managed to put hydros on, but hadn't given it a paint job nor switches so that it would hop or bounce as he drove down the road. This was unfortunate because the cool thing to do in high school was to drive around the school at least twice, right after the final bell rang, to show off your car or at least that you had a car to drive in (even if it was technically your dad's beat-up work truck); especially if you had a loud-ass stereo system installed in your car.

When we would drive in this particular friend's car, he would suggest that we jump up and down in our seats to at least give the illusion that his hydraulics were fully functioning. We'd be cruising down the street next to one of the high school buildings, our upper bodies hopping up and down, mainly in the back seat, and we could feel the car's bounce picking up momentum each time our ass cheeks landed on the back seat. We laughed as the car bounced next to some girls walking down the street, giggling at us, due to our attempt at manmade hydraulics. I wish I had the power of astral projection in that moment, or to create a duplicate of myself by just thinking about it so I could see how ridiculous we looked as the Cutlass bounced up and down in unison to the rhythm of our bouncing bodies.

That was the closest I had gotten to riding around in a lowrider, or more a mock-lowrider.

In college I had a friend by the name Cesar who had been fixing up an Impala to convert it into a lowrider. One weekend he rolled up with the car; it still had the primer on and he parked it in front of the house that me and six other roommates were renting at the time. Even with the very dull gray primer on it the Impala was still nice to look at, plus my friend had installed a decent sounding stereo system, that when turned up, must have made many of our geriatric neighbors look out their windows to see what ruckus us Mexican college kids were getting up to now.

You see, we were the only college kids in the neighborhood at the time and on top of that, we were Mexican. The very predominantly White and retired neighbors must have believed we were bringing down the property values around *their hood.* It didn't take long for one of those neighbors to walk across the street toward us.

My friend lowered the volume on his system and I was just waiting for the old guy to complain about the noise coming outta the car us "whipper snappers" were blasting.

"Fuck me," I thought to myself, "more complaining."

But instead the man said, "Nice car. Is it yours?"

El Cesar smiled and replied, "Yes. Thanks."

"I haven't seen one of these in a long time," the old man said.

From there he and El Cesar talked about the car but I didn't pay much attention, I was just relieved the old neighbor man didn't come over to complain about all the noise or threaten to call the police because there were too many Mexicans in a group standing in front of a "cholo car."

You should have seen the smile on that man's face though. He was admiring that Impala but you could tell he had been transported back in time to his own youth, possibly even to a time in his late teens or early twenties when he cruised around in a car like that with his friends. He might have even owned one and had many memories sharing that backseat with the woman that was now his wife. If he did own one, he was maybe now melancholic regretting having to part ways with his own Impala back in the day, because perhaps his wife told him to get rid of it. He possibly remembers the day he had to sell off his own Impala more than or just as much as the day he married the woman who made him walk away from his first love.

Nevertheless, there was nothing stopping him from admiring the beautiful machinery that had caught his attention; he even communed with us Chicanos to eyeball this vehicle; now that right there, comes to show the power of an old Impala that was being worked on progressively. It had the power to take this older man back in time, but along with that, it had the power to lessen the gap between generations and just as importantly, between ethnicities.

I eventually heard that my friend El Cesar finished fixing up the Impala; paint job, upholstery, stereo system, and all. But instead of keeping it, he sold it online to a foreign buyer. I was surprised, because the whole time he had been working on the car I thought it was going to be his own to keep. I don't recall what country the buyer was from, but wherever that is, that's where the car resides now. Maybe for El Cesar it became more about the actual build; once built he must have been satisfied but figured it's the actual process of taking a vehicle like an Impala from "before" to "after," and not so much keeping it. The satisfaction was in finishing and being able to beautify a car with his own two hands and skills. From there, he let someone else take ownership of the car, and let them admire it and keep up with the maintenance.

Having sold that car, I heard El Cesar bought another car or two he started working on, going through the process all over again.

I understand why my Chicana/o Studies profe made the statement about the amount of time and money spent on a car; when there are so many other issues that would benefit from both, whether it be for the comunidad, or even for a person's own family or other personal necessities.

I get it.

But in my perspective, lowriders *are* a valuable cultural commodity, and being that currently our books have been banned, it would be nice for Chicana/o Studies to try to hold on to these cultural artifacts.

What's to say that someday a backwards-thinking politician won't come up with the following bright idea:

"Hey! I know! Why don't we ban those lowrider

cars all those Chicanos spend so much time and money building?! Besides, those vehicles represent the Chicano/a criminal element. Well I'm an ignorant politician; therefore I believe all Chicanos are wrongheaded criminals that seek to create disunity through Chicano Studies courses and their cultural artifacts. We can take all the money and time it takes to build one of those vehicles and place it in a fund for our own stuff. What stuff? Well you know, stuff!"

Maybe that's too extreme. Maybe that will never happen. I hope it doesn't because it was pretty cool seeing my friend's Impala, lowrider-in-progress, bring about unity amongst a couple of men from different generations and ethnic backgrounds. As far as I'm concerned that's time and money well spent.

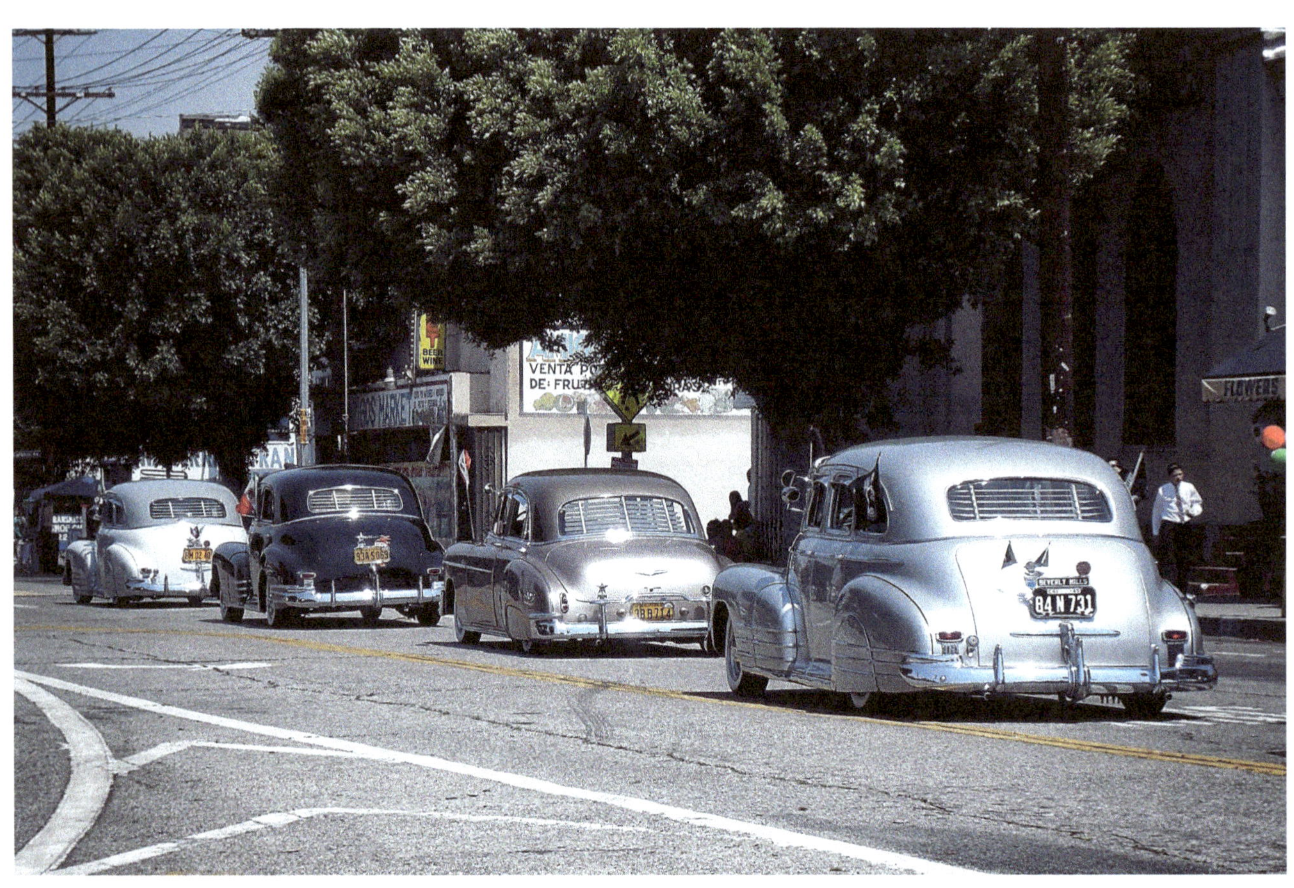

Cruising Cypress Ave. – Chevy Bombs

Take A Little Trip With Me

By Robert Flores

I am 16 years old,
it's 1975 and I drive a Lowrider
It's a 1968 VW painted with 3 shades of brown,
I have that stenciled on the side rear windows:
SHADES OF BROWN
It has more speakers than I need.
A little white steering wheel.

The city I live in is rife with gangs and car clubs
but I don't roll like that.
Soy nerd con cuatro ojos.

I am 16 years old and I play the sax,
and I drive a Lowrider.

I play in every band at my high school,
marching, jazz, orchestra.
I also play on weekends in a band called SUAVE,
like the car club
that the rest of the band is in.

We play for the car club dances
Weddings.
Quinceneras.
You name it.
We play oldies and the new stuff for that day,
WAR , EWF, TOP.

After school one day
this friend comes up to me:
“Robert this dude is looking for you,
I think he wants to kick your ass!”
Orale..
His name is Bobby Colin and he’s driving a 1953 Ford,
primer green.
Mas feo.

He asks me to be
in his band,
SAUVE.
Sure, and get paid?
Hell yeah!
I am 16 years old and I go to Catholic school,
and I drive a Lowrider

My high school is 90% White
8% Brown
2% who gives a fuck.
My grade school was almost all Latino
so this situation is a little strange
for both the gabachos
and us brownies.
They think we are all in gangs
or gardeners.
Well some of them do.
They dig the Lowrider.
What choice do they have?
Or I'll get my gang on you!!

We do get along,
we party
cruising the streets of SanTana.
Good times.
The city is divided
into at least four different gang territories,
FTroop,
Dogtown,
Delhi Aces
and SantaNita.

Now I have friends in all of the territories
so I have to be careful
when I cruise around town.

Once a friend who lived in Dogtown
was at my house.
We went to go get beer,
(yes, we were in high school)
and this girl called him out:
"Where you from?"
Holy shit!
He got in my car and said:
"Drive! Drive!"
I got out of there and asked him:
"What happened?"
He was all shook up.
"This girl asked me 'where you from'
and it wasn't like 'hey handsome,
where YOU from?' it was,
'Hey, where you from, ese?'"
Daaaamn.
At least he had bought the beer before
we had to jam.

I'm 54 years old now,

I drive a Toyota Tundra,

but when I was 16…

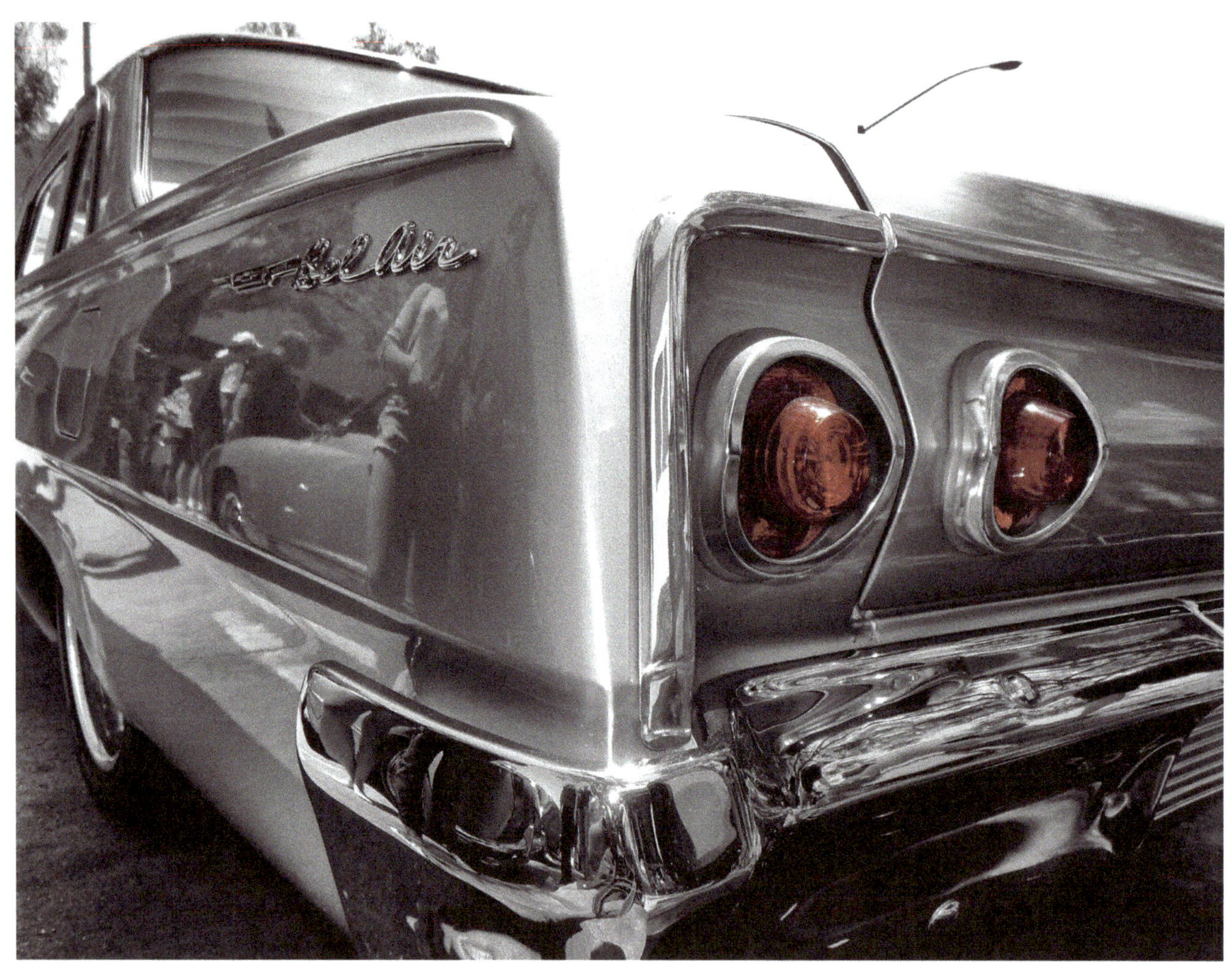

Liquid Steel – 1962 Chevrolet Bel Air

1969 Impeccable White Impala

By Ricky Luv

Friday evening, classes over, Lucas and I sat on the shingled roof to our Animal House frat, smoking a bong à la Cheech & Chong, Led Zeppelin's "Whole Lotta Love" blaring out our room window, when a 1969 impeccable white Impala drove into the driveway. Our cotton mouths dropped. We'd been ogling *les belles* on their bikes who lived next door at the *La Maison Française.* A couple of the *güeros* in our house even had a Benz or Beamer, but not a real car like an Impala. It was as if out of a soft sunlit dream or better yet, a photo I had seen of my Pops as a younger man leaning back cool against the hood of his very own 1969 impeccable white Impala with a cigarette in one hand and a beer bottle in the other.

Pops always talked about how much he loved that car, how he had sacrificed to scrape together enough money as a sous-chef at a Beverly Hills restaurant in order to buy it, how much he loved to show it off to his many girlfriends…until he crashed it.

But who on campus would drive such a car? Out stepped a brown, squat dude with aviator sunglasses, a white tee, tan khakis and black shoes that looked orthopedic.

"Chespirito?!" Lucas and I simultaneously

turned and uttered to one another.

Chespirito was the nickname we baptized him with not because he was a comedic genius like Roberto Gómez Bolaños but because he was diminutive and his gravity was comical to us.

We climbed off the roof, slipped in through the room window and bounced down to the second floor. Chespirito had a corner room from the stairway, and we beat him to his door. He took off his sunglasses like some CHiPs Erik Estrada.

"What's on your mind, gentlemen?" he said and furrowed his brow, making his frown hang lower, and the pores to his pock-marked face open wider.

"So how does a guy like you have a car like that?" asked Lucas.

"Just because I'm an engineering major doesn't mean I'm a square," he countered.

"We hadn't seen it before. 1969?" I intervened.

"Maybe. You know about cars?" he asked.

"Did you buy it?" I asked.

"I wish. It's my uncle's. He asked me to look after it for a few days," he said and crossed his arms.

"Is your uncle on the lam?" asked Lucas.

"It's none of your business, but no," he said.

"Is there any way we could take it for a ride?" I asked.

"No way. I wouldn't trust you guys with my grandmother," he snapped.

"We don't want your *abuelita*, just your wheels for a spin around the block," said Lucas.

"I told you, they're not mine. Now excuse me, I got work to do," he opened the door to his Spartan abode, desk by the door, bed in the back; no posters, no *nada*.

He moved to close the door on us when I stepped in, "We got a double date tonight--"

"We do?" said Lucas.

"Yeah, with the two from the tutoring group, remember?" I smiled extra big at Lucas so he would go along with it.

"Oh, yeah!" Lucas said, "The one with the bust, and the other with the butt."

"Really? You going out with some ladies tonight?" asked Chespirito, suddenly interested.

"They wouldn't have a friend for me, would they?"

"Man, I'm afraid not. But you'd be doing us a big-time favor if we could borrow your car for just a couple of hours tonight, so we can drive the ladies around campus and show them a good time?"

"Whattaya say, brother?" said Lucas, extending his hand out for the keys.

"I'm not your brother," Chespirito said.

"Not frat brother, but still a brother," I added.

"What do I get out of it?" asked Chespirito.

"We'll put in a good word for you with the ladies…so they can set you up with one of their friends," I offered.

"Really? You'd do that for me..?" asked Chespirito.

"If you hand over the keys," said Lucas.

Chespirito took a key off his key ring and was about to hand it over when he stopped.

"I don't want you guys drinking or doing drugs and then driving."

"Who? Us?" said Lucas. "Perish the thought."

"I'm serious, man. And no hanky panky in the backseat either. Got it?" he added.

I pulled out my driver's license.

"I'm driving. Clean record."

"I want the car back by 10. No later," he said.

"Party starts at 9," said Lucas. "How about midnight at the latest?"

"You better. I'll be waiting for you guys," he finally relinquished the key to me.

We bounded downstairs into the car. The exterior was impeccable, gleaming in the sun; but the inside wasn't as pristine; the leather interior was worn and cracked here and there. But hell, we didn't even own bikes.

"Dude, we forgot the bong!" said Lucas in his most excellent Bill & Ted accent.

"Dude, he said no drugs," I reminded him.

"Dude, you're not actually going to listen to that peckerwood, are you? It's not like we're driving to San Francisco, just around campus. *Un poco de leche*."

He didn't wait for me to answer as he flew upstairs and down in record time with our 3-foot bong. He packed a bowl, but I stopped him, "Let's at least wait till we're away from here."

I turned the engine on. It was like an airplane purring awake. I didn't know shit about cars but it sounded like a car should as I pulled out of the driveway, cruised down the street to the next stop sign, turned the corner and pulled over.

"Now what?" asked Lucas.

"Nothing. Let's hit the bong," I said ripping a huge hit that made me fill the car with lungfuls of smoke.

Lucas snatched the bong away and did the same. We sat in a dense fog and couldn't see shit out of the windows. And we didn't lower them either because we wanted to breathe in all the smoke and not waste it.

I swam and saw that my eyes were bleeding red and swollen in the rearview mirror. Normally I looked like a Chicano Clark Kent with my black-frame glasses, but now I looked demonically possessed. Lucas looked in the mirror too. He looked more like a young Joe Pesci.

I started the car again but this time I really felt like I was driving an airplane down campus road. The car felt as wide as the two lanes and as long as a block. I turned the radio on, which was missing a knob, and changed it from some sappy pop station to a classic rock station that was in the middle of playing Santana's "Black Magic Woman." It couldn't get any better.

I had grown up in a dusty border town, and some of my first memories were of me as a toddler standing next to Pops as he drove a beat-up, blue 1950 Ford pick-up with a spotlight on the roof. During my elementary school years, we had a 1970 olive Mercury Marquis with a white leather roof that was peeling off. In high school, I finally got to drive my Pop's run-down 1976 brown Thunderbird Continental.

Pops always bought used cars, never new, because we couldn't afford it and because he claimed he wanted a car made of metal and not plastic. But I never cruised through Main Street in the T-Bird, not when the kids from my town were parading 4x4s that they bought with their drug money. My best buddy at the time drove a 1964 red convertible Mustang we did cruise in, despite the fact that the other kids didn't think it was cool to ride in a car that old.

Now here I was cruising around Stanford University. Lucas didn't have a license even though he grew up in East Los Angeles because his experience growing up, like mine, was a sheltered home life at best predicated by excelling in school in order to escape the hood. But he lived in a real hood where there were gangs and drive-by shootings; whereas, I lived in a trailer park simply endangered by poverty.

In college though, we felt like *Goodfellas*, free to do what we wanted, with impunity from parents and authority figures.

We had succeeded in getting into the top university in the U.S. at the time, learned to work the system during our freshman year and expanded our consciousness by experimenting with marijuana, mushrooms and acid our sophomore year. The world was ours for the taking. And we finally had a craft worthy of delivering us to the "Promised Land."

I was going in circles, with no destination in mind when Lucas rolled down his window.

"Slow down," he said.

He stuck his head out the window as we passed two blonde coeds in short shorts out for an aerobic walk.

"You girls wanna a ride?" he said in a perverted and slurred intonation that made them stare us down with total disgust.

"Go back to East Palo Alto and leave us alone!" said one of the blondes.

The other raised her key chain with a small canister at the end.

"We got mace, you creeps."

Lucas stuck his head back in as I screeched away.

"Dude, what the fuck were you thinking?"

"Fuck those racist white bitches!" he said.

Is that how they really looked at us? I always did notice how we ended up in the corner of beer-soaked frat bars, set aside and afar while they, the *güeros*, hogged up the bar and cavorted in front of us, and how the ladies avoided us. And when they did look us in the eye, it was only to give us the stink eye; the *bruja* eye, and wish us dead.

Chale! What a buzzkill!

*

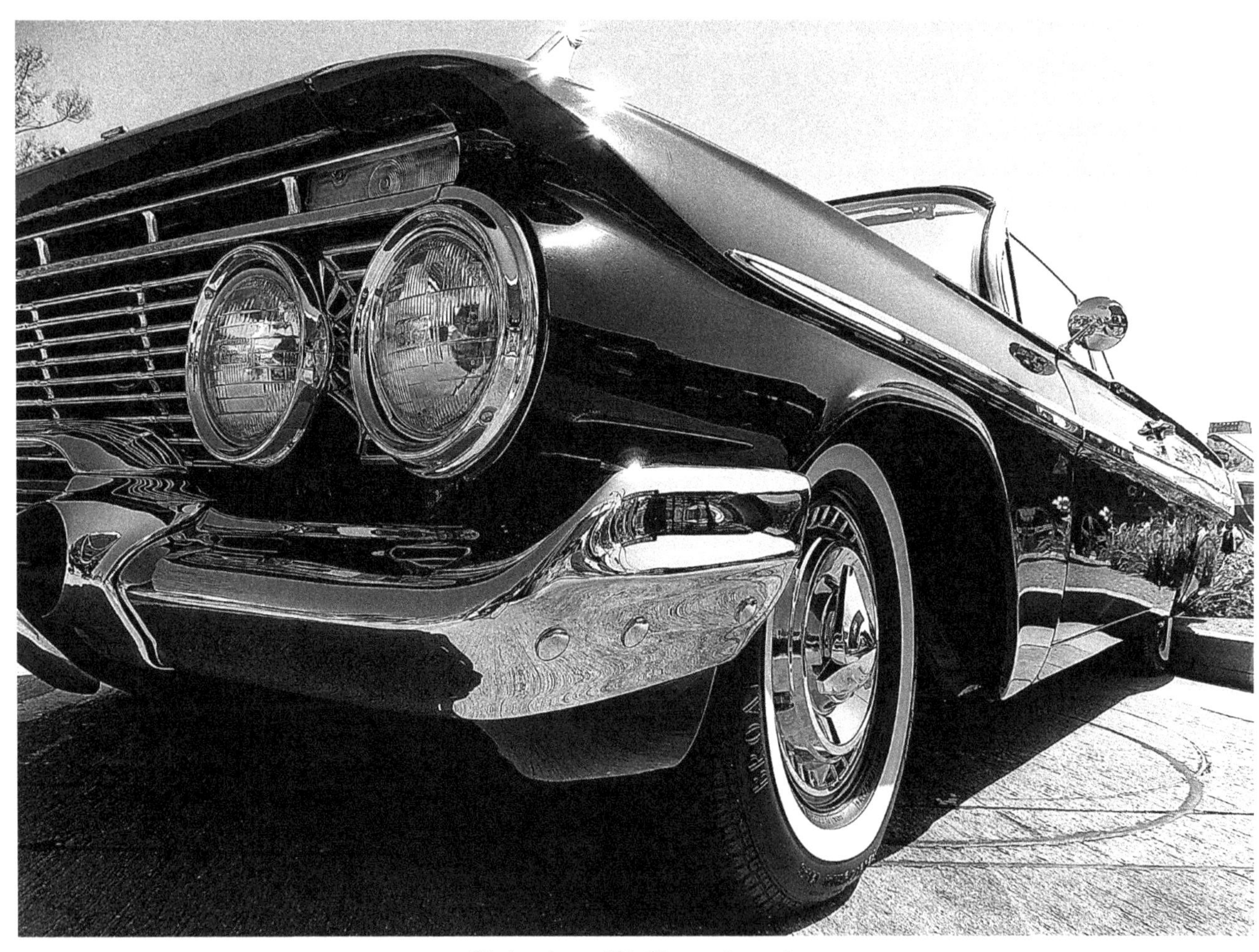

61 Angles – '61 Chevy Impala

I felt like turning around and returning to our frat, which is the only frat that would take us because they had Chicano engineers and the Benetton of minority rejects (one guy even had a metal plate in his head, no shitting). But they rescued us from ending up in another freshman dorm from hell where we would have to sit at our own table and get the stink eye from all the politically correct goody two shoes who complained that we partied too much and that we shouldn't join a frat because then we'd become a bunch of misogynistic alcoholics.

Fuck that noise! We were in college for fuck's sake! We could do what we wanted whenever we wanted however we wanted with whomever we wanted! They weren't our parents!

I turned the car around.

"Wait," said Lucas. "There's Sandy's dorm."

"Sandy's a prude," I said.

"Just cause she didn't give you any."

"She's never gonna give anybody any," I shot back.

Still, I parked out front.

We found her room, knocked on the door which had a stupid Polaroid of her with her big ole round glasses and waited.

Nobody home.

I tore the photo off and handed it to Lucas.

"Now, now, don't go coo-coo for your cocoa puffs," said Lucas and stuck it back on the door upside down.

As we passed by the kitchen on the way out, Lucas bee-lined for the fridge and started in on the big combination lock at the door. Feigning my most excellent Bill & Ted accent, I reminded Lucas, "Dude, you gotta' know the combination first."

The lock clicked open.

"Sandy," he said.

"We can't take anything anyway," I said and pointed to a whiteboard next to the fridge where students wrote their name and what they consumed.

"Do I need to say it?" asked Lucas.

So I wrote Sandy's name down while Lucas produced a six-pack of wine coolers.

"Fuck, no beer?" I asked. It didn't take us long to down the coolers.

Disappointed about living on a lame campus and the lack of adventure, we headed back to the frat.

"Why'd you tell Chespirto we had a double date?" asked Lucas.

"That's all he talks about: chicks. Or chicks around campus he would like to meet. He's a just a *horniado* like the rest of us. I knew that if I even hinted about chicks he'd lend us the car," I explained.

"And with a double date, he couldn't come along," nodded Lucas.

"Bingo."

"Speaking of bingo," said Lucas, "Looks like a rager over there." He pointed as we passed a dorm with cars parked out front and students standing by them drinking and smoking. I almost jumped the sidewalk as I rubbernecked. Pulled a u-ey and drove right up.

I truly felt Ray Liotta-cool as we stepped out of our 1969 impeccable white Impala, even in our shorts, tees, and *huaraches.*

We were on the fringe of campus. I never even knew this housing existed; it was more like a side porch where they were gathered, lit only by the street lamps. We walked up to the keg and filled up red disposable cups. No one gave us the stink eye or even looked our way really. They looked like students, but edgier, more punk and goth, more burned-out.

Just our crowd.

"Hey, I've seen those girls at the drug frat a couple of times," I told Lucas.

"Who? Broom Hilda and the Hamburglar over there? They're both witchiepoos!"

Lucas had a knack for pegging people with nicknames.

Frumpy, Broom Hilda was all cackles with a terrific hook for a nose. Now Hamburglar, she had a nice shape; long legs crossed precariously, about to tip to one side or the other, in striped black and white tights, black skirt and sweater, crossed arms, face pale but pretty, long straggly hair and a dark cloud over it all.

"I got Hamburglar," I called it.

"Do I have a choice?" Lucas asked.

I walked right up to her and asked, "You wouldn't know where to get some shrooms or acid, would you?"

"Who's asking?" she said.

"My buddy and I have seen you and your friend around?"

"You a Narc?"

"More of a curious observer."

"We had some coke earlier. You got a cigarette?"

"Got a bong in the car."

"Weed's so old." She said and brushed aside a strand of hair and eyed the 1969 impeccable white Impala, "Yours?"

"Of course," I said and half-smiled.

"Whose is it?"

"Guy in my frat. How'd you know?"

"Don't lie to a liar."

"Right. Wanna go for ride?"

"Why?"

"I don't know. We can go get some cigarettes?"

Arms still crossed and head down she made her way to the Impala.

"What about your friend?" I called out to her as I looked back at Lucas and Broom Hilda laughing up a riot.

I ran to open the door for her, but she beat me to it and slammed it closed herself.

The smell of patchouli filled the car as I revved the engine. She sat perfectly still, like a cadaver.

"Where you from?" I asked her.

"LA."

"Yeah? So's my buddy, Lucas."

Silence.

"I'm from Arizona, on the border with Mexico."

More silence.

"So you're Chicana?"

"I don't know what I am."

Yeah, I get that feeling sometimes too. Especially when I'm really high, like it almost doesn't matter."

The silence was killing me so I turned on the radio. "White Rabbit" by Jefferson Airplane was playing. Coincidence, omen, I couldn't tell anymore.

"You got any Chili Peppers?"

"No tape. Just radio."

She turned it off.

"Hate old music."

"What, Classic Rock? I mean I like a little of everything. Really like New Wave too, like Depeche Mode--"

"So old."

"Depeche Mode, really?"

"Saw them when I was in junior high."

"Well I didn't get out much. Not till now anyway…"

The hole was getting deeper. Luckily, we arrived at the gas station mart. I got out of the car and went around to get her door.

"Marlboro Red," she ordered.

The fluorescent lights were such a buzzkill as I entered the store and bought the cigs. The Impala looked good outside through the clear glass, and I even had a chick with me in the passenger seat. But it was all looks.

She lit up as soon as I got back in the car. It was the most alive I had seen her.

"So what are you studying?" I ventured.

"Econ."

"Cool. I'm doing English and French Lit myself. But I'd like to write someday."

She turned and blew smoke in my face.

"You're not gonna like me."

"Why's that?" I asked.

"I just wanna make money."

"Everybody's gotta make money, right?"

"Not writers."

I didn't feel so cool driving a 1969 impeccable white Impala anymore. I didn't feel so good about anything anymore.

She jumped out the car and walked over to her friend as soon as we returned.

"We're out of here," she said to me.

"I'm Ray, by the way. What's your name?" I said.

She planted a full kiss on my lips, "You'll see me around," she smiled. She actually smiled.

They took off. I could still taste her cigarette.

"So what happened on your little excursion there?" asked Lucas.

"That was the highlight," I said with a dumb grin on my face.

"Dude, they still got a keg."

"And we still got a bong!"

Of course, I don't know what we talked about or did from there on in because all I could think about was her. I don't even know what time we got back at or how we got back, just that the pounding on our room door was the last thing I wanted to hear competing with the pounding in my own head.

Lucas was still passed out in the upper bunk bed. I un-pasted my face from my own bed and got the door.

Chespirito practically ran me over, face bloated red – he couldn't spit the words out fast enough.

"You, you, you guys, really fucked up this time!"

"Why what happened to the car?" Lucas suddenly jumped down from his bed.

I went to the window and climbed out. Lucas and Chespirito followed. We stood on the roof looking down at the front lawn. There were long tire tracks across the yard and a loop and the car facing the street. Lucas ran back in and downstairs for a closer inspection.

I squinted hard.

"I don't see any dents or damage."

"That's not the point!" Chespirto threw his hands up. "Where the hell were you guys last night?! I waited till midnight, 1 A.M., 2 A.M., 3 A.M., and you guys never showed up! I almost called the cops, but I didn't want to get you guys in trouble. Can you believe that? I didn't want to get *you* in trouble!"

Lucas barged back in.

"Not a scratch!" He handed the bong over to Chespirito, "Here man, smoke a bowl and chill the fuck out."

"You guys were all drugged up, weren't you?! I should've called the cops!" continued Chespirito.

"Look man, sorry we were late, but we did get the car back to you in one piece, alright? And I did ask our dates about a friend for you, but their friend sounded weird, not good enough for you."

"Oh really? I mean, wait a minute! Bullshit! I can't trust you guys worth nothing anymore!" he said.

I handed the car key over to him.

"Thanks for lending us the car. You're alright, man."

"Yeah, you're not as uptight as I figured, Chespirito," Lucas added.

"Who's Chespirito?" he asked.

"A cool Mexican comedian," I said.

"Oh," he said scratching his head and took off.

Lucas and I sat on the roof once more, ripped a bong hit, and watched on as Chespirito got into the car below and drove it off the lawn and away. How I wished I could have my very own 1969 impeccable white Impala.

††

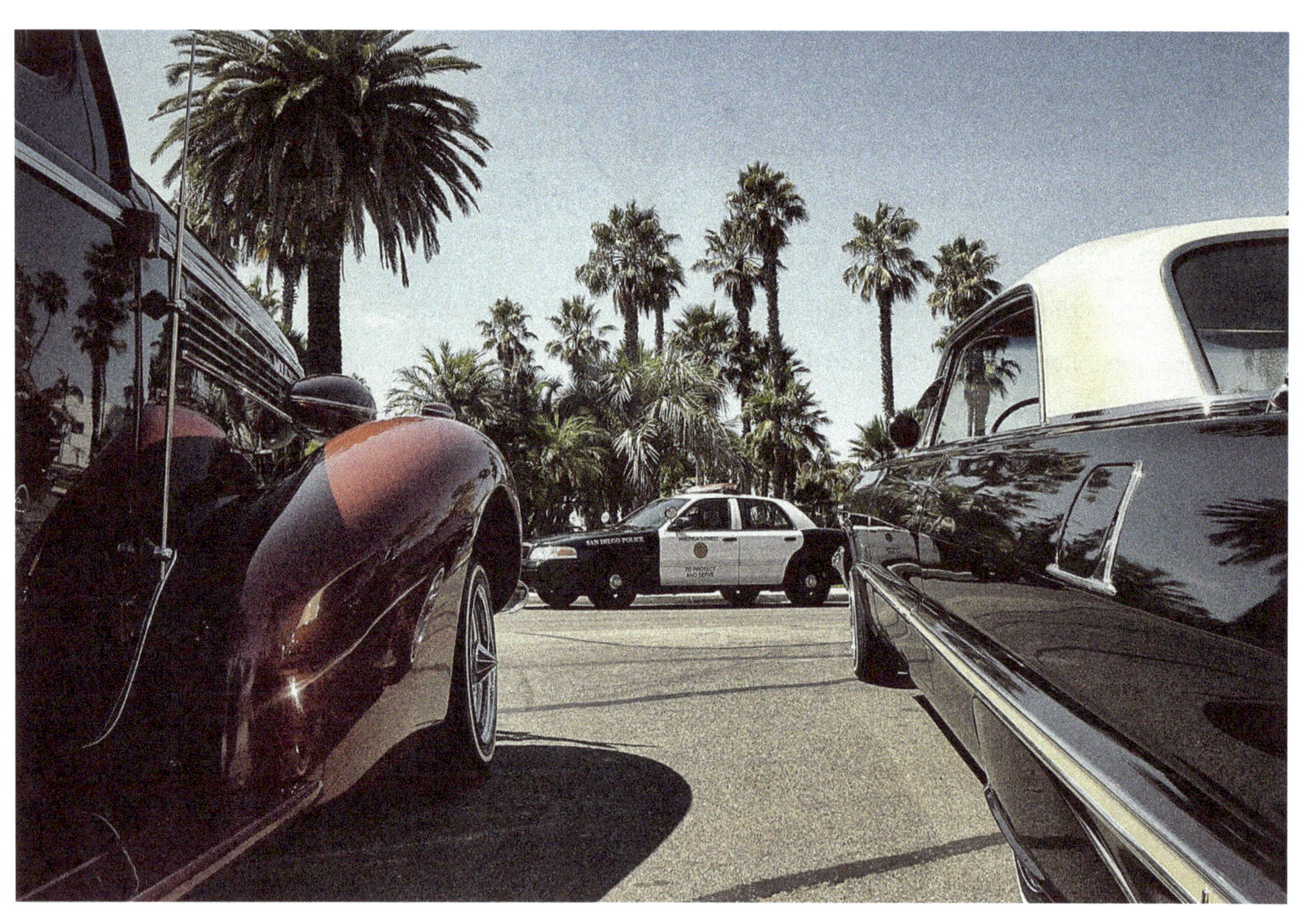

At Odds – ‘38 Buick, ‘63 Chevrolet Impala

Memories of Whittier Blvd:

By Roberto 'Dr. Cintli' Rodriguez

I am bleeding profusely from my forehead, handcuffed face down on the corner of Whittier Blvd and McDonnell Street in East L.A. Because of a riot stick attack to my body, including my forehead, I am immobile, unable to lift my head, yet, by looking into the pool of blood in front of me, my own blood, I see a reflection of people scurrying about, running from riot-stick-welding Los Angeles Sheriff's deputies, in all directions. The pool of blood keeps getting larger and larger. I know I was unconscious, but I don't know for how long. What I am aware of is that I have been on this cold street for some 10-15 minutes. They have now put me in the backseat of a police car. It is now perhaps 1 A.M. and I continue to bleed profusely. They leave me in the car again, alone, for another 10-15 minutes. Finally, they return and the deputy on the passenger's side points his riot stick at me, threatening to "finish the job" if I act up… They drive through an alley, and then proceed slowly to Santa Martha's Hospital in East Los Angeles. While the doctors there stop the incessant bleeding, they cannot actually treat me there. I want to tell the doctors and their attendants what has just happened to me, but now that I know that the deputies will be transporting me elsewhere, I am scared to speak.

They had threatened to kill me earlier if I opened up my mouth.

Four to five Sheriff's deputies assaulted me with riot sticks, on Friday night, the opening night of *Boulevard Nights*, for photographing a brutal beating of a young man in a sarape on Whittier Blvd in East L.A.

Because of the gravity of my injury to my forehead, and because I cannot be treated at Santa Martha's, I figure that if I am killed by them, the deputies could assault me again with their riot sticks and claim that I died from my [original] severe injuries.

Up to this point, I had probably bled continuously for perhaps 30-40 minutes and possibly an hour, as I did not actually clock the bleeding. If I were killed, the doctors at Santa Martha would testify that indeed, the injuries were too severe for them to treat me there, thus a ready-made alibi for the deputies if they indeed wanted to "finish the job."

So I keep quiet as I want to live. Rather than make a phone call, which they would overhear, I save my call until I "safely" arrive at the jail ward of the L.A. General Hospital, which is where they say they will be taking me.

We leave Santa Martha's after about a half an hour. On my mind, as they drive me to the LA General Hospital, is the recent execution of David Dominguez, a young homeboy who was kidnapped and executed by a rogue Sheriff's deputy from the San Gabriel Valley the year before. I think about him because I attended the trial of the deputy who executed him.

The ride is traumatic as I have received a brutal beating and these deputies have threatened my life. Even though we are on the freeway, the ride is slow as we arrive at a juncture at the Soto off-ramp. To the left is General Hospital, which can be seen clearly as it is the largest multi-story building in the entire region. To the right is an isolated and empty field with no lights, near one of L.A.'s most dangerous neighborhoods. It is perhaps 2 A.M.

While they act confused, they turn right. Up till then, I had been relatively calm. But when they turn right, I tell them the obvious.

"General Hospital is to the left!"

Clearly, they sense blood. They see and sense fear. It is at this point that I accept that I will be executed. In an instant, my entire life flashes before me. The slow ride into darkness continues. All I can think of is not to beg for my life - to die with dignity.

About two blocks down, they make a left into a service road that leads into the hospital. Knowing that I am in fear, they both burst out laughing and give each other a high-five.

More so than the beating, it is this sequence of events that will cause resentment within me for the rest of my life. When we reach the parking lot, the deputy on the right raises his riot stick, issuing yet another [death] threat against me.

As I am led out of the car and into the back elevator, I leave a long trail of my own blood in the parking lot from my wind-breaker jacket and blood-soaked pants. While in custody, I find out that I have been charged with attempting to kill four Sheriff's deputies with my own camera. When I leave on Sunday, they do not return my pants.

*

This is part of my testimony, from March 23-25 1979. It is part of my memories of what was to become my living hell for the next seven and-a-half years – to be relived in detail in court in 1986. I have written at length about that part of my life (*Assault with a Deadly Weapon, 1984 and Justice: A Question of Race, 1997*), about nearly getting killed by special enforcement bureau sheriff's deputies patrolling Whittier Boulevard that night and that weekend. That was the night of the premier of *Boulevard Nights*, a movie about cruising and lowriding on the Eastside. At the time, I worked for *Lowrider Magazine.*

It took a year to have the criminal charges dropped against me, after which I filed the lawsuit. It took another six years, and a 36 day trial, to win the lawsuit.

Today, I am a professor at the University of Arizona and the above narrative is also the basis for a forthcoming memoir titled: **Yolqui: A Warrior summonsed from the Spirit World.*

It is about my battles against torture, political violence and dehumanization and it compares the violence in the streets of the United States, inflicted upon primarily peoples of color, with the violence in Central America. Many of my close friends are from Central America and the violence here, in a sense, is not comparable to the violence there, because of the torture, disappearances, death squads and many murders… And yet, I do find a connection.

The violence against youth of color in this country and the skyrocketing criminalization of these youths has exploded the nation's ever-expanding prisons, filled with Black and Brown youths, resembling warehouses. It is a situation that Human Rights Watch has called a "human rights crisis."

**Yolqui refers to warriors from the spirit world, summonsed to fight in this world.*

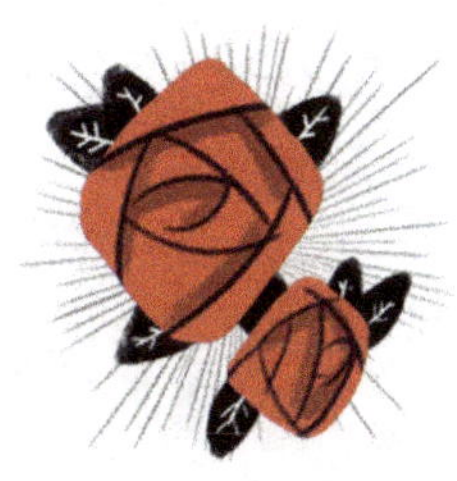

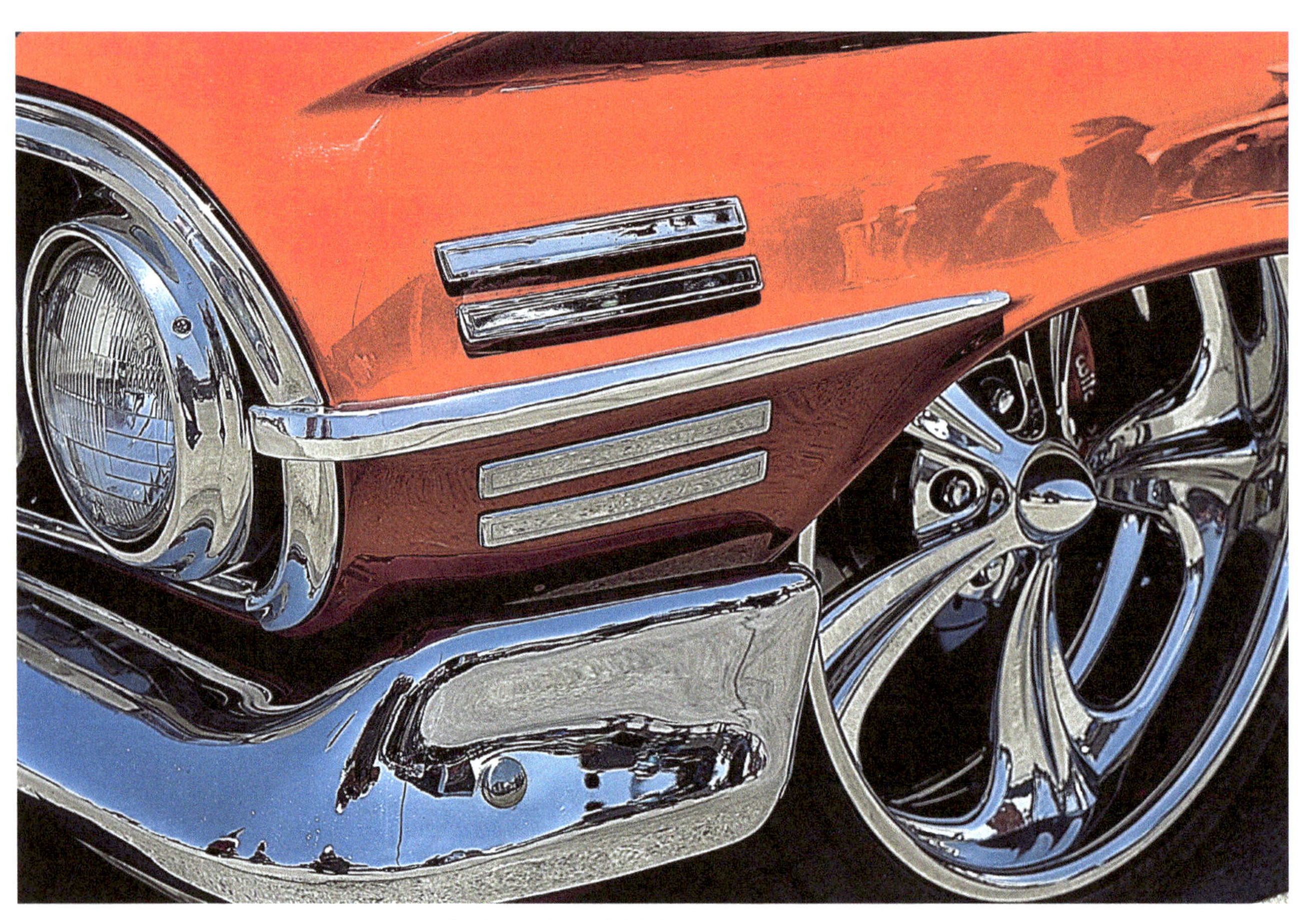

ChRomED – 1960 Chevrolet Impala

this wheel: ancestors

By Lizz Huerta

I lowride ghost ranch
sleep in tumble,

awaken to glowride dawn with
my stranger road, mi canto.

we slowtide knowing, welcome
the shatter, dream sea of desert,

sun guide, gentle, leap off pier, this
sister mother hustle, chrysalis,

post pride ghost dance, bees come
for my throat eat each moment,

crow bride medicine bag, your
words feathers I swallow.

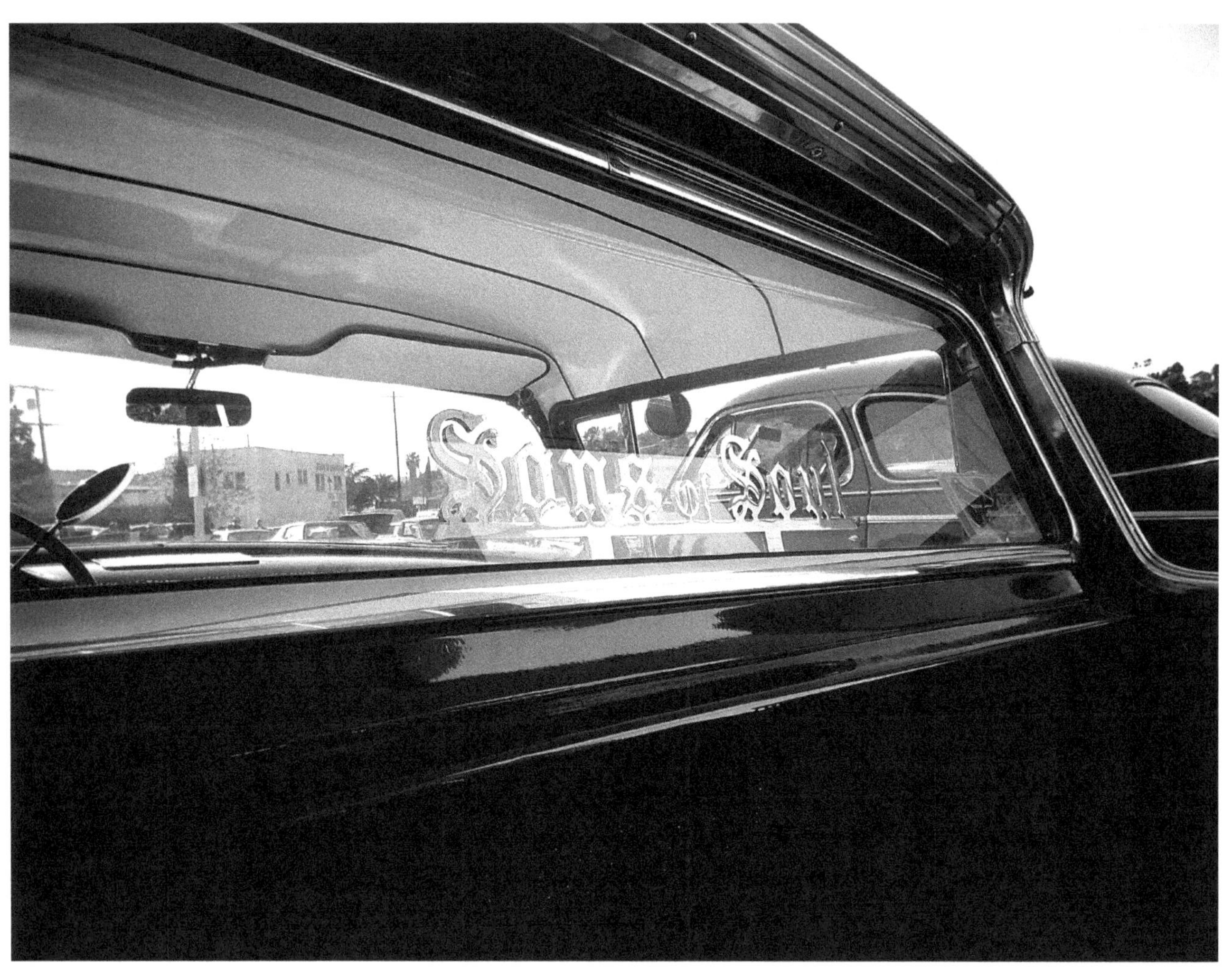

Sons of Soul – 1957 Ford Fairlane

Spring of 1996

By Angelo Sandoval

After being locked up in private school
lost in a world of self-righteous classmates
confined in a system that devalued my cultural identity
I graduated from high school
It felt good to be free
to explore the world
and celebrate my success
Baile y musica,
familia y amigos
Graduation gifts of hard earned cash
led me in search of a new ride
I found a flamantita 1990 Ford Ranger
clean inside and out, one owner who took pride in this troquita

My new troquita
blanca with a brown interior, original.
two wheel drive, not much of a work horse
yet perfect for a show horse.
Saving money to transform my troquita
Three years later the beautification transformation began

Lowrider veteran, mi Tio, giving advice to me:
new paint
rims
hydraulics
El Veterano con El Novicio in the game
cruise to Orlie's Hydraulic Shop in
Corrales, Nuevo Mexico.
Two chrome hydraulic pumps,
shiny like a mirror,
we saw our reflections on the tank
and the motor of the pumps.
My troquita had dance moves
like two love birds bailando
to a Ranchera or Cumbia
dancing to la musica de mi Querido
Notre de Nuevo Mexico
With my Tio behind the paint gun
We gave my troquita a solid white exterior
accented with a gold pearl
my troquita rolled in style
Thirteen inch Crown Wire Wheels
and don't think I forgot the one inch
white wall tires.
My troquita kicked ass

the first in Española aka Spaña with hydraulics
fluid flowing from pump to cylinder
turned heads as I cruised
Spaña's main drag, Riverside Drive
Los pueblos de
Córdova,
Chimayo,
Las Truchas,
Rio Chiquito,
Alcalde,
Velarde
y todo el Norte
Gathered in Spaña
Lowrider Capitol of the World

Warm Sundays al medio dia
the Homies gathered at the car wash
on La Joya Street
la musica blasting
We brought out the shine in our ranflas
the way love brought out the shine in our eyes
My troquita joined Spaña's cruise line
earned its respect
Among the classic old school ranflas;

Cadillac

Cutlass

Grand Prix

Monte Carlos

Bombas.

Lowriding

in my troquita

cruising Spaña's main drag.

Pride in my troquita,

a youngsters welcoming into a brotherhood

of shared respeto y carnalismo.

Land of Poco Tiempo

Lowriding isn't a hobby

but a modern art form that is the

keeper of how life has always been,

low and slow

no rush, no hurry.

I cruise into

the brightness of

the full moon

ending a Sunday afternoon.

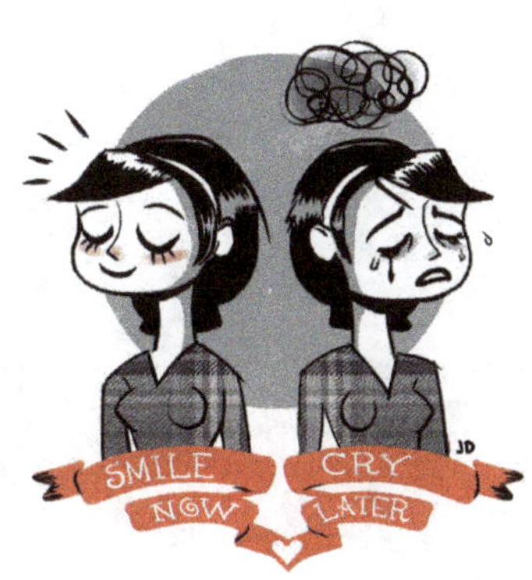
SMILE
NOW
CRY
LATER
JD

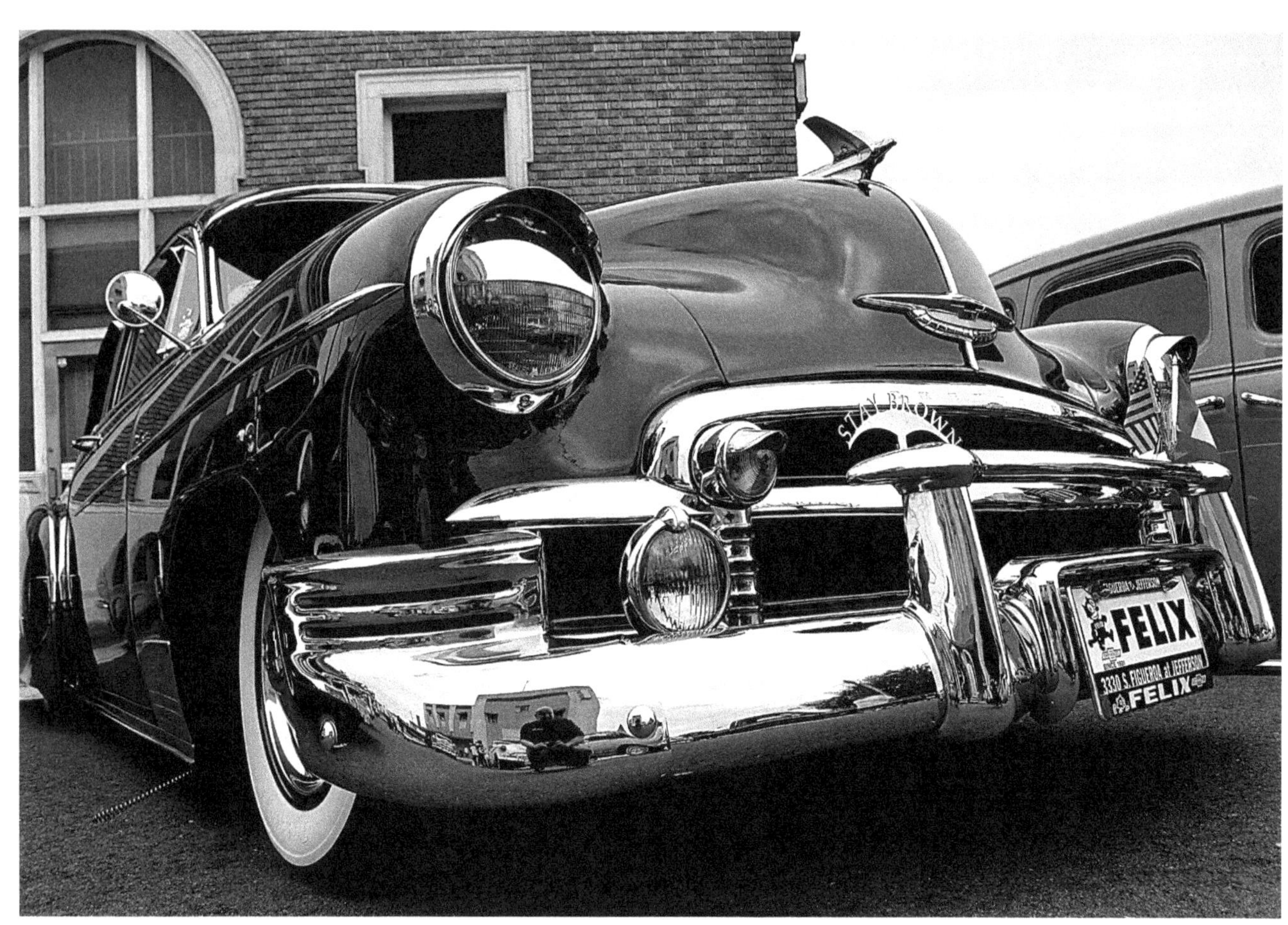

Stay Brown – 1950 Chevy Deluxe

A Father's Gift

By Richard Vargas

I have a list of "firsts" stored in my memory; age three, my first slice of pizza, (I threw up) age seven, my first bicycle, (a beat-up hand-me-down my mom picked up at a police auction for five bucks,) and age thirteen, my first French kiss with one of the "A" list girls at Hosler Junior High, when she cornered me under the mistletoe, (definitely one of my prouder moments.) But right up there at the top of the list, I have to include the one time I came close enough to reach out and touch the white powder my father injected into his arms. I was only four years old.

He pulled the car into the driveway, already regretting not shooting up in the garage where he had purchased the heroin. When he sat down and pulled out his kit, the guy who sold it to him said he had some business to attend to, and he would have to go somewhere else. Now, he would have to shoot up at the house. Smoking a joint in the comfort of his backyard or the privacy of his bedroom was one thing. Closing the door, locking it, preparing a syringe and sticking it into his vein, while his wife and kids were in the next room watching TV, was another matter. The thought of it made him uncomfortable.

The smell of carne cooked in red chile, rice, fresh beans, and homemade flour tortillas greeted him as he walked through the door, but the aching chill in his bones was getting worse, growing into a desperate and more demanding appetite he could not put off for much longer.

"My daddy's a cowboy," I used to proclaim to my classmates in kindergarten. Watching him roll his own cigarettes with the pungent tobacco he kept in a shoebox is one of my favorite childhood memories. How he would sprinkle the dried weed into the coarse, yellowed paper, roll it between his fingers, and then with one fluid motion swipe the tip of his tongue along the glued edge. I had watched John Wayne do the same thing a hundred times in the movies, but he had nothing over my father.

Another ritual was the washing of the car, every Saturday morning. The chrome was polished until it sparkled in the warm, midmorning sun, and I could see my reflection in the Chevy's glossy, customized, baby-blue paint job. Then I would climb in on the passenger side and in a time before seat belts, stand up and hold on as we took the car for a cruise, my slick lowrider father and his mijito driving slowly through the streets of downtown Compton.

He rolled up the windows and lit one of his cigarettes. The cloud of secondhand smoke didn't smell harsh like regular cigarette smoke, but was sweet and pleasurable as it filled my little lungs. Everything slowed to a crawl and the shop windows displaying women's shoes and the latest fashions drifted by like a hazy summer dream.

Ray Charles or Bobby Darin sang on the radio as my father's friends pulled up alongside us at the red light, their dark hair combed back slick and shiny from greasy gobs of Tres Flores pomade. They passed information back and forth about the weekend's parties and dances, where the prettiest babes would most likely show up and who scored what. Then they always nodded in my direction, "Shit, Richard. He looks just like you, *ese*. Hey, little man! You doin' all right? You keeping your old man in line?"

They would laugh as the light changed and pull ahead to the next familiar car on the road, collecting and disseminating news about the neighborhood like a switchboard on wheels.

His son and his two daughters were playing in the backyard. They came running when they heard his car pull up. He knelt down to hug his babies, opening his lunchbox and pulling out three Tootsie Rolls. They kissed their father on the cheek and heard their mother call out from the kitchen, telling them the candy was for after dinner. He sank down into the secondhand easy chair with the tattered upholstery in the sparsely furnished living room. His children started untying his work boots, tugging and pulling until they finally came off his sweaty feet. All the time, he kept thinking about the balloon of white powder in his pocket calling out his name: "Richard! Richard! I'm right here, baby, what you waiting for?"

After dinner, he locked himself in the bathroom, unpacked his kit, and focused on what he had to do. The plan was to get high in the bathroom, then retreat to the bedroom for the rest of the night. They could forget about having family time tonight—no "Bugs Bunny Show," no bowl of popcorn drenched in melted butter as they all huddled around on the floor, crunching the kernels in unison and laughing at the antics of Bugs, Yosemite Sam, and Daffy Duck.

Tonight was his to spend in his other world, alone.

*

I can remember the Friday night our mother loaded us up in the car and took us to the drive-in, without him. I was a month shy of starting the first grade. It was payday. They had groceries to buy. Mouths to feed. Where in the hell was he? I knew she was upset when I heard her say aloud to no one in particular as she backed the car into the street, "Let him come home to a dark and empty house, goddamnit…"

When we returned home, the headlights of the car swept across the front yard as it turned into the driveway, lighting up the figure of my father face down and passed out on the cold, wet lawn. Our mother jumped out of the car, knelt down at his side, lifted his head, leaned in close to make sure he was

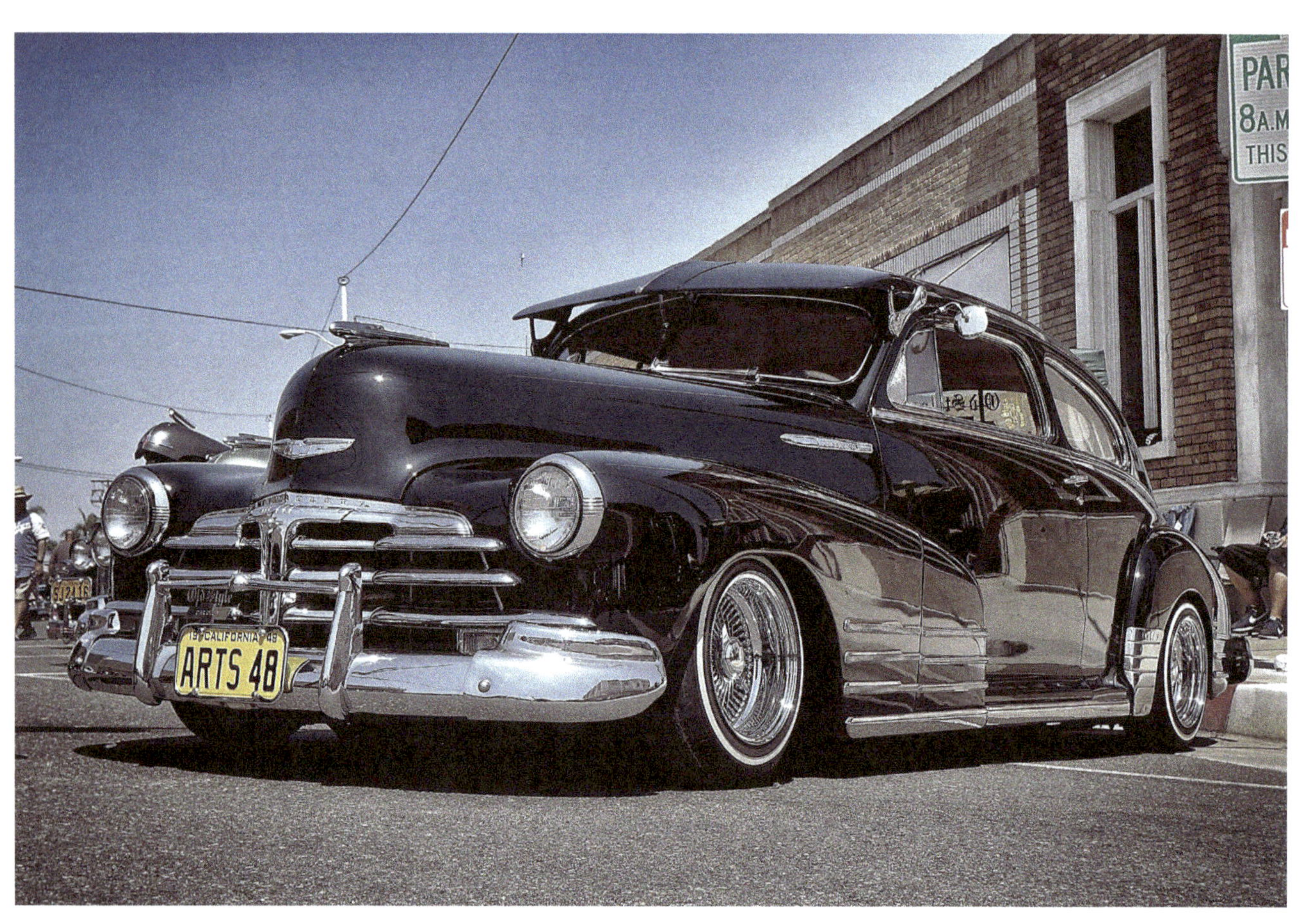

Art's '48 – 1948 Chevrolet Fleetline

breathing and slapped him hard to wake him up.

We were still in the car looking out the windows, wondering why our father was sleeping outside. We watched our mother try to lift him up. She called out to tell me to go next door to get help. I ran to our neighbor's house and knocked on the door. He answered, took one look, realized our dilemma, and ran over to give us a hand. Without saying a word, he helped Mom lift our father off the ground and carry him into the house. They sat him down at the kitchen table. We were rushed off to bed, as our mother stayed up the rest of the night, nursing her husband back from the brink.

He had poured the contents of the balloon into the measuring spoon and was going to add drops of water, when he heard the sounds of feet dancing on the other side of the door. The hunger inside was gnawing at him and the only thing he needed was so close. "Daddy, I have to pee!" Through the sharp pain wracking his brain, he heard the urgency in the boy's plea. His five-year-old son had no idea what he was going through. The only thing that mattered was his son had to pee, now. He heard the doorknob as the child jiggled it back and forth. The dancing noises were getting frantic. He took off the leather belt around his arm's bulging vein, picked up the implements of his habit and stashed them behind the shower curtain in the corner of the tub. He unlocked the door, let his son in, closed the door and waited in the hallway. His son ran in, pulled his pants down around his ankles, aimed his penis for the center of the bowl, and let out an "Ahhhhh..."

I once witnessed my father being arrested. It must have been the summer before I turned five because I wasn't in school yet. I was home watching my favorite afternoon cartoon, "Tom and Jerry." The front door was open, but the screen door was closed. I heard a knock, and although I knew better than to talk to strangers, I went to see who it was. Standing on our porch were two white men. I stared at this odd couple. The one at the door was trying to peer in from the other side of the screen as his partner was scanning the outside of our house, as if he was looking for something. White people didn't live where we lived. We didn't know any, except for the man whose car was parked in my aunt's driveway every Friday and Saturday night. (His name was Mike, and the grownups in the family did not like to talk about him.)

The men at my door were dressed funny. One was wearing a denim jacket and jeans. The other was dressed in a black jacket, white T-shirt, and blue jeans. The white men I saw on TV always wore shirts and ties, and when they got home from work, they slipped on cardigan sweaters and slippers before they smoked pipes in the "study" and read the newspaper. Their wives wore clean, crisp housedresses, and they called each other "dear." The white men always wore pajamas at bedtime. They and their wives always slept in separate beds. The fact that my parents slept in one bed, not two, was one more way I thought white people were better than we were.

"Hi, sonny. Is your dad home?"

Snapped from my spell, I turned around to look for my mother. There she was standing behind me. She directed me back to my cartoons, and then told the men at our door she didn't know where my father was, or when he would be home. She closed the door, and less than a minute later, we heard noises coming from the backyard. We went to the kitchen and opened the backdoor. He was between them, his arms handcuffed behind his back. They had found him hiding in the garage. Neighbors were peering over the fence from all sides of our backyard. He saw me and told my mother to take me back inside. For a brief moment, our eyes met, as if we were saying goodbye, and then he was gone.

My childhood transformed into a blur of memories: weekend visits to various jails or the men's state prison in Chino, and always remembering to reply that my father was in the Navy and out to sea whenever asked of his whereabouts.

His release brought unannounced nighttime visits by tired-looking parole officers, who asked a lot of questions and took notes as my parents smiled a lot. They tried to look so happy it was scary. As they introduced me, my sisters, and a recent arrival, my baby brother, I have to think we must have looked like props, pieces on a set arranged to convince the parole officer we were a normal American family.

On Fridays, after the family trip to the market to stock up on groceries, we all took a ride to the methadone clinic. We sat in a dark parking lot waiting for half an hour. My mother told us our father had an appointment to see a doctor, and he was getting better. He always came back to us a more mellowed and subdued man.

Eventually, it got better for us. My father was hired on as an apprentice welder. He was learning a trade and making decent money. The parole officers faded away. The clinic appointments finally ended.

I knew we were turning a corner the day I got a brand new bike. My police-auction special was on its last legs, but I had never complained. Then, one day my father came home from work and said, "Let's go for a ride. Just you and me."

He took me to a bicycle shop and once inside, asked me which one I liked. I knew the minute we walked in that it was the one with the banana seat, biker handlebars and sparkly gold, metal -flaked finish. It wasn't a Schwinn Stingray, but I didn't care. It had taken me nine years, but I finally had my first, brand new bicycle.

Christmas that year was the best. We had a real tree, flocked with fake snow. I would sit and stare at the colored lights flashing in the dark. I never tired of looking at my distorted reflection peering back at me from the globe-shaped red and green glass ornaments. The smell of pine filled my nostrils, and I knew this was a real Christmas, at last. And the presents! They were stacked higher than I could ever hope or dream. Christmas morning was one continuous shout of glee as we ripped the wrapping paper off G.I. Joes and toy tanks and skates and puzzles and board games and plastic models of my favorite monsters (Frankenstein and the Wolfman) and even a small airplane with a real gas motor to propel it through the air. My sisters also got Barbies and dollhouses.

Everything was better and new. It was only a matter of time before we would take our place alongside the other families who had the latest model of station wagons and houses with white picket fences, who took summer vacations and did things together. The struggle was over, gone like a bad dream. Only good times were ahead. Or so it seemed.

*

A few weeks later, on January 16, 1965, I woke up to my mother shaking me, telling me to get up and get dressed. It was a Saturday, and I pulled the covers over my head. It was a game we often played. Then she would sing to me, belting out some god-awful song she made up on the spot. Since she could not carry a tune to save her life, (a trait I've unfortunately inherited,) I would stick my fingers in my ears and plead for her to stop. This time, she wasn't singing as she went from one bunk bed to the next, shaking my sisters and brother, yelling for all of us to wake up.

I threw the covers back and saw my father's only brother. My uncle stood in the doorway, head down, as tears rolled down his cheeks. My mother's eyes were red, and she looked as if she had been crying for a long time. Then, she announced in a low, but calm voice, "Your father is dead." I wish I could say she held me and gave me comfort as I burst into tears, but I cannot.

Later, I found out he had been hanging out with his old friends, slipping back into his old habits. On this particular night, he had scored some heroin that had not been cut right. It was more pure than the usual drug on the streets. He immediately overdosed. A lot of time was wasted because almost everyone involved was on probation or on parole, and an incident like this could send people back to jail.

Someone dropped him off at the home of friends from the old neighborhood, who in turn drove him home. My mother had left us alone, asleep in the house, as she rushed him to the emergency room in the early morning hours.

While my mother sat next to my father in the ER and waited for medical attention, a doctor passing by stopped, took one look at my father slumped over in the chair, took his pulse, and said casually, "This man is dead."

The week that followed was another series of blurs. I vaguely remember sitting in my grandmother's kitchen, as my father's brother talked about going across town and confronting some people, and my grandfather telling him how foolish and dangerous that would be. I remember that the funeral home had some really good donuts. I remember the matching dark-green sweaters that made me itch and the black slacks my brother and

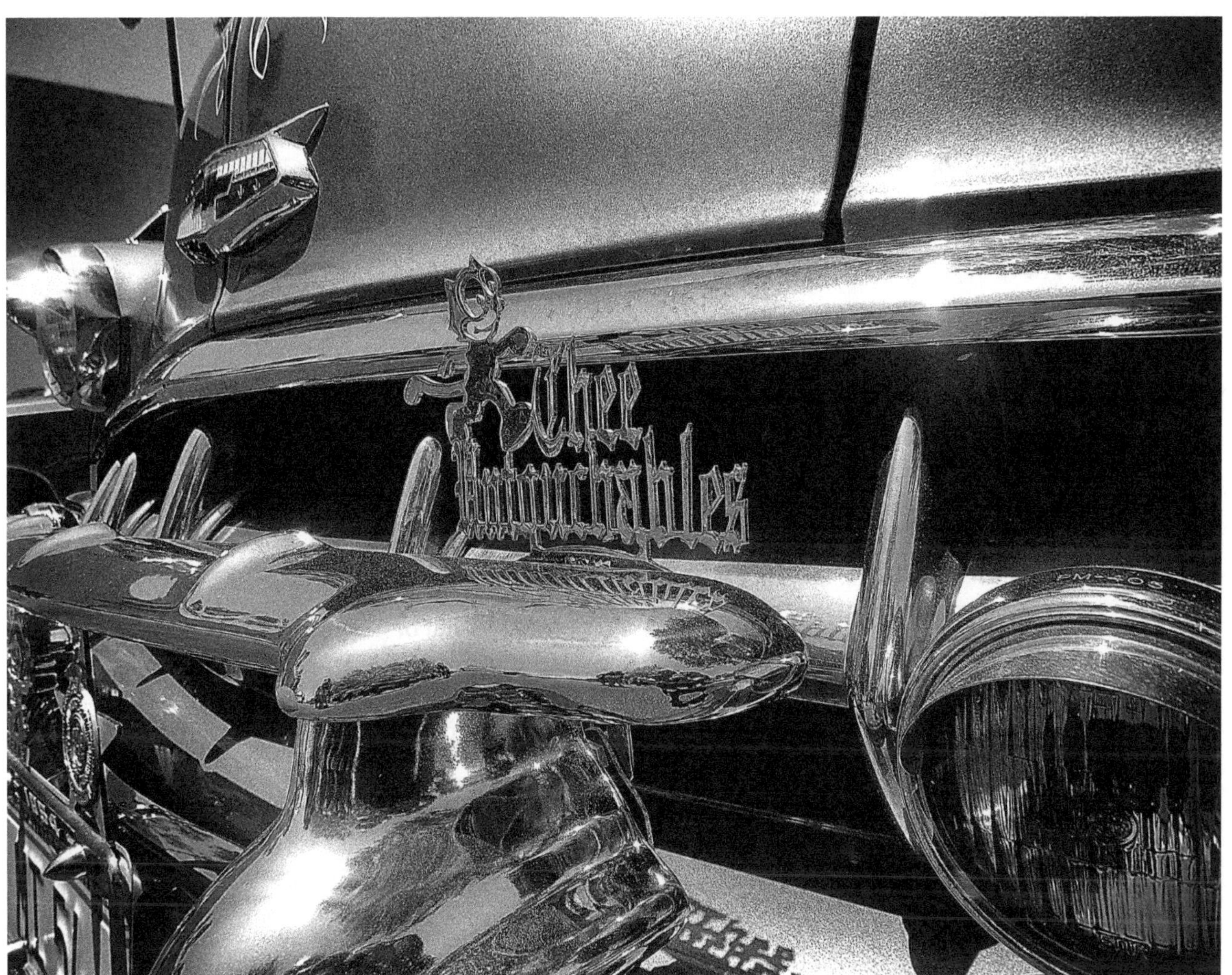

Thee Untouchables – 1954 Chevrolet Bel Air

I had to wear to the funeral. I remember the thick, nauseous smell of too many flower arrangements in one room. I remember the new lie we were coached to tell whenever someone asked how our father died, "My dad had a heart attack."

And I remember another time as if it were yesterday: I was five years old, jumping up and down in the hallway, begging my father to open the bathroom door and let me use the toilet. He unlocked the door and let me in. I made a beeline for the bowl, pulling my pants down around my ankles, standing on my tiptoes, and taking aim. He stepped out and closed the door as the splash of my pee sounded like music to my ears. I began to take note of my surroundings, when I saw the needle on the corner of the tub, partially hidden behind the shower curtain. The needle could only mean one thing, my father was sick. I had been to the doctor often enough to know that. What I didn't understand was why my mother's measuring spoon was in the bathroom with white powder in it. Even more confusing was the blue balloon. Did the doctor run out of candy suckers? I finished my business, pulled up my pants, and opened the door. My father was standing outside the bathroom waiting.

Why I never said a word to anyone, I'll never know.

I didn't know it at the time, but my childhood was taken from me that day. I know some will read this and roll their eyes. *Christ! Another writer whining about his tragic and pitiful life. Can't these people find anything else to write about?* I have, and I do. But what I've come to realize is no one has the perfect childhood. We spend a lifetime trying to unfuck ourselves, recover from the sins of our mothers and fathers, and then turn around and hope we don't do the same to our own kids.

I grew up hating my father. The choice was simple, heroin or me. He chose heroin. The bitterness poisoned my heart. The sense of rejection tainted my relationships. I pushed people away or left them before they could leave me. Some people have a hard time with it, but I never had a problem saying, "I love you." It's easy when you don't really know what it means. I knew from the time I was a teen that I did not want to have children, a promise I've kept to myself all these years.

It wasn't until thirty years after his death,

during the mandatory midlife crisis and the ensuing sessions of therapy, that I revisited my past looking for answers.

Catching up with strangers who cut me off on the road for the simple satisfaction of giving them the finger, confronting coworkers over the most insignificant thing and hoping someone would throw a punch, family gatherings that always fell apart once my sisters found something to scream and argue about, a brother who casually left his wife and one-year-old daughter when he got his best friend's wife pregnant, and an insecure mother (who didn't care what her current husband sold to pay for their comfortable lifestyle) were all too much. I was looking for the source, and all arrows pointed at my father.

My therapist asked and probed, and I recalled most of the memories I've already written about. But she kept pushing me, helping me remember things I had blocked out over the years. One memory stood out from the rest: I'm shivering in the dark, under the covers of my bed, shaking uncontrollably as the chills overtake my small, eight-year-old body. My teeth chatter. I am waiting for my mother to return from the store with urgently needed over-the-counter medicine. We cannot afford a doctor. I turn my head and see him standing in the doorway. The light from the hallway behind him creates a dark silhouette. I cannot see his face. He walks into the room, bends over me, and tucks the blankets around me, snug and tight. He puts his rough hand on my forehead and my cheek, trying to gauge my fever. He doesn't say a word. Then he lies down next to me, holding me close. He is taking deep, deliberate breaths. I can hear and feel his heartbeat. His body heat begins to wrap around me, heating up the blankets, until I am in a warm cocoon and the shivering has stopped. My breathing naturally synchronizes with his, and my eyes begin to close. The last thing I remember before I doze off is feeling safe and loved.

This is how I finally came to realize my father loved me, and never stopped loving me. The demon he battled had nothing to do with me. But it could have. That night while I stood in the bathroom, peeing, it had made its presence known to me, smiled and winked as if we were destined to become close friends.

My father was a heroin addict. It was his curse to bear and had nothing to do with me. I like to think, somehow, he knew his early exit would make sure it stayed that way.

And in my mind, that's the only truth that matters.

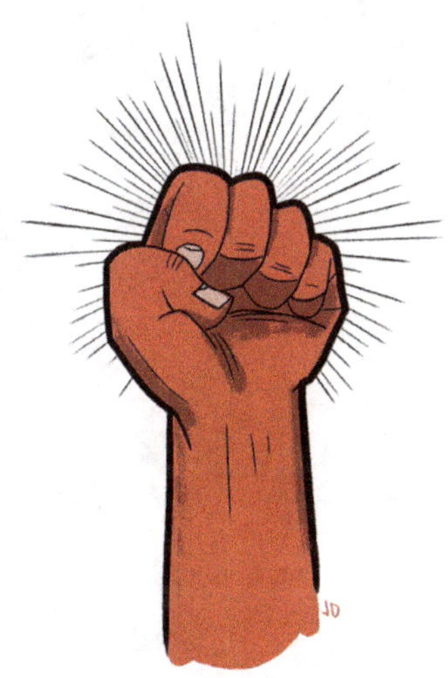

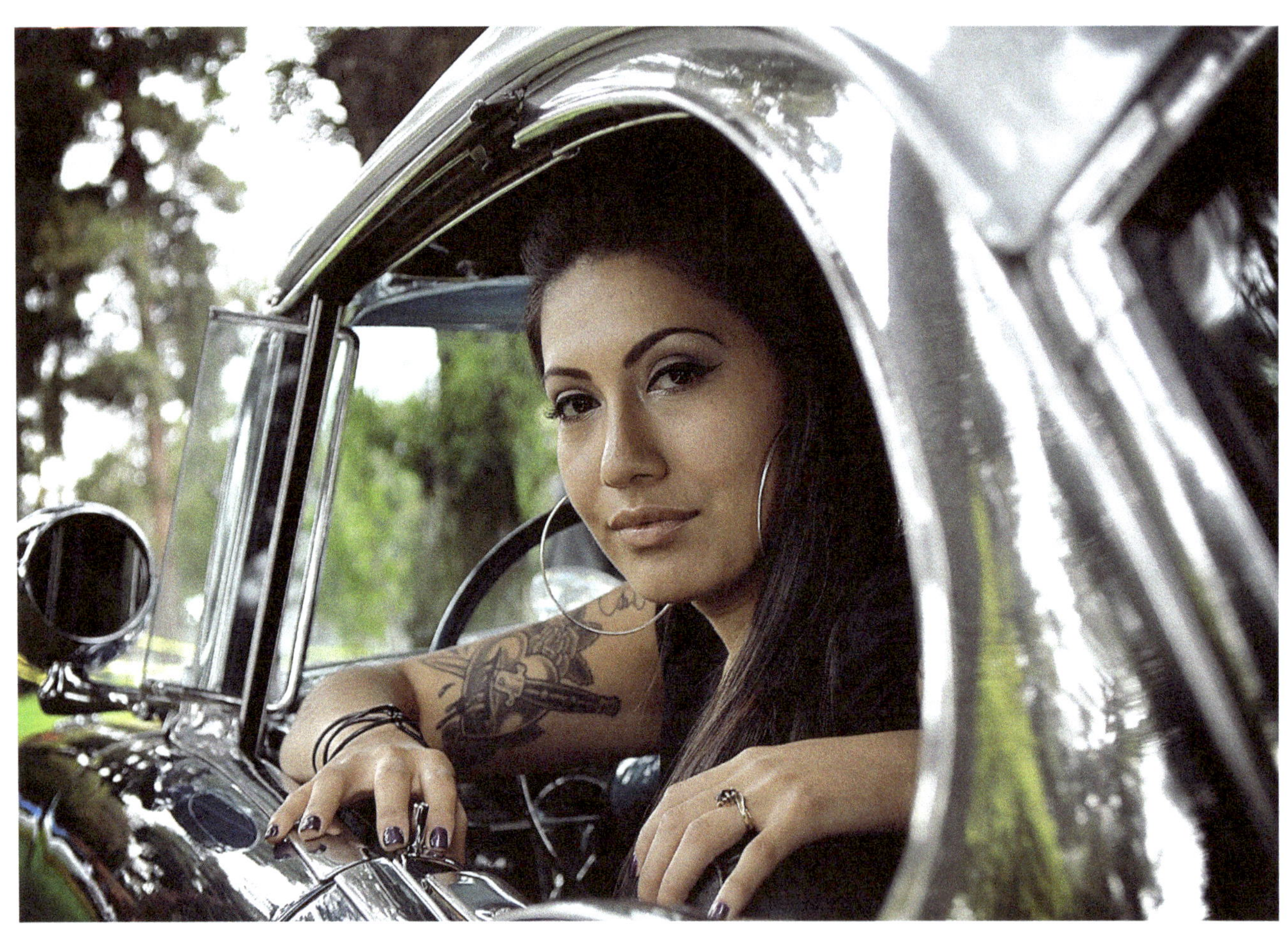

End of the Line, Mayra Ramirez – 1956 Chevrolet Bel Air

End of the Line

By Santino J. Rivera

This is the ruca in my dreams
It's not what you think, ese
and I know what you're thinking, aye
Every time I jump in the '48
she gives me this pensive look
with those eyes
Mas firme
Chingona
Chauuu!
before pushing her stiletto on the gas pedal
as far as it will go
Each night we end up in a hail
of twisted metal
fire and blood spatter
¡quemando llanta!
on the highway at the edge of my mind
Each night I know better
and yet I always climb inside
and sit next to her.
There are no words
between us
barely even a glance
the rush of the screaming wind
and trails of lights passing by
are enough to make my heart explode
Her name is on my lips
at the moment just before impact
and each morning I wake up
to echoes of her laughter
c/s

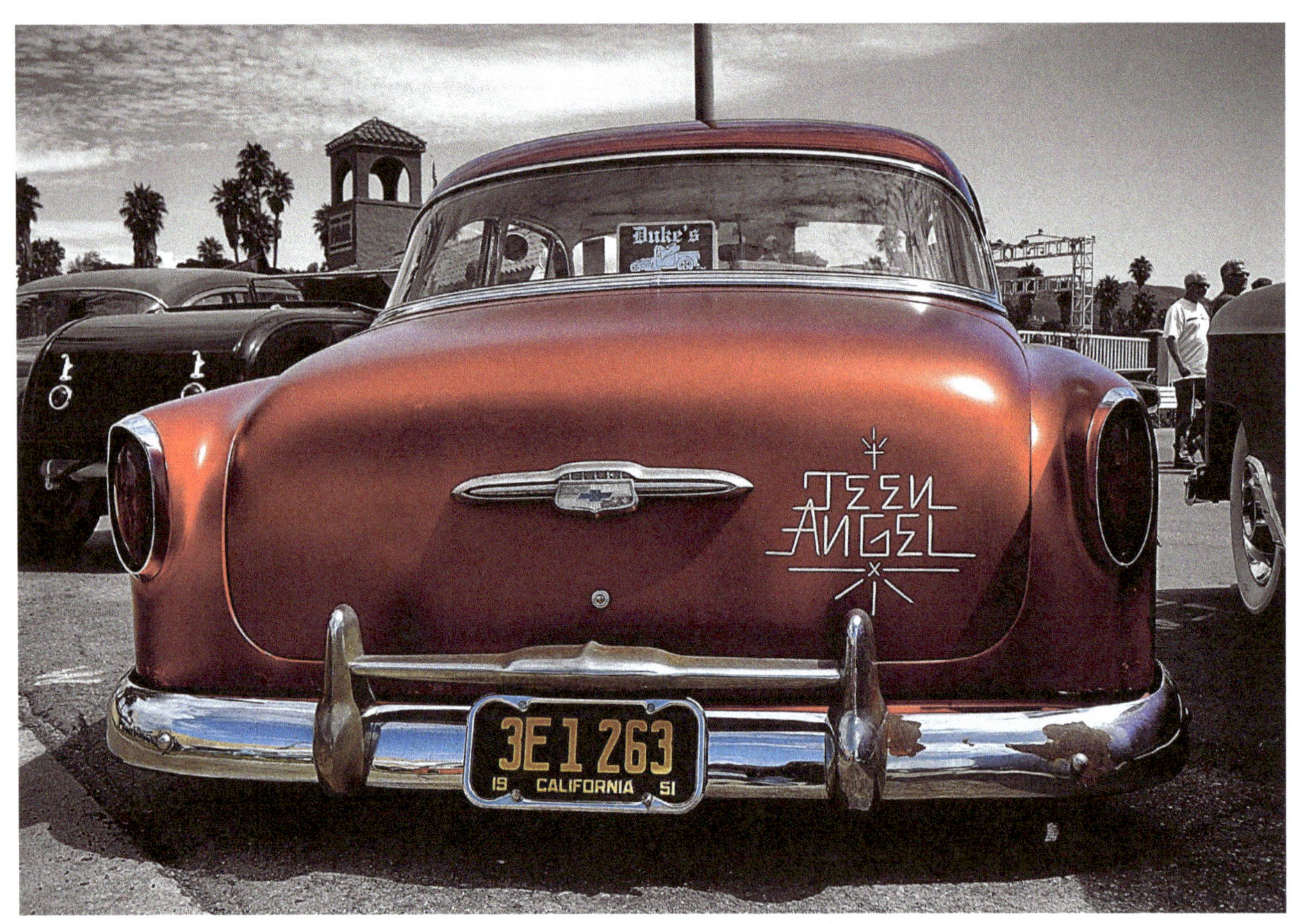

Teen Angel – 1953 Chevrolet Bel Air

Little Stevie's Sweet Ride

By Alvaro Rodriguez

She had no right to sell it, pinche puta madre. 1971 Monte Carlo, candy purple haze, white walls shinybright, 315, V8. I get mad just thinking about that damn car.

It was Esteban's. They called him Little Stevie even though there was no Big Stevie. He was my father. I think.

My mother, La Puta Ybarra of the Echo Park Ybarras before gentrififucktion when they ran them out for gabacho shabby chic cottages and shit, claims Little Stevie's mess went up in her one hot summer night and nine months later, out I popped like a brown baseball from a pitching machine. The fact is it could have been one of a dozen cholos she was doing back then.

I'm not exaggerating.

But Little Stevie's sweet ride, complete with the decal of two fighting roosters on the back window – in your cara – never openly claimed me. Child support? You gotta be kidding. But I have his eyes, his mouth. At least that's what La Puta Ybarra says. I look in the mirror and I can't tell.

Maybe.

So that's my herencia, am I right? She had no right to sell it. It all went in her arm anyway, in the space of a month. And I'm walking or taking the pinche bus…which sucks!

He let me drive it when he was too drunk to take his ass home from this bar or that party. I kicked it heavy duty, taking the scenic route so I would be seen in that cherry ride. He never lived with La Puta Ybarra, always stayed with his Moms in Whittier. Arrested development, they call it. Like father, like son.

And now I have a girl and a baby on the way. I don't give a shit; I'd have put a car seat in the back of that ride. That's a fine Dad-mobile, '71 Monte – candy purple haze.

Thirty-five hundred bucks she got for it. Beautiful ride like that. I think he fucked with the odometer. No way that thing had less than 75,000 miles on it. But a new engine. Gleaming chrome. Fuck. 3500 bucks.

Pinche puta.

My girl's name is Sherrie. She's Mex, don't get me wrong, but she looks white. Kinda like Rose McGowan in that zombie flick where she loses her leg and gets a machine gun leg. Sherrie still has her leg, though.

Nice calves.

Baby bump getting bigger every day.

Nice can.

Not Kardashian, but just right. Like Baby Bear's porridge in that story. Abuela said porridge was like atole but without any canela sticks. That's Abuela Ybarra and she was never no puta.

Watch your mouth.

You know what? I coulda got seven, eight grand easy for that ride. But I wouldn't have sold it. I'd have taken good care of it. Cruised Whittier Boulevard, dumping and pumping. That's the shit right there. A king's chariot – shit, royal candy purple haze!

I got time so I took up painting. Not the regular Mexican shit. No Virgens, no tattooed putas, no sleeping Aztecs. They're called abstract. Colors and shapes and shit.

Feelings.

The things I see when I close my eyes. But now when I close my eyes, I see thirty-five hundred bucks. A 71 Monte Carlo. I don't think I could even make that shade of candy purple if I tried. So I don't try.

If you want to write to me, I'll write you back.

When I get out, I'm going to find a job and support Sherrie and the kid. But I don't think it's gonna last. She hasn't visited me here in Victorville.

Not once.

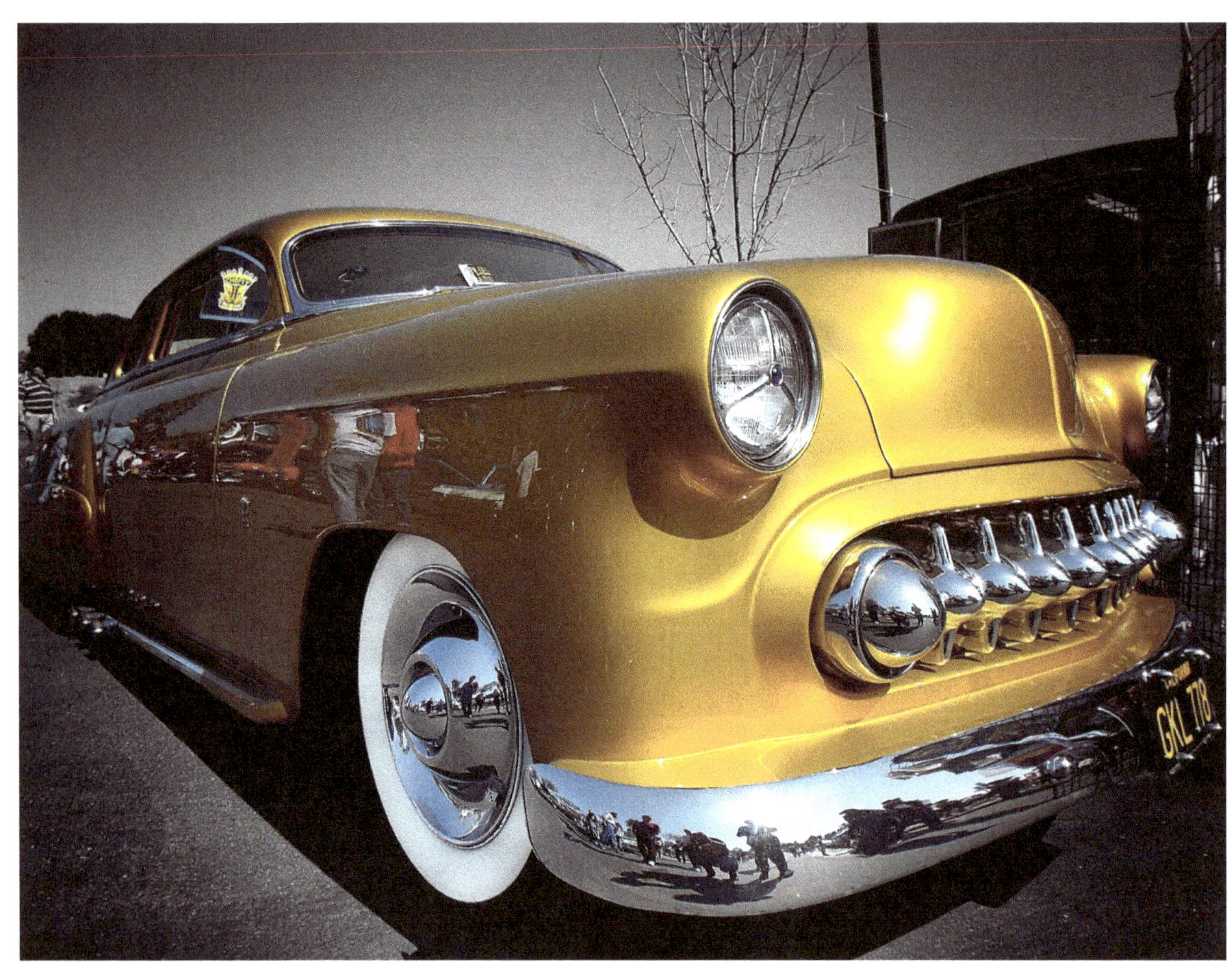

Inca Gold – 1953 Chevrolet Bel Air

A Lowrider Named HUITZIL

by Lawrence Gandara

"More bounce to the ounce"
blasting through the speakers
of this sweet, sweet, sweet ride.
The name: HUITZIL.
Let's create and destroy,
you and me.
Let's fill the void
of our thoughts,
hearts,
and soul
like the space in between
the tires of this jumping
MACHEEN.
Anything but...
Anything but a machine now.
It is neither the up or down,
but both and in between.
Here you can extract the nectar
of an orangy chalkish concrete flower brick.
The nectar of the Project's

that enters the blood like gasoline
to this sweet, sweet, sweet MACHEEN.
My wings are like the switch, enable my being
to go side to side, up and down.
I am the embodiment
of the four directions and elements.
From Dog Town to Palestine to Chiapas.
Not even the sweetest flower
can decompress this struggle.
This ranfla bangs on the pavement,
bangs on the system.
Not only like Rage Against the Machine,
but MACHEEN
against the system.
You too are HUITZIL,
you too are like this sweet, sweet, sweet ride.
You are a MACHEEN!!!

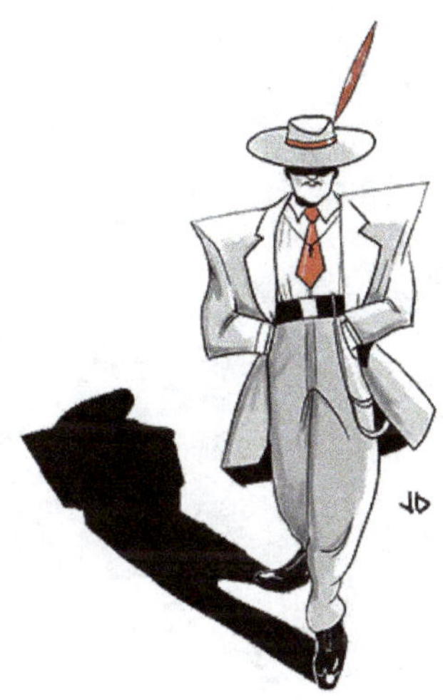

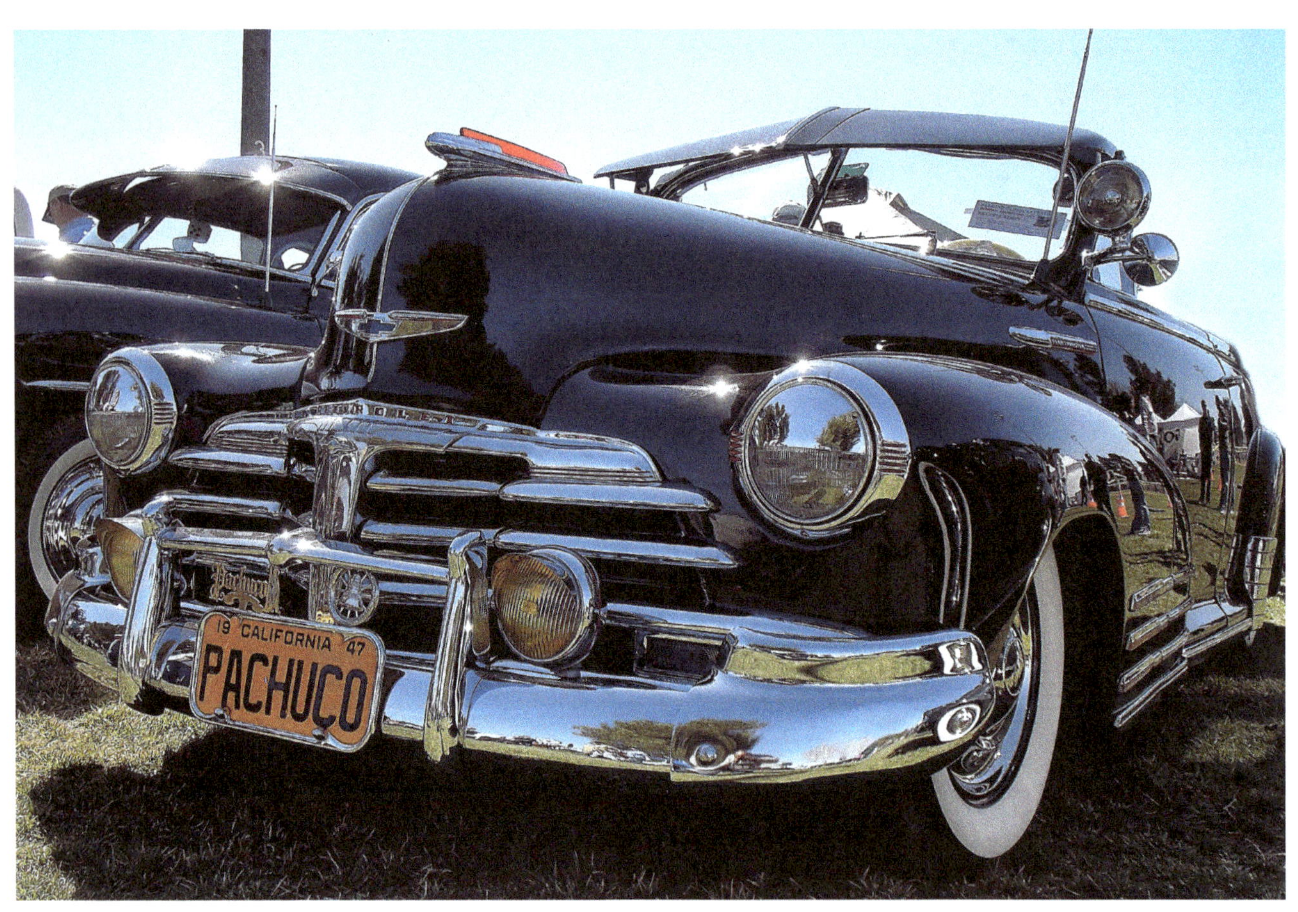

Pachuco – 1947 Chevrolet Fleetline

Carchitexturas

By Steven Alvarez

G L Y P H[1]

image: prophetik CHALEY CHASTITELLEZ

than than tharán[2]

& that brownish skin of history

limned in all imageswords

nouns & verbs

---

[1] estereotypical caricatura

[2] as they still sing of him in cantinas & countrystores. In those ranchos where viejitos gather at cool dusk w/ Johnny Walker red passed around clockwise a-smokin & a-listenin to old canciones & cuentos of other days. "He breaks before he bends—& cuts a dashin figure" dijeron these old bastards. "A man a man 'twas a man." They also make albures abt his "stuffing his own shaved scrotum in his mouth puro huevón ja ja JA." Órale: "another Latino Dedalus—what this world needs eh" / "slightly Byronic in slouch / more Oneigen in shape" / "belonging to that most vile category of social fauna / human rubbish" / yes at times / "claims life hostile to him" / "& so harbors brown resentment" / "mapped betweeness folks in this business call it / & where Dedalus had god & Ireland / he's got Guadalupan Aztecs / & Massico" / "& both shape poetry" / "when born his pappy sd 'this pinche huevón will be a poet prophet—look at the size of his mouth' / & right then still slippery w/ his birthjuices his pappy lifted that chavalito & dedicated him to the Sun & to that flowery death of poetry / so sure enough he's here sung abt / & sings too" /

context: this AZtlán moment pulsating
caged temporal & spatial configurations
nadie cd ever imagine dead imagine
a huevo—indeed—Tucson
written in *Codex Moja'odicus* never happened /
never each time
time cycles recycled cycles

e(s)pic: & all Chaley sees yepa—
neck resting on a yellowed whitewall spare tire behind his
head reading solito in that parked beater
eseventydos Datsun he rolled / what folks in AZtlán
called "birth control" for C's lackluster destiny
for "eseshual" conquests / five colors of sun
rusted away no bumpers / screwdriver in ignition
no passenger window
C browsing through his magazines
w/ images of high heeled bikini-clad rucas
posing w/ glittery love machines
w/ wire wheels / one C had his eye on
violet flaked azure pearl lilac ghosts
choptopped tricked-out troka / Toyota
dancing pickup bed

shaved taillights y todo /
ah dreams / sweet dreams / relaxing
in his parked beater Datsun just off Calle Brazos
Panadería Estrella's lot / frowning down his mag
& up C's eyes fixed on bluest sky he'd already known
bluest azure pearl bluer than any ma-ching
the blues of ol AyZee
these skies nothing more than postAZtlán sky grand
& yet tinted bluely differently
from gilded styrofoam towers & hollow pyramids
plastic bodies & concrete cacti
& suddenly prophetic C sees in all he sees
in all his Pochovisions
funneled to this quasimomenteeTEEto
güey up high—that spot—¡güey! ¿what the shit is that?:
some damned green birdsnake w/ owl's eyes screeching

¡ATENCIÓN!

¡ATENCIÓN!

¡ATENCIÓN!

diving from somewhere down from that tainted Arizona sky

& only C sees this flapping madly plumedsnake

for since no one truly looks up in AZ (esp. bc doing so cd burn one's eyes blind)

& yes look to this: how clouds emanate from this animal

& veils of cloudfog surround—descends or ascends he can't tell—

& frankincense scents

soften into darkened foggy neonglows curtaining him

& as his gaze presses on looking further into this birdsnake's

owl's eyes C sits up no longer in that pick-up's bed

¿& his lowrider mag? snails w/ candypaint shells

sliming trails of salsa verde / ¡de veras!

now a barrio forest

untouched thick brush / ponderosa pine / sitka spruce

as in Alaska again

& up & walking on

tugging up his ethnocentric misogynistic chicansmo loincloth

& pushing on & on thru veils of cloudfog & on

he encounters *her* that ruca in 'is magazine

cheenga kay yes

& Chaley peering thru

smoke [cough] fir needles singeing

her bronzely freckled skin / *she*

posed on saplings ferns & ocelot pelts

eyes inaccessible

legs closed

heels high

her hair the ocean

& C behind some alders

& she on her petate of saplings & furs

arching her back

magueyes walling her

& her knees bend her legs open & C sees

glisten . . .

& well—pos—taco de ojo—he stiffer than times

of global credit crises / boom ready to bust one cd guess

& his thoughts flash bulbs of black enlightening him yes

& right where he thinks Tucson *was*

there's her & whatever happens . . . no / ni modo

& just then her curls leap & she sways & jerks

convulsively & again that green birdsnake

screeches

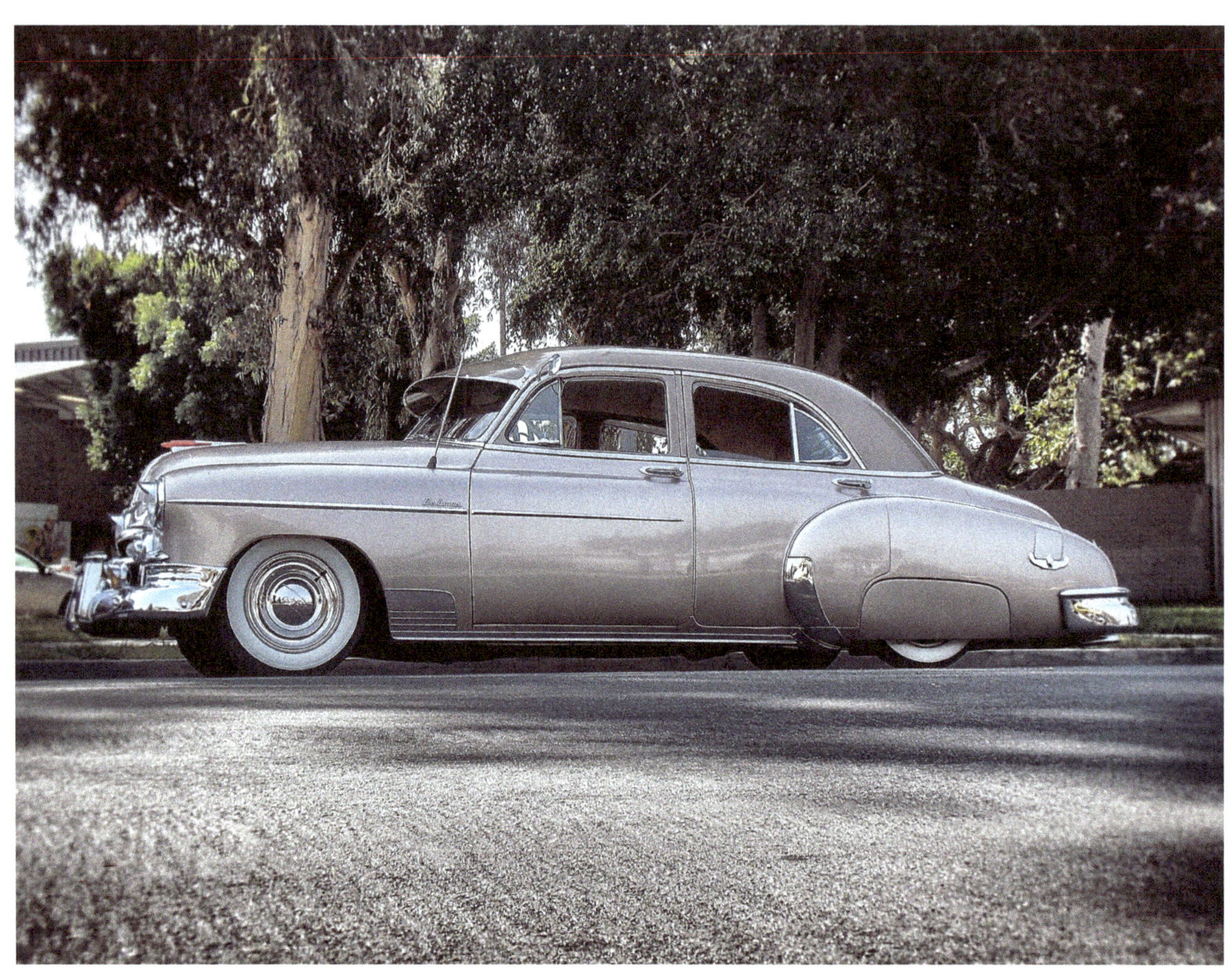

Champagne Deluxe — 1950 Chevrolet Deluxe

¡ATENCIÓN!

¡ATENCIÓN!

¡ATENCIÓN!

¡ATENCIÓN!

& wacha C / mark how it soars & its claws
firmly gripping eyesockets
of one nice skull lit like dark stone [¿*trans*?]
& C thinks to himself stigmata
¡joder!

& now
here
Tucson

¿& la ruca?
limp headless

yes manches some serious Zetas booshit

& up & up flies that birdsnake w/ owl's eyes & her skull in its talons

UP & UP to that winedark violet
smoking volcán

shit: C: that: Puebla.
Es la verdad. ¡Great storms of luz!

& C shuts tight his eyes terrorized
sways & damp stardust tumbles
& wind whips him

smoke gone
as he hears shouts

of bass from some eseventytres Monte Carlo at this stoplight
next to his Datsun Chaley finds himself returned to . . .

or he never left quizás didn't he can't sey . . .

but truchas sweet baby santo niño there his lowrider mag
& as he rises from that bed & marvels redcandyapple

flake / w/ pearl ghostpatterns calaveras

chromegleam of wirewheel rims
godly gold spinners
    yes de veras / Chaley calls out to these carnales
    over Ice Cube explaining why that day was a good day
NOT having to use his A-K & such Chaley
    sez to these gentlemen YO: ¿ya'll see that plumed snake flying?
    he shouts this three times bc bass drowns his voice
    & finally that pelón passenger volumes down their song
    & Chaley asks again abt flying feathered serpents screaming attention
    & these two dudes gesture signs w/ their fingers
    concoctions of knuckle & wrist twists accenting mano
    acrobatics & communicating to Chaley
    they prefer no verbal interaction & as they speed away
    BOOM b a s s BOOM BOOM b a s s
    BOOM b a s s BOOM BOOM b a s s
    Chaley glimpses airbrushed trunk mural
    soaring Quetzalcoatl pinching C's severed head in his talons
    y verla fea headless heeled ruca corpse walled in maguey
  & abuelo Popocatépetl crying for his children . . .

        újule

pero ain't no sin to take off yr head & baile in yr bones

& C scratches his cabeza

asks if & why

Datsuns divinations in Tucson ache

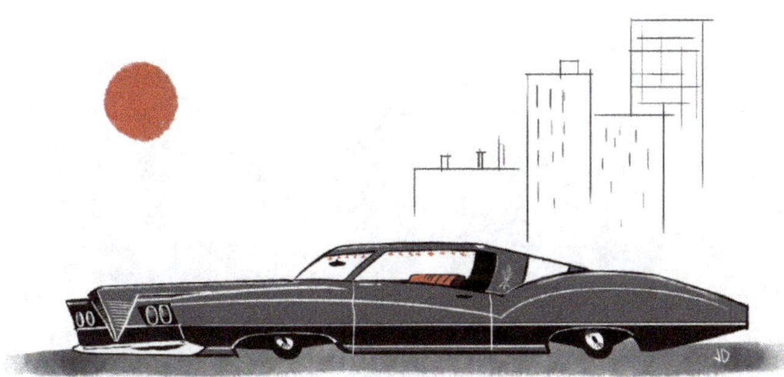

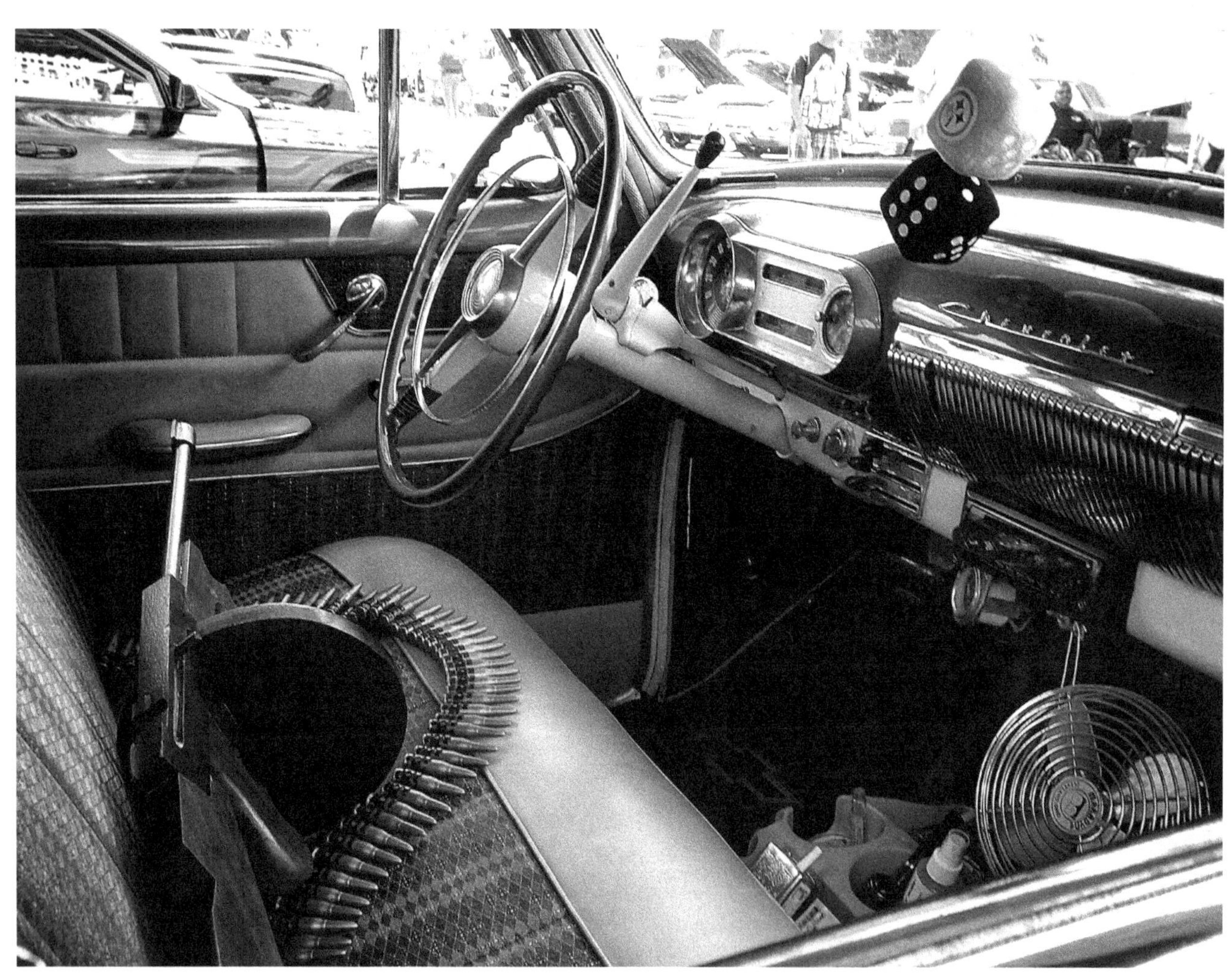

What Car Alarm? – '54 Chevy Bel Air

South Sixth Tucson Summer

By Steven Alvarez

1

bowtie taillights

hitting scene with D's

juiced ton-&-a-half Amurkan machine dancing

placa
patterns
                    flake skirt murals

y no hay chota

2

twice told tale

tangled

AZ's finest pendejos

chotas cruising for cruisers

however

this led
to confrontational relations
between chotas

&
Tucson residents
Chaley's southside barrio
bc residents believed
chotas imagined gang & criminal estereotypes
to predicate
stops

"you wear gang colors"

"you're out too late"

"thugs match yr description"

"there were reports of shots fired / car like yrs"

"more than three browns in the car"

"you look suspicious"

"violating noise ordinance"

"over-tinted windows"

"hanging rosaries or objects from rearview mirror"

"parked in a known gang area"

3

make space for the ride
mechanical body moving thru spacetime

on the wings of internal combustion

interior luxurious pleasure zone

barrio logos

barriology pues

segregation & marginalization of Xicanos

by capital / by the pinche state

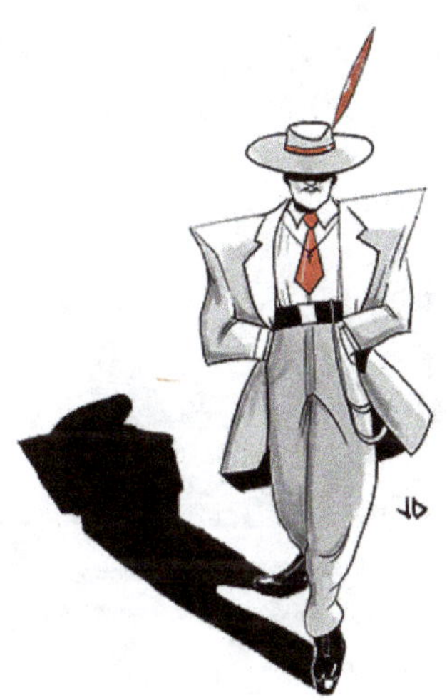

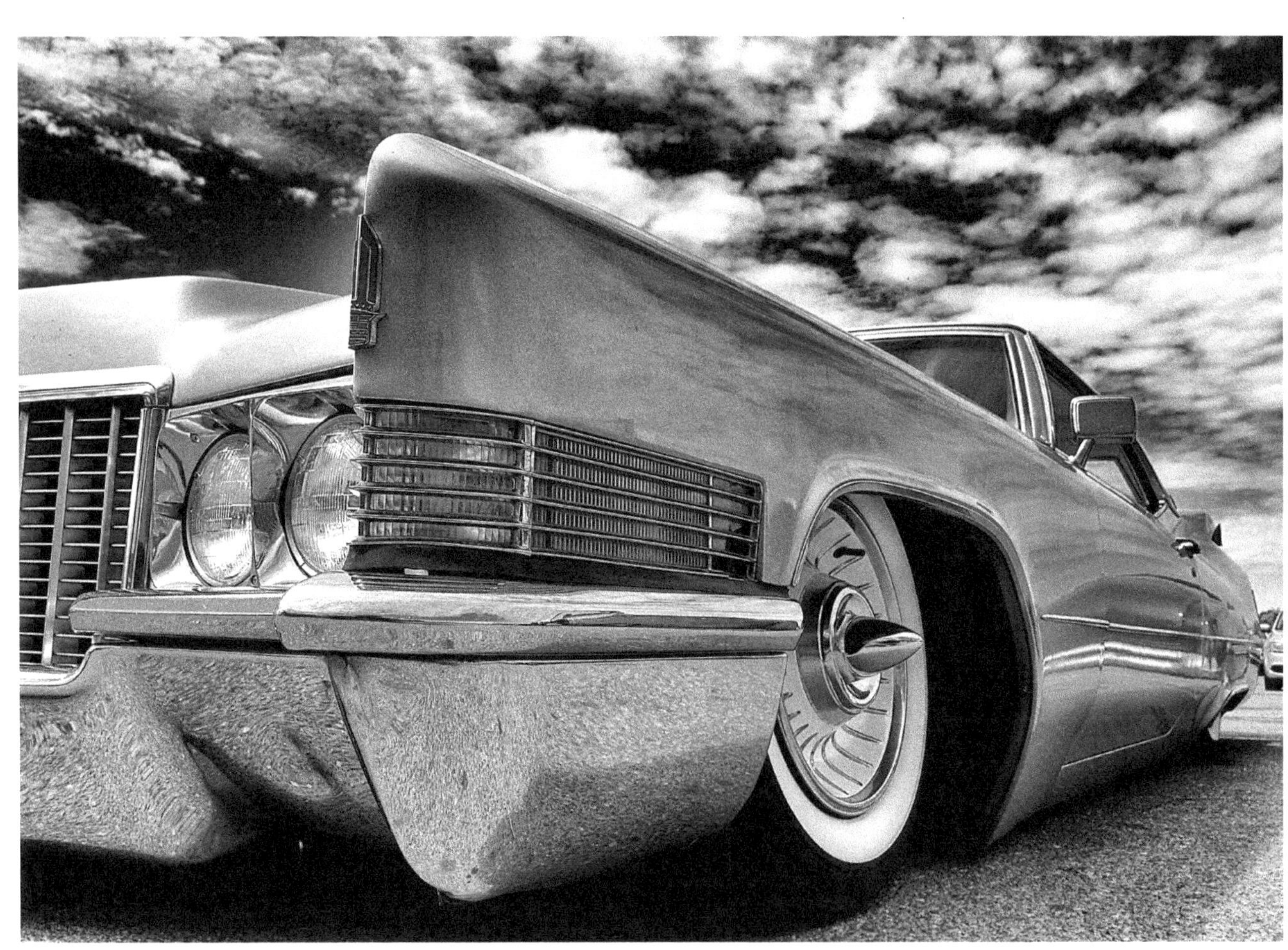

A Cadillac King –1970 Cadillac DeVille

Coker's Cadillac

By Gustavo Arellano

I was born to drive old cars. The earliest auto I remember was a teal-green Ford Thunderbird, a beast with eyelid headlights that my dad drove in my infancy. After that, he bought a 1963 Dodge Dart, the vehicle where I learned how to drive in the parking lot of the Anaheim Indoor Swap Meet over a year of Sunday mornings and which he scrapped right as I received my driver's license, a fact I rue to this day. In high school, while my peers dreamed of BMW, Mercedes Benz, Ferraris, and other marks of conspicuous consumption, I wanted a Karmann Ghia. As my baby brother grew older, I instilled in him the following rule: you're not truly a man until you buy a classic that you trot out when it's time to show off—this means you're well-off and take pride in yourself.

But I never thought I'd actually *own* an old car. See, I'm pragmatic by nature, which is a polite way of saying I'm a cheap bastard. I respect those who can afford to keep a *ranfla* in their garage, but that wasn't going to be me. Whenever I had extra money, I gave it away to causes I supported—the revolution may not be televised, but it always needs a few extra pesos. In my junior year of college, I bought a new 1999 Toyota Camry—I don't regret the purchase, because the car is still running and took care of me (my baby brother now drives it. He's not a man—yet). But when I bought that era's epitome of Orange County middle-class aspirations, a little part of me died.

Salvation came in the form of the *OC Weekly*, the alternative newspaper. I started working at the

OC Weekly in 2001, and it's the only job I've ever had during my professional career (my current title: Mexican-in-Chief). It was a ragtag crew of misfits, all revelations to my sheltered pocho experience, and everyone drove the appropriate vehicle to fit their personality. Boss man drove a Beemer; my best pal on staff, a lanky gabacho named Nick Schou who's now my managing editor, drove a Ford Explorer that took him all the way down to Chiapas and back (yet it didn't survive a random drive on the 405 Freeway near Huntington Beach that left the Explorer engulfed in flames—go figure). Staffers who were parents drove minivans; the single folks, compacts.

The one glorious exception was the managing editor at the time, Matt Coker. Every day, he'd drive to work in a glorious 1974 Cadillac Eldorado convertible. Oh, how happy I was when I'd see Coker swing that boat into the parking structure—navigate, actually, is the better term, and not just because it completes the metaphor. The 1974 Cadillac Eldorado was one of the largest cars Detroit ever produced for the general public: Three tons and 18+ feet of American steel, more than six feet wide, with an 8.2 liter V8 engine that sounds like a jet and purrs like a kitten going 80 miles per hour. It screamed power and respect—which was funny because Coker is one of the most unassuming, laid-back *cabrones* you'll ever meet. Top down, Howard Stern blasting on the speakers, Coker's Cadillac was everything I had ever dreamed for. It was in nearly mint condition—the story he told was that some old guy bought it brand new off the lot, drove it in a Palm Springs garage for about 25 years without ever using it again, then died. His heirs sold it to a Cadillac dealership in Hollywood, where Coker found it and gave it a great home.

The Eldo served as inspiration: I would work as hard as I could so I could buy an old car. Nothing that big, though: it simply didn't match my personality—I still wanted a Karmann Ghia. All that changed, however, in 2007. The *Weekly* had undergone a schism—three-quarters of the staff quit to start a new paper in Long Beach. Coker had guided those of us who remained through one of the hardest times of my professional career—and just as everything seemed to be settling, Coker shocked us by announcing he was quitting to helm an alt-weekly in Sacramento.

None of us begrudged him—he deserved to be *jefe* somewhere. Nevertheless, it was going to be sad seeing him go, not seeing him drive that Caddy into work.

Then, one day, I noticed something on his car's window: FOR SALE.

I ran to Coker.

"Why are you selling it?" I wondered.

"I gotta move up to Sacramento," Coker replied. "And I can't take the car with me."

"How much?" I shot back, and the car was mine within the week.

Dream fulfilled, yes, but now that car meant more than prestige. It had always brought happiness to me, always took me back to the calm days of the *Weekly*, of the trust Coker and others had in me to join the paper. To see Coker gone would be a tragedy; to see the Caddy leave the *Weekly* family was unacceptable.

I bought it, and promptly left it in our parking garage for two years until management forced me to move it (starting it was a laugh—we had to spray ether on the carburetor, which promptly caught fire). Part of me wanted to just leave it there as a museum piece, a reminder of the good times. But when I finally needed to get it out of its dungeon, I realized it was time to properly restore it. Time to be a man.

I took the Cadillac to Tijuana, home of the best restorers around. Over the course of a month, they stripped the car down to its shell and rebuilt it. New upholstery. New paintjob. A fresh chroming. A shiny ragtop. A proper tune-up. Such a job would've run into the five figures stateside; I paid about $4,000.

Later on, I installed a new stereo system in addition to the original 8-track player-stereo set '74s came with.

It's not my daily driver, but come summertime I take it wherever I go, getting approving glances from everyone. I'm never going to put hydraulics on it, or lower it, or give it a mural—it's perfect as it is. Oh, and Coker returned to the *OC Weekly*. Peace is restored.

Still haven't got that Karmann Ghia, but I currently own a '68 Volkswagen Bus—it'll do for now.

††

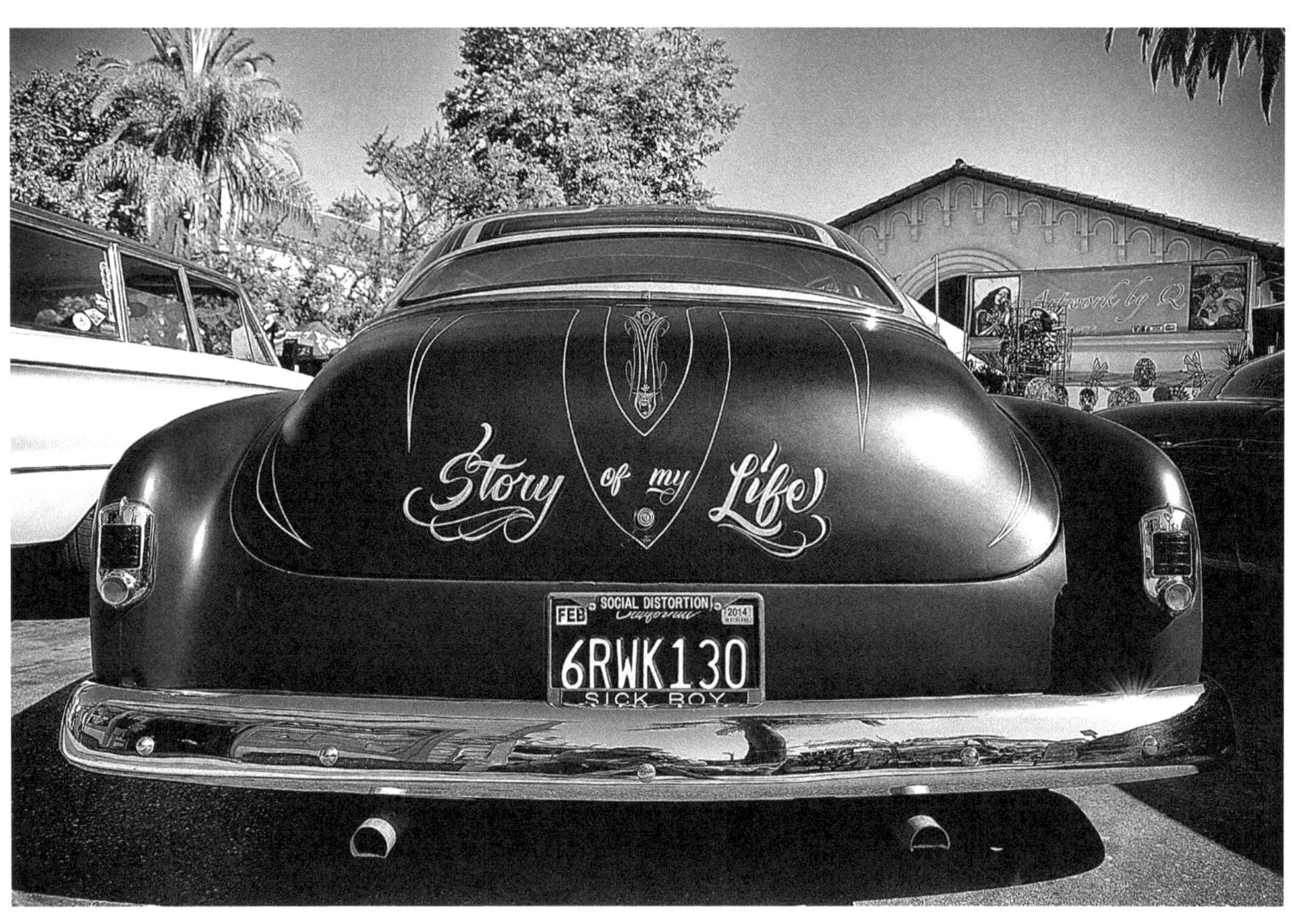

Story of My Life – 1951 Chevrolet Deluxe

About the Authors/Artists

Angel Diaz

My name is Angel Diaz, born May 23rd, 1980. I've been an artist all my life, living out of Oakland, CA. I'm heavily influenced by my Mexican roots, lowriders, and Chicano folk art. I paint what I see; a lifestyle, a way of being. You can see more of my work at: www.puesorale.net.

Art Meza

Art Meza is a third generation Chicano, an L.A. native and a lover of classic cars. These elements are uniquely represented in his photography – photography with some "Chicano Soul."

Lalo Alcaraz

Lalo Alcaraz is perhaps the most prolific Chicano artist in the nation, according to his own bio, which he wrote while grooming his goatee. He is the creator of the first nationally syndicated, politically themed Latino daily comic strip, "La Cucaracha," which is read in American newspapers nationwide, including the Los Angeles Times and not Lowrider Magazine. Lalo's comics are syndicated by Universal Uclick, home of "Doonesbury," and several talking dog & kitty cat comic strips. Lalo produced editorial cartoons for The LA Weekly from 1992-2010 and now creates editorial cartoons in English and Spanish for Universal. Lalo's books include "Latino USA: A Cartoon History," (2000 by Basic Books), "Migra Mouse: Political Cartoons On Immigration," (2004). Alcaraz also authored the first collection of his daily comic strips, "La Cucaracha," (2004, Andrews-McMeel Publishing.) His upcoming book is "Imperfect Union: A contrarian history of the United States, 2014 by Basic Books. Lalo teaches Editorial Illustration at Otis College of Art & Design in Los Angeles. He is a staff writer for an upcoming secretly titled animated TV show on Fox, set to debut in Fall 2014. He is the co-host of KPFK Radio's wildly popular satirical talk show, "The Pocho Hour of Power," heard Fridays at 4pm in L.A. on 90.7 FM, and co-founded the seminal Chicano humor 'zine, POCHO Magazine. Alcaraz also co-founded the political satire comedy group Chicano Secret Service. And he is Jefe-In-Chief at Pocho.com. Lalo is married to a hard-working public schoolteacher and they have 3 extremely artistic children.

Luis J. Rodriguez

Luis Rodriguez has published fifteen books in poetry, the novel, short stories, memoir, nonfiction, and children's literature. He is best known for the bestselling memoir "Always Running, La Vida Loca, Gang Days in L.A." Luis is also co-founder of Tia Chucha's Cultural Center – a bookstore and cultural space – in the San Fernando Valley as well as founder/editor of Tia Chucha Press, a poetry press publishing poets from throughout the country's diverse communities. His latest book is the sequel to "Always Running" entitled "It Calls You Back: An Odyssey Through Love, Addiction, Revolutions, and Healing."

Danny De La Paz

Danny De La Paz is a well-respected actor, writer, and director, with over thirty-five films and television projects to his credit. He is perhaps best known for two iconic performances in the films Boulevard Nights and American Me, which established his reputation as an actor of intensity and honesty. He is regarded by many to be a cultural ambassador for Chicanos, a position he takes quite seriously.

Andrea J. Serrano

Albuquerque native Andrea J. Serrano has been writing and performing poetry since 1994 and is published in Malpais Review; the Mas Tequila Review; ¡Ban This! BSP Anthology of Xican@ Literature, as well as La Bloga: Online Floricanto and The Duke City Fix. She has performed at numerous venues including the Nuyorican Poets Cafe in NYC, Galeria de la Raza in San Francisco and was part of the Librotraficante Caravan

Reading in Albuquerque in 2012. Andrea was also a panelist at the Tucson Festival of Books in 2013. Andrea is the youngest of seven daughters and credits her family, her ties to land, language and culture and the experience of growing up Chicana in Albuquerque with influencing her writing. Andrea is a member of the band Cultura Fuerte, and is the creator and host of Speak, Poet: Voz, Palabra y Sonido, a monthly poetry venue.

Anna C. Martinez

Anna C. Martinez lives in Albuquerque, NM. By day, she is a struggling civil rights attorney/partner in her firm, AEQUITAS LAW. By night, she is an aspiring performance poet. She was born on Normandie Ave, Los Angeles, at the height of its civil rights movements to a closet-singer mom and a Chicano activist mural painting dad who quit his illustrator job with the aerospace industry in refusal to design warheads for use in the Vietnam War, and moved his family to his childhood home in Santa Cruz, NM. Unable to paint or sing, Anna discovered her art by writing love poems for horny teenaged friends in exchange for quarters to buy Hot Fries from the Tom's machine at Española Valley High. A fierce activist on Facebook, Anna has been blocked by many a friend and family member who cannot handle her sexual advocacy or political truth. She is the oldest of five, mom of four, grandma of two, wife of none, and Nina to too many. She was first published in 2012 in the anthology La Palabra: the Word is Woman. She is in-house poet at Las Pistoleras Instituto Cultural De Arte in Taos, NM, and holds titles as Albuquerque City XXX Haiku Champ, and City Chicana/o Slam Champ with her performance of "Chimayó Chevy Pickup."

Allen Thayer

Allen Thayer is a music lover, researcher and writer specializing in soul music and its many global and cultural permutations from Brazilian Soul to Lowrider Oldies. Allen is a regular contributor to Wax Poetics magazine and has been published in The Fader and the Utne Reader as well as contributed liner-notes for Light In the Attic, Luaka Bop and Plug Research record labels.

Enrique Arroyo

Enrique grew up in a lowrider family in the heart of LA. In addition to writing poetry and reading banned books, he enjoys spending time with family and friends.

Jason Hoyt

Jason Hoyt is a father to be who grew up in the Barrio Sesto near downtown Houston. A college graduate in General Liberal Arts. He currently resides in Pasadena, Texas.

Nancy Aidé González

Nancy Aidé González is a Chicana poet and educator. She graduated from California State University, Sacramento with a Bachelor of Arts degree in English Literature. She attended Las Dos Brujas Writer's Workshop in 2012. Her work has appeared in Calaveras Station Literary Journal, La Bloga, Everyday Other Things, Mujeres De Maiz Zine, La Peregrina, Huizache The magazine of Latino literature, DoveTales, Tule Review, and Seeds of Resistance Flor y Canto:Tortilla Warrior. Her work is featured in the Sacramento Voices: Foam at the Mouth Anthology (2013). She is a participating member of Escritores del Nuevo Sol, a writing group based in Sacramento, California which honors the literary traditions of Chicano, Latino, Indigenous and Spanish-language peoples.

Nikkeya West

Nikkeya West is a third generation Chicana living in Idaho. Her family has originated from both Juarez, and New Mexico. With a white father that was never present, Nikkeya has learned to indulge in Chicano culture and what it truly means to be biracial. She graduated with honors in Spanish and a member of the Multicultural Group. Today she continues her education and is currently working on a Bachelor's degree. She is juggles life as a wife, mom of two, and a student with high hopes of becoming an immigration lawyer one day. Her love of cars comes from stories from her grandfather and his inspiring rags to riches life. This poem was inspired by a car her grandfather once owned as a young man.

Luis Alberto Urrea

Luis Alberto Urrea is an award winning Chicano poet, novelist and educator. He was born in Tijuana, raised in San Diego, and banned in Tucson. He is the author of several books, including Vatos, By the Lake of Sleeping Children, Across the Wire, The Hummingbird's Daughter, Into the Beautiful North, The Devil's Highway and Queen of America. Urrea was a Pulitzer Prize finalist in 2005 and is a member of the Latino Literature Hall of Fame.

Tara Evonne Trudell

Tara Evonne Trudell, a mother of four, is full-time student working on her BFA in Media Arts with an emphasis in film, audio, and photography. It is through this expression of art, combined with her passion for poetry that she is able to express fearlessness of spirit for her family, people, community, social awareness, and most importantly her love of earth.

Jim Marquez

Jim 'The Beast' Marquez. Born & Raised East Los Angeles. Author. Self-Published 14 Books. Has written dozens of pieces for arts & cultural mags (Google the bastard).Taught English as second language for 15 Goddamn Years. Backpacked across Europe solo 7 times. Attended four World Cups in Person. Books: www. LuLu.com/spotlight/JimMarquez. Social: www.facebook.com/JimThe Beast Marquez. No kids. And a Scorpio, Motherfuckers!

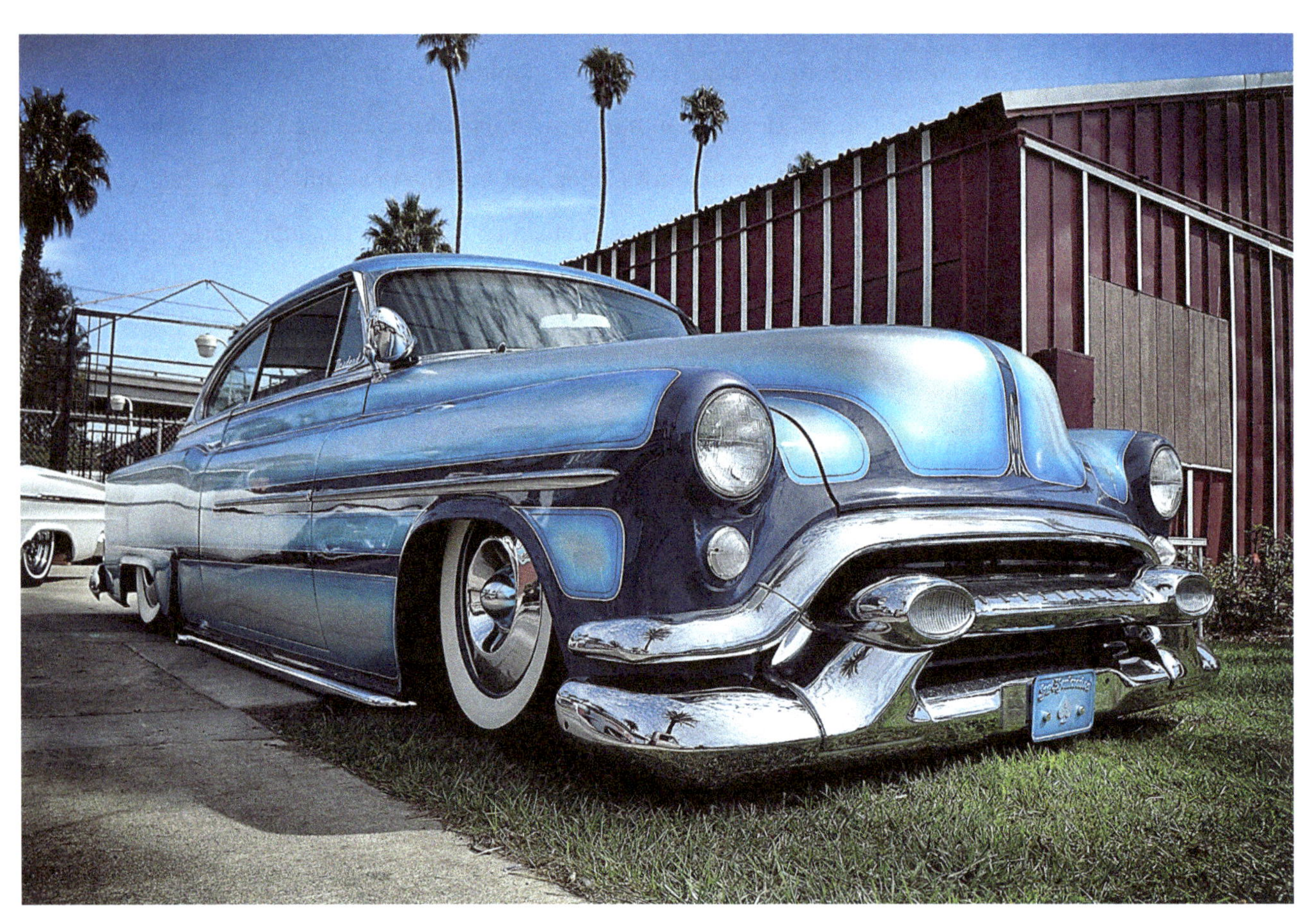

Ol' Blue – 1953 Oldsmobile

Gina Ruiz

Gina Ruiz is a writer of strange tales about chanclas and aliens; chupacabras, Lloronas, ghosts and life in East L.A. She has several blogs: on food, books, writing and poetry which you can find by visiting her at GinaRuiz.com. Her poetry has been publishing on Poetic Diversity, while her book reviews have been published on Blogcritics, La Bloga and Xispas. She volunteers each year for the Cybils Awards, a book award for Children's and Young Adult literature in her capacity as the Young Adult Nonfiction Chair. This year, Gina has the honor of being a finalist for the 2014 PEN Emerging Voices Fellowship.

Daniel Villarreal

My name, as it is, Daniel Villarreal, born on planet Earth. Raised in my grandmother's home. I became aware of my own existence when I moved to L.A., Boyle Heights, in 1973, at the age of 12.

I did well in Junior High School and dropped out of High School. I was more interested in gangs and drugs at that moment in time. Eventually I enrolled at East Los Angeles College.

I began working for the Los Angeles Unified School District off and on for the following 8 years as a teacher's assistant. Along the way in my teenage years I took up writing and photography. I became a poet, then a performance artist and eventually an actor in Hollywood. I was in Stand And Deliver, American Me, Speed, Menace II Society and a handful of other films and TV shows.

I have worked in film production for over 25-years, co-wrote and co-produced a feature film, Never Trust A Serial Killer. I am currently seeking funding for a feature I co-wrote and am co-producing, Brother Jonas. I write screenplays and I am also in the middle of writing a book, my coming of age story, Straight Out Of Dreamland (Crazy Motherfucker Named Sleepy). Finally, I am currently developing a documentary series featuring myself finding and mentoring young artists in a program that travels through 6 generations of Chicano art.

Gloria Morán

Gloria Morán is a scholar, filmmaker, transmedia artist, and author. Originally hailing from the Bay Area, her second-generation Chicana upbringing greatly informs her work. Merging theories and practices of Ethnic and Cultural Studies, Gloria's work seeks to highlight issues of race, ethnicity, and class. Gloria's current film screening nationwide in festivals, The Unique Ladies, takes a feminist look at lowrider culture and practice through the eyes of the all-women lowrider club Unique Ladies. Previous, Gloria directed and produced a short documentary about gentrification in the Mission District of San Francisco and one San Francisco native's interpretation of this change titled Homes for the Homies, and was reviewed as SF Weekly's "Best Pick." Her current transmedia project and feature length documentary, Save The City, delves into the rampant gentrification and eviction crisis in her hometown of San Francisco. Gloria has taught as an adjunct lecturer in Film and Latina/o studies in addition to frequently guest lecturing on the subject area of lowriding and Chicana/o popular culture and its impact on culture and community. She earned a Bachelor of Arts degree in Latin American and Latino Studies and Journalism and a Master of Arts degree in Social Documentation, both from the University of California at Santa Cruz.

Noelle Reyes

Noelle January Reyes is a 3rd generation Chicana, raised in El Sereno, near the heart of El Pueblo de Nuestra Señora La Reina De Los Angeles. Born on a rainy day filled with hope and glitter, Noelle was always meant to be fierce, original, and fearless. Armed with hoop earrings, and her iconic red lipstick, she has become an advocate for artists of the eastside. Influenced by her own roots and culture, as well as nuwave, lowrider and art scenes being born in the City of Angels. A "do-it-yourself" state of mind empowered her to manifest her dream to create a legitimate outlet for art and expression in her own community. As an art lover and art maker it seemed only natural to open a space to host community artist and events, as well as a platform to showcase her own talents, and eye for beauty. Thus, Mi Vida Boutique was born. Although it has transformed, through years, much like it's very founder, the original message/love not only remains but grows. Unquestionably, both she and her boutique have become a staple in the Los Angeles Art scene. Adopting and adapting to the ever changing art and mediums that exist, it is evident that both Noelle and her projects are much more than meets the eye, filled with surprises, love, and always one of a kind.

Mother-Daughter-Sister-Comadre-Artivist

C/S

Raúl Sánchez

Raúl Sánchez comes from a place south where the sun shines fiercely, where Indigenous and European cultures collided. An avid collector of poetry books, a self-proclaimed "thrift store junkie," he occasionally volunteers as a DJ for KBCS91.3 FM. He conducts workshops on The Day of the Dead, and his inaugural collection, All Our Brown-Skinned Angels was nominated for the 2013 Washington State Book Award in Poetry.

Manuel Gonzalez

Manuel is from Albuquerque, New Mexico. He identifies himself as being Chicano. The history, culture, and spirituality of his people are among his inspirations. "I'm proud to be from New Mexico, and to me it's more than just green chile and desert. It's seeing the value of famila and respect. It's the Rio Grande valley and Santuario de Chimayo. It is feasts, dance, poetry and prayer." Looking within oneself and examining ones roots is the essence of the type of poetry he works with. Emotions, feelings, experiences, and prose in an historical and cultural context is the goal of his workshops. Self-esteem, finding something to say, figuring out how to say it eloquently, and letting your voice be heard are just some of the benchmarks in Manuel's workshops.

Viva Flores

Viva Flores began her ambitious writing career at the age of eight, when her Valentine's Day poem was placed at the center of the construction paper heart on the classroom door by her third grade teacher, Mrs. Fairbanks. She is now a grown woman who silently carries flammable stories and poems in nondescript shopping bags.

Xicano X

Xicano X is currently planning his escape from the Ivory Tower. You can read his rambling nonsense at xicanox.blogspot.com.

Robert Flores

Robert Anthony Flores. Born in SanTana. Lives in SanTana. Drinks in SanTana. Mexi-American. Juaneno Indian. “Someone told me there’s a girl out there with love in her eyes and flowers in her hair.”

Ricky Luv aka Ricardo Lira Acuña

Drunk on Bukowski, high with a little help from his friends, on the road with Keroauc, fear and loathing with Gonzo and Buffalo Brown, lost in the Twilight Zone, office zombie by day. Writer by night. www.rickyluv.com

Roberto “Dr. Cintli” Rodriguez

Roberto Rodriguez, PhD, – or Dr. Cintli – is an assistant professor, Mexican American Studies Department, at the University of Arizona. He is a longtime-award-winning journalist/columnist who returned to school in 2003 in pursuit of a Master’s degree (2005) and a Ph.D. in Mass Communications (Jan. 2008) at the University of Wisconsin at Madison. He is the author of Justice: A Question of Race; it documents his 7 1/2 year quest

for justice in the courtroom, stemming a case of police brutality that almost cost him his life. His research focus at the University of Arizona is on Maiz culture on this continent, and its relationship to the Ethnic

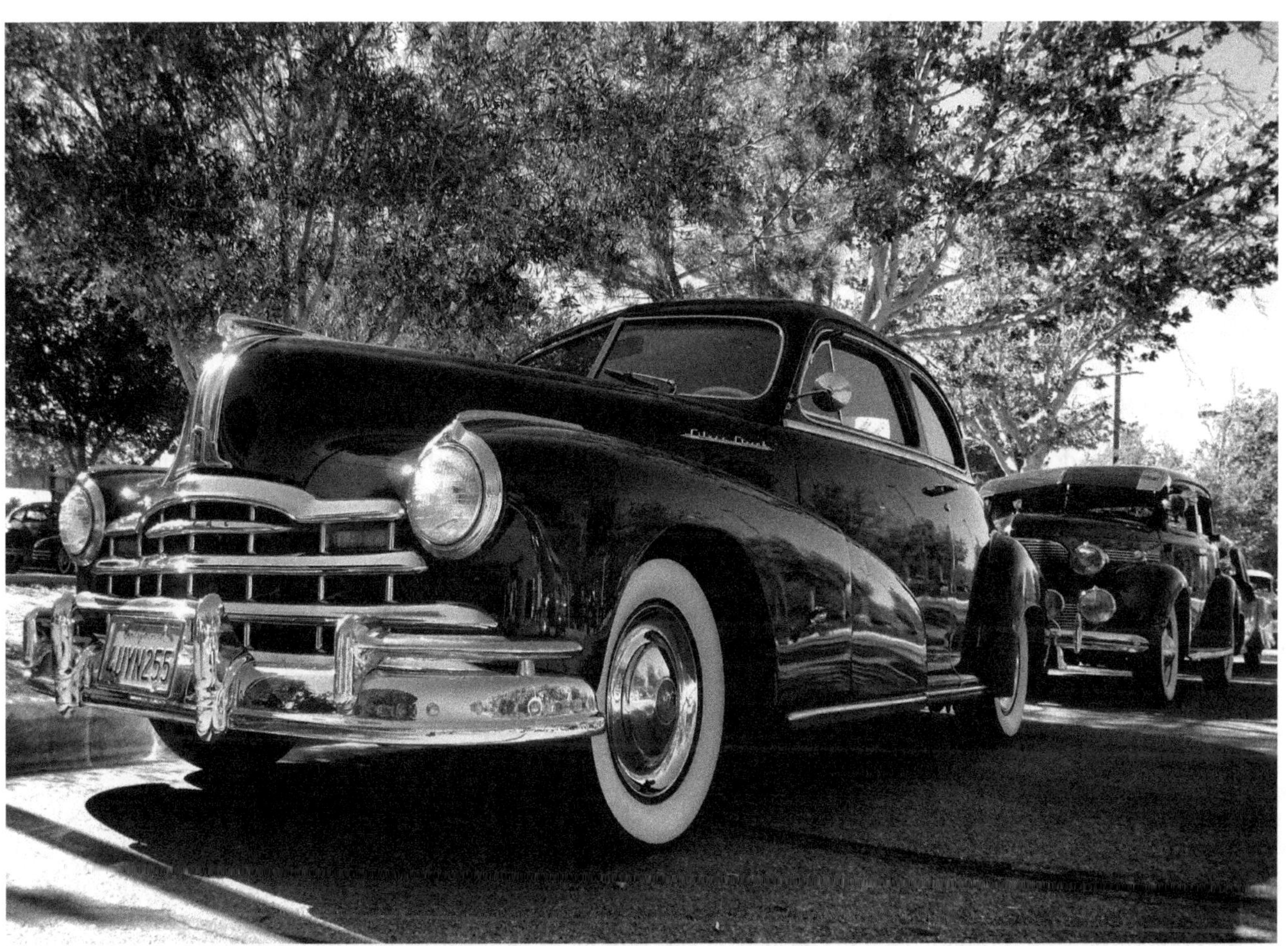

Black Beauties – 1948 Pontiac 1939 Chevrolet

Studies controversies. He has a forthcoming book “Our sacred Maiz is our Mother: Nin Tooanantzin Non Centeortl (University of Arizona Press 2014). He works with the concepts of elder-youth epistemology and running epistemology and was the 2013 Baker-Clark Human Rights award from AERA. He can be reached at: XColumn@gmail.com.

Lizz Huerta

Lizz Huerta is poet, fiction writer and educator from Chula Vista, California. Her work has appeared in ¡Ban This!, ZYZZYVA, The Portland Review and Toe Good Poetry. She is currently working on a young adult fantasy novel.

Angelo Sandoval

Angelo J. Sandoval hails from the Sangre de Cristo Mountains in Northern New Mexico. He grew up in the small town of Córdova. Angelo was raised around lowriders since he was a baby. Angelo attended Northern New Mexico College and New Mexico Highlands University where he received his Masters degree in Social Work. Angelo is a photographer and aspiring poet. His drive to be the best photographer and poet comes from his two daughters, Esperanza and Isabella. Lowriding for Angelo isn’t just a hobby, but a tradition and a way to remember his family and friends who introduced him to the cruise culture of Española, NM.

Richard Vargas

Richard Vargas was born in Compton, CA. He earned his B.A. at CSU Long Beach, where he studied under Gerald Locklin. He edited/published five issues of The Tequila Review, 1978-1980, including poetry by Gerald Locklin, Alberto Ríos, Jimmy Santiago Baca, and others. His first book, McLife, 2005, was featured twice on Garrison Keillor’s Writers Almanac, in February, 2006. A second book, American Jesus, was published by Tia Chucha Press, 2007. A third collection, Guernica, revisited, is currently scheduled for publication in 2014.

Vargas received his MFA from the University of New Mexico, 2010. He was recipient of the 2011 Taos Summer Writers' Conference's Hispanic Writer Award, and was on the faculty of the 2012 10th National Latino Writers Conference. Currently, he resides in Albuquerque, New Mexico, where he edits/publishes a biannual poetry magazine, The Más Tequila Review. http://www.amazon.com/Mas-Tequila-Review-Poetry-rest/dp/1491297395/ref=sr_1_1?s=books&ie=UTF8&qid=1381721248&sr=1-1&keywords=the+mas+tequila+review

Santino J. Rivera

Santino J. Rivera is an independent author, publisher and owner of Broken Sword Publications. Born in Denver, Colorado, Rivera cut his teeth as a freelance journalist, street poet and later as an EMT. His books collect and feature material unlike anything else currently on the market today. In 2012 Rivera published ¡Ban This! The BSP Anthology of Xican@ Literature, as a response to continued censorship and book banning of Chicana/o authors in Tucson, Arizona. The book was featured at the 2013 Tucson Festival of Books live on C-SPAN. In 2013 Rivera's indie pub house released the controversial collection of comics, 'Josh Divine's Ducktown,' from Colorado artist Josh Divine. Rivera has lectured and performed spoken word coast to coast - from Aztlán to the mean streets of the dirty South. He is passionate about free speech, Xicana/o activism, the printed word and giving a voice to those without. Rivera currently lives with his family in Saint Augustine, Florida.

Benjamin Quiñones Reyes

Benjamin Quiñones Reyes is a writer born on the same day as Oscar Wilde in San Luis Rio Colorado, Sonora, Mexico. He grew up in Boyle Heights/East L.A. where most of his influence and inspiration comes from. He is active in building a better community in Los Angeles and promoting peace globally. He loves to read, write and drink lots of green tea while listening to Tupac Amaru Shakur and Rosalino "Chalino" Sanchez. He can reached at BenjaminQR@Gmail.com

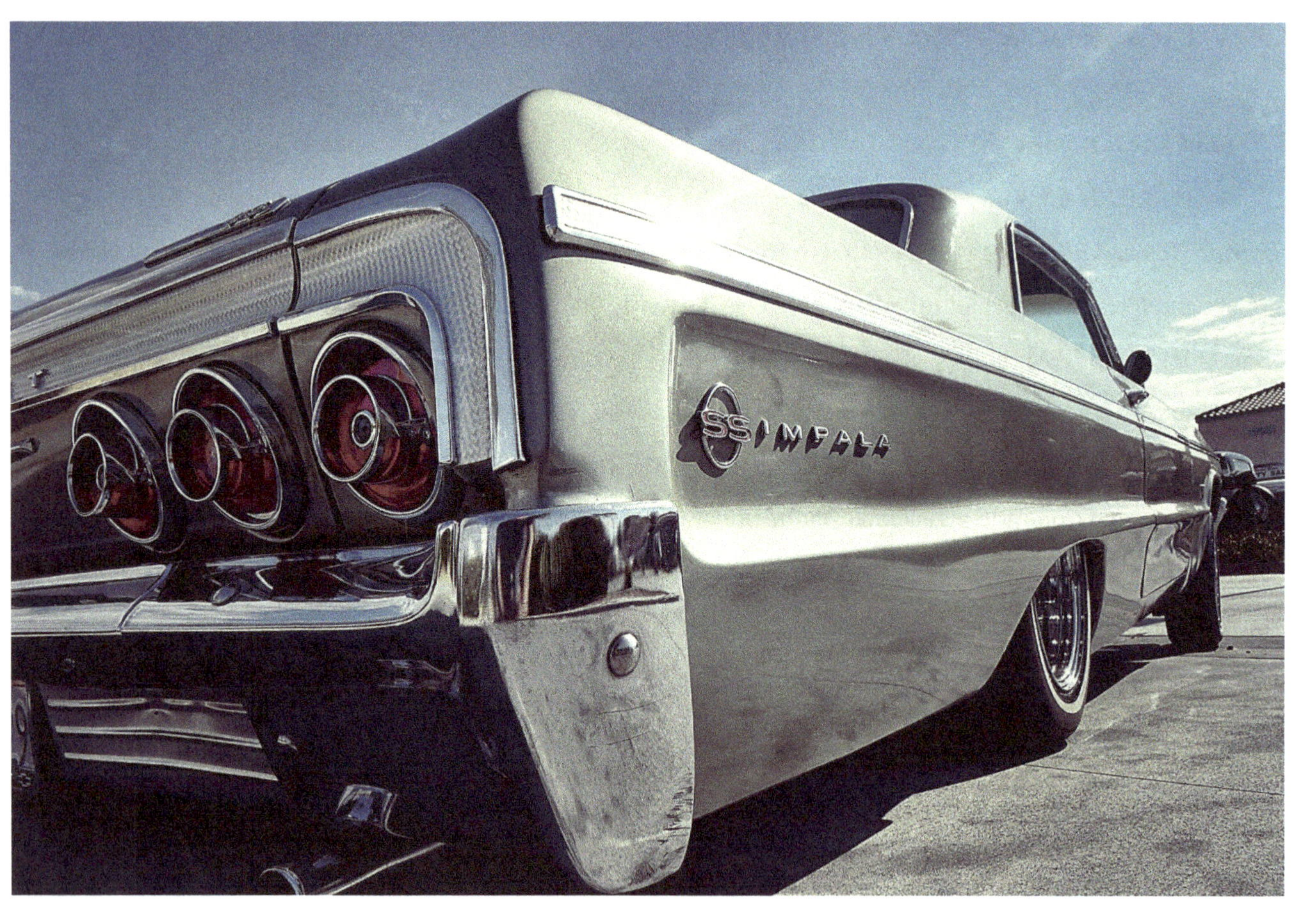

Vintage '64 - 1964 Chevy Impala

Alvaro Rodriguez

Alvaro Rodriguez is a screenwriter living and working in Texas. His short fiction has appeared in AFTER DEATH (Dark Moon, 2013), ALONG THE RIVER (VAO, 2011), POPCORN FICTION, and others. He is the co-writer of the film MACHETE (2010) and is currently writing FROM DUSK TILL DAWN: THE SERIES (2014) for the new El Rey Network.

Lawrence Gandara

I grew up in what is called Angelino Heights. However, home to me was always a place called Dog Town (Housing Projects), the womb of my community. I am one out of eight siblings, seven brothers and one sister. My grandparents raised me. At the age of nineteen I lost my mother to a drug-related death. My family's history is rooted strongly in the Chicana/o culture. I am now a community and student organizer who will most likely be the first of his family to earn a university degree (Senior at Cal State Los Angeles), but always keeping in mind that family and community are not detachable.

Steven Alvarez

Steven Alvarez is an Assistant Professor of Writing, Rhetoric, and Digital Studies at the University of Kentucky. He has authored two novels in verse, The Pocho Codex (2011) and The Xicano Genome (2012), both published by Editorial Paroxismo. He is originally from Safford, Arizona. Read more of his work at www.stevenpaulalvarez.com.

Gustavo Arellano

Gustavo Arellano is the editor of OC Weekly, columnist behind ¡Ask a Mexican! and part of ZOG.

Mayra Ramirez

Mayra Ramirez is an art curator, model, blogger and artist that currently resides in her Oakland, California home with Señor Bernie the Chihuahua. As a result of the widely popular images that depict her, as well as the art shows she curates, she is commonly recognized as an icon and activist of Chicana culture. Being a first generation Chicana that grew up in both northern and southern California, Mayra was exposed to the diverse lowriding scene which she immediately fell in love with and began to immerse herself in the culture. With her work she seeks to create a new style of classic chola beauty and Chicana social consciousness, showing respect for her Pachuca elders while embracing a new evolution of Chicana identity.

Emilio R. Medina

Born in Tijuana Mexico and raised in National City CA for most of his life, Emilio currently lives in Westchester CA. with his wife Gillian, two daughters Danielle & Isabella and their two rescued dogs. Emilio is the Creative Director and owner of muyCreative design studio based in Los Angeles CA. Emilio is always keeping busy creating art for his clients as well as taking on projects that are geared towards education and bringing awareness to social issues. He received his B.A. from San Diego State University and has been dedicated to his craft as a Graphic Designer for over 15 years. muycreative.com | emilio@muycreative.com | @ muycreative

Josh Divine

Josh Divine is a professional illustrator, graphic designer and the author of *Ducktown*. Josh provided spot illustrations thoughout this book and handled the layout and design. His work can be seen online at *joshdivine.com.*

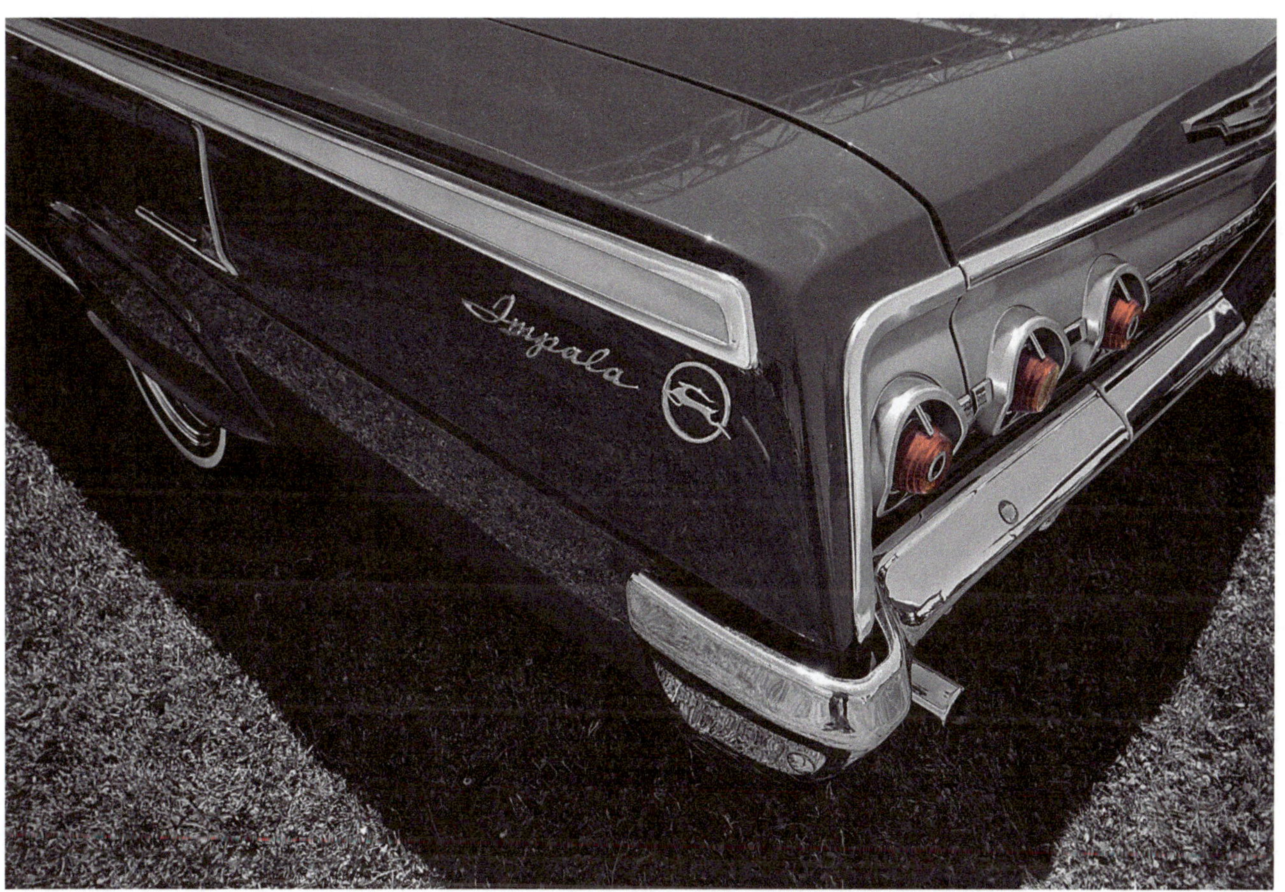

Black & Red – '62 Chevy Impala

Photo & Artwork Index

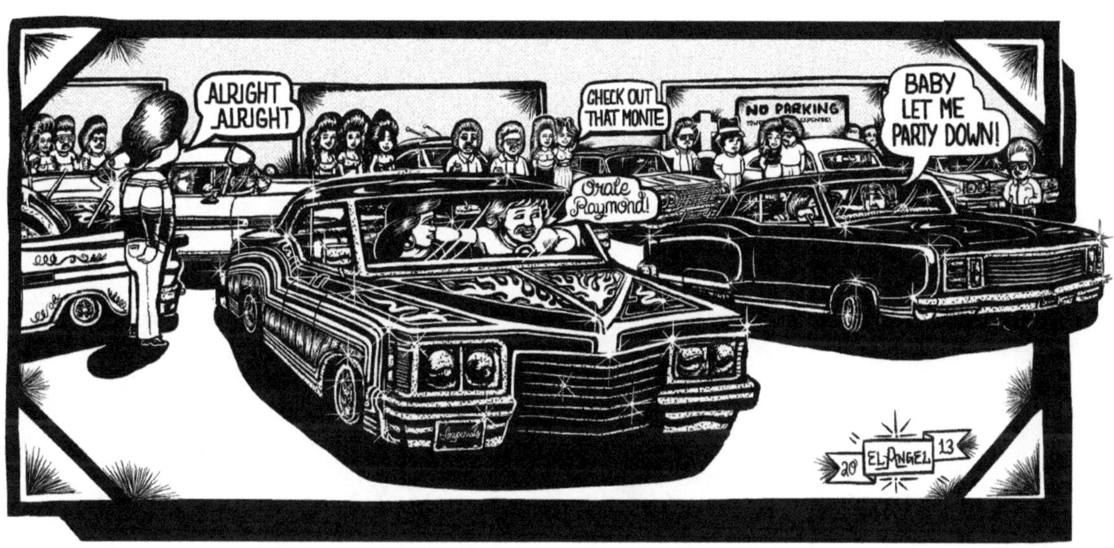

Boulevard 1 by Angel Diaz

www.ingramcontent.com/pod-product-compliance
Lightning Source LLC
LaVergne TN
LVHW081402110826
845149LV00010B/1635

* 9 7 8 0 9 8 9 6 3 1 3 1 0 *